APERTURE

THE LIGHTS TRILOGY

S. CARO

Nymeria Publishing, LLC

First published in the United States of America by
Nymeria Publishing, LLC, 2022

Nymeria Publishing
PO Box 85981
Lexington, SC 29073
Visit our website at www.nymeriapublishing.com

Print (paperback) ISBN: 978-1-7363027-7-4
Ebook ISBN: 978-1-7363027-8-1

First Edition: 2022
Printed in U.S.A.

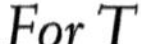

For T

PROLOGUE

The room is sterile, claustrophobic with too many people -
in this case, too many angels and Nephilims —an oversized cherry oak table, and at least eight mesh-backed chairs,
perfect for ergonomics. Laine Saint has been in this conference
room in the heart of Cross Medical Center more times than she
can count, probably more than the number of years she has
been on Earth so far.

254 long years, not that she's counting or anything.

"How many times do I need to tell you?" Jeremiah
Graham's voice rings through the already too small room,
rattling through everyone's ears.

Arlo Wesley and Lawson Saint flank on either side of
Laine. None of them flinching at Jeremiah's words, at least
outwardly. On each side of Jeremiah are the Nephilim, Cael
Malach, and Zera Young. Jeremiah's white coat is tight on his
lanky shoulders and seems far shorter than the rest of the
doctors at Cross Medical, but that's probably because he stands

nearly six foot and five inches. The wrinkles around his eyes create divots in the bags under them.

His piercing eyes are directed towards Arlo, who's dressed simply in a plaid button down and fitted khakis.

"We don't have the time to wait! These human children in Edge need to be taken care of. We are losing souls everywhere to the darkness and we can't afford to lose anymore. You don't want me to get the Guides involved do you?"

The room tenses at the threat of the Guides. Laine knows that they wouldn't take the time to involve themselves in something so trivial. But she has also spent enough time with them and with Jeremiah to know that this threat isn't hallow and she can't risk it with Nola there.

"No Brother, there's no need for their involvement-" Arlo starts.

"We will help you, Brother Arlo," Laine chimes in stiffly.

She rubs her damp palms on her blue uniform pants, the only indication of her nerves then motions to her son, Lawson.

"Sure, a single Protector and barely a Nephilim," Jeremiah spits out.

Lawson moves closer to his mother's side and puts his hands on the back of one of the mesh-back chairs. His knuckles go white with the pressure of anger building up in his tense shoulders. He's heard this particular insult plenty of times, especially from Jeremiah, but each time is worse than the last. He made his choice, and he wishes this bitter old angel would just get over it.

"What about your other offspring, Sister Laine?"

If Jeremiah was truly interested, the only indication is the slightly higher tone at the end of his question. Instead what drips through his words is disgust. Disgust at Laine's decision to procreate with a human and she knows it.

Now, both Laine and Lawson tense up. Laine's hands ball into fists at her side as the chair in Lawson's grip groans with the strain. They both knew that was coming, having discussed what they were and weren't going to say about Nola during this meeting. They agreed, Lawson taking a bit more convincing than necessary, that any talk of Nola would be off the table. But now faced with the question outright, Laine's mind goes into full Protector mode with the added motherly fierceness.

"She's not ready yet." The words come out through Laine's tense lips.

"You've mentioned that several times now, Sister Laine. I hope this is not another instance with your first," Jeremiah's eyes flick to Lawson then back to Laine.

"When will the... Nephilim," he spits the word, "be 21 in human years?"

Lawson opens his mouth to answer but his mother places her hand on his forearm to stop him. He knows that touch, it's a touch he's felt most of his life, and decides to begrudgingly keep his mouth shut.

"Soon." Laine gives a vague response, but she knows the answer as her heart beats in time with the number of days left until Nola turns 21.

Exactly five days.

Absentmindedly, she thinks of the brown-haired toddler running around so carefree and wishes Nola was still that way. Not just days away from possibly figuring out all about this world.

Goddess forbid, she becomes a part of it.

Jeremiah groans impatiently from the other side of the room, breaking Laine's train of thought.

"Sir, we need to go," Cael's soft voice cuts through the tension.

He had pulled a small device from the pocket of his light blue scrubs, putting it back as he spoke. His young eyes are slightly larger behind his glasses.

Suddenly, Laine is very grateful for this young Nephilim.

Zera has already moved around Jeremiah and Cael to head towards the door. She was far too quiet during this meeting, choosing to keep an eye on everyone instead of voicing her opinion. In a way, that made Laine more on edge than when Zera does decide to speak her mind.

"Right," Jeremiah starts, boredom returning to his natural tone. "Brother Arlo, I want a report back to send along about the souls in Edge. Don't disappoint me. And Sister Laine," he turns his head to her as the rest of his body shifts towards the door, "I would love to hear about Nola and her progress, 'soon.'"

If it wasn't so off-putting, Laine might have laughed at Jeremiah's feeble attempt at air quotes. Instead, she dips her head in a nod at him. He gives her a knowing look then turns without acknowledging Arlo or Lawson and leaves the conference room.

The heavy wood door shuts behind him with a click.

"Fuck," Arlo lets out with a deep sigh. "Thanks, Laine, for covering my ass there."

Laine's face cracks into a smile.

"It's the least I could do with you keeping an eye on Nola for me."

"Ahh, it's no problem. Though if she keeps hanging around

the café, I may have to give her a job," he says as he nudges Laine's shoulder.

"Might not be bad for her," Lawson chimes in. He has moved to lean against the wall behind them, arms folded across his chest.

"You know, just in case," he shrugs as Laine gives him a watchful look.

"Don't worry Laine. I'll be right there no matter what happens," Arlo reassures her.

"Thank you. You have no idea," she smiles at him hoping that all her gratitude pours out into that simple expression.

Arlo nods at Laine and pulls her into a hug. It's awkward as angels don't typically touch one another but the longer Laine spends on Earth, the more comfortable she becomes with the basic human interactions.

"I better get back," Arlo says over Laine's shoulder. He breaks away from their hug, heading towards the door.

"We'll see you around," Lawson calls after him and they nod at each other.

Arlo gives one last look at Laine, a look of hope but also one of sympathy. They all know what's about to happen and soon they won't be able to deny it anymore.

The door clicks behind him leaving mother and son alone in the conference room.

Lawson kicks off the wall, surprisingly his smart black suit he had been wearing all day in court still looks good.

"Mom..."

"I know, Lawson, I know." Laine runs her hands through her auburn-brown hair.

"She's going to know sooner or later."

Laine knows this. She knows her daughter and knows the

chance of her getting her wing. Her thumb brushes over the two black wings on the inside of her left wrist, but she can't bring herself to have this conversation with her son.

The only thing she has left in her is hope.

Hope that her little light won't get her wing. Won't become a part of this world and be thrown into the middle of this war. She looks at her son, thinking about how she couldn't protect him from this world glancing down at his single black wing peeking out from the cuff of the sleeve of his suit.

"She doesn't have to. Not yet."

ONE

The cool October breeze, warmed only by the sun, blows through the open window. It rustles the leaves making the burnt orange and candy red colors dance with the brown and green as they fall to the ground. Through the blinding sun rays peeking through the window, the dust pirouettes in the air.

I watch as a yellow leaf on a tree in our backyard, barely holding on to its branch, sways in the wind. Idly, I hope that it can hold on but I know that one mighty gust will sever it from its branch and it'll finally join its family on the ground. Maybe it's wrong of me to wish this prolonged loneliness on the leaf, we all return to our family in the end, right?

I know the last couple of days here at home in Cross have been needed. This fall break has been more relaxing than I could've imagined. I've always loved being able to focus on my family, talk about nothing over meals, running around, and keeping my rambunctious nephew, Max, entertained is all I could've asked for of this momentary distraction.

Even now I can hear Max running around downstairs trying to get his Halloween costume together, no doubt bothering his mother and grandmother to get it perfect. The wind shifts outside, and I can smell the burgers on the grill just below me. I know Lawson is out there manning the grill, taking a moment to find his own peace. He and I share that aspect of our personalities, needing at least a single moment to ourselves in the day.

It's something we got from our father. The need for just a moment to look around and gather ourselves. I remember watching my father in this very room, which we lovingly called "The Artist's Cave" because of how much time he would spend here, sitting in the brown suede recliner that has since collected dust.

I look over to the ghost of a loved chair and force myself not to think of the way my father's eyes rolled up to the ceiling so many years ago or the way his pale skin was so ashen that it nearly matched his white t-shirt that he was wearing that day.

Instead, I think about all the times I found him in here bent over a new art book or looking over old photographs from his travels collecting art all over the world. Many times, he sat here in silence, enraptured in the colors, the mood, each particle, or brush stroke from the artist. It was like he was reading a story in every painting or picture. And he would tell those stories to me. I guess it's safe to say that's what inspired me to go into the best Art History program at Edge University.

Because when dad... died... I wanted- no, I needed to see the stories he saw. I needed to see the world just as he saw it in those small colorful moments.

"I didn't expect to find you here..."

My mother's voice comes from the doorway of The Artist's

Cave. I jump slightly from where I'm sitting on the old couch, well really, it's just a loveseat that used to be a part of a set in the living room. The floor creaks as she takes several steps across the room and brushes her hand lightly on the back of my father's chair.

Her emerald green eyes, the same as mine, take in the old fabric and I can almost see the memories playing behind them. A sad smile lifts one side of her mouth and she takes in a deep steadying breath.

"This room has always felt different since your father... passed," she says solemnly. "I am glad you're in here though. It feels...right having you in the magnificent Artist's Cave. Very fitting for him, and for you."

I give her a small smile.

This room has changed in his absence, it's darker because he took all the color with him. But if we're being honest, the color started fading long before he passed. I would never tell my mother this, but I stopped seeing the magic in this room, in my dad, when I found him that first time when I was 12. The needle was still stuck in his arm.

That needle injected him with his high, but it also sucked all the color from his face... from my world for the longest time.

"Yeah..." I answer as I wipe a tear that starts to escape. "Actually, I just came up here to take a moment away from the tornado that is Max."

She smiles fondly, no doubt thinking about the energetic blonde boy that we both love dearly. Her eyes crinkle a bit at the edges, showing the only signs of the years of stress and aging on her otherwise flawless face. She grabs the opening of her brown cardigan and wraps it around herself as she moves to sit on the cushion next to me.

"You know I love the kid but sometimes it's nice to escape," I smile back at her knowingly.

"Yeah, he is great but sure is a ball of energy. Sometimes I can't help but feel all the years when I watch him run around."

Her eyes sweep over my face before she turns her head towards the open window. I watch her eyes close and take a deep breath in, I'm sure smelling the food as well as the staleness of the room. A smile creeps onto her face and she opens her eyes slowly to look out at the scene of dancing colors in her backyard.

I can't help but see the similarities in our features. Same green eyes, same brown with auburn highlighted hair, even our face shapes are similar. It's not hard to see how some people would mistake us for sisters instead of mother and daughter. The only difference in our appearance being that I'm nearly six inches taller than her, getting the height from my dad.

"I know what you mean, most of the time I feel old trying to keep up with him," I sigh.

"Oh hush! You're only 20. Until tomorrow at least..."

Her voice shifts from reprimanding to melancholy. I look over as she picks at her left sleeve.

"Well don't sound too excited," I chuckle.

She looks up and meets my half smile.

"It is exciting! It's just... you know, dumb mom stuff, my baby's growing up."

She shrugs lightly but I catch something else shift behind her eyes.

"Yeah, okay," I decide not to push her.

"Do you have any plans to celebrate?"

"Um, I haven't actually given it much thought. Maybe Ash

will want to do something or force me to do something," I roll my eyes at the thought.

Ash has been one of closets friends since we started rooming together freshmen year. We bonded quickly in our first Art History class, Historic Preservation, our freshman year. She and I share our dreams of becoming teachers after graduation, Ash preferring middle grades, but I favor high school. She is an amazing artist, brilliant, beautiful, and probably the only person who has been my main drive to get out of my shell while in college. Well, she and Harley are a tag team at this point.

"I don't know, I think just staying in would be nice..." I shrug and stare at the soft beige curls of the Berber carpet beneath my feet.

"Don't let Harley hear you say that," she warns as if she can hear my thoughts, "they would have a cow. Besides, that doesn't sound like a very fun 21st."

She says nonchalantly but playful joking laces itself in her tone.

"Mom, are you telling me to go out and party?" I gasp at her as dramatically as possible, lifting my hand to my mouth.

She laughs at me.

"All I'm saying is that maybe you could use some fun, you only turn 21 once you know. But also, I'm still your mom, so I'm going to tell you to be safe and smart," she says sternly. "I've just seen how distant you've been this weekend and thought maybe... it would be a nice break from school too," her concern overwhelms me.

So, she did notice.

I don't know why I thought the one person who could read through me wouldn't catch the small moments that I drifted away. I have found myself the past couple of days during moments of silence or when the conversation wasn't on me, lost in the memories of the past. Memories of my dad, drowning in all the grief that comes with those. And more recently memories of Sean, who even now can't seem to get the hint as my phone vibrates in my pocket once again.

It also hasn't helped that I chose this room to get away in. But maybe that's just because this is home and home comes with so many painfully claustrophobic memories.

"Don't worry, it's been a refreshing break."

The emotional and mental pain of being home is something I've grown used to over the years and most of the time I'm able to keep it locked up and still enjoy the time with my family. But I would be lying if I didn't say that being away at college is my saving grace to get away from it all.

"Oh?" she asks, trying to keep the eagerness out of her voice. "Is there something else?"

I take a deep breath and my stomach growls with the smell of the burgers.

"No," I say, averting my eyes back to the open window and the beams of bright yellow sunshine. I know that I should tell her how much pain it brings me to be back but seeing how happy she is every day that I am here... I can't hurt her like that.

"You know you can tell me anything right? If you want, my little light," my mother pushes, subtly trying to get me to spill.

I smile to myself at her endearing name for me. It brings me back to my childhood faster than being in this room does.

"Yeah, I know."

I let the silence hang between us, deciding on what to tell her. I watch the yellow leaf that is still holding on for dear life finally let go and freefall to the ground. Certainly, meeting the sea of colors below.

"It's nothing mom, no need to worry."

I sigh and take a moment to watch the sunlight dance across the colors too nervous to look at my mother. After a moment she speaks earnestly.

"I'll always worry about whatever is bothering you," she does nothing to hide the anxious tone in her voice.

The corners of my mouth rise in a knowing smile. I may have gotten a lot from my father, but my mother and I share the same anxieties. Those monsters of worry that pester us at the worst times.

"I know."

I reach across the small gap between us to grab her hand, hoping my touch brings her as much comfort as her hand does in mine.

She smiles as she rubs her thumb across my palm and stops momentarily looking at the inside of my wrist and turns it over like she is examining a wound. I watch as a line forms between her eyes and concern flashes across her features. She opens her mouth to say something but is cut off by the tell-tell bounding steps of a hyper toddler running down the hallway leading to the room my mother and I occupy.

"I found em!" Max shouts as he comes through the door.

I look past my mother to see Max skipping the few feet towards us. The floor creaking and his blonde hair flopping with every skip. His big brown eyes are mischievously playful, and the grin spread across his face could make even the most cynical person crack a smile.

What catches me off guard is his outfit. Not 20 minutes ago, Max was wearing jeans and a t-shirt and running at about

30 miles per hour around the house, not even fazed by the chilly fall weather. Now, he has nearly stripped to nothing except an oversized cloth diaper, far too big feather angel wings on his back, and a small bow and arrow in his tiny grasp.

"What do you think No-No?"

He stops right in front of me and stares up. His eyes shine with excitement as he turns and shows off his costume. I can't help but smile and join in on his excitement.

"I think you look like the best cupid. Even better than the real one," I wink and poke his little belly. His rosy cheeks spread farther with his grin.

"And what bout you gam?" Max turns to my mother expectantly.

She smiles lovingly at him and grabs him around his waist to pull him close to her. He fights it for a second but lets her cradle him in her arms. He leans into her chest and closes his eyes.

"You look amazing my love," she kisses the top of his head.

"But it is far too chilly for you to be out there tomorrow night in nothing but this."

She pats his behind covered in cloth to nudge him off her lap. He giggles and jumps off and fully sprints to the brown chair, my father's chair, his grandfather's chair.

I wish more than anything he was around to meet this little blonde ball of energy.

"Gam and No-No says I look great mom!" he shouts towards the door. His large angel wings sit crooked on his back causing him to sit crookedly in the chair.

"Oh No-No, Harwey is downstairs threatening to eat all the food."

I laugh and shake my head. That kid never ceases to make any moment feel lighter and yet grounding all at the same time.

"Let's go then, Max! We can't let them eat everything!" I say playfully and he laughs as he jumps off the chair and starts a full run back through the doorway.

My mother is now standing in front of me holding out her hand and my stomach growls instinctively. I stand and wrap my arm around her shoulders, and we head down the hallway filled with the scent of grilled food, cookies still in the oven, and Max's laughter.

TWO

After lunch, I sit on the couch in the living room that hasn't changed much since I moved out, with Max's head in my lap. I run my hands through his hair, soothing him just like I used to when he was a baby. It's hard to think that now he's nearly grown, well as grown as a four-year-old can be. But he's no longer the tiny infant, squishy and helpless. Now, he can run around and bounce back from all bruises and scrapes, and he can tell us what he needs and how much he loves us. Most importantly, he can understand when we tell him we love him and how much we mean it.

Looking up I see his parents, my brother, Lawson, and his wife, Flynn, on the love seat next to us. Lawson has his arm around Flynn's shoulders, and she cuddles into his chest, an easy kind of love radiates from them constantly. I can't help but feel a twinge of jealousy at the ease of their relationship knowing that it's something I've never experienced. It certainly wasn't easy with Sean.

I hear my mother fiddling around in the kitchen, more than likely putting away the food and dishes and packing me something for my ride back to Edge. I look past Lawson and Flynn to the dining room table where Harley sits leaning back in the chair, just as stuffed as I feel and just as comfortable as if this was their house. Granted, it might as well be. They are as much a part of my family as Flynn is.

Hell, I've probably spent and spend more time with them than I do my own brother. Though now, Harley and I may be grown and only communicate mainly through video or phone calls, but we're still up to no good when we're together, which seems to be always, especially when I'm home.

Dressed in a simple oversized band t-shirt and dark ripped jeans that I'm sure might be unbuttoned secretly under the table, they laugh at something on their phone at the same time my phone vibrates. I smile knowing already that they sent me whatever it was that made them laugh. Looking back at Max I feel his breathing slow as he starts to drift off.

"Wow, we should keep you around more often," Lawson says quietly and I smile down at the sleeping boy.

I look back up at my older brother. His eyes are so much like our father's, a caramel brown and soft but so serious all the time. His hair is almost the same shade of dirty blonde as well. Sometimes it hurts to see so much of our father in his face but it's also so comforting.

"Don't worry, I'll give him some candy before I leave so he's wired for you guys later," I wink at Lawson.

"Now that is just cruel," Flynn chimes in.

All three of us laugh together quietly. Just then my mother walks into the living room and sighs.

"While I love hearing you guys laugh and having you all

under one roof, Nola it's probably time for you to head back so you're not driving at night, right?" she smiles sadly at me. "Same thing with you Harley," my mother glances over at my best friend.

"Ah, Laine, you know I got this," Harley waves their hand dismissively but smiles their golden smile at my mother. "I could probably drive to Low in my sleep at this point."

My mother's whole body turns with the roll of her eyes.

I keep my mouth shut but smile all the same. It's no use in arguing that I drive perfectly fine at night as well, so I just smile back at my mother when she looks back my way. Always reassuring her that I will be fine, trying to ease the concern written on her face.

"Of course, let's see if I can shimmy out of this."

Slowly, I wedge my hands under Max's head to hold it steady while I shift my body out from under him. Using my full concentration, I move carefully. Max stirs a bit, but he doesn't wake. I let out a breath that I didn't realize I was holding in. Deciding to use the old "switch-a-roo" technique, I grab one of the throw pillows on the couch and place it under his head, standing still, willing him to not wake and notice the change. Once I realize he isn't going to wake I turn to his parents and point at my chest.

"I'm a pro," I whisper and grin at them, Lawson just rolls his eyes in response.

"Wait up," Harley whisper calls as I stand upright. "I need to grab my bag up there anyways and I'll help you get your shit together," they smile ruefully at me as they come around the couch, passing me to head up the stairs.

"Ha. Ha. Harls. You know *that* will take more than just the two of us."

I hold in the bubble of laughter at my self-deprecating humor in my chest, but Harley lets theirs go as they take the stairs quickly, knowing this house like the back of their hand.

I leave Lawson, Flynn, and my mother in the living room silently watching the television and praying that the quiet lasts with Max asleep. Taking the steps up quickly, I'm in my too small childhood bedroom with its bright sapphire walls before I know it. I can hear Harley in the room over which has now been donned the guest room but is really just for Harley. Stepping carefully as not to make the floor creak and wake the sleeping giant downstairs, I pace my room grabbing the clothes I had thrown lazily around, putting them in my bag. I tiptoe to the bathroom to grab my toiletries and shove them in my bag on top of the clothes.

You should really be more organized... my subconscious berates me in a voice similar to Harley, but she should know by now that organization is not my strong suit. In fact, she's been yelling at me since high school and even more so now that I'm in college, to get my life together.

But alas, her voice is hoarse and I shrug her off as I grab a few shirts and a pair of jeans from my closet that I had left here, forcing them into the stuffed bag. I yank the zipper closed while looking around the room one more time to make sure I have everything. My eyes catch the small collage of pictures from high school above the bed.

I walk over to look through them, feeling a bit more nostalgic with every step. Most of them are of Harley and I and our many adventures. I'm almost immediately transported back to the moments from each of these time capsuled images.

Our beach trips with my family on the Fourth of July. The one time we hopped the fence at the park down the road from my house and Harley had to talk the cop out of calling our parents. Our many sleepovers and the times we went to football games together.

And prom... I nearly tear the photo from the wall. I had forgotten that that one was up there and the memory of that night, still fresh even after all these years, nearly forces me to rip the image into tiny pieces and burn it.

Sean smiles at me from the image. His arm around my waist, wrinkling my shimmery peach gown, and even now I can feel his fingers digging into my side. Seeing the forced smile on my lips, I'm surprised that more people didn't notice me screaming behind my eyes. But the important people saw the pain I was hiding.

"I can't believe you still have these," Harley's voice comes from behind me, and I hear the familiar squeak of my bed as they sit.

"Yeah..." I say sadly. "Some of these are too good to get rid of though."

I smile as I pull one of my favorites off the wall. I took it right after Harley had jumped into the freezing lake up north in May. Harley's face is mortified that I had snapped the picture as they reached out to try to take the camera from me. I remember how our laughs echoed on the lake for hours after. Present day Harley looks just as mortified as they hold the tiny moment in their hands.

"Like I said, can't believe you still have some of these," they grimace at the picture in their hands. Harley looks up at the prom picture that I was just looking at and says, "especially that one."

"Ah, yeah... I honestly forgot that one was here until just now," I answer.

I thought it was a memory that was in the past with no physical evidence but apparently, my younger self kept her pain as moments posted on her walls. Maybe I haven't changed much. I pick at the corner of the picture, looking anywhere but at Sean's face.

On the other side of the picture is Harley dressed in a long black sleeveless dress with their date, some junior they decided to drag along with our small group.

"Hey, what was this guy's name?" I point at the guy next to them in the picture.

"I think his name was William or Will... or was it Phil...?"

"Damn dude, I'm sorry," I say to the mystery guy, shrugging it off.

In the picture, Harley and their date are in the same awkward prom pose but their arm is outstretched towards me, their hand closed around mine. I can still feel their tight grip, the only thing that grounded me that night was them. Placing the picture back on the wall, I put it next to another one of our beach pictures. Using the beach to cover Sean, leaving Harley, her mystery date, and me to shine in the photo.

"You sure you don't want to burn that one?" Harley asks honestly, disgust lacing their tone. They know more about what happened with Sean than anyone else in my life. So, their disdain for that asshole is warranted.

I take a moment to look at the picture and realize it's not about him.

"Well, I'm hoping, since I can't actually rip him out of my past, maybe I can just cover him up with the good memories. Or replace him with new ones," I turn towards Harley.

"Speaking of which," Harley's face shifts into something

more mischievous. "Any new prospects in the love department?"

They wiggle their eyebrows at me, I'm sure, in an effort to be suggestive, causing me to laugh harder at their ridiculous question.

"Um... absolutely not," I say between laughs.

"What? I don't understand how that could possibly be that funny," they say with false hurt. "You're stunning Nola! Which brings me to tomorrow, we're fucking doing something for your birthday and I don't want to hear anything about it," they pause but not long enough for me to protest. "We need to get you laid."

"That's not a problem," I compose myself enough to wiggle my eyebrows at them this time. "Besides, I don't really have the time to get involved with anyone right now. I'm slammed with school, photography club, oh I don't know, trying to graduate and get out of here."

I wave my hands around my tiny room. The moment the words are out of my mouth there is a second of relief at the confession, then almost immediately the guilt comes down at finally voicing those words out loud. These words have flurried through my mind several times over the weekend of being home and many times before but now they float in the air between Harley and me.

"You don't have the time or are you not wanting to put in the time?"

Harley's question hits me like a ton of bricks. Of course, they already know the answer as their eyes flick back behind me to the picture on the wall. Harley stays silent as their brown eyes find me again.

"That's not fair, Harls. I don't know if I'm ready or if I'll be ready to have someone in my life like that again..."

"Maybe, but you'll also never know if you don't put yourself out there again."

I let their words sink in as my heart constricts. I know they're right, but it doesn't make it any less painful to hear.

"Besides, I don't know what's so bad about being here," they look around, leaning back on my bed. They lift their hands up behind their head, brushing the dark hair over the shaved half of their head.

"You don't know the half of it..."

The words are out before I can stop them. I clamp my mouth shut with fear and regret. Harley, my oldest and best friend, who had been there for everything with Sean, still doesn't know how deep those wounds go. They don't know about the year leading up to prom night, covering up the bruises at his hands.

Worst of all, I never told them what really happened to my father. They held my hand at the funeral, stood by through the depression that followed. But I could never tell them about his addiction. I could never tell them how it plagued my family for years. They don't know that this house, this home is filled with so much darkness. Harley has been fortunate enough to still be left in the light with all the colors.

I won't be the one to drag them into the dark with me.

Suddenly, Harley sits up and pulls me down to sit next to them. They look down at my hands, turning them so that they are palm up. Harley takes a deep breath.

"I wish you would tell me," Harley whispers in a confession.

My heart races with both pain and resolution.

"I wish I could," I say through it all.

"What I really wish is that you realize that no matter what you have going on in that brain of yours, it's not going to make me love you any less."

Harley's eyes search mine and I can see the sincerity in them. It nearly breaks me. I open my mouth to let it all flow out, let the darkness go but nothing comes out. The darkness is at home within me, and it doesn't want to let go.

Instead, what comes out is, "shouldn't you get on the road?"

I can see the resolution cross their face. Harley lets go of my hands to pull out their phone to check the time.

"Shit yeah. Alright, I'll call you tomorrow to figure out what we're doing for your birthday."

"Absolutely!" I say with the biggest smile I can muster.

It's better to let them think I'm totally not going to spend the first half of the day studying, then probably on the couch the rest of the night. Harley squints their eyes at me in doubt but pulls me in for a hug anyway.

"Let me know when you get to Edge."

"And you let me know when you get to Low safely," I say into their shoulder. "I miss you already."

My heart swells with love for this crazy kid that chose me to be their best friend when we were just kids.

"Bitch, I'll see you tomorrow."

I laugh as they pull away, giving me a wink. Harley grabs their bag that I didn't even realize was on the ground and gives me a salute as they leave my bedroom. I hear Harley's rushed goodbyes downstairs to my family, our family. Instead of following them down, I sit in silence for far too long, letting the weight of the weekend push me further into the bed. Or maybe it's just the weight of the eyes from the photos boring into me, judging me for letting the pain of being home and ghosts of my past keep me in the darkness.

The thought of being back in Edge pushes me to my feet and as if on cue, my phone buzzes with a text.

I glance at my phone for the first time all day and smile at Ash's message:

When the hell are you coming back? I'm dying of boredom.

After her message comes several exaggerated emojis of her metaphorically dying of boredom. I quickly type out,

OMW, don't die (:

I quickly grab my bag, leaving my old bedroom and all of its pictures of my pain on its walls. I continue my march down the stairs, expertly avoiding the tender spots in the floor that give way to loud groaning creaks. I don't get far down the stairs before something catches my attention.

In hushed voices, I can hear Lawson and our mother speaking quickly to one another at the bottom of the stairs.

"So, you haven't told her?" Lawson questions.

"Not yet... I noticed something today and was about to tell her, but you know the rules. Then Max, then lunch... I just wanted to have one more normal day," my mother responds quickly.

"Yeah, one more day... after all, her birthday is tomorrow. But I think she still needs to know about..."

Distracted and confused, I try to get closer to hear their conversation. My foot falls on a step that reveals my presence

　　　　　　　　　　　　　S. CARO

with a loud groan. They both fall silent, while I quickly try to gather myself, pretending I hadn't been eavesdropping. I continue down the stairs without missing a beat.

"Oh, Nola!" my mother says, overly excited. "I packed up some cookies for you to take back to Ash."

She quickly turns around to grab the container from the kitchen table. While she is turned away, I look up at Lawson as he watches our mother walk past him. His face and shoulders are pinched in frustration. He turns back, meeting my eyes. He appears to relax a bit, but I can tell the frustration is only eased by a new emotion flashing behind his brown eyes, pity. He half smiles at me, as if that would help any.

Our mother returns with the container full of cookies.

"Here we are!" she nearly throws them into my hands.

"Umm... thanks," I fumble with it for a second before getting a grasp on it.

"It feels like you guys are throwing me out of the house," I say jokingly but I watch them intensely. Neither one of them giving anything away.

"Not at all! Just want you to be safe on the road and get there before dark. You know this," my mom pats my shoulder, ushering me towards the living room.

"Sureeee," I drag out, tiptoeing back in. I place my bag on the floor next to the couch where Max is.

Walking up to Max, blissfully asleep, still, in the same position I left him in, I balance the cookies in one hand as I bend down to kiss the soft waves in his hair.

"I love you," I whisper to him. He smiles in his sleep.

I straighten up and head to Flynn.

Giving Flynn a quick hug, "Good luck with the sugar rush he is going to have tomorrow."

I give her a knowing look as she slaps me playfully on the arm.

With a quick smile, I turn to Lawson.

"I'll see you soon," his words seem heavier than usual.

I tilt my head to question, but he just shrugs it off, wrapping his arms around me.

He releases me quickly to grab my bag on the floor, heading out of the house towards my car sitting in the driveway. I lock arms with my mother, who's standing in the doorway, both of us walking out of the house together.

"Thank you for putting up with me this long weekend."

I say to her as we reach my car, putting the cookies in the passenger seat.

"You know you're welcome any time. Always. The house is too quiet most days anyways," she smiles softly at me.

"Just have Max over and you'll be begging for quiet in no time," I wrap my arms around her as we both laugh.

"Happy birthday, my little light."

She says lovingly into my shoulder with the same hint of pity, or maybe sadness, in her voice that flashed through Lawson's expression.

"Thank you," I say pulling away from her.

Part of me wants to ask her about the conversation. About what she needs to tell me or what I need to know, but the concern in her eyes stops me, instilling a new sense of fear. It's a fear I haven't felt in a long time, a fear of the unknown. My rational side wants to think nothing of it. The side of me that keeps me sane, puts it all into the box I've created for myself with all the pain and darkness that comes with home far out of reach.

I pull open my driver's side door firmly shutting the box in my mind labeled "home" and opening the box labeled "college". Looking up at my mom through my passenger side window I give her a smile and a wave.

"Love you," I say to her.

"I love you too," a smile brightening her features again.

Throwing my car in reverse down the driveway, I catch my mom, Lawson, and Flynn standing together on the porch waving to me. I shoot Lawson a look hoping he understands the cavern of unsaid words between us.

THREE

The papers around me shift and the wooden table creaks under the pressure of my hand as I flip through the pages of my Art History textbook, jotting down notes for our current topic. Soft piano music comes from the speakers of my laptop, filling the small soundproof study room with an ethereal, peaceful feeling, perfect for studying. Classes haven't resumed yet from fall break, but it doesn't hurt to get ahead.

This tiny room has been my go-to study spot for the past two and a half years, second only to studying outside. It's so small that it only holds two chairs, a wooden table, and one of my favorite paintings on campus that hangs on the wall opposite of the door. The room is nestled in one of the corners of the third floor of the library and its one window on the wall perpendicular to the door looks out over a small courtyard.

This space has been a safe haven, a place for me to go to get some peace and quiet. Or at the very least, a place to escape the elements outside. When it's blistering hot or when the heavens are coming down or even when the salty air turns dry and cold, I know this room will always welcome me with open arms. Most of the other study rooms in the library are occupied most of the time, more so when finals roll around, but with this room being so small most groups don't even bother coming up here.

My library room, my little peaceful corner of the world, feels different today. I can feel myself sitting a bit more rigidly, the wooden part of the chair digging into the backs of my thighs.

Maybe it's because I'm older today... I can feel it. Most of my birthdays feel no different than the day before so why is today any different?

The music changes and in the silence between songs I hear a group of loud footsteps approaching the room. Several voices accompany the footsteps and I squint at the wooden door blocking my view.

No one should be talking on the third floor.

Annoyed, I start to stand to figure out what's going on or at least tell the group to fuck off. My knees crack with stiffness as I stand but that's not what knocks me back into the chair.

Instead, it's a blinding heat radiating up my left arm, like I just stuck it into a fire. I feel my spine hit the back of the chair as the air gets knocked out of me. I try to get enough air in my lungs to cry out in pain but before I can, the burning pain is gone just as quickly as it came.

"What the fuck was that?" I say out loud, but my words only reach the other empty chair in the room.

It takes me a moment to collect myself. Looking down, I grab my wrist with my other hand and massage it, examining the area. But there's nothing.

Odd...

Maybe a slight discoloration on the inside of my wrist but no physical explanation of the burning sensation beneath my skin. With every passing second, the pain slowly subsides and my heart rate settles into a relatively normal rhythm.

You're fine, my subconscious says, trying to ease the worry still nagging at me.

My phone buzzes aggressively on the table next to me. I pick up my phone and check the new text.

***Happy Birthday Nola from Flynn, Max, and me!**
Oh and Max drew you this masterpiece:*

The next message is a crayon drawing of my likeness if I can call it that, with a birthday party hat on. The ones that are triangular and striped, purple and blue. I can't help but smile at the scribbled mess and think about the concentration that had to be on Max's little face as he drew the picture carefully, picking each color purposefully.

Looking back up at Lawson's name at the top of the text box, my smile drops as I think back to the hushed conversation between him and our mother yesterday. They made it sound like it was my last day to be normal, but I just don't understand how this changes anything...

The same unease that had started to subside returns full force like a sack of coal in my chest. My hands itch with the message I want to send. Confronting him for answers. Ask him about the conversation and what it meant. But instead, my thumbs are still, hovering over the screen not knowing where to start. I put my phone down on the table, running my sweat slicked hands along my jeans. The suffocating feeling rises in my throat and my feet move before I can stop them. Pacing behind my wooden chair, I run my hands through my hair. This feeling is like nothing I've ever experienced. Even in my darkest moments, I could still breathe, if only just a little.

I stop pacing and close my eyes. Forcing my lungs to cooperate, I take a deep breath.

There's no reason to panic, Nola. The choice is yours to ask Lawson or not.

She's right and I know it. I open my eyes and stare out the window, down to the courtyard below. Today is supposed to be a good day and now my own brain is making it miserable with its ever spinning web of thoughts. Through the noise in my head, I can faintly hear my phone buzz once again behind me.

Another birthday message, I'm sure of it.

I turn back to the table having decided, it's my day, and confronting Lawson is only going to pull me back to that suffocating feeling when all I want to do is breathe. I grab my phone and type out the quick message.

Thanks. Tell Max I said it's his best work yet.

It is only a few seconds before his response comes through.

I hope you get to enjoy your day. We love you.

I read over his message several times and it has the same ring as our mother's voice yesterday, only concerned with me enjoying my birthday. It's a near mimic of her words...

My phone buzzes insistently again in my hand, breaking me away from the memory. Glancing at it I see Harley's name and face on the screen.

"Hey, Harl," I say into the phone already knowing that this

conversation will go like the others this morning but still happy to hear from them.

"Woah, your excitement is palpable," they say sarcastically. I can hear their smile through the phone and laugh.

"Sorry. Let me adjust..." I clear my throat dramatically. "Hello, Harley! I have so missed you and can't wait to hear what you have to say through this electronic device!" I laugh.

"That is much better! HAPPY BIRTHDAY NOLA!" they shout.

I can hear a few mumbles on the other end, which means they're more than likely in public and just yelled. My cheeks flush red from the embarrassment even though I'm not there.

"Jesus, Harley! You didn't have to shout..."

"Yeah well, you're the big 2-1. Welcome to the club!"

I think back to their very own 21st birthday in August before junior year started.

"You been keeping my place warm?" I smile.

"Yeah yeah, you can't make any more old jokes now that we're in the same boat. Anyways, how do you feel? Do you feel any different?" Their voice shifts from joking to serious quickly and it throws me off guard.

"Ummm..." I pause, my mind racing over everything.

Nothing makes sense.

"No, not really," I lie. "Feel just about the same as I did yesterday, except now I guess I can drink... legally."

"Okay good..." they pause, and I can hear the concerned shift in their voice.

"So, I have some bad news."

"Oh no..." I hesitate.

"Unfortunately, I won't be able to make it to Edge tonight and celebrate with you, but I'll make it up to you soon, I promise! I just got wrapped up in some schoolwork."

My heart drops, they were my only saving grace for whatever Ash has planned for tonight.

"Booo..." I frown at my phone. "Screw schoolwork."

"Like you aren't sitting in the library right now studying," I can hear the smile on their voice.

"Woah... how did you know?" I look around looking for a hidden camera or something.

"I probably know you better than you know yourself, Nola Rae," they say with complete honesty.

"So, what do you have planned for tonight!?" their voice overpowered with excitement.

"Well, I think Ash is planning something but I'm not sure what just yet. I'm sure I'll hate every second of it," I say sarcastically and I can hear Harley laughing on the other end.

Just then my phone buzzes against my ear.

Speak of the devil.

"Hey Harl, Ash is actually calling me now. I'm sure to break the news," I roll my eyes and laugh. "I already miss you and hate that you won't be able to make it tonight."

"I know, I miss you too," Harley says.

"I'll talk to you later?"

"Of course! Good luck. And happy birthday Nola... Enjoy it!"

The line goes dead, and I quickly answer Ash's call.

"Hey, Ash! What's up?"

"We have it all arranged," she says a bit breathlessly. "Dinner at the café at six, then getting ready at the apartment. We've already picked outfits, well costumes really..."

I groan.

"Hush, you'll love it," she counters quickly. "And then Horizon at 11."

"We? Horizon?" I say hesitantly.

My mind tries to picture the club that has quite the reputation as one of the more reputable clubs in this small town.

"Yes, and I won't take no for an answer or Jess will actually murder me."

Jessika Conti is our mutual friend that Ash and I met our freshman year during one of the school sponsored events. She often joins us when we study or on the rare occasions, we go out. She's headstrong, her words always sharp, like every syllable is weighed and calculated before leaving her mouth. Jess is the kind of friend that keeps you grounded when your head gets stuck too far in the clouds, which mine often is. I smile knowing full well that she actually might kill Ash if I disapprove of tonight's festivities. Especially if they've already been planning this.

"Ugh... fine. Do I at least get to know what costume you guys have planned for me?" I beg.

"Nope. You'll see it tonight."

The call ends with a definitive click.

Normal. I can do normal. I can go out with my friends tonight of all nights. That's what everyone does.

I can do this, I say to myself as my subconscious takes several shots of clear liquid courage.

Tonight, the café is busy with students grabbing to-go meals quickly to finish getting their costumes together for the multitude of parties. Some of them come in fully dressed in their costumes already, a handful are half dressed in normal clothes and half in costume. Others, like us, are still in jeans and jackets.

Arlo Wesley, the one and only barista in this place and part owner, is at the counter taking orders while simultaneously preparing drinks. In the spirit of the day, he wears a simple orange button down with tiny black outlines of pumpkins all over it matched with dark pants. His sleeves are rolled up so that they're out of his way.

Pierre, his partner and chef, is running back and forth making orders just as fast as they are coming in. He's wearing a similar button down but it's white with black outlined ghosts, although the majority of the shirt is covered by his apron. They're not only fantastic business partners but an adorable couple. They dance around each other, almost like they can predict each other's next move. I smile as they playfully bump into each other in an attempt to throw the other one off. Arlo looks up and notices me watching, he smiles in return and waves. Blushing, I feel like I've just been caught doing something I wasn't supposed to, and wave back.

"Nola Rae, are you going to finish eating or just pick at it?" Jess says, bringing me back to our small table.

I look down at the half-eaten sandwich, which would normally be gone by now, and my stomach turns a bit. Too nervous about this evening.

"I think I'm done... mom," I smirk at her.

"Yeah, well I'm just trying to make sure there's something in your stomach before tonight," she rolls her eyes.

"We can always pick up something if needed," Ash chimes in with a shrug.

She takes another bite of her sandwich and Jess sips at the

steaming mug in front of her. I continue to pick at my food, trying to avoid their watchful gazes. My eyes catch on a group of girls who've just walked in, talking loudly in line.

"I really wish you guys would tell me what costumes you have planned," I say to Ash and Jess as I take in the group of girls and their elaborate costumes.

"And ruin the surprise?!" Ash nearly chokes around the bite of her sandwich.

"Absolutely no way," Jess agrees.

"Can I at least get a hint?" I clasp my hands together, crumbs falling onto the table in front of me, and meet both of their deep brown eyes.

They both look away from me, sharing a knowing look. It's like the look that Harley and I give each other when we're communicating only with our eyes.

A look only best friends know.

"Fine," Ash turns back to me. "You're gonna look hot."

She smiles showing all her teeth like that should explain it all.

"That doesn't help," I frown at her.

"We're all going to look hot," she continues, completely ignoring me. "We're gonna get so many numbers, well..." she pauses. "You and I will, Nola. Jess and Ben are doing their couple thing."

Ash turns to Jess and makes a face like a kid who doesn't get their way. I'm honestly surprised she doesn't stick her tongue out.

"Wait, Ben is coming?"

"Oh, great Ash, thanks," she raises her hands up in defense. "Nola, I was going to ask you if that was alright since you know Ben and he loves any excuse to come down to see all of us."

Normally, I would prefer just the three of us because I always enjoy our girls' nights but having Ben might help balance out our group. At least with him there I might not be the only one left out of the Jess and Ash dynamic. Besides, I do like him, he's good for Jess.

"Yeah, no that's totally fine!" I say, painting on an encouraging smile.

"Great, so are we ready to head out and start getting ready?!" Ash says, nearly bouncing out of her chair.

"Yeah, let me say goodnight to Arlo and Pierre and I'll meet you guys at the car," I say, getting up from our little table and grabbing our trash.

Crossing the café quickly, I stop at the part of the counter where Arlo has been placing drinks to be picked up. I grin up at him as he places yet another coffee on the counter.

Arlo has been one of my many constants in Edge. I met him one evening during finals my first semester. I needed to get off campus and study somewhere else, that's when I stumbled into this café. Arlo was standing exactly where he is now, and all I remember was the amount of care he put into every word while asking me how my day was going. We ended up chatting for an hour about finals and how I was liking Edge. Talking to him felt safe and so much like home, like talking with my father.

"Hey there Nola," he barely looks up, but an endearing grin spreads across his face anyways.

"Are you guys heading out?" he asks, finally meeting my eyes. "We could use the table you've been hogging."

"Wow, some way to treat the birthday girl," I feign hurt. "And here I was coming to say goodnight and thanks for the food as always!"

"We are always here to feed you, especially on your birthday!" he gestures wildly. "Speaking of which, wait here."

He spins on his heels and heads to the back of the kitchen.

There is a bit of a lull in the line of customers ordering, but a few come up in front of me to grab the remaining drinks on the counter. Before I can feel too awkward, Arlo is back with Pierre by his side. In his hands is a small white cardboard box.

"Happy birthday Nola," they both say in unison. Arlo gives me the box. The top of it is clear so I can see a small round cake in the box. It's red velvet, iced simply but elegantly with a few flowers. I look up and meet both of their smiles with my own.

"Thanks, you guys!" I reach up and hug Pierre tightly around his neck.

"Anything for you love," Pierre says as he kisses both of my cheeks, the ghost of an accent in his voice. He breaks our hug and starts to walk away, back to work.

"Have fun tonight!" he calls back. "Call us if you need anything," he waves.

I wave back but Pierre doesn't see. Back already turned as he vanishes into the kitchen.

"Thank you, seriously. You guys didn't have to do this for me," I say turning back to Arlo.

"We know, but we wanted to! You only turn 21 once and even adults get cakes," Arlo smiles and wiggles his eyebrows at me.

I scoff and roll my eyes as I reach up and wrap my arms around him. The hug is strong and quick.

"Anyways, what are you guys getting into tonight? Nothing too crazy I hope?"

His smile shifts as concern starts to leak into his expression.

"We're just going to Horizon. Jess and Ash are dragging me

really. But it should be fun," I shrug.

"Jess and Ash... anyone else?" he questions like only an overprotective father would.

"Uhh, well Jess's boyfriend, Ben is meeting us there..."

"Hmm..."

He pauses, eyes boring into mine. I shift uncomfortably under his gaze, feeling like every move I make is being analyzed. Arlo tends to be a bit overprotective, but I know there are good intentions behind the pushiness. I break away from his gaze and land on his hands across his chest. I notice that he's rubbing the inside of his left wrist over a small tattoo there. I've seen the small wings before but seeing them now, it stirs something in me, comfort maybe?

Absentmindedly, I touch the inside of my own wrist.

"All I ask is that you're careful. Have fun and enjoy but be careful."

He lifts his arms and wraps them around me in another quick hug, but there's a hint of a warning in his voice.

"Call if you need anything," Arlo says sternly next to my ear.

Arlo waves as he turns back around to continue the working dance with Pierre. I turn to head to the door, confused about why it seems like everyone keeps telling me the same thing. Like they know something I don't.

Whatever it is, it's starting to irk me. The anger crawls under my skin, making me shiver a little. I push open the door of the café more aggressively than I intended.

Looking up, I see Jess and Ash laughing next to my car. Well, if everyone wants me to have a normal birthday... I'm going to have a normal 21st birthday. I grin as I reach them, deciding to welcome whatever chaos is in store for tonight.

FOUR

"Cheers to Nola finally reaching the ripe old age of 21!" Jess raises her shot glass to me.

"Ha. Ha. Very funny," I respond sarcastically, letting our glasses clink in the air. The familiar burn of the tequila washes down all my worries of the day, really the past few days, and settles warmly in my stomach.

"Hey! You guys started without me!" Ash complains as she rounds the corner into our tiny kitchen.

Her dark cape billows behind her nearly catching on the edge of the counter. Ash is decked out with a black cape, a black velvet mini dress, and fishnet stockings. She pairs her outfit with black shiny stilettos that accentuate her long legs beautifully, this is her version of a sexy vampire. Ash overdid her makeup a bit, but somehow the silver eyeshadow, a shimmery highlight that contours her cheekbones perfectly, and bright red lips look elegant.

For me, she picked out a "sexy" wildlife photographer

costume. Which meant I had to squeeze into khaki shorts, that were short and tight, paired with a cheetah print tank top, and a fake plastic camera to carry around. I couldn't help rolling my eyes at the whole idea, but I play along. It also didn't take much for me to give in and let her put a full face of makeup on me without any complaints. While I'm sure she wanted to go all out, she settled for a dark brown smokey eye to enhance my green eyes. I dug into the back of my closet to find my old brown combat boots to round out the outfit.

Jess and Ben had already planned out their outfits over the weekend. They decided on a couple of red devils. Jess's vivid red leather dress compliments her skin tone beautifully. She too is wearing fishnet stockings but instead of stilettos, she is wearing candy red platform boots. I didn't know exactly what Ben would be wearing but I had a feeling it was going to be a suit in a similar shade of red. Jess's makeup is darker than ours and she has pulled her hair up into a tight bun. She places the mini pitchfork she's meant to carry around in her bun, holding it all together.

"Here," I say, pouring another round of shots in the glasses in front of me on the counter.

"Oh no, I'm good. Someone has to make sure we all get home tonight," Jess says, waving her hands in front of her.

I look at the three shots and slide one to Ash.

"More for me," I shrug and down the two shots quickly.

"Woah. Alright, I like this version of Nola," Ash cheerfully clinks the now empty shot glass in my hand, downing her own.

"Like I said, one of us has to get us home," Jess shakes her head but smiles.

I smile back, cheeks flushed and already my vision blurs slightly. Jess's phone chirps and she glances at it quickly.

"Our cab is here," she winks mischievously. "Are we ready to go gals?"

I look over to the couch, hearing it beckon me. But the alcohol dances around in my stomach, making me flush as it promises to be a distraction for the night.

"Fuck yes!" I say, grinning widely.

Horizon used to be much smaller than it is now. Overcome with the ever-growing college population, the club expanded out of its small main building and added on a second bar and outdoor area. From the outside, it's one of those clubs that if you passed it during the day, you would have no idea that it was a club. It's only distinguishing feature from the buildings around it is a bright green door with a burnt orange "**H**" on it.

Our cab pulls up to that bright green door after a short drive. Even though it's a Monday night, the club is bursting at the seams with college students dressed in all sorts of costumes. A lion is out front smoking a cigarette, passing it back to what I assume is his animal tamer, a guy dressed in a khaki short sleeved button up and matching shorts. A group of girls with barely-there dresses are waiting outside the front door of the club, trying to flirt their way past the bouncer.

We all file out of the cab, getting in line behind the group of girls. As we wait for them to be ushered in, the music from inside rattles the door and I can feel the bass beneath my feet. A cool breeze brushes at my exposed legs, sending a small shiver up my spine. Luckily, the girls file in the club a moment later so we don't have to stand in the cold for too long. We quickly flash each of our IDs at the large bouncer, but he lets us in without so much as a grunt of acknowledgment. If my stomach wasn't already filled with the shots of tequila, there might have been butterflies fluttering from the excited nerves.

Once through the door, I'm immediately overwhelmed by the blaring music, felt deep in my chest, and the overpowering scent of floral perfume mixed with sweat and cologne. We're immediately swept up in the sea of bodies on the dance floor. It takes a few minutes for my eyes to adjust to the darkness and ever-changing colored lights beaming down from the ceiling. My ears ache with the music until they too become accustomed to the noise. I try to decipher what song is playing but the music morphs and changes as the DJ does his thing in his booth at the corner of the room opposite the bar. The music, while overwhelming, is infectious. I find my body moving with the beat before I can control it, getting lost in the melody. I feel someone grab my hand and pull slightly. Looking at the source I see Jess motioning her head towards the bar.

"Ben is over here! Let's get some drinks!" she shouts over the music.

I nod and let her lead me out of the crowd, shoving our way through the crowd. We cross the room to the bar in no time and I catch Ben leaning against the bar casually. Like I suspected, he's wearing a bright red suit, no doubt already sweating. His light brown hair is cut shorter than the last time I saw him.

Ben's eyes scan the crowd and land on Jess and me. His face splits into a wide grin taking in Jess. We reach him and she releases my hand to throw her arms around his neck. He picks her up and squeezes her around her waist. They kiss lovingly and I turn away, a flash of green envy hits the pit of my stomach.

I see Ash standing nearby, chatting animatedly with a few

people who I recognize from our major class together. Reaching over I grab her arm to get her attention.

"Hey, Ash!" I shout when she looks over.

"Hey, guys!" I say to the group of people around her.

If only I was better with names. I'm sure we've all been introduced before, but for the life of me, I can't remember a single name in this group. I smile at all of them, and they smile politely back. One of them sways slightly and I can't tell if it's because of the music or the alcohol spilling over the side of the clear plastic cup in her hand. If I had to hazard a guess, it's the latter.

"Hey, girl! We gotta get you a drink!" Ash shouts back to me.

When she turns, she's holding a drink in her hand. I think it is orange, but it changes colors too quickly under the lights for me to be sure.

"Yes! What're you drinking?!" I say loudly in her ear as I pull her to where Jess and Ben are now talking to each other.

"It's a tequila sunrise. Basically, just tequila and orange juice! I figured I'd stick with tequila tonight," she smiles.

"That sounds amazing!" I feel my mouth water at the thought of the cool orange juice.

Ash and I squeeze in next to the rest of our group.

"Hey, Nola! Happy birthday!" Ben shouts from the other side of Jess. He still has a grin plastered on his face.

"Thanks, Benny-boo!" I joke, using the same nickname that Jess calls him. "It's so sweet of you to make the trip just for me," I wink at him, nudging Jess in her side.

Her answering look of annoyance sends me into a fit of giggles.

"There goes your chance of me buying you a drink tonight," Jess says with a smile playing on her lips.

"Oh shit! Well, that's alright," I lean around her. "Benny-boo, can you get me a drink pretty please?" I clasp my hands in front of me, begging.

Jess pushes me away and we all laugh. In between laughs, I catch Ben waving his hand slightly to get the bartender's attention.

"What can I get you guys?" she shouts clearly over the bar.

Leaning slightly over to give us her full attention, her lip ring catches in the light as her lips form the words.

"What do you want, birthday girl?" Ben asks me.

"Oh, we have a birthday?" the bartender looks excitedly at us. "Who's birthday is it?"

"Mine," I answer, alcohol taking away my shy filter. My cheeks don't get the memo though as they blush, embarrassed.

"Happy birthday! What can I get you?"

"Umm... I'll take a tequila sunrise," I say quickly.

She nods then expertly begins pouring the drink. It only takes a matter of seconds for her to gather the ingredients, skillfully pour everything into a cup, and place the bright sunny drink in front of me.

"Here you are. On the house. Let me know if you need anything else!" she smiles and quickly turns to walk towards another group at the opposite end of the bar.

"Well damn. We should go out more often for birthdays. Free drinks!" Ash says excitedly. I smile, taking a sip of the drink. It's sweet and a bit tangy but delicious.

"Come on!" Ash grabs my free hand, shouting as the music changes. Her eyes sparkling in the lights as she pulls me, "let's go dance!"

Jess and Ben are too busy talking to each other in their own little bubble to notice us walking away. As I let Ash lead me back to the dance floor, her cape flows behind her, the end of it tickling at my knees as I trail closely behind. Continuing to sip my drink as we squeeze back through the bodies, I welcome the cool liquid as the heat radiating off the crowd becomes overwhelming. We come to a stop in the middle of the floor, looking down, I realize half of my drink is gone.

Oops...

The room tilts around me but I try to ignore it, letting my body be swept up by the upbeat music.

Ash and I have gone out several times before this but usually just to some house parties around town. Each time I could feel myself coming more and more out of the shell that I've buried myself into. Ash has helped pull me out of it slowly but surely and tonight is no different. She sways to the music, bouncing slightly on her heels to the beat. I smile and mimic her moves, adding little shimmies to my bouncing. We both laugh. We dance like that for a bit, making complete fools of ourselves. As the music changes, I look over her shoulder and notice two guys watching us.

One is taller than the other, but both have blonde hair tucked underneath baseball caps. They are wearing matching baseball uniforms, I guess they're a part of a team costume.

Real original, my subconscious rolls her eyes.

The tall one locks eyes with me and nods to the other before heading towards me. There's something about him that is oddly familiar, I try to rack my brain to place him, but it just swims with the alcohol.

He stops right in front of me, smiling, and I'm hit with the scent of cheap cologne and beer. His smile is charming enough and he's definitely attractive. He leans down to speak directly in my ear, I feel his hand grabbing my waist.

"Wanna dance?" his words are loud and slurred.

Looking over his shoulder, I see Ash dancing with the other guy he was talking with. I brush off the unease and shrug.

"Sure!"

Blondie smiles wider, showing off perfectly straight white teeth. His hands find my waist and I awkwardly put my arms around his neck, letting him lead me in time with the music. The dance is a bit off, but we sway together as the music picks up. Suddenly, he turns me around to where my back is up against him. I feel his hands travel down my thighs. Closing my eyes, if only to stop the spinning of the room, I let the music take over my senses. I sway my hips and bounce to the beat of the song... or was it two songs already? I lean back into the guy to steady myself and his hands travel upwards. The movement quickly snaps me out of the dance. The last person whose hands were on me like that were Sean's. Without thinking I spin on my heels and for a second, his reflection flashes across blondie's face.

"I... I gotta go," I stutter, just loud enough to his stunned face.

I don't give him a chance to respond before I turn to head back to the bar. My body begging me to run right out of the building.

Sean isn't here.

He can't be.

Not today.

The room spins with every pulse of the bass and somehow my hands land on the cool top of the bar. My drink spills a little on the counter and I down the rest of it, slamming the plastic cup back down. The combination of ice cold and the warm feeling of the alcohol eases some of the rattling in my chest and buzzing in my brain. The alcohol doing its job tonight, keeping the memories and lies locked away. His voice, his hands, the bruises they left.

"Hey," a deep voice comes from somewhere far away, startling me. "Are you alright?"

I peel my eyes away from the melting ice in my cup to find where the voice is coming from. To my surprise, it's right next to me. Well, he is right next to me. I blink a few times, trying to get my eyes to focus fully.

Fuck this guy is gorgeous!

His eyes are bright blue, like the base of two flames, but they change every few seconds beneath the ever changing lights. The stubble of a 5 o'clock shadow perfectly frames his jawline and lips. His jet-black hair is disheveled but in a devil-may-care way. I feel laughter bubbling up my throat and before I can stop it, it escapes with a cough.

This guy can't be real. It's got to be a cosmic joke. He looks like every leading man in every movie, tv show, or book I've ever read. And yet, he's sitting on the barstool next to me and just asked me if I was alright.

Shit. The music changes to something softer that doesn't need to be yelled over.

"Um... yeah. Sorry. Yes, I'm alright," I answer finally.

He leans closer to me and a wave of warmth comes with him.

"Good," he says with a smile playing at the corners of his mouth. "Can't have someone as beautiful as you not having a good time."

I nearly choke on the noise that comes out of my throat. I feel my cheeks flush and this time it's not from the alcohol.

"Ha!" is the only coherent thing that comes out in response.

"What?" his voice and face shift to one of innocence.

"Nothing... just, coming on strong there buddy."

Buddy? Really? My subconscious smacks her hands against her face in disbelief.

He leans back, taking the warmth with him.

"Apologies," he starts. He grabs the beer in front of him and takes a sip. Placing the beer back on the countertop he reaches out his hand to me.

"Name's Blake."

The music changes and the bass assaults my ears once again. I desperately wish I had another drink to deal with the music and the fact that I'm going to have to yell again. I reach out my hand and grab Blake's outstretched one. His grip is strong and damp with condensation from the beer. His hand radiates the heat coming from him tenfold and shoots through me like an electric current. I release his hand quickly.

"Nola," I say recovering from the shock of electricity.

"A beautiful name for a beautiful woman," he smiles.

I can't help but smile back even as I roll my eyes.

"Charming," I say back to him.

"That's what they say," he shrugs. "Can I get you another drink?"

Blake's blue eyes glance briefly down at my empty cup and then back up to me.

Oh, this guy is good.

My subconscious sits up from her slouched drunk position and adjusts her boobs. She's ready to get his number and go home with him and I can't blame her really. I'm floating happily above the surface of the waves of emotions over the past few days and the alcohol is my life raft.

"Birthday girl!"

The voice of the bartender comes from in front of us startlingly me away from Blake.

"Are you ready for another drink?" she asks excitedly.

I didn't realize he had leaned back in until I feel his warmth next to me once again.

"It's your birthday?" Blake's voice is close to my ear and his warm breath sends shivers down my spine. I can only nod my head in response.

"Well, you have to let me buy you a drink now."

I can hear the smile on his lips more than I can see it and I can't help the intoxicating pull of my own mouth spreading across my face.

"You really don't have to..." might as well play hard to get.

He turns away from me, the smile on his lips is now a full grin.

Did I just make him smile like that? Fuck that's a good smile...

"We will take another round please Casey," he says to the bartender.

She, Casey, gives him a polite smile in return, turning to go make the drinks.

"So, you know the bartender?"

Blake shrugs his shoulders and it's the first time I've let my eyes wander past his face. He's dressed in a dark plaid button down that looks either blue or green, sometimes with hints of orange depending on the lights. It's unbuttoned revealing a dark t-shirt underneath. He's also in dark jeans.

If he is wearing a costume, I don't get it.

"I know a lot of people around here," he answers simply. "I'm surprised I haven't seen you around. Do you come here often?"

"Did you really..." my face splits further into a grin as I start laughing. "Did you really just give me that line?"

He shrugs again but keeps silent, encouraging me to answer. His blue eyes flick with interest and something else as he looks back at me. I can feel my heart in my chest and this time it's not thumping in time with the bass. Casey returns with our drinks, and I thank her quickly, greedily taking a sip of the sweet liquid.

"Um... yeah no I haven't actually been here to Horizon before. Today is my 21st and my friends thought it would be fun," I answer, words tumbling out without much thought behind them.

Blake nods like it's the most logical thing but that can't be right because the words don't sound right on my tongue.

"And are you having fun?" he tilts his head in interest, eyes locked in on mine.

I can't help but stare with the same intensity. There's no way this guy is this interested and yet he's staring at me like I'm the only person in this crowded room. My heart continues to beat against my ribcage like it's never beat a day before in its life. I peel my eyes away from the blue flames and back to my drink. I take another hearty sip hoping that it'll make me more fearless. If this guy really is interested, what's the harm in testing the waters? The next words out of my mouth are words I don't think I would've said if I wasn't drowning in orange liquid courage already.

Fuck it.

"I could be having more fun..." my eyes flick back up to his and I can feel the lust on my tongue. As I lean towards him, he shifts to face me more.

"Do you want to dance?"

In one smooth motion, he downs the rest of his beer and holds out his opposite hand to me. I quickly finish my drink as well and smile as I take his hand. The warm electrical current is still there but it's muted, like everything else around me. I stand too quickly and sway slightly on my feet. Okay, so I may be drunk, but what else could I have expected for my 21st? I wanted to have fun and let loose. Have the "normal" birthday everyone wanted me to have.

And so yes, I may be drunk and about to dance with a complete stranger but sue me.

Blake quickly moves his other hand to my back to steady me. We're swept up quickly in the crowd, pushed closer together just to make room for those around us. I can feel the sweat starting at the base of my neck from the heat of the alcohol inside of me and the closeness of Blake at my back.

Focus, Nola. All you have to do is sway to the music.

We reach an opening in the middle of the crowd and I turn to face Blake. His gaze is just as intense as before and never leaves my face. The burning blue glows mischievously in the lights. Running my eyes over his face, he grins widely at me. Instead of the uneasy feeling of blondie, Blake's smile only brings me comfort. I reach up and wrap my arms around his neck, as he towers over me. In the same motion, his hands find my waist and we pull each other closer. I can see the confidence in his smile, but his eyes show how hesitant he really is, questioning every touch. I lean in closer, wanting to be as close as possible to him. It pulls at me in a way I've never felt before, not even with Sean.

Blake sways to his right and I follow a second later. Everything moving sluggishly with the slosh of alcohol in my stomach. We dance slowly, far slower than the song would suggest moving as everyone around us is jumping excitedly to the beat. I think the music changes, but it sounds so far away, not piercing the bubble surrounding Blake and me. He leans his face down, making my heart jump in my chest. No way he is about to kiss me. His cheek brushes up against mine and I feel the soft stubble press against my jaw. My subconscious deflates from her expectant pose, and I can't help but deflate a little with her.

"I have to say," Blake says low in my ear, drowning all the other sound around us out, "you are quite breathtaking, birthday girl."

I smile as his words send a rush through me. I can feel them, warm and tingly through my brain, fluttering in my stomach, making me weak in my knees. It flows like the burning electricity that seems to be charging the air around us, between us. The feeling almost as intoxicating as the tequila.

I pull his face closer so that his forehead is resting on mine. I try to look in his eyes, but they're too close to focus on. Instead, I land on his mouth. His lips full and a smile tugs at the corners. It might be the alcohol talking, but I want his lips on me, all of me. It's a strangely powerful feeling that I've never had before. I pull against his neck, pressing my body as physically close to his as humanly possible. At this distance, I'm sure he can feel my heart beating against my chest. My eyes close as his lips brush lightly against mine. I expect them to come crashing down, but they don't. My eyes open and his face is next to mine, once again whispering in my ear, hot breath on my neck.

"I want to kiss you. But are you sure?"

I could see the question dancing in his eyes before he even asked it.

That's so sweet... my subconscious applies a vigorous amount of lipstick.

"Fuck it," I say, crashing my lips against his smirk.

A light laugh vibrates from his lips to mine, but only for a moment. I intertwine my hands in his hair as his hands break away from each other, one still resting on my lower back, holding me close to him, as the other travels up to my face. Tracing every dip and curve as it moves, sending shivers along my spine. He kisses me roughly but passionately and I can't help but reciprocate. Not able to get enough. To be close enough to him. The electricity continues to crackle around us, pulsing in time with the music.

Suddenly, the burning heat that was simmering around us shoots through me and turns into a raging inferno, centering itself on my wrist. It's the same fire that burned earlier today in the library but that doesn't make sense. The only thing I know is that the fire sobers me up quickly from the intoxicating pull of his lips. I gasp as I break away from him and grip my left wrist trying to calm it but the fire rages. The pain radiates through my hand and shoots up my arm. I take a few steps back, away from Blake. I look up at him, seeing the confusion and concern flash behind his eyes.

"Are you alright?" he asks through the cold distance between us.

I try to think of something to say but the room spins with the new pain.

"I'm sorry... I," I search for words through the fog, "I shouldn't have done that."

Looking around Blake, I beeline to Ash.

"Nola?" I hear Blake call out as I pass him. He reaches out for me, but I flinch away, not able to meet his eyes.

The fire rages as I grab Ash's arm, yanking her away from the boy she's wrapped up in.

"What?!" she shouts angrily, looking over, confused. "Oh, what's going on Nola?"

She takes in my pained expression and her mood changes quickly from irritation to concern.

"I need you to come with me to the bathroom," I say as casually as possible, not even acknowledging the other guy standing there.

"Err... yeah okay. Excuse us," Ash shouts to the guy as I tug on her arm. I feel slightly bad for pulling her away, but the fire continues to burn, drowning out everything else.

I catch Blake's confused blue flames of eyes. Turning away quickly, I leave him helpless on the dance floor.

Ash locks arms with me as we push our way through the crowd again. I lean on her trying to keep me steady from the blinding pain radiating up and down my arm. We reach the bathrooms at the back of the building quickly and luckily there's no one waiting outside the door. Bursting inside, I unlock my arm from Ash and head straight for the sinks.

"So, what's going on? It looks like you guys were hitting it off?" Ash says casually behind me.

I turn the sink on full blast, throwing my wrist under the flood of cold water in an effort to relieve the burning slightly. Something I've done when I've accidentally burned my finger cooking or straightening my hair.

"Um... yeah... Sorry to have to pull you away like that. It's just..." I hesitate, trying to focus on anything but the burning. "It's just, I don't really know. This pain just started and..." I look at my wrist and there's a slight discoloration that wasn't there before. It's dark red and raised.

Ash hovers next to me.

"Hmmm... it looks like some sort of rash or allergic reaction..." She shrugs.

I know she's just trying to help but her comment irks me a bit. If only she could feel the burning flames that are radiating through my arm, she would know that this is something more. Something different than any rash or reaction I've felt.

I watch her in the mirror as she turns away, entering one of the stalls behind us. Focusing back on my wrist, suddenly the dark red mark changes to a light brown.

I feel the panic start to rise in my throat.

"What the fuck?" I whisper to myself.

Just then the door to the bathroom opens and I look up to see two women walk through. They are both dressed in sparkly flapper dresses, one in silver and the other in gold with matching masquerade masks and satin white gloves. They look a bit older, maybe late twenties, a bit odd for a club like this. The woman in the gold dress has fiery red hair, styled perfectly in ringlets. The other has short straight blonde hair. Both have piercing blue eyes, but the rest of their features are obscured by the masks.

"I hope you're having fun tonight. It was a good night to go out. I mean did you see that guy I was just dancing with... what a babe," Ash says dreamily as she exits the stall. She stops at the sink next to me and begins to wash her hands.

"That guy you were dancing with too. Damn Nola, bringing in the hotties."

I nod slightly, distracted by the pain that still hasn't subsided and by the two beautiful women who have yet to enter any of the stalls. Looking back down at my wrist, I see the light brown mark is still there, but the edges are changing. Morphing before my eyes into a hard outline in blueish black of a... a wing?

That can't be right...

Peeling my eyes away from the strange burning mark, I meet two pairs of blue eyes in the mirror. Something flashes white before my eyes and then everything goes dark.

FIVE

The stench of something metallic mixed with mildew floats in front of me and startles me alert.

What is that?

I try to decipher the smell, it's like old mop water that has been sitting on the floor for far too long. A light drip, as if on cue, falls and lands on the floor somewhere in the distance...

or is it closer than that?

Listening as hard as I can, but my senses can't keep up with the racing thoughts in my brain. I try to open my eyes and get my bearings, only to be met with darkness. Something is covering them.

A blindfold.

Straining to see through or under the blindfold, I only catch a glimpse of some light pushing through overhead. I feel the panic rise like bile in my throat.

It wraps around my chest and squeezes like a snake intent

on killing me. My lungs try to push against it but the only oxygen comes in in short bursts. Sweat builds on my temples, rubbing against the blindfold. A fucking blindfold... the snake constricts again. What the fuck is going on?

Come on, keep it together. Focus. My subconscious keeps me company. *Assess your surroundings, Nola.*

That's something they always stress in all those true crime documentaries I watch. I know that I'm blindfolded but there's light beyond it. Shifting my hands, I feel the rough pull of rope holding them together behind my back. The rope bites at the burning on my wrist, though it has subsided a bit.

That's good, right?

My subconscious rolls her eyes. *Never mind that now! You're tied up!*

Metal, a metal chair. I can feel the familiar cool, smooth texture of it beneath my legs. I go to move my legs, but they too are tied at the ankles to the legs of the chair.

Okay, so moving isn't an option.

Focusing with all my might, I can now hear the drip of water clearly. It's coming from behind me around five feet or so. The muffled sound of a speaker playing music is also coming from the same area.

Horizon... So, I can't be far from people. Would they hear me if I scream?

I start to open my mouth, a scream building in my throat but another noise stops me.

A voice.

"Are you sure it's necessary to do all of this?" the voice, high and airy, says.

"Listen, it's the only way to get the point across. She has to know something..." a deeper hushed voice responds.

"Okay, but did we have to take both of them?"

Both of us? Who else... fuck, Ash. The realization sinks like a brick in my stomach.

"Maybe it'll motivate her to talk," a third voice hisses.

I crane my head to try to hear for Ash. Is she close? Why can't I hear her?

"Ahh looks like someone's with us now," the third voice says. Menacing excitement clear in her voice.

Light footsteps cross the distance from the voices to me. Followed by another set of lighter footsteps that stops about halfway to me. I brace myself for the unknown as my heart pounds in my throat. Whoever these people are, this can't be good.

Wow, understatement of the century Nola. My subconscious has her hands balled in fists in front of her. Always the fighter that one.

Suddenly, the blindfold is ripped away and I'm momentarily blinded by the fluorescents overhead. As I blink several times against the light, something shiny catches my eyes. Finding the source, I see the woman in the gold dress from the bathroom. Her fiery red hair is still perfectly placed around her shoulders. The only difference is now the mask is gone showing off her features fully. Her cheeks are cut sharply and jut out making her look almost feline. She's beautiful but she also looks like someone you wouldn't want to cross.

Behind her is the woman with the silver dress, her features are softer but still strikingly similar to the other. They could be related, maybe sisters.

Next to the blonde in silver is a short, stocky man. He looks uncomfortable dressed in a dark turtleneck that nearly covers his plump chin. His dark hair sticks to his sweaty forehead as his brown eyes dart back and forth between the two women in front of me. I catch his eyes once, but he looks away quickly. I swear in just that brief moment I can see panic and fear flash in his eyes.

What does he have to be afraid of? I'm the one tied up.

I struggle against the binds once again but to no avail.

"Hello Nola," the third voice from before says. Looking up I see the owner of the voice, the woman in gold.

"How..." I swallow my fear, trying to gain confidence. "How do you know my name?"

"Oh..." the woman laughs, the sound is shrill, reverberating off the walls. "We know plenty," she grins menacingly at me, white teeth shining in the fluorescents.

I flinch at the sound of her voice, my confidence quickly shrinking back to its original size.

"Listen, Nola, we need to know where it is," the woman in silver chimes in, her voice stern but kinder than her friend.

The pit in my stomach widens as the confusion rings in my ears.

"Where what is?" I question, my voice coming out stronger than I feel, shrugging my shoulders only to be answered by the rope's bite against my skin.

"Ha!" the redhead shouts causing me to flinch at the sudden noise. She turns back to the man still on the other side of the room.

"Are you sure this is Laine's daughter?" she asks him, and he nods nervously.

Mom?

What does my mother have to do with all of this? My mind flashes to her pained face, always concerned about me and I, her. But what's her connection with these people? Why would these people take me? Is this what she was trying to warn me about? All those vague 'be careful's. The brick of fear is still sitting heavy in my stomach, but a new pit has opened up, swimming with confusion and frustration.

"What does my mom have to do with any of this?!" I shout at the woman, obviously the leader of the trio, and she turns back to me.

"Ah, there's that spark," she smiles with all of her teeth, rubbing her hands together. I want to scream again, but I stay silent, waiting for her to continue.

"You must be her's. Laine and I go way back," she waves her manicured hand dismissively.

"Nola, just tell us where the Euch is, and we'll let you guys go," the blonde says. Annoyance rises in her voice but I can tell she's trying to keep the peace.

I look around and land on Ash, several feet from me. She too is tied up with her hands behind her back and legs tied to the chair. The cape of her costume is torn at the shoulder, barely hanging on. She's blindfolded, and her head is slouched forward. She must still be unconscious.

Fierce, protective rage radiates through my chest.

"I don't know what you're talking about," I say sternly, still looking at Ash.

Each word leaves my mouth like a threat. If these three don't let Ash go, they are going to regret it. I've never been one to fight but the instinct to protect flashes through me in a blinding frenzy. Ash has nothing to do with this from what I can gather, and I could care less what they do to me...

Suddenly, a sharp pain radiates across my right cheek from

my jaw to my temple, causing my head to turn in the opposite direction. My ear is still ringing and it takes me a moment to recover from the shock of being slapped. A hand grabs my shirt and yanks me forward, nearly lifting me off the chair. I feel the ropes protest as they dig into my skin. I look up and meet furious blue eyes.

"Pathetic little girl! You're going to tell us or much worse will happen to you!" the red-headed woman spits with fury.

I wince at the onslaught and feel a welt already forming on the side of my face, but again I stay silent. The woman tilts her head slightly, the way a cat would when examining with a wounded animal.

"Hm, maybe you'll spill by other means..." a wicked smile spreads across her face, she angles her face towards Ash but never takes her eyes off me. She starts to straighten up, loosening her grip on my shirt and my heart jumps in my chest.

"No," I whisper desperately. "I really have no idea what you're talking about. I don't know what a Euch is or why I would have it or any of this really!"

The last part comes out louder than expected, as panic overrides my earlier bravery.

Her eyes bore into mine, examining my words. Suddenly she reaches out her hand and I flinch away, afraid that another hit is coming but instead she moves slowly, deliberately. For a second, I see a familiar mark on her wrist, but I can't quite place where I've seen it before. Her hand stops when it reaches the top of my head, and she begins to stroke my hair.

"Poor girl," she says with mock kindness, the wicked smile still playing on her lips. "You have no idea what you are."

Just then, something crashes against the wall on the side of the room where Ash is. I look over and see her stirring slightly, finally coming to. Glancing above her head, I see the door still vibrating on its hinges. Through the door, someone bursts into the room. I strain my eyes, trying to make out the familiar figure.

Arlo? Why is Arlo here?

Confusion swarms my brain, but I try to focus on him. I watch as his eyes land on everyone in the room, finally his protective gaze landing on me. Concern and relief wash over him as he takes in the situation. I'm sure he can see the welt forming on my face. His eyes flash towards the woman in front of me. His concern immediately shifts to white hot anger, and I can almost see it fuming off him. He controls it expertly, taking a few steps towards the trio, watching each of them carefully.

"Sister Katherine," he nods towards the redhead.

"Sister Hannah," his eyes shifting towards the blonde.

"And Brother Abraham," the man in the back nods slightly back at him.

I watch as all three of them take several steps back as Arlo approaches them. Arlo's hands are raised slightly, he radiates an eerie calm with each step he takes. Hannah and Abraham nervously flick their eyes to Arlo and Katherine. Katherine on the other hand, while retreating, nearly growls at him.

"Well... hello Arlo? Is it now?" the name dances on her tongue. "Not sure if I like that name, you've had better..."

Arlo's eyes find my confused expression. He's had other names? What does that mean? I tug at my wrists, but the rope doesn't budge. He switches directions, taking several steps towards me keeping his expression calm both to me and the trio.

"I would've thought you kept better watch," Katherine's voice is laced with disgust. "Over your little pet project."

Arlo reaches me and mouths a *sorry*. He walks behind me, and I can feel his hands brush against my wrists. The rope tightens for a moment as he loosens the knot. Finally free, my arms fly in front of me, wrists still stinging from the rope. Across the room, a soft groan comes from Ash's chest. I don't wait for Arlo before I immediately start to work on the knots around each of my ankles. Out of the corner of my eye, I can see Arlo walking around me, all his focus back on the trio.

"Guys, there was no need for any of this," Arlo's voice is calm but stern, similar to the tone he used earlier tonight. He shrugs and waves his hands around the room.

"Wasn't there?" Katherine hisses. "You know that we need the Euch and you and Laine are deliberately hiding it from the rest of us. The ones who can actually use it for the mission!"

"You know that isn't true," Arlo replies simply.

"Brother, you know the Euch and its power — her power — can end all of this," Hannah pleads.

"Listen, it's not safe to talk about this now," Arlo turns his head slightly and I catch a glimpse of the sorrow that fills his eyes as he looks at me.

So many questions swim around my mind and I pour them all into my look back at him.

As soon as my ankles are loose, I stagger my way to Ash. My body moving with nothing but adrenaline at this point. My brain on the other hand is a jumbled mess, consumed by all the information swirling in this room and stress filling my lungs.

I can't think about that right now though because Ash stirs again in her chair. Getting her out of here safely is more important than anything else pounding in my head.

I cross the small room to her and will my fingers to work quickly with the rope tying her up.

"Anyways, I think we should all go our separate ways unless you would like this to be reported to the Guides. I'm sure they would love to know how their plan is going rogue," Arlo says casually, turning back to Katherine, Hannah, and Abraham.

My ears strain to keep up with their conversation, trying to keep up with the new words that I've never heard before. I free up Ash's hands and move to her feet. I reach up and brush my hair out of my eyes and wince as my fingers brush against my cheek. I can feel hot tears filling up my eyes. Tears of fear. Tears of confusion. Tears of anger. My chest heaves with the panicked breaths desperately trying to escape my lungs by any means necessary.

"You wouldn't dare," Katherine's words reach me as I stand slightly to get the blindfold off Ash's eyes. Her eyes are still closed but she's stirring more and more. The panic of the situation hits me all over again, I need to get her out of here.

I look back to Arlo, his back still to me as he sizes up Katherine. It's a world class pissing contest that isn't necessary right now. He must know we need to go so why is he just standing there?

"I would," Arlo answers her.

"That would probably hurt you more than it would us," Katherine says nonchalantly.

"Arlo..." the panicked word bursts out of me and floats through the room with a mind of it's own.

I stumble before getting my feet under me as I haul Ash up with one of her arms over my shoulders. Catching Arlo's eyes as he turns away from the trio, he quickly crosses the room and is by my side in seconds, getting Ash's other arm around him to help.

"Guys," Arlo looks back at the trio. "We can settle this another time without the Guides' involvement. Sound good?"

There's a moment of silence from the group as they look at one another. My heart, which hasn't stopped pounding against my ribs this whole night, feels like it's going to burst with the anticipation. Are they going to let us go?

"Well, what a fucking waste of time this was," Katherine says finally.

Without missing a beat, Arlo takes most of Ash's weight from me and starts to turn.

"Come on," Arlo says gently, placing a hand on my back to guide me.

"You'll be hearing from us soon Brother Arlo," Hannah calls from behind us.

"I will be expecting it," he answers.

We turn together towards the door, where the music gets louder from the club above us.

"Don't forget, Brother Arlo," Abraham warns behind us, his voice sounds closer which makes me turn and look at the stocky man. "You know who's coming," he tilts his head toward me.

With one last pitiful glance from him, I'm ushered out the door of the musty basement room. We take the stairs quickly, leaving the trio still talking behind us. I struggle with my own weight, or maybe it's mostly Ash's, but Arlo seems to be an expert at rescuing people who've been kidnapped because he's barely breaking a sweat. Some relief washes over me as we reach the top of the stairs and back into the crowded club. But the relief only lasts for a second, as the panic that has been sitting right at the surface of my chest rears its ugly head.

Everything is too loud, too stuffy, too hot, and it almost makes me stop, paralyzed by the weight.

"What the fuck just happened!?" I shout to Arlo, not able to keep it in anymore.

I can feel his grip tighten on my back and he nearly pushes me forward, towards the door of the club. No one seems to notice what is happening around them. They don't notice that I'm nearly shouting and having a breakdown or that Ash is still unconscious between us. I feel the burning anger mix with the fear and panic. They fill my chest at the same time the burning in my wrist returns.

Something pulls me to look up and almost immediately I see Blake's eyes on me. He's back at the bar sitting next to the guy that Ash was dancing with and another pretty blonde girl. I can't believe he's still here. Confusion fills his eyes as he takes in my face, lingering on my cheek for a moment too long. His eyes move from my face and land on Arlo. I watch as his face morphs into something I've never seen before. It's a mask of anger, fear, and disgust. He turns away quickly and goes back to talking with the girl next to him.

Arlo pushes again, shoving my attention back to him and Ash.

"No!" I protest, my whole body shaking. "Tell me what just happened!"

Arlo looks over my head to the door of the club and finally, I can see the cracks in his cool façade. I can see the panic simmering under the surface there.

"Everything will become clear soon," Arlo says, looking deep into my eyes.

His voice is clear and steady as the weight behind his words fill my mind. This time when he moves, I move with him. I don't have any more strength to hold back and truthfully, getting away from Blake, the trio, from the burn that won't stop, away from this disaster of a birthday, and out of this overcrowded club seems to be the things that move my feet forward. I let him push me the rest of the way out of the club. Guiding me to whatever answers lie beyond.

SIX

Steam rises up from the mug in front of me. The dark liquid nearly touches the brim, but I can't bring myself to take even the smallest sip. I know Pierre was just being kind when he placed the tea in front of me a few minutes ago and it would be rude to not at least act like I'm drinking it. But just the thought of something so mundane as drinking tea seems so trivial when the world around me is cracking at the seams.

The bell on the door rings as someone enters the café. That chime would be abnormal at this time of night, but I knew she was coming. Arlo called her on his way to come rescue us from the basement and I'm sure she was in her car before they disconnected.

The steam continues to swirl in the air, making itself at home in front of me. I watch as it manifests and disappears all in a matter of seconds, over and over, as she takes a seat in the chair opposite of me.

Can the steam feel the cracks within me or the world around me? Maybe it'll stay around long enough to fill the gaps.

"Nola, my little light..." my mother's voice is soft, hesitant. "I'm so happy that you're alright."

I keep staring at the wisps of white rising from the mug. For whatever reason, I feel like the moment I look away from it, my world really will shatter, like this one over-poured mug is the only thing holding it all together.

"Thank God Arlo was there," she continues. "I can't imagine what... they would've done if he didn't come in when he did..."

My cheek twitches and I feel the lingering soreness of the slap from earlier. I nod and slowly peel my eyes away from my safety mug. Landing on my mother, her face is painted with concern. Her eyes are wild with it, along with hesitation and a focus I haven't seen. Ever.

"I'm so sorry that all of this happened. That you got dragged into the middle of this... I wanted you to have a normal 21st birthday and I hoped for more time before we had this conversation," she takes in a deep breath, breaking eye contact. "I just, I don't know where to start..."

"Start with this."

I lift my arm up to show her my wrist. The mark that started to appear in the bathroom at Horizon is now a solid black wing on the inside of my left wrist.

"Ah, yes," she says, taking in the mark.

Hesitantly, she rolls the sleeve of her hoodie on her left arm, moving it to where the cuff now sits halfway up her fore-arm, showing me a nearly identical mark on her wrist. The only difference being instead of one solid wing, there are two. The same mark that was on Katherine and Arlo and I'm sure the others as well if I had the opportunity to take a closer look.

Not that I wanted to.

I remember seeing the mark on my mother's wrist every so often when I was growing up. One time, in my innocent childhood curiosity I asked her what it was. She wrote it off as a tattoo, something silly she got when she was younger. It had always piqued my interest but in my childlike mind, I laughed with her and went about playing with the other kids in the neighborhood, never giving it a second thought.

Until now.

"I'm assuming it's not some adolescent mistake in a grungy tattoo parlor?" I ask her sarcastically.

"No," she smiles slightly. "This," she turns her wrist, "this is the mark of angels."

My jaw collapses to the floor as the shock rattles through me.

There's no way...

"There's no fucking way..." my words voiced out loud instead of in my head. My mother sits in silence with pursed lips.

"Angels?" I question, trying to recover. "Like actual fucking angels? Like halos and fluffy wings and all of that?"

My mind rakes through all the information from my short years as a church going child/pre-teen.

We were never super religious. Sure, we went to church every now and then but when my father was deep in his addiction, my faith shattered, and I never really grasped any of it after that. Before that, I remember in after-school programs at our church I would have to read chapters in the Bible, coloring pictures from the stories. A few had angels in them, always floating high above the scene with bright wings on their backs and golden halos.

"Ha!" my mother scoffs. "No, not at all. But you know what, your brother said nearly the same thing. I guess I should've realized..."

"Lawson? Lawson is an angel?" I think back to all our fights, how much he picked on me growing up. I would think he was a little devil, not an angel.

"Well, technically, he's a Nephilim. Like you."

"Nephilim..." I repeat, the word feeling funny on my tongue.

"Yes, half angel, half human..." she pauses, searching my face.

I feel her eyes on me more so than I actually see them because I find myself staring back down at the mug. The steam has calmed as the tea has cooled but some small tendrils still float in the air. I wrap my hands around the mug, feeling the ombre of warmth of the thick glass. My body moves without my mind telling it to and I bring the mug to my lips, letting the sweet, earthy, warm liquid heat my core.

A Nephilim... I'm a Nephilim. I am half angel... I force my mind to try to make sense of any of it. I don't feel much different... Surely, I would feel... I don't know, 'angelic,' right? None of this makes sense.

"And you?" I say, staring into the mug watching the tea ripple with my shaking hands.

"I, well, I'm your mother."

She reaches across the table and places her hands on mine around the mug. Pulling my hands towards the table, the mug lands with a slight thud against the wood. She doesn't remove her hands, instead keeping them holding the outside of mine. I don't flinch or pull away because even if she is something more, she's right – she's still my mother. She's still the one person who can bring me comfort in the smallest ways. I meet her kind eyes and she smiles softly at me.

"But I'm also a Protector," she continues, and her face turns into something more pained. "A part of one of the factions of angels sent to live here on Earth for several years to protect, save, and guide humanity to the light. Arlo and I are in the same command."

Factions of angels? Plural, there are multiple factions. How many are on Earth? Where else would they be? Is there a Heaven, really? The questions spin in my head, the room spinning with them. It's an unsettling reminder of how much I drank tonight. Even though I've sobered up mentally from the shock of everything, I can feel the alcohol slosh like an ocean in my stomach.

Focus Nola, one thing at a time. I take a steady breath and the last wisps of steam blow away from me.

"And those people from tonight?" I can focus on what happened, I think I can process that at least. "Katherine, Hannah, and Abraham?"

"Also Protectors, but a different command. One that has apparently gone rogue."

"They were looking for something... a Euch? What's that?"

"The Euch... of course..." she pauses a beat, shifting uncomfortably in her chair. "Um, well the Euch is a sword. A very powerful sword crafted by the same smith who created Archangel Michael's flaming sword. It's a steel sword bathed in holy oil, making it deadly to... darker creatures..." she hesitates. "Really the darkest one."

"The darkest one? You don't mean?" I search her serious eyes for the answer.

"Yep, the Devil himself," she nods, watching my every move.

"And why would they think I have a sword like that? Or that you would?"

"Well," she hesitates, and I can see the thoughts crossing her mind behind her eyes. There's a pause as she weighs what she wants to say next. It gives me some time to bring the mug back to my lips and take a steadying sip.

"Short version is: there's a war going on my little light," the words leave her mouth with all the pain behind her eyes. It hurts me to see how much it hurts her to tell me these things almost as much as the shock that pummels me in the chest.

"A war?"

The shock wins out, pushing the two words out with a rushed breath.

"Yes, it's a war that's been waging for thousands of years," she shifts once again, turning more professional like she's had this talk a million times. "The war between light and dark. Angels and demons. And like with all wars, there are weapons. Sister Hannah, Sister Katherine, and Brother Abraham apparently are on a mission now to get the Euch to help us," she pauses again to search my face to make sure I'm following along or maybe to wait for more questions, but all the questions stick in my throat.

She continues after a moment of silence, "My thought is that they took you to get to me. Because I'm a descendent of Archangel Michael, making our bloodline noble. And noble bloodlines tend to have arsenals passed down through the generations," she shrugs and looks beyond me. "But what they weren't expecting was how little you knew so that might have helped things. What I don't understand is why they would want it when it's basically useless in their hands..." her voice trails off in thought.

My head spins with the new information. There's a war. A war between angels and demons? So, demons are real? It feels like my head is swimming, overflowing really, like the tea in my mug. Even with my small sips, with every new question answered, there's not even a dent made in the hot liquid or in the mountain of questions that keep piling up. I try to wrap my head around the fact that not only am I not fully human but I'm half angel but I'm also a descendent of an archangel and apparently there's an arsenal... I take a few deep breaths to steady the thoughts racing in my head, but it doesn't help.

Every other word coming out of my mother's mouth comes out in a shout. I know she isn't yelling. I can see her mouth moving around the words. She's being deliberately gentle, business-like even, which is something I'm so grateful for considering the circumstances. And yet, from the time her carefully crafted words leave her mouth and travel the small space between us to my ears, the volume is deafening. This isn't something I'm unfamiliar with. Most of the time when I would get stressed in school or at home as a kid, or hell, even now, the panic would cause everything to be louder than what was around me. But it doesn't help that the lights above are screaming with electricity and the drip of the sink behind the counter sounds like a rainstorm in my head.

"Shut up," the words leave someone's mouth in a rushed shout. It takes a minute to realize they're my words.

"Nola, please..." my mother's words still come through as a gentle scream.

"Can you give me a second?" the words sound level coming out but I'm not sure.

My eyes flick around trying to find something, anything to silence the noises overcrowding my head. With a deep shaky breath, I grab the lukewarm mug, like it's my only lifeline, my only connection to a past life.

It feels like a lifetime before I muster enough courage to speak again. My mother, my angel of a mother sits patiently.

"So," I start, testing the waters. The storm of panic and noise still rages in my mind, but the tide is shifting slowly. "They assumed that I knew what I was... but I didn't because you kept all of this from me. Kept me in the dark until I was kidnapped!" my voice raises as the anger builds.

"I only kept this from you because I wanted you to have a normal life. As normal as possible, at least until you came of age," she rationalizes. "Then I guess, I hoped that I would be more prepared for this conversation. I didn't expect any of this to happen. For you to be thrust into all of it. In fact, I prayed that you wouldn't ever become a part of this."

"What do you mean?" anger still simmering on the surface.

"I mean that most Lights," she pauses when she sees the confusion on my face. "Sorry. We call Nephilim, the Lights... My little light..." she reaches across the table, grabbing my hands to hold in hers, and gives me an endearing smile before continuing. "They come of age at 21 and sometimes they get their wing..." she turns over my hand to show the wing and somberly rubs her thumb over it. "And sometimes they don't."

"If they do?" I ask hesitantly, staring at the new wing. "What happens then?"

"Well..." my mother gulps, debating on something behind

her eyes. "Currently, it's not pretty... which is why I hoped that you wouldn't get your wing."

"Well, I did. So, tell me," I say, voice stronger than I meant it.

She reacts as if I just smacked her across the face but recovers quickly, back to her serious demeanor.

"Most Lights are being wiped out. Killed by angels and demons," I feel her hands shake around mine as her whole-body shutters. "The few that are still left are in hiding, able to blend in with humanity. Or there's a small fraction of them who have joined some commands of Protectors to help humans, to help fight in the war."

The cracks in my world deepen as new ones split and tear at new sections. My life, my seemingly normal, college life, tilts on its axis. Nothing can be normal again, can it? A part of me wishes that the little black wing didn't exist, that none of this existed. No angels. No Nephilim. None of it. My life wasn't and isn't perfect, but it was normal...it was human. I guess that's still an option. Be human, undercover, in hiding for the rest of my life.

But you know you can't do that. I think to myself.

Not with mom out there. What if she needs my help? Or Lawson...

"What about Lawson?" my mind flashes to their hushed conversation, he knew something and wanted me to know too.

"He works alongside our command," she says matter-of-factly.

I nod, pretending to take everything in. I stare past her, out into the dark night through the window of the café. Questions fly through my mind. Why are the Lights being killed? Or should I say... why are we being killed? What does it all mean?

My mind automatically goes into pros and cons mode, weighing each decision. I open my mouth to speak but am cut off.

"Listen, Nola," I focus back on my mother. "I know that this was a lot of information. And I know you have a lot of questions, decisions to make. I can see all of that rattling around in your head," she smiles sadly, knowing me better than myself.

"But none of those have to be made or asked tonight. Take tonight and think everything over. I only ask that you be careful... There are things out there..." she tilts her head towards the door. "Things in the shadows – demons... that are going to try to hurt you."

"Don't forget the angels," the sarcasm drips out of me.

"Yes, them too. You can't trust anyone," she says sternly.

"Am I supposed to trust you?" I ask, feeling the hurt building in my chest.

She hesitates for a second, pulling back and crossing her arms over her chest. She gives me a look I've seen many times in my life. It's the look you get after you've done or asked something stupid. Her eyes squint slightly, weighing the options in front of her. Taking in a deep breath, she softens once again.

"Of course, you can, my little light."

"Really?" I push back. "You expect me to trust you after you've purposefully kept me in the dark about who... what I am. Not to mention my life is in danger from both angels and demons oh and there's a fucking war going on?!"

"Nola...I know it's a lot to take in—"

"Understatement of the fucking century mom."

"Let me finish," the dreaded mom tone fills her voice, silencing me. "Like I said, I know it's a lot to take in and there is a lot for you to think about. You need time to process but, in that time, I need you to be careful. And I need you to know that you can trust me and Lawson. We are still your family," she reaches back out to me, but I pull back, taking my mug with me.

"We've been through so much together. With your father..." she pauses with her hands flat on the table in between us, her eyes glued on the wood. My heart skips with the grief that comes with the memories of my father.

"You were so strong through all of it," she says as if she can see all the memories running through my mind. "I know you'll be strong through this too."

I laugh through the cracks in my world. Does she not see how the world is coming down around me?

"I honestly don't know if I can," I say at the end of my laughter.

"You will," her statement seems reassuring but carries its own weight.

"I just need you to promise me that you'll be careful," her eyes search mine, protective fierceness filling them. "While you take however much time you need. Can you promise me that?"

She needs the reassurance as much as I need hers, that's how we've always been. Each other's rocks when we need them the most. But how can I promise something like that when this new world has only just been opened to me?

I nod anyway.

"Good," she lets a puff of air out between us. "Can you also promise me that this stays between us? You can always talk with me, or Lawson, or even Arlo if you need to talk," I hear a shuffle by the counter and turn to see Arlo standing there, busying himself by wiping the countertop.

How long has he been there? He must have dropped Ash off at our apartment already.

"But it needs to stay between us..." my mother finishes.

Suddenly, I'm back in that hospital lobby after my father's first overdose. Just a scared kid that didn't know what was really happening and with the same weight of keeping everything between us as a family. My mother asked me to trust her then and is asking me yet again here to trust her enough to come to her if I need it.

Betrayal filled hurt stitches the cracks in the walls of my world.

Maybe I can't trust her, or any of them really, just yet but I can hear the words she isn't saying. It's not safe to talk about this. She's warned me not to trust anyone. Panic rises as my mind flashes to Ash. She's already been through tonight, being kidnapped with me because of some rogue angels thinking they could get information I didn't even know out of me. If angels can do that when they don't know that I know nothing, I can't imagine what they would do if I did know or if Ash knew anything... Let alone what demons could do. So many people in my life are now in danger because of what I am.

But maybe they don't have to be.

"Okay," the word is somber, defeated as it leaves my mouth.

I look over to see Arlo still standing by the counter, no longer pretending to do work. He nods his head, a promise.

"I need to head home," I say, stronger this time as I turn back to my mother. The weight of everything sits heavy on my bones, fighting my movements as I push the chair away from the table.

"You'll call right?" my mother asks nervously.

It pains me to meet her eyes.

"Of course," I lie to her.

She's right, of course, she is. It's a lot to process and now I know I need to figure out where to go from here. And I'm not sure yet if I'll go to her. The questions that still are unanswered filter through the murk of emotions in my mind. I catch each one, putting them in a box, to be filed and sorted later.

For now, I stand on new legs that drive my heart and mind away from my mother. The footsteps following me are my only indication that Arlo is right behind. Protection detail that I'm sure was agreed on between him and my mother long ago. Together we walk out into the darkness and whatever lies beyond the shadows.

SEVEN

The car ride back to my apartment was awkward to say the least. Arlo doesn't fill the silence with small talk, and I can't bring myself to indulge in the mundane task as well. The only sound that fills the car is the overbearing thumps of the road beneath the wheels. My mind too busy reeling with exhaustion and grappling with the truth that the guy sitting beside me in this car is an angel.

An actual fucking angel.

Oh and so is my mother.

And I'm part angel and so is Lawson.

The thoughts still don't feel real, even as we pull into the parking lot of my apartment complex and I'm not sure if any of it ever will.

"Um... thanks?" my voice cuts through the silence for the first time and even I can hear the pure exhaustion lacing itself within each syllable. "For saving me and Ash tonight. And umm, taking me home too."

My eyes flick over to Arlo in the driver's seat. He's turned, facing me, his own face illuminated by the soft orange glow of the streetlamp outside. His eyes are kind, they're always kind, even when he's being a sarcastic prick or just seriously overprotective. But now his expression is something like sorrow or pity like he just witnessed someone losing a loved one or that person just got a death sentence.

"It's no problem at all Nola," he says and even though his face shows his pity, his voice is nothing but honest.

I nod, turning away from him. I can't stand it anymore. The look on his face makes me feel like I'm something that's broken. Hell, maybe I am. The cracks in my head, in my world, are still there but for now they are taped up. Taped up with betrayal, pain, and exhaustion but taped up nonetheless.

"Right," I say as I open the car door.

"Wait Nola," there's pity in his voice now.

I sigh, one foot on the ground, one foot still in the car.

"I just wanted to let you know that I'm here too. If or when you are ready to talk..."

It's kind, it really is. I know that, at least the logical side of me knows that, but the other side of me is too hurt to accept it. Instead, I'm just annoyed. I know we have only known each other for the past two and a half years, but that was still time he kept this all a secret from me. He and my mother have been working together all this time and yet I had no idea.

"Thanks," is all I say. It comes out clipped with annoyance as I swing my other leg out, shutting the car door a bit too aggressively behind me.

There's nothing more that I have to say or even can say to him or my mother or any of them. At least without a world of regrets that come with it. The bite of the cold stings my legs as I walk through the small parking lot of my apartment complex, but that's not what chills me to my bones. It all comes back about demons and whatever else in the darkness that could be lurking in the shadows.

What if... no that tree just moved because of the wind... I'm sure of it.

My steps pick up anyway as I nearly sprint up to the third floor. I fumble with my keys for a second before I'm back into the safety of our warm apartment. Before the tension in my chest chokes me. I let out a breath into the darkness of our living room at the same time my phone vibrates aggressively in my pocket.

"Shit!" I shout to the darkness but quickly slap my hand over my mouth.

The moment of relief from being back in the safety of my apartment rushes out of me. It's replaced by something different. Worry that Ash might be nearby or hear me, wake up, and then what? Would I have to come up with some excuse? Figure out what to tell her.... Can I even tell her? How would I possibly tell her everything that I know now when none of it even feels real to me right now.

I move blindly, the room only partially lit by the blue glowing letters on the stove telling me the time.

2:47

Fuck... I have to get up for classes in a few hours.

Classes... college... I can't help the small rush of air that comes out of me. I think it's supposed to be laughter because of course I'm worried about getting to classes when I just found out that I'm a fucking Nephilim. It's all some sort of cosmic joke at this point, I'm sure. Because it still goes on. Still a part of me, my humanity. A wave of need rolls through me. A need to hold on to some sort of normal even while this new world stretches out before me. A world filled with Protectors, Lights, demons, the Devil, and who knows what else. A world balancing between life and death, at least for me and those like me.

I know I need to hold on to my human side, the only side that I've known. But I can't help but wonder where I would fit in or if I even would with this new side. Where do I go from here?

I pull my phone out of my pocket to give myself some extra light through the hallway and stop at Ash's door. Leaning close I can hear her soft snores. Another wave of relief flows from the top of my head to the bottom of my feet. I have some more time. A conversation with Ash isn't something I need to worry about right now.

My phone buzzes once again in my hands.

Who the fuck-

The names staring back at me aren't surprising which makes me even more annoyed.

I open the first one from Sean.

Happy Birthday beautiful. I miss u so much.

I delete it without a second thought. He has no right.

The next one is from my mother:

***My little light... I trust you made it home
safely.***

I scoff at my phone as I walk the few steps to my room, throwing the door open. Like she doesn't know.

I'm really sorry that you had to find out this way. But please know that you can come to me if you need to talk. About anything, You're still my little light and I'm still your mother. I love you.

I feel like I'm floating. No, not floating. Maybe more like I feel torn, split. Yet I'm still in one piece, still whole even if now, I'm split in half. Half angel. Half human. My world may have shattered and turned upside down, but I'm still me. I think. Maybe now I'm just a newer version. Whether that's a good thing or not, I haven't decided.

My humanity is begging me to forgive my mother. The part of me that wants to bury itself into schoolwork, hide away from this new world, and forget about it completely. This part of me that has grown up in a relatively normal life, give or take all the bullshit. But hiding away is what my mother has forced upon me without me even knowing. Can I keep that up? Maybe she would be able to help fill in some blanks about this new world, my new world, but the anger from earlier still simmers below the surface.

She kept me in the dark, on purpose.

I throw my phone on my bed, turning away from it, from my mother. I shower quickly, letting the warm water wash away the night, relaxing the knots in my muscles, and clearing my racing thoughts. But of course, it doesn't help completely. No matter how long I stay in here the day won't flow down the drain like I want it to.

So, I make another decision as I dry my hair. I pick up my phone and tap on the one name that I know will help me.

Someone who wanted me to know in the first place, Lawson. I quickly type out my message.

I know. We need to talk.

I press send with a new purpose.

The air's cold. So cold that I can almost see my breath against the bright blue sky. Sitting in the park behind my apartment, I look up and see the oak trees here are finally changing colors. The orange and yellow leaves burn with the sun. I smile with nostalgia... I've seen this dance before.

I grab my camera, which is conveniently sitting next to me, and stand up from the ground. Dead leaves crunch beneath my feet as I walk closer to the trees. I snap some pictures as I go, a picture of my shoes half buried in the piles of leaves, a great action shot of a leaf falling from the tree, another of a squirrel standing to attention before he scurried up a tree. I look through the many photos, smiling at some of the really bad ones but not caring.

I stop at one to admire the depth of focus on a leaf hanging precariously on the tree branch when I see something in the background. No, it can't be... my heart sinks to the pit of my stomach. A dark figure stands in the background of the picture. How did I not notice that when I was taking the picture? The hair on the back of my neck perks to attention and the familiar pit of fear opens at the bottom of my spine. What's new is the dull burn on my wrist where my wing is.

I look around still, needing to know.

It has to be somewhere...

I turn around, facing the pond where I took the picture.

"There you are," I say to the figure propped casually against the same tree.

How convenient.

Not quite sure if I should close the distance between us, I feel everything from the night before - *or was it a few nights ago?* - come flooding back. Memories of his lips on mine, the need to be closer, a buzz of alcohol in time with music, and all the intensity from before tingles on the surface. It flitters though the air with the same electricity buzzing through invisible wires. With the familiar feeling of terror and excitement filling me, an even stronger emotion comes into play, curiosity. I march over to him with determination.

"You really are a curious one, aren't you?'"

I flinch as Blake's deep voice stops me in my tracks, he's still several feet in front of me but somehow his voice sounds like it's right next to my ear.

He half smiles as he takes the hood off his head, revealing dark brown hair which is partially flattened but he quickly fusses with it, lazily styling it. He closes the gap between us in a few long strides.

"You should really be careful about that whole curiosity thing Nola," he shrugs with a smile. "You know what they say..."

I tilt my head with the confusion I feel and then it clicks. Curiosity killed the cat. Is he really making that joke right now?

"You know you ruined a perfectly good photo with you being creepy over here," I accuse him. "What are you doing here anyway?" I ask in the brief pause between us.

"Well. I am ever so sorry Nola, for ruining your picture. But you should really pay closer attention to your surroundings," he gestures around the park, and for the first time I realize how dark it's gotten.

"Hmm... that's strange... wasn't it just midday?" I ask out loud, half expecting him to answer but his silence lingers between us as his blue eyes stay locked on me. "You didn't answer me, what are you doing here?"

His shoulders lift slightly in a shrug, but his eyes never leave mine.

"Oh you know... just strolling around," his tone is nonchalant but there's an edge to it.

I tilt my head again, "Just strolling around in my neighborhood?"

Blake's eyes finally leave mine and take a look around for the first time. As he takes a moment to do so, something shifts along the edges of the woods somewhere around us.

I catch my breath. Something isn't right. I know that somewhere in my mind at least. But it seems so distant like reality is right there yet it's something that I can't grasp. My wrist flares again as Blake's eyes find mine once again. His face has shifted with the darker shadows that are moving between us. He looks down at my wrist and takes a step back.

"I suppose I was curious too," he says evenly.

The blue flames flick back up to me and the fire rages in my wrist with the same intensity of his stare.

"And now I know."

~

I wake in a cold sweat.

Absentmindedly, I rub the inside of my left wrist. There's a faint sting and heat rising from my black wing. There's no way that was just a dream, it felt so real...

Half dazed, I get out of bed to get ready for the day. I have three exams today, because apparently scheduling them right after fall break was a genius plan, according to my professors. I'm exhausted and unprepared, but somehow, that's not what I'm concerned about. Right now, my mind only drifts to the sounds coming from our tiny kitchen.

Ash.

There's no avoiding this morning and all the moments from last night come flying back. My super NOT normal 21st birthday started out so great and now I'm faced with this new reality as the wing on my wrist stares back at me. That's the biggest piece of evidence right there. I throw on a hoodie and pray that it's cool enough outside that I won't sweat all day. Okay, so maybe some version of my new world can still be hidden but Ash is no doubt going to have questions.

I tie my shoes slowly. The last step of this panicked zombie movie that was me dressing after getting almost no sleep, with what little sleep I did get being occupied by that very strange dream about Blake. More questions about that rattle in my brain, buzzing with the other questions that seem to never have left since last night. It's starting to feel like a test that I haven't studied for or even taken a single class on inside my head.

Speaking of...

I grab my bookbag next to my door. With one more quick look at the bags under the eyes staring back at me in the mirror behind my door, I take a deep breath.

"Here goes nothing," I whisper to the girl I barely recognize.

At the same time that my door opens, the anxiety that was

just simmering at the surface crashes down on me. My hands feel slick as I take the few steps down the hallway. The buzzing seems louder drowning out the questions, but in their place is sheer panic. My head pounds with it. Or maybe that's just the alcohol from last night or the lack of sleep. Regardless, my brain is a jumbled mess still wading through everything. If Ash has questions, how am I supposed to explain what happened last night? How can I tell her that I'm a Neph-

"Good morning, Nola!" Ash's voice reaches me through the void in my head. I wince at her excitement, feeling the full force of the headache.

"Oof, sorry about that," Ash's kind brown eyes meet mine and she lowers her voice with a smile. "Wild night huh?"

I can feel my heart pounding in my chest, I'm surprised she can't hear it in the tiny space between us.

"Yeah..." I rub at my temples.

That's a completely normal thing to do, right?

"Who would've thought you turning 21 would've been such a rager?" she turns back to finish buttering the toast in front of her. "I mean I can't remember most of the night... which is odd, I didn't think I drank that much..."

I turn away from her as I reach into our pantry to grab a breakfast bar. My stomach flips in time with my heart, maybe I'll just be sick right here and that's how I can get out of this conversation.

"I guess I blacked out," she takes a bite of her toast.

I see her shrug from the corner of my eye, so I bite my tongue. A flicker of hope flashes through the panic, maybe she doesn't remember...

"I just hope I didn't embarrass myself..." she continues.

"Oh shit, or you Nola. I'm so sorry if I did anything really stupid!"

The hope grows even more. She really has no idea...

"Well, you did almost make out with some random guy..." I tease her.

"Jase?" she tilts her head at me and her eyes glaze over. "Oh no, I remember that... I could've just eaten him up..." she bites her lip seductively.

"Ew."

"Like you have room to talk! I saw you with that guy!"

Heat rushes up the back of my neck, centering itself at my cheeks. It's embarrassing how quickly the memory of Blake's lips on mine comes flooding back, short circuiting my last remaining brain cells. Almost as quickly as the burn on my wrist that tore me away from him.

"Right..."

"You guys seemed to be hitting it off," she wiggles her eyebrows at me and winks. I can't help but smile at her as I take a bite out of the breakfast bar. "I have loads of questions about what happened with that situation..."

She pauses briefly to make her point. I open my mouth to tell her that it was nothing, but she continues.

"And then I remember you dragging me to the bathroom and then nothing. Do you remember what happened then?"

I nearly choke on the food in my mouth as my heart stops. Coughing, I search her eyes. I'm met with nothing but concern, probably because I'm nearly choking in front of her, and genuine curiosity.

She really doesn't know what happened last night. She doesn't remember being taken or the angels. She doesn't remember Arlo taking her home after dropping me off at the café. She's completely oblivious that at the café, I learned what I am and the new world I'm a part of and the world that she was dragged into. But she doesn't remember...

For that, I'm grateful. Maybe it's better she doesn't remember. Ash was already put in danger, and she didn't know then, I can't imagine what would happen if she actually knew what I was.

Suddenly my mom's voice fills my head: *only come to us if you need to talk.* Meaning, don't tell anyone our secrets. My subconscious nods her head, she knows our mother is right. Ash is better off not remembering what happened last night. For her own safety, I can't tell her what I am or what really happened. That only leaves me with only one option.

"Well, we went back to the bar," I lie.

I head towards our front door. My body apparently has a natural reaction to lying: try to escape the conversation by any means necessary. Sometimes that means changing the subject. Other times it means finding the nearest exit.

"Had a few more drinks with Jess and Ben and a few others," I keep listing as I hear Ash following behind me. "The music got really lame and then Jess called us a cab back home."

"Hmmm..." I hear her shuffle with her bag.

"Sounds pretty lame. I'm sorry about that, Nola."

Ash sounds genuinely upset. Like it was her fault that this fake scenario was so 'lame.' I turn to her quickly.

"No, don't be sorry! I had so much fun last night! And a headache to prove it," I tap the side of my head with one hand while I open the door with the other. I'm hit with a brisk morning chill.

"Come on, we're gonna be late," I give her my best smile. I need to sell this.

She smiles back as she shoves the rest of the toast in her mouth.

"I guess I shouldn't be surprised that you would think lame would be fun," she says through her full mouth as she passes me out the door.

"Ha. Ha," I roll my eyes at her.

My phone vibrates in my pocket as I lock the door behind us.

"Are you gonna tell me about this tall dark and handsome man you were sucking face with last night?" Ash's question sounds far away as I check my phone.

It's a message from Lawson, finally answering me from last night. The message is simple and to the point:

I'll meet you at the café tonight at 8.

Resolution fills me. Lawson will give me answers tonight. I hope he can fill in some of the gaps left by our mother. I feel the simmering anger still holding me hostage at being kept in the dark. It's stifled only by the thought that Lawson wanted to tell me before. He's still not getting off scot free about that though.

"Earth to Nola?"

Ash waves her hands at me over the top of my car.

How did we get here so quickly?

"It's freezing, can you unlock your car?" she pulls at the handle.

"Right, sorry," I put my phone away unlocking my car with a beep. We both scramble in.

I've taken up the mantle of taking us to class every morning since we moved off campus. It was my idea after all to do so, although this has kinda been my punishment. Not that I mind it. I like driving, always have, and living off campus is worth it. I smile to myself. There I go again, falling back into the normal college kid side of everything. Humanity.

"Are you thinking about that guy?" Ash asks next to me.

"What?"

"You're smiling like an idiot," she says like it's a fact.

"No... I was just thinking about classes," I lie again.

Ash turns her whole body to look at me as if I'm some science project that she can't understand.

"You. Are. So. Strange."

I hit her shoulder as I put my car in reverse. She hits me right back and we laugh together. It's all so easy.

"You shouldn't hit the driver," I say through the laughter. "Anyways, you were telling me about Jase, was it?"

She dives into everything that she can remember from the night before. The spotlight effectively turned off me, I let out a sigh as I smile and nod along with her. The less I have to think or talk about last night with her, the better. I pack away me being a Nephilim, the thoughts of Blake, and the creepy dream into a box. I dust off the box that says college, unpacking the notes for the three tests I have to take soon.

So, cheers... to this absolutely normal college day I'm about to have.

EIGHT

I watch the time tick by while I sit in the warmth of my car, something I've been doing a lot of today, just waiting for the minutes to go by. Waiting for time to pass in classes today, not even paying attention to the lectures, to that old reality of my life. In fact, most of the day I just felt like I was floating through these different realities, still not sure which plane of existence I should exist on. Normal college student or Nephilim...

It's been exhausting.

Now a nervousness, a ball of hesitation and fear, knots my stomach. It's been there all day so it might as well set up its own house, feeling content to not leave me alone. I try my best to ignore it as I scan the darkness around my car. I still haven't gotten used to the fact that it gets dark at 5 o'clock. But now that it's the beginning of November, I really shouldn't expect anything less.

This darkness feels different though. Heavier. Filled with

eyes, and who knows what else watching me. Maybe it's all in my head but I swear, every now and again, I can see the darkness moving. Breathing, spreading, and enveloping everything it touches. Sure, there was a finality to the darkness before but the fear that comes with it now is something I haven't felt since I was younger. I always had to sleep with a nightlight on, just to keep an eye on the shadows. Now that old fear is resurfacing, and I find myself frantically searching the dark for some source of light to fend off the awaiting shadows.

The bright green numbers of the clock on my dash flip to 7:45.

Enough stalling Nola, my bossy subconscious berates me.

She's dressed battle ready, armor and all, ready to get the answers to the list of questions in her hands. The ball of fear knots tighter in my stomach as I open my door, letting the cool darkness inside. I quickly glance around, half expecting someone...or something...to be standing next to my car or by the building that's just a few feet from me. My paranoia thickens as I look over my shoulder, feeling as if there are warm eyes on me at every turn.

But maybe it's just that, paranoia.

Nothing moves in the darkness, but that doesn't stop me from nearly jogging from my car to the door of Café Blanc. It doesn't stop the breathless pants escaping my lungs as I burst through the door, startling the lone student sitting close by. He looks annoyed over the top of his laptop.

I give him a small apologetic smile and sidestep past his table. Looking up, I spot Arlo at the counter, a white hand towel draped over his shoulder. A spray bottle full of blue liquid sits on the counter next to him. Arlo is talking in a hushed voice to another man, his dirty blonde hair slightly tousled.

Lawson.

Of course, he's here early. Ever so punctual, my brother would be early to his own funeral if he had it his way.

"It's rude to talk about people when they aren't here to defend themselves," I say as I approach the counter, voice cheery despite the wad of nervousness at my core.

Lawson turns, giving me his signature "annoyed brother" smirk.

"Don't worry, Arlo already knows all your horror stories. Like that one time that you split your pants on the playground in front of your whole class. In front of... what was his name?" Lawson drapes one arm over my shoulders as I elbow him in the side.

"Shut up Lawson!"

My cheeks flush as I glance up through my lashes at Arlo. A smile plays on his lips but he just pretends to go back to cleaning the counter. My eyes land on the wings on his wrist.

There it is again, my old-world colliding with my new one. Here we are, my older brother joking around and doing what he does best, embarrassing me. But he's embarrassing me in front of an angel. An actual angel. One who is connected to my mother, our mother, through some faction of other angels. And my brother... my stupidly overprotective, annoying older brother, is a Nephilim.

Like me.

I shake off Lawson's arm and grab his wrist to turn it over, I have to see it. He pulls away from me slightly, but I hold on tighter. He's wearing our father's old watch. The brown leather is cracked from the years it spent on our father's wrist. Through all of his travels and even to the very end. This watch has seen it all, but now it's covering the one thing I need to see.

If only for my own sanity, I need to see Lawson's wing, just to make this all more real. Without moving our father's watch anymore, I see the single black wing peaking around the cracked leather. I push his watch further up his arm so that I can see it completely. His black wing stares back at me as I bring my left wrist up so that they are side by side. His wing is upside down from my view, but nearly looks identical to mine. The only difference being that his wing points up further.

"You should've told me," I say to our wrists. My chest deflating with the words.

When I look up at Lawson's eyes, they're full of sadness and regret. He glances around, finally landing on the guy still buried in his laptop.

"Not here," he says, pushing the watch back down, taking a few steps around me before he disappears into the kitchen.

I glance over at Arlo and he just nods his approval. It doesn't help. I still feel like I'm violating their personal space as I follow Lawson through the back of the café. He moves through the small kitchen full of oversized appliances as if he has been here a million times before.

Maybe he has...

Everything is clean and organized, tubs of different ingredients carefully tucked away and clearly labeled. Flour, sugar, cinnamon, nutmeg, and on and on it goes. Lawson comes to a stop at a door tucked away towards the back of the cafe. Inside, is a small office. Two leather chairs sit on one side of the desk with a larger black leather chair looming on the other side. Lawson sits in one of the smaller chairs and turns the other to face him. He holds out his hand, motioning me to sit.

"If you had any idea how bad I wanted to tell you..." he begins as I sit across from him, not wasting any more time.

"It was torture. But the rules are so clearly laid out and I just had to wait. I know how in the dark I was... How betrayed I felt..." he shakes his head at the memory. "I didn't want you to feel the same way, I wanted you to have someone you could confide in," his words float heavily around me.

"I tried to tell mom how I felt. There was something in my gut that just knew that you would get your wing. I tried to convince her to tell you ahead of time. Give you time to prepare or teach you...or I don't know... I just knew that it would happen, but she just kept insisting to let you have normalcy," his hands fly up in air quotes, "'just in case.'"

A noise escapes his lips like a cough or a sigh.

"I heard you guys talking when I was home..." I confess.

"I figured you did."

"Why didn't you tell me then?" I press.

"I almost did. But when I looked at you," he gives me a small smile, looking down at his hands. Nervously, he rubs them together. I know this move, he has always done this since we were kids. It's a tell for how uncomfortable he is.

He continues anyway, "I just saw my baby sister. Someone who I needed to protect, like so many times before," he pauses a moment as I'm sure he's remembering all the same times I am. Our father's addiction and the pitfalls that came with that. And I know he had some idea about what happened with Sean, not that he could've protected me from him.

"And I guess mom's words started to sink in and I had hope that maybe, just maybe, my gut was wrong. That you wouldn't be dragged into all of this," he waves his hands around, defeated.

"Well," I hesitate. "I hate to say this, but I was kinda physically dragged into all of this with the whole being kidnapped thing."

Lawson shifts, his shoulders pinching with anger as he speaks through gritted teeth.

"I heard. That's definitely not how I wanted you to find out. Those three are going to get what's coming to them..."

I've seen this anger before from Lawson. It's that overprotective brotherly anger that he would get when someone pushed me down on the playground or took a toy from me when we were growing up. It's also the same protectiveness that would fill his features when I would be crying in my room about a boy in school that didn't like me. And don't get me started on how this anger would appear when our father overdosed time and time again. This kind of anger used to scare me as it came out of my brother but over time, I realized that that anger was just what came out when he was scared or facing something he couldn't control. Our mother used to say how that's how our father was when they first met, and I think that thought scares my brother more than he lets on most days.

"I mean," I say, trying to calm him down, "it was a good thing Arlo was there."

"Right," he takes a deep breath, closing his eyes. I can see the thoughts running in his mind trying to steady himself. "That's what mom said. Shit, you should've seen her when she got back home..."

Lawson shakes his head and opens his eyes again. Those brown eyes, our father's eyes, meet mine with such intensity. Something in me shifts, it's partially the anger that's still there intensifying. The other part of me is upset that I wouldn't think how my mother would've reacted about the whole situation. I was too blinded by my own hurt, maybe I still am.

"We are forever grateful that Arlo was there to help. And he knows that."

"You sound like mom," I say to him, bitterness on my tongue.

"I know you're angry with her," Lawson's tone is level. "No one can blame you for that. I was angry for a long time too..."

"Then how did you get to where you are now? Working with mom and Arlo I mean?"

A sad smile tugs at the corners of his mouth.

"It's a long story," he starts. "But short version, it took me a while to come around to everything. To really accept it all. Do you remember the semester I studied abroad?"

I nod remembering the long months where I didn't get to talk to Lawson much while I was still in high school. He was off in Germany studying environmental law in European coun- tries. We talked every so often while he was away, but it was sporadic with his service and the time difference. I thought I was going to lose my mind with how much our mother smoth- ered me during those months. I guess now her neurotic behavior during that time makes sense. Lawson had just turned 21, had just found out he was a Nephilim, and now he was in a different country trying to figure it all out. Our mother was a basket case, to say the least, and I had just written it off that she was worried about him. I had no idea it was deeper than that.

"I take it you weren't just studying law while you were there?" I ask, already knowing the answer.

"There was law... but there was also a lot of other research I was getting into. I met a few Nephilim while I was there, and we talked about everything. Shared stories about what we've learned about the war. A couple of them fought alongside angels. The majority though preferred to stay out of the fight," he says matter-of-factly making my mind spin. "It's also where I got my first taste of what lies in the darkness..."

I try to keep up with everything he's telling me now but it's like wading through mud. My heart rate spikes with the fear of what he's saying.

"Demons?" the word still doesn't sound normal coming out but there it is, settling in the air between my brother and me.

"Yeah," I can feel him watching me as he talks. "Don't get me wrong, it was terrifying being in the face of that kind of darkness, but I knew then I couldn't sit by while those creatures lurked around. So that's when I made the decision to figure out how I fit in with the faction of protectors that mom is a part of."

"Wouldn't it have been easier to just avoid it all? I mean you mentioned some of the Nephilim that you met weren't in the fight, right?"

I can see the pause in Lawson as he takes a moment to consider my questions.

"You do know about what is happening to Nephilim right?" he asks instead.

I nod, "Yeah. Mom mentioned that the ones that are around are either getting killed off by either angels or demons," I swallow the pain and fear that brings up. "Or some are in the protector faction, helping. And few are in hiding."

"Those that are in hiding, the only way they can hide effectively is if they have damaged their souls," he looks down at his hands, rubbing at his watchband. "Some have kids, knowing that's one way to split their souls. Depleting it further the more kids they have. Others...well, others go down darker paths. Splitting their souls through other means.

Painfully and shamelessly until there's nothing left," he shivers.

"Nothing left... what do you mean?"

"I mean, that they're no longer themselves. They walk around no longer whole," his words are laced with sorrow filled with whatever memories that are passing through his eyes.

"But why? Why would anyone want to do something like that? What's so special about Nephilim?" the questions spill out of me with my heightening anxiety.

"From what I've gathered over the years," Lawson answers, picking his words very carefully, "it's all about souls."

I tilt my head, not quite understanding.

"I don't know the nitty gritty of it when it comes to Heaven. But Nephilim souls are like a beacon. If they're whole, they're powerful. You're powerful, Nola."

Those last four words take the longest to sink in.

"And being powerful is dangerous on both sides," Lawson continues, not giving me time to take it all in. "A threat to both sides. So, you have to be careful."

I take a deep breath. So, it's not simply hiding. Not something as simple as just keeping my head down. I would have to change my very being, to go undetected. But who's to say that that would work? Or would that be the best option when there are demons lurking in the dark? If I'm so powerful, wouldn't that help in keeping the darkness at bay? Wouldn't that help to protect my friends and family if I was still whole?

My options are:

1. Possibly get killed.

2. Split and deplete my soul to go into hiding, change what makes me, me; or

3. Fight.

My subconscious bounces with joy, a wide grin spreading on her face. As she jumps up and down, the armor on her shoulders clanks together. She has really come into her own with all of this.

"I won't do that," my voice unwavering.

Lawson's head snaps up.

"I won't change a part of me, the core of who I am. I can't. Just to become someone I'm not to feel safe," I shake my head. My eyes land on my wing.

"I'm going to fight," I hear Lawson take in a sharp breath. "I'm going to fight with you all."

I look up to Lawson, his jaw nearly on the ground as he searches for words in my face.

"You honestly couldn't have expected me to sit on the sidelines," I say incredulously to him.

"You can't be serious!" Lawson nearly shouts, finally finding his voice. He frantically runs his hands through his hair as he searches my face.

"Obviously, there's so much I need to learn. How to fight being one. I want to learn everything," I say to him, ignoring his outburst. I really should've tested the waters with this as I watch every range of emotion cross my brother's face. It flashes through fear, confusion, and lands on anger.

"Nola, I can't. I won't let you do this! You're putting yourself in danger when there's a way out."

"You would rather have some sliver of me walking around, a ghost of who I was than all of me?" I press.

"I would rather have any version of you than nothing at all Nola," tears well up in his eyes as the anger subsides and I watch as fear washes over his face.

My heart breaks taking in my older brother's expression.

Someone who I always thought was strong, the strongest of us all. Especially when our father died, he never shed a tear in front of us. Always our rock. That same man, now sitting in front of me, something bigger than he once was, with fearful tears in his eyes. It nearly makes me change my mind and give up a piece of my soul right here, right now.

But I can't trade in who I am for some shadow version of myself.

"You don't get to choose for me Lawson," I say hesitantly. "But I would love to have my brother by my side, my big brother to help guide me. I'm going to fight, with or without you," I look to my brother like so many times before. "I would love if you could teach me, but I'm sure Arlo would be happy to help too."

Something in my last words triggers something in Lawson. He sits up straighter, quickly wiping at the tears still threatening to fall down his cheeks.

"I just wish that you would stay out of all of this. You're jumping in with no real idea of what you're up against," he takes in a shaky breath, slowly getting back to his business demeanor.

"I guess I wish you didn't have to know about all of this," Lawson says hopelessly.

I stay silent as I watch Lawson's chest rise and fall with steading breaths. The anxiety knot makes itself known again in my stomach by rolling over. I know he knows that I meant it when I said that I would fight with or without him. I don't need his permission. But having his support would be better. It would be easier when our mother finds out. She has a harder time resisting the both of us when we're on the same side. And I know eventually, I'm going to need her on my side with this decision. After all, I would be joining the faction she's a part of too.

"I can't teach you everything," he says finally. "Not tonight at least."

My heartbeat picks up speed. Of course, a lot of this can't be taught or talked about in one night. If anything, the amount of questions I came in with has doubled.

Is he actually agreeing to this?

"I wish you would stay out of this..." Lawson repeats, his voice is resigned, somber. He reaches across and grabs my hand.

"I can't."

"I know," a sad smile lifts the corners of his mouth.

"Always the fucking rebel," he shakes his head. "And I'm stupid enough to stay by your side."

"What are big brothers for?" I say grinning at him.

"Apparently I'm only good for guiding my little sister into this crazy world before she does something stupid," he rolls his eyes at me but that sad smile doesn't waver.

"I would never..." I half joke with him. It's easy to fall back into our sibling banter.

"Sureee..." he drags out. Lawson leans back in his leather chair looking both like a weight has been lifted and like a new one has been added. I can't help but feel the same.

"I'll put some things together for you to read over and start training," he continues. "Are you going to tell mom?"

The weight in the room intensifies. I'm beyond grateful that my brother decided not to put up much of a fight about me joining the faction, but my mother is going to be another battle.

"Do I have to?"

"Yes," he answers without hesitation.

I groan right back at him.

"I'll be there if you need me to but it's a conversation that you need to have with her."

I nod, still flipping through my options in my head. My subconscious has already created a Venn diagram of pros and cons.

"And Nola?" I meet my brother's intense gaze. "On top of you not doing anything stupid, you need to lay low. You have a target on your back and while Arlo is here to help protect you, you need to be diligent too."

I nod, feeling the full intensity of his words. It only adds to the fear building in my chest.

"At least until we get you training, be careful out there. The darkness and what lies within it is dangerous."

The gravity of my new reality floats around us. Not daring to burst the bubble of my old reality. Inside here, we're still just Lawson and Nola. Outside, we are two Nephilim, descendants of Archangel Michael, with targets on our backs with demons and angels alike.

NINE

I type into the search bar, my pinky hovering over the enter key.

It's a harmless distraction, I tell myself as I glance around the nearly vacant library.

Ash sits across from me, head buried in one of her textbooks as she scribbles in her notebook. We've been in the library for a couple of hours at this point, deciding to sequester one of the light wood tables on the second floor instead of my library room on the third floor. At least here we can still whisper about the upcoming test in our Art History class.

With what started out as us deep in our shared homework, quickly shifted to us working on separate assignments as we finished. Ash working on what looks like biology notes, and I've turned to editing some photos for my next photography assignment due in a couple of days. But while I've been trying to stay on topic, stay focused on both my schoolwork, a normal college life for the past couple of days, I've had this other side of me pulling at me.

It's a side that needs to know more about what I am. My phone has buzzed several times, each time I get my hopes up, thinking that it's Lawson sending me whatever it was he was going to send. Instead, all the texts have been from my mother wanting to talk. I know I need to. She's always been one of the only people I can turn to for just about anything, and yet the bitterness is still there.

So here I am, staring at my computer's internet search bar with the word "Nephilim" staring back at me instead of editing the photos I need to or working on any of the other numerous assignments I need to get done before Thanksgiving break in a couple of weeks.

I look around the library once more.

Ash still occupied. Check.

Other students on the other side of the floor. Check.

No one behind me. Check.

Fuck it, I think to myself.

I hit enter a bit too aggressively and hold my breath as the webpage loads.

Everything is out of focus for a second when it finally loads. It's like I've never learned English as I read through some of the words on the page. Words like 'beasts,' 'giants,' 'fallen angels,' 'abominations...' none of them make sense.

And the images...

I hover over some of them, making them slightly larger. Massive creatures, some human-like and others dark winged animal-like beasts that I've only seen in movies or tv shows. These terrifying depictions with bloodied hands and feet slashing away at smaller humans or other winged creatures. My hands start shaking with fear.

This can't be real...

I move on to some of the links. The first couple lead to some religious encyclopedia pages breaking down several versions of the Bible and what it mentions about Nephilim. These pages are kinder in their descriptions but not by much. Mentions of Nephilim in the books of Genesis back in the same time as the creation of Earth, according to the Bible. My mind flashes to the many afternoons at the church we used to go to, reading bible stories and coloring along. Nothing looked as dark and creepy as these images on my screen. The images from my childhood were always light and colorful and now those colors are being muted, replaced by these creatures.

None of this makes sense. If Nephilim are supposed to look like this, how am I still me?

Tears start welling in my eyes as I shut my laptop. The sound reverberates through the library causing a few heads to turn my way. Even Ash looks up from her work with concern in her eyes.

I blink back the tears, giving her a small reassuring smile.

"You alright?" she whispers, not being fooled.

"Yeah, yeah, I'm fine," I lie. "I just, I'm hungry and can't focus anymore."

I'm the farthest from hungry. In fact, where my stomach should be is just an open pit, as dark and cavernous as some of the backgrounds of the images I just looked at. It's the only lie that comes out of me naturally. Ash looks back down at her work for a second, then back up to me and sighs.

"You're always hungry."

"Are you saying you're going to pass up on some food and coffee right now?"

She squints her eyes at me, yet I can practically hear her stomach growl from the other side of the table.

"Fuck you."

"Awwww, I love you too," I whisper back at her, placing my hand over my heart. "You want the usual?"

"Yes please," she resigns as I put my laptop in my bag. "I need to find Jess anyways. She's got better notes on this biology crap."

"Ooo don't let her hear you say that."

Jess, being the studious science major that she is, would have Ash's head if she heard her disrespecting biology like that. Ash and Jess have even broken out into an argument about the best subjects in school before, neither one wanting to give up that they were right. It ended with all of us laughing through ridiculous stories from high school on the floor of our living room.

"You better not tell her," Ash shoots daggers at me.

"I would never," I slide my finger across my heart and wink at her.

"Okay okay, are you gonna go get the food or just sit there?"

"So pushy…" I throw my bag over my shoulder. Ash has already pulled out her phone and is typing away, I'm assuming a message to Jess to meet her at the library.

"I'll be back in 20," I say as I pass by her.

She waves a hand at me.

My bookbag feels heavier as I walk out of the library. Weighed down by the secret of my new world sitting in the search bar of my laptop. Crippled by the lies that are starting to come easier and easier with Ash. Sure, they're little white lies right now but I can't help the feeling like I'm lucking out with every conversation with her so far.

I pass by my car parked on the street next to the library. There's no need to move it from this prime spot when the café is only a few blocks away. And while it would be nice to get this weight off my back, a walk sounds nice.

The sun is just starting to set behind the campus buildings. As the breeze picks up as I round the corner, I zip up my jacket. Maybe I should've chosen the car. But it's too late now, I've chosen this path and I'm nothing if not determined to get to the café and get some food for at least Ash, but more selfishly to talk with Arlo.

I cross the street and can see the sign a block away. Café Blanc with its white façade, open window front, and small parking lot next to it. In my old life , this place held so much peace, but now it holds so much more, pieces of my new life and the secrets that come along with it.

Opening the door, I'm hit with its familiar scent of baking pastries and brewing coffee. But something new mixes with it, the memories from several nights ago. The café is crowded with students and tourists, each of them talking loudly with others or sipping their coffees too loudly while they type away at computers. My eyes linger over the small wooden table and the very seat that changed my life. Now occupied by a young woman quietly reading, oblivious to the world around her as her mug of coffee sits on the table no longer steaming. The only indication that she has probably been sitting there for a while consumed by the fantasy world within her hands and ironically not knowing of the one that's around her.

"Hey Nola," Pierre's voice startles me out of my staring.

I somehow made it all the way to the counter without even realizing it.

"Oh, sorry Pierre," I clear my throat, refocusing on what's in front of me. "How are you?"

"I'm doing well," he gives me a small smile. It's part pity and part teasing. "And you?" his tone shifting to serious.

"Ummm..." my hands clasp tighter on the straps of my bookbag.

How am I? Simple answer is, not great. Honestly, I've been freaking out since I found all of this out. Feeling out of control and left out of so much which stresses me out beyond anything I can think of. Feeling like I have a weight of the world on my shoulders trying to make sure everyone I love stays safe with me being a part of this new world with angels and demons and trying to navigate how I'm supposed to fit into it all. None of which I want to load on to Pierre.

"I'm alright," not a total lie.

But the questions are still rattling around in my head. What does it really mean being a Nephilim? What's it like being an angel? Is there a "god"? Lawson explained it some but not enough. I need to know more.

I need to talk with Arlo.

Pierre's brown eyes crinkle at the corners as he tilts his head. He knows I'm bullshitting. I just pray he doesn't push it.

"Good," he says finally. "Arlo is in the back if you want..."

How did he get so good at reading my mind? I think to myself. Or maybe he knows? He has to know about everything right? How could he be married to an angel without knowing? I add these questions to my list to ask Arlo.

"Right, thank you."

"The usual for you too?" Pierre asks as I start to sidestep the counter to head to the kitchen.

"Oh yes and one more sandwich and coffee for Ash as well, pretty please?"

"I'm not running a charity case here Nola, you're gonna have to pay eventually," he rolls his eyes.

"Sureeeee..." I drag out with a smile. He shakes his head at me, and we both laugh.

I watch as he quickly scribbles my name on two to-go cups all the while taking the next person's order. Slipping past the door, I head through the kitchen, back to the office Lawson and I talked in just the other day.

Staring at the different shades of brown in the wooden door, I inhale the faint scent of cinnamon and sugar, trying to gather some courage. I know I shouldn't be as nervous as I am, it's just Arlo. One of the main men in my life that's been a constant for the past couple of years, except now I know what he is. An angel. An angel that has been keeping tabs on me for my mother. She's probably going to hear about this conversation. Hell, she probably already knows about the one I had with Lawson. Maybe that's why I haven't heard from him yet. He might still be working out the repercussions of telling me what he knows.

My hand lifts to the hardwood, my knuckles make contact in a loud knock. Or maybe it just sounds too loud and aggressive to me.

I hear a faint, "come in," from the other side as well as a couple of other muffled noises.

I feel my hand tremor slightly on the cool handle, but push aside the nervousness and open the door with a new purpose.

"Brother Arlo," an annoyed voice on the phone next to Arlo

greets me. "There has to be more than that. You know how upset they will be if the report is not complete—"

Arlo meets my eyes and quickly picks up the phone.

"I have nothing more to report," he says simply into the phone and hangs up quickly, effectively ending the conversation with whoever was on the other end.

Immediately, all awkward nervousness turns into awkward embarrassment.

"I'm so sorry," my hands go up as I try to close the door. "I thought you said to come in and I'm just... I'm sorry I didn't mean to interrupt."

"Nonsense," he waves a hand at me, motioning me inside the office.

"That conversation was over before you got here. You kinda saved me from having to repeat myself a millionth time."

Arlo shrugs and leans back in the larger leather chair. He looks at me, gesturing to the chair across from him.

"Please sit. What can I do for you, Nola?"

Here comes the nervousness again. Tingling in my fingertips as they brush along the leather of the chair across from him. Making my heart skip several times in my chest while my mind races with which question to start with first.

"I..." I stutter, my legs giving way to sit. "Well, I'm sorry-I just don't know where to start..."

"I'm sure you have a lot of questions. Your conversation with Lawson went well?"

His question sounds more like a statement. He already knows what we talked about; he's just being polite.

"Yeah, it helped but there's still so much I don't know and I just thought you... well, you could help fill in some gaps," I look at him hopefully. My words are rushed, flooding out of me, now that I've started I can't seem to stop. "Lawson said he would give me books or something for me to look over and study and he just hasn't so I started doing my own research and it just didn't help. Like last I checked in the mirror I'm not some giant... I mean sure I'm taller than most girls my age but like not a giant. And just nothing makes sense—"

Arlo's phone vibrates on the desk between us.

I hadn't noticed that he started to smile while I was speaking, I'm sure thinking I'm as crazy as I sound but that smile quickly fades as he looks at the screen. He groans as it continues to ring.

"Nola, I'm so sorry but I have to take this."

"Oh... yeah no, no problem..." I start to wave my hand in front of me feeling deflated.

"But I do want to have this conversation. You have a right to know what is real and what is just internet crazy," the corners of his mouth rise a bit. "Are you free on Saturday?"

I try to think ahead. My only plans for Saturday were to study, get things prepped for the next week, and go out to take pictures for my next photography assignment. Just a typical Saturday.

"Yeah, I can be free on Saturday."

"Great. Meet me here at 10, okay?"

I nod. The studious side is cursing me for giving up a perfectly good Saturday to get ahead but my curiosity got the better of me. My subconscious is jumping up and down ecstatic about whatever is in store.

Arlo stands from his seat, and I follow suit. His eyes are shifting from me to his phone to the door behind me. Right, whoever is on the other end, this needs to be a private conversation. For a moment my mind flicks to my mother. Is that who is calling him? He walks past me to the door, opening it for me.

"I'll see you, Nola," his voice thoughtful.

It's hard to not let the disappointment sink. Disappointed that once again my questions are left unanswered, at least for right now.

"See you later," I say, leaving the office. He smiles at me as I turn away to head back to the kitchen.

Whatever happens on Saturday, I know I need to get Arlo to trust me if only to help me get more answers and guidance on all this angel business. They're all going to have to trust me eventually and stop leaving me in the dark.

After a quick and awkward goodbye with Pierre, I speed walk through the door of the café. Feeling rushed to get back to Ash before she actually murders me for not bringing her food. In a hurry and unaware, there's no time to notice someone standing at the curb just outside of the cafe until I run right into them, knocking them off the curb with a resounding splash of coffee hitting the road.

"Fuck! I'm so sorry! I didn't see you there..." I stop, taken aback.

No way, no fucking way he's right here.

"Blake?"

Blake's bright blue eyes are what meet me first and I'm taken back to the night in the club. Staring into those eyes as they shifted in the ever-changing lights. I feel heat rising in my cheeks as my eyes move down to his lips. Those lips that I fully made out with not too long ago. I have to look at something safe. I land on the right sleeve of his jacket; the leather now drenched in coffee. It glistens in the light of the lamps on the sidewalk that are just starting to glow as the sky darkens more.

"Ahh, hello Nola," his deep voice reverberates through my chest. It's odd to hear his voice clearly and not muffled over pounding music.

Yet, it sounds so familiar...

"It's not a problem. It's just coffee," he's polite, too polite, and every word sounds like a warning.

"Well... still... I'm so sorry. I was just... never mind, my head is in the clouds. What are you doing here?" I stare between his coffee-stained jacket to the cup that is laying on the ground.

"Don't worry about it. It's a small town, only so many places to get coffee," he reaches down to pick up the cup. "But this wasn't that great anyway," he shrugs.

"Don't say that too loud or Arlo will have your head."

He laughs like there was some joke in that, "Good luck with that."

Confused, I just look up at him, hoping he will give me an explanation. His smile is so wide, revealing perfectly white, straight teeth, it reaches his eyes, and they crinkle a bit at the corners. How is he this beautiful?

"Never mind," his smile starts to fade but still a ghost of it lingers on his lips. "You really should be more careful. You never know what kind of creeps are lurking in the shadows out here."

I swear his eyes flick a brighter blue. But maybe not. This isn't the first time I've heard this warning. My family's voices pop into my head. Blake can't actually be talking about demons too, right? That's not possible, he must just be joking about normal human creeps.

"Ha ha. Sure. You think I would walk around without keeping some sort of protection on me," I tap the side of my bookbag where my keys jingle in my hand. I lift them up to reveal my pepper spray.

"Woah. Be careful where you point that thing," he smiles briefly, but then his face darkens.

I tilt my head in confusion, or is it fear? The way his face changes sends a shiver up my spine. Suddenly, I realize that I am out on the side of the road with a total stranger. Sure, he's a stranger that I've made out with before but a stranger, nonetheless. Anything could happen right now. I take a few steps back, heading towards the café doors and more importantly the light.

"Good," he nods as he watches me retreat.

"Just be careful," again, a warning. Except Blake's warning feels like it comes from somewhere else, something more menacing.

Just then my wing flares with a dull burn as a black car pulls up to the sidewalk. Blake opens the car door and looks back at me briefly, the flames flick in his eyes once more, and then he's gone. Disappearing into the darkness.

I watch as the taillights of the car turn the corner and finally let out a breath, that I didn't realize I was holding in. I feel a sudden rush of relief. The fear flows out of me in waves but only for a moment. That whole interaction could've turned out much differently than it did. I shiver and look around, double checking my surroundings, making sure I don't see anything in the shadows. It's nothing I haven't already been doing since finding out about demons but I still don't know what to look for. Will I ever know what a demon actually looks like? It's a question to add to the list for Saturday. Quickly, I pull out my phone to call Ash as I half walk, half jog back to the library. As I close in on my destination, the burn on my wrist completely fades.

Never mind that as the streets get darker, I see a pair of burning blue eyes at every corner and down every alley.

TEN

I look over at Ash in the row of desks next to me, as I circle the last answer on my Art History test. She's casually checking her nails as one would do after just getting them done. She must feel my eyes on her because she suddenly looks over and winks at me.

I stifle a chuckle, brushing off her fake flirtatious advances. Rolling my eyes, I notice the clock as it strikes four in the afternoon. Classes are over for the day.

Finally.

I pack up my things, hand my professor my test, and head for the door with the rest of the class.

"Dude," Ash says as we make it through the door. "That test was too easy. I think Professor Mills is getting soft in his old age. Or maybe he just gives the easier ones to his favorite students," Ash links arms with me as we walk down the overcrowded hallway. Good thing we're both tall enough to see over the majority of heads to break through rather quickly.

"Oh, no doubt. Half my answers were already circled when he handed it to me. What a softy," I nudge her with my elbow, and we both laugh.

"Anyways, now that that's over. What are we doing now? Should we see what Jess is up to?"

"She probably has something else to study for. I have a couple of assignments and things to get done for next week. Do you want to head to the library? Ooooo... we can get food delivered!?"

Ash lets out an exasperated sigh, "We were just there yesterday! How can you still study on a Friday?"

I shrug at her as we weave our way through the crowd.

"You're such a nerd. It's disgusting."

"So, you're in?" I smile brightly as we reach the stairs at the end of the hallway.

"Ughhhh... fine," she fanes disgust. "But I won't enjoy it."

I smile at her as I pull out my phone from my back pocket, letting Ash guide us, arm and arm, down the rest of the stairs and out the door of the art building. Just as I'm about to hit send, I feel a shove from Ash.

"Woah. I'm so sorry. I didn't see you guys there!" the voice is deep with a slight southern accent.

"Oh, no no, that's our bad..." Ash responds in a joking manner. "Wait... Jase?"

"Holy shit! Ash!?"

I finally get a look at the face the voice is coming from. Faintly, I recognize him as the guy from the club that Ash was dancing with. Now in the lights of the hallways, I can fully see him. Jase's a kind looking guy, fair skin and blonde hair. His deep brown eyes remind me of Sean but the expression in this guy's eyes is nothing but kindness. Next to him is a guy who looks similar to him except this guy is taller, but not by much, and has dark hair. Both of them are eerily attractive.

"What are you doing here?" Ash asks him, completely surprised.

"We have a class in this building," the snarky response comes from the guy next to him. His voice condescending, like he's talking to children.

Jase turns to him with a glare, but he just looks back down at his phone and types furiously.

"Sorry, don't mind him," Jase says, turning back to Ash. His eyes seem to only find hers. They stare at each other only long enough to make it uncomfortable.

Geez, get a room already.

I clear my throat loudly, tugging slightly on Ash's arm.

"Oh shit – sorry," Ash looks between me, Jase, and the ground. Is she blushing? "Nola, this is Jase. Jase, this is Nola."

"Name's Jase Floyd," he sticks out his hand.

Oh, so we're using full names here?

"Nola Saint," I unhook my arm from Ash and reach out.

The moment our hands touch, a burning flame flashes through me and centers itself at my wrist. I've only felt this kind of burn once before, the night of my birthday. I break away from Jase probably too quickly and I hope Ash doesn't notice. Jase's brown eyes search my face quickly. I know there's curiosity behind his eyes but something uneasy settles in my stomach. If he felt something too, he doesn't show it.

The burn lingers as Jase clears his throat, nervous. "Um. And this is my brother, Azel."

Azel, nods his head in acknowledgment, never lifting his gaze from his phone. He types frantically on the touch screen. I don't know if it's the serious look on his face or the way his eyes are hooded and expressionless, but I'm hit with the same wave of uneasiness that nearly knocked me off my feet last night with Blake.

Fear, that's what this emotion is.

"Heh. Don't mind him. He's dealing with some family business," Jase says.

The way Jase says that, makes me very nervous. The ball of fear wraps itself up and travels up my chest. I place my hand on Ash's shoulder and give her a slight pull.

"It's alright. Um, it was nice meeting you guys but um - we should get going."

Something instinctual takes over my body. I need to get Ash away from them and I don't know why but the unsettling feeling of fear is only growing. I nearly have to drag Ash away.

"Right, Ash?" I continue, hoping she can hear the plea in my voice.

My grip tightens on her shoulder, and she finally turns to me with a look of annoyance, but with one look in my eyes, I think she understands.

"Right," she answers turning back to Jase. "I promised this bookworm here that we would go to the library... again," she rolls her eyes meant for me.

"It was really nice seeing you again, Jase. We'll talk soon?" her voice full of nervous hope.

"Of course, I won't keep you girls from what you need to do."

I pull back again and give him a small polite smile. Ash waves, giving Jase her best flirty smile.

"We'll see each other soon," Jase promises as he smiles, eyes only on Ash.

We get a few feet away, out of ear reach when Ash complains.

"Damnit, Nola. That man could be my first husband and you just had to pull me away," she exaggerates every word.

"Yes, I'm the worst, I know," better to agree with her then let her know how I'm really feeling about the two boys behind us.

"Jase..." she says dreamily. "What a total babe huh?" she skips a little as we walk down the sidewalk towards the library.

"Yeah, he seems alright..."

Alright at a distance but not near you Ash, the thought pops into my head from somewhere inside of me. It doesn't make sense. I squeeze my hand at my side, still feeling the warmth of Jase's hand and the fading burn at my wrist. I look down at my sleeve at what I can't see. My wing.

"I can already hear the wedding bells..." she smiles broadly, blissfully unaware.

I force a smile, but my mind is reeling.

There was no electricity when I shook Jase's hand like the electricity that bubbled between Blake and me that night. But there's the similar warmth that came from Blake. I thought at the time it was just the alcohol flowing through me but now, it feels different. The memory changing, morphing with everything that's happened since that night The warmth that radiates from them is like touching the glass of a candle after it has been lit for too long. A heat that shocks you when you touch it but isn't totally unbearable. I don't remember Sean being that warm. If anything, he was cold both emotionally and physically. There was nothing warm about his presence.

My mind goes in another direction, taking a leap of faith. An angelic direction. Could Blake, Jase, and Azel be connected to the angels? I filter through all the interactions with my family and Arlo, do they run warm too? Is that what this is? Maybe Arlo will have some answers tomorrow...

A car horn blares beside us on the street. It startles me out of my own head. I hadn't realized we were already walking up the stairs to the entrance of the library. I store my questioning into the deep reassesses of my mind. No use in thinking about that now. No answers will come from my spinning mind.

"Earth to Nola?" Harley's voice comes from my laptop sitting on my desk.

I almost forgot about our weekly calls until my laptop started ringing with the familiar tune 20 minutes ago. Ash and I got back from the library a couple of hours ago, had a quiet dinner and then we went our separate ways. Ash to catch a show she's wanted to watch and me, to work on the photography assignment I've been putting off. Finding color where it's least expected.

I've come up empty on ideas so far, having done some research on the greats to get some inspiration but nothing has come up. Most of the images remind me too much of my father so it's been a lot of opening and closing of different pictures. I finally closed out of the tab for Nephilim and replaced it with a photography search when my laptop started ringing with Harley's name across the top. A part of me didn't want to answer, officially tapped out of talking for the day, tapped out of thinking really.

But we always answer each other's calls.

No matter what.

"I'm sorry," I refocus back on Harley's face on the screen. "What were you saying?"

"Just that I murdered three people today," they answer casually.

"Wait what?"

They roll their eyes, "I'm kidding, it was only two people."

"Ha. Ha," I search their face, but they give me nothing. "For real, what were we talking about?"

"You were telling me what's got you so distracted."

Harley crosses their arms. Leaning back in their chair, they wait.

What can I even tell them? Where would I even start?

"Well Harl, you know how I turned 21 last week?" I play the conversation in my head. *"Well, I'm a Nephilim. I know what you're thinking, 'what's that?' It means I'm half angel and half human. My mom is an angel, so is Arlo. Oh, and Lawson is also a Nephilim. They all fight with the angels in some war with the darkness. And I've decided to fight along with them to help protect you and everyone around me. I know it all sounds crazy but that's my life now. Oh, and I have exams coming up that I need to figure out. How silly to be worried about school. And how could I forget, there's Blake too. I'm not sure about him. He was just this random guy I made out with but there's something about him that I can't seem to shake. So basically, I'm just trying to figure my own shit out while still keeping up appearances because what else am I gonna do?"*

"I was just thinking about this photography assignment I have coming up," I say instead. "I have zero motivation to get it done."

Harley stares at me through the screen. The look is similar to the look they gave me when we were home. It's intense like they're trying to read my soul. Which at this point, they probably could.

I grab my notes on the side of my laptop and flip through them. Trying to distract myself from Harley's intense gaze and the shaking of my hands. I know I can tell Harley anything. Hell, they know just about everything. But the truth... I'm still trying to figure out the truth myself. I can't put that on them as well. I just hope that Harley can't see through the façade I've worked so delicately to put in place with Ash and everyone here.

"Right..." Harley's voice brings me back to them. "Well, you're the best photographer I know, Nola. I wouldn't have given you that camera all those years ago if I didn't believe that. You'll figure it out," they smile at me.

"Unless you want to bounce some ideas?" of course, Harley would want to help.

They've always been that way. A dedicated and fierce nurturer for those they love. They can be a hardass most of the time but I know that behind that tough exterior is such a large heart. It's hard not to have hope that if I did tell them, Harley would be the first to accept this new part of me and try to figure out some way to not let it feel like the burden it already feels like.

But I can't.

"I would love that," I smile at my best friend.

ELEVEN

The road crunches beneath the tires of Arlo's SUV. It feels different this time. Last time I was in his car, he had just saved us. The only thing I remember was Ash snoring softly in the back seat on the way to the café. It was probably the shock of the evening that made everything blurry, like seeing it all through a fogged glass.

Now though, everything is clear. Well, maybe not crystal clear with the number of questions that are begging to burst out of my chest, but clear enough to focus on the silence filling the air between us, the passing cars, street signs, and buildings. We turn down another street that I don't recognize.

"I trust you're not taking me somewhere to murder me?" my hands tremble slightly but my voice stays steady in the joke.

Arlo laughs deep in his chest. I can feel it around me. It's comforting enough to make me smile back at him and ease into the passenger seat a little more.

"I would never..." he puts his hand over his heart. "Besides, it would be hard to murder you where we're going."

His shoulders lift in a shrug as he turns the car down another street.

"Ha. Ha. But for real, where are you taking me this early on a Saturday?"

"We're here," Arlo answers simply, pulling into the parking lot.

The red sign reading **EMERGENCY** catches my eyes first.

Then the flashes of red and white from a nearby ambulance rushing into the hospital entrance. My throat closes as the memories flash behind my eyes. Memories of those same flashes but in the back of that ambulance was my father's barely conscious body. His once deep chocolate brown eyes were pale and lifeless when my mother placed her phone in my hand, pushing me to call 9-1-1. To be strong even as a kid. It was a strength I never knew I had to watch the color drain from my father that day and then to be standing there as my world filled with new bright flashing lights.

"Why," something sticks in my throat making the words thick on my tongue. "Why are we at the hospital?"

"Well, I figured you would want to see what I do," Arlo stares out the windshield at the hospital doors. They slide open as an older man pushes a woman in a wheelchair through them. He lifts her carefully into a waiting car.

"What your mother does," Arlo continues. "What all of us do really."

"Us?" I turn to him. "You mean the angels?"

He turns and gives me a knowing look. With a simple nod, he turns off the car.

"Right..." the word comes out in a whispered breath. I don't know if Arlo hears me or not because he shifts again. This time opening his door to get out.

Leaving me alone in the silence.

Even in the still of the car, my senses are overloaded. Flooded by the memories of my past, my complicated human past, with each faint siren passing. Combated with the curiosity of this new world in front of me. I stare at Arlo's back as he leans against the hood of his car. Giving me the space I need to decide. He has answers and is willing to show me more, which is more than what my family has given me since I've found out.

With a deep breath, I push back the memories of my father into the box they came from and open the car door.

Arlo gives me a small smile as I stop next to him at the front of the car.

"Alright, let's do this," he says, locking his car behind us. He leads the way through the parking lot to the sliding doors of the hospital that older couple came out of.

"It's probably a bad time to mention how much I hate hospitals, right?" I ask as the first double doors slide closed behind us.

The yellow fluorescents buzz overhead, battling with the other sounds of the lobby. Coughs, cries of pain, groans of all kinds, steady footsteps, and the occasional squelch of hand sanitizer dropping into the hands of some waiting patient or loved one. The smell is just the same as the hospital in Cross, metallic and sterile, like bleach was just used on all the surfaces to clean whatever bodily fluids might have just been spilled, and yet it still can't cover up the smell. My whole body shivers with disgust.

"It's definitely too late to mention that," Arlo stifles a laugh, covering it with a cough.

"Thought so," I say back to him.

He stops at the wide receptionist area, leaning on the counter. I stay a step behind, not really sure where I should be, and glance around at the waiting room. There are several people waiting, all of different ages and states of dress and distress. Some have makeshift bandages stopping blood, holding together wounds on various parts of their different bodies. Others are bundled up, shivering, while others are barely dressed and visibly sweating still. Occasionally, someone coughs or sneezes and it makes me want to bathe in hand sanitizer almost immediately.

"Can you page Dr. Miller?" Arlo asks the receptionist. She looks no more than 21 with her dark blonde hair pulled back in a tight bun. She looks at Arlo briefly before typing away on the computer in front of her.

"Who's asking?" her voice is snippy, annoyed with us already. Her eyes skim over Arlo, then land on me for a moment.

"Tell her her 9 o'clock appointment is here," Arlo's voice is all charm.

The young receptionist squints her eyes at him, the look makes her seem much older. I wonder if she's at the end of her shift because she doesn't seem to give his statement much of a second thought. She reaches into the front pocket of her bright pink scrubs and pulls out what looks like a phone. She types away at it.

"You can wait over there," she motions to the waiting area before going back to her computer. "She'll be here in a moment."

"Thank you so much, Jackie," Arlo gives her a warm smile.

"Yeah yeah, whatever, Arlo."

Arlo moves to a couple of chairs on the far side of the waiting area. Away from most of the patients waiting.

"So, you two know each other?" I question looking between them.

He sits down in one of the navy plastic chairs and grabs a magazine that has a handsome couple on the front with a massive house behind them. I sit next to him, avoiding the armrests that probably haven't been wiped down in a while. It's been a while since I've felt this way, irked by everything in my surroundings, especially in hospitals. Probably because I've avoided them for years, ever since the last time... where I was too late to even say goodbye.

"I know everyone here," Arlo answers simply flipping through the magazine.

"What was with that whole... interaction then? She didn't seem to know you, actually, she seemed pretty annoyed..."

"Because Arlo is annoying, that's why."

The warm voice comes from behind us. I shoot out of my chair, fear skyrocketing in my throat but fortunately, I stifle the scream. The source of the voice looks alarmed at my reaction. I watch as she composes herself quickly.

"I'm, I'm so sorry," I say to her.

She looks kind as she gives me a gentle smile. Shifting in her white coat, she lifts her sleeves casually. I can see the two black wings peeking out as she adjusts her clothing.

Right, this an angel. A new angel standing right in front of me.

"No need to be sorry dear," even her voice is kind, the smile never wavers, crinkling her hazel eyes at the corners. She brushes back the falling pieces of brown hair from her bun pulling the rest of her hair back.

"It should be me who's sorry for startling you."

"Nola, this is Althea," Arlo's now standing beside me. She reaches out her hand. "Althea, this is Nola."

I quickly wipe my hand on my jeans, hoping to get rid of some of the sweat that has started to build there. Will I ever be comfortable meeting angels?

"Hello," I grip her hand and shake.

"It's a pleasure to meet Laine's daughter," she smiles.

Of course, she knows my mother. I wonder if they're all in the same faction. Someone coughs nearby, a reminder that we're in public. I know I shouldn't ask here but the questions dance on my tongue.

And as if Althea can read my mind she says, "come on, we can chat more elsewhere."

She turns to walk away, white coat flowing behind her. I catch Arlo's eyes as he starts to follow close behind. He nods, giving me an encouraging smile. I know I can trust him; I have to.

"Thank you for taking the time to meet with us Althea," Arlo says to her back. Althea leads us through a heavy metal door opened only with the swipe of her key card. Beyond the door is a long beige and white hallway filled with dozens of rooms.

"Always so gracious," Arlo continues.

"I don't know why you're buttering me up Arlo but you can stop now."

I watch as she shakes her head but I can hear the smile on her lips as she turns down another identical hallway and stops at a large elevator.

"Besides, I know you're here for a reason. Both of you," her kind eyes flash between the two of us.

"Always straight to business," Arlo says as the elevator doors open.

"I'm not sure I follow what you guys are talking about..." the words fall from my lips, finally finding my voice. The nerves have constricted my throat so much so that the 'hello' from a few minutes ago felt like a choked breath.

"Nola, I did bring you here for a reason," Arlo turns to me from the other side of the elevator. It beeps with every new floor.

"The main one being that I figured you had questions about us," Arlo glances at Althea. "And I think the best answers you're going to get is from seeing."

"Seeing? Seeing what?"

The elevator dings one final time as the doors open. Althea steps out first, leading us with confidence. Notice the sign overhead reads **CARDIOLOGY**.

"Welcome to my home away from home," Althea waves her hand in front of her.

The two nurses sitting at the desk look up and wave at her. From the rooms around us, it's relatively quiet except for the beeps, rhythmic and steady. The smell is still the same here as it was down in the waiting room. It's starting to settle and churn in my stomach.

"So, you're a Cardiologist?" I ask timidly.

"Althea here is the head of cardiology!" Arlo answers with a prideful grin.

"Shhh," Althea shushes Arlo. "And some of my patients are trying to sleep here."

Her voice drops to a whisper. She waves back to the nurses,

and they go back to their individual work. We walk around their station, Althea glancing every so often into rooms as we pass.

"What do you do here?"

The question seems silly as it sits in the air between us. It's a question with an obvious answer if you're human. But she's not, Arlo's not, and I'm... not...not fully at least. I just hope that Althea can hear the real question, what're angels doing at a hospital, this hospital.

"I help humans," Althea answers.

So, she did catch on.

"Any way I can," Althea continues, her eyes landing on mine. "My post here was an easy decision to make all those years ago. Helping the hearts of these humans, keeping them alive to guide them towards the light, that's what I do. But I also help when I can't help them here. I can help their souls get to... well what you would call Heaven."

I know she's speaking in simple words but for whatever reason, they aren't connecting.

"I'm sorry," I say. "You do what now?"

Arlo and Althea share a look while smiling at one another.

"She really doesn't know, huh? Laine didn't mention anything to her?"

"Not that I know of," Arlo answers.

"I'm right here guys," I speak up. "And no, my mother never mentioned any of this to me. I didn't even know what I was until a few weeks ago," I look at Arlo, he knows this.

"Right," Arlo nods. "Althea, do you mind?"

"Of course," Althea stops at a door towards the end of the hallway.

All the other doors had rhythmic beeps coming from them. But this one, the beeps only come every few seconds.

"This is my patient, Mr. Howard," Althea says as she opens the door.

There's a single bed in the middle of the room with a tv across from it playing softly. A leather chair and a small table with wheels sits on either side of the bed. Within the beige and white sheets is a thin figure.

"He's been here for the last 5 years," Althea and Arlo walk further in the room but I can't make my feet move.

"He's been through several surgeries and treatments. Howard here," from where I'm standing I watch as she reaches the side of his bed and takes his hand, "is on the transplant list but unfortunately, I don't think he's going to make it until his number is called."

The monitor beside his bed beeps weakly.

"I've done everything I can to prolong his life here on Earth. To keep his body going... but his time to move on is coming, soon."

"What is that?"

It takes me a moment to realize the words, the question, is mine. Because something else has completely captured my eyes. I didn't notice the soft glow when we first walked in, it just looked like the reflection of the overhead fluorescents off the white sheets. But no, it's something else. Something bigger, its glow burning brighter over Howard's chest.

Another beep.

"Nola? What do you see?" this time the voice is Arlo, closer than I thought he was. It tears my eyes away from the glow back to his face.

"There's this, like this glowing ball of light.... It—" I look away from him, back to the man in the hospital bed. "It's crazy but it's right there! Can't you see it!?"

"What you're seeing is his soul Nola," Althea says calmly. "Though it is strange that you can see it..."

Her head turns curiously towards me, still standing in the doorway.

My eyes back on the glow. His soul... I'm staring at a human soul. The realization hits me all at once. This man is dying, and I can see his soul. It's so beautifully tragic this golden glow. This man is dying, right in front of me, and I can't help but watch this golden light morph and grow larger. This man is dying...

I think I'm gonna be sick...

Althea gently places her hand right over the golden orb. My feet move forward, more into the room, even when everything in me wants to run out of here. Althea leans down as she places her other hand on Howard's head, brushing his wispy grey off his forehead.

Another faint beep.

I strain my ears to hear over the buzzing lights overhead and I catch something else, a faint hum coming from the golden soul. Althea's mouth moves at Howard's ear, but I can't hear what she says. Prickly tears fill my eyes as I catch Howard's mouth move at the corners, I think it's a smile. Althea moves her hand that was over his soul up and the golden orb travels with her hand, completely out of his body. A prolonged beep comes from the machine next to him. The only indication that his heart has stopped.

He's gone.

But yet he's also still here. His soul sits in Althea's hand.

I think Arlo moves, shutting the machine off. The beeping

stops but it's still ringing in my head. Althea lifts her hand further, nudging the soul up towards the ceiling. It floats there for a moment as Althea brings her hand back to her side.

"Go on," she speaks gently to it. With a final nod, the golden soul vanishes up and out of the room.

I stare at the spot on the ceiling like somehow, it'll make this feel more real. Because everything I just saw couldn't be real, right? How could any of this be real?

My eyes drift slowly back down, landing on Howard's lifeless body.

Suddenly, the whole room tilts and spins on its axis. I'm blinded once again by the memories. Howard's body morphs into my father's lifeless one the last time I saw him. I was too late to say goodbye, too much of a child and too consumed with what I thought was love. But what Sean did that night was one of the final straws that broke my back, broke my trust and love for him. I'll never get that night back. I'll never be able to say goodbye.

I'll never be able to spend those last moments with my father like I just did with Howard.

Was it as beautifully peaceful as this was?

My knees give way as I collapse on the tiled hospital floor. The tears that were only just starting before are now free falling. I feel my chest split in half. There's not enough air in here. It's stale and something putrid fills my nose. Sobs escape my chest and everything rattles within me.

"Nola?" Arlo's voice is now right beside me. Distantly, I feel his warm hands on my shoulders.

"Are you alright?"

What a silly question... can't he see that I'm not alright? Not in the slightest.

"What," the word comes out with a sob, "the fuck was that?!"

"Nola, take a deep breath for me please."

Arlo inhales through his nose and out. I can't follow so he does it a couple more times. It reminds me of something my mom would do or maybe has done, before when trying to calm me down. I smile through the tears streaming down my face and I try to bring in more air into my lungs. Arlo guiding me along.

"Good," he takes another deep breath in as he wipes at the tears on my face. "What you just witnessed is what we do. We help and protect humans here on Earth for as long as we can. Guiding them to the side of the light, away from darkness. And when it's time, we guide their souls home."

Arlo glances over to Althea, still standing by Howard's bed, his face now covered.

"Althea did a beautiful job. Probably because she was trained by the best," Arlo smiles turning back to me.

"That man is dead..." I whisper.

"Yes, he is. At least here. But you saw for yourself—which is incredible by the way—his soul, that perfectly golden soul, is on its way," Arlo's tone is comforting.

But nothing can calm me when there's a dead body just on the other side of the room.

"How..." I try to form a question, any question through the haze. "Am I supposed—am I going to have to—to do...that?"

Arlo shakes his head at me.

"No, at least not right now. There are loads of steps before we get there..."

My mind spins again. At least it isn't the room this time.

My stomach still flips all the same and it nearly makes me lose everything in it.

"Oh..." sweat starts to pool in the palms of my hands and down my back.

"I trust you've chosen to work with us," the intensity of Arlo's gaze ramps up as the seriousness in his tone increases. "At least that's what I gathered when you came to see me the other day?"

Of course, Arlo knows more than he lets on. Even though we didn't talk about much that day, he still knew what was left unsaid. That's why he took me here, to answer some of my unspoken questions. But even now more fill my brain.

Maybe the questions will never really end.

But I do know one thing, that my decision is exactly that. To work with them, to help protect my friends and family and all of humanity, and maybe one day I'll be able to do what Althea just did. Just not today.

"Yes," I say, feeling stronger, more steady by the minute.

Arlo takes my hands in his and nods. It's so silly how this man I didn't know three years ago is now such a huge part of my life. An angel grips my hands, my half angel hands, both of us kneeling on a hospital floor with another angel standing by.

It was real. It is real.

"Then we have work to do," Arlo says with a smile.

TWELVE

R estless. That's how I would describe last night. Everything from yesterday replaying over and over in my mind. Sometimes in real time, other times slowed down to a painful crawl. Howard's face would morph in my dreams from his own to my father's waking me up in a cold sweat.

The bell above the door chimes, announcing my entrance. They must have unlocked it just for me, at least Arlo must have. We decided yesterday after another silent ride back to my apartment that we would meet again today, bright and early. He mentioned something about training, but my brain can't... no...won't wrap around that thought. Probably because I've only gotten a handful of minutes of sleep and I might be the only crazy person awake at this ungodly hour on a Sunday.

The sun is lazily rising on the horizon, casting a golden blue hue in the sky. Another person walks by the café, yoga mat slung over their shoulder.

Okay, so maybe not the only person up.

"Nola! You made it! And you're on time!" Arlo's cheery voice rings in my ears causing me to wince.

"Jesus, I'm still not fully awake yet," I bring my hands up covering my ears, and smile at him.

He grabs something from behind the counter as he walks toward me. A warm blueberry muffin and a travel mug of hot liquid might just be the perfect sight this morning. A smile plays across my lips as I am hit with the scent coming from the mug. Earthy, floral, and sweet, my favorite tea.

"You're a godsend," I smile and take a large gulp, the tea burning slightly but doing the job of waking me up. That is if one could be woken up without actually being asleep at all the night before.

"Well, actually..." Arlo smiles, laughter bursting out from him.

I tilt my head not understanding what's so funny.

Did he miss the part of me being not completely awake?

Slowly, t clicks and I can't help but join in with his deep joyous laughter.

"Right, you actually are," I take a large bite of the muffin. It melts in my mouth. I close my eyes and relish in the sweetness.

"Fuck, Pierre!" I shout to the back of the café. "You're also an angel. This muffin is amazing!"

Pierre pokes his head out of the door to the kitchen, smiling at me.

"Thank you, love. You enjoy! You better get going now," his eyes shift lovingly to Arlo. "Go easy on her won't you, babe?"

My face flushes at the sweet interaction.

"I'll try," Arlo winks at me and turns back to Pierre. "I love you. We'll be back in a few hours."

"A few hours?!"

The words fumble out of my mouth around another large piece of the muffin. He can't actually mean we'll be training for that long. My muscles start to ache in protest. I haven't been active for that long in well, a long time... The nervous knot that now has a permanent address with mail deliveries in my stomach rolls again.

Arlo laughs, I'm sure amused by my ridiculous expression. He wraps one arm around me and waves the other one to Pierre who blows him a kiss in return. We're met with the rising sun and cool breeze as he ushers me out the door.

We walk a few blocks in silence while I finish my muffin and tea. Arlo leads me to a part of the city that I've only been through in passing on one of my meandering journeys. Journeys that are usually guided by my need to get new pictures for an assignment or just for my own enjoyment.

The brick storefronts are silent other than a few workers setting up mannequins or heating up kitchen equipment inside. We stop in between a small boutique and a shop that smells like it swallowed flowers by the thousands, almost bursting to explode with the scent. I glance at a window to find the culprits of such an onslaught of smells and my eyes are met with piles of all sorts of soaps. Some are round or square, others oblong or star-shaped. Colors range from beautiful pastels to neon headlights.

I crinkle my nose as we walk further down the alleyway in between the two shops. I guess it's more like a small sidewalk in between the two buildings, barely able to fit two people walking shoulder-to-shoulder down it. Arlo walks a half step in front of me, finally stopping at the midpoint where a side door sits. It's a solid metal door with a keypad lock atop the handle that has a keyhole in the center.

"Are we breaking into one of the shops?" I question, speaking for the first time since we started our walk.

Arlo gives me a childish grin.

Slowly shaking his head, he doesn't even look as he punches in the code. Instead of stepping through the open threshold, Arlo steps to the side. Panic creeps up my throat as I look in the darkened inside. It's the same panic that's been following me over the past few days. Especially since learning what lurks there.

I look hesitantly at Arlo, he wouldn't lead me into anything dangerous. *Right?* He responds simply by tilting his head towards the inside.

"It's okay," he says, "we're not breaking and entering today."

The panic dissipates as laughter escapes my lips. That slight encouragement moves my feet forward.

As I step through the threshold, my feet land on something that gives way slightly.

Odd.

The metal door clicks, locking shut behind me at the same time that lights flick on overhead. Yellow fluorescents cast a warm hue, illuminating the room. As my eyes adjust to the harsh light, I notice that half of the room is covered in matted flooring while the other half is occupied with weights of all sizes, a few treadmills, a contraption with bars and bands that I've never seen before, and boxing equipment.

With a gym set-up like this... it's both impressive and intimidating. Frankly, I'm not sure where to start...

"Don't be worried," Arlo's voice startles me. I didn't even hear or feel him move next to me. I let out a sigh with my hand over my chest, feeling the pounding of my heart beneath it.

"Worried? What makes you think I'm worried? Other than the obvious..." I babble.

"Ha!" his laughter echoes off the high ceiling. "All you have to do is let your instincts take over," he shrugs and smiles.

"What instincts?" I ask honestly. "I've never trained for anything in my life, let alone what it means to train to be a part of a faction of angels in the middle of some war that I still know nothing about."

"You'll see. But first cardio," Arlo winks as I groan back at him.

He starts towards the treadmills, not even checking to see if I follow. I have half a mind to just turn and walk back out the door but the whirlpool of fear and curiosity at my core forces me forward instead. Maybe my fear and my instincts are one and the same.

"Okay, but don't laugh if I can't make it a mile," I say as I stop next to one of the treadmills.

Arlo is already standing on one as he removes his blue hoodie and drapes it over the arm of the machine. Toned muscles peek out from the short sleeves of his shirt and he fixes his mussed hair in the mirror in front of us.

"I would never," a deceiving smile plays on his lips as he looks at me through the mirror.

"We will start slow. Just warming up for now and then we can push it up," he reaches over and turns on my treadmill before messing with his. The resounding beeps wake the machines alive. For a moment I'm reminded of the beeps from the hospital yesterday all over again.

I step up as it starts to move. It's a brisk walk but nothing I haven't done around campus or the city. The time starts to tick up along with the steady increase in the mileage tracker as my breathing evens out with the pace.

At five minutes, Arlo looks over, casual as ever.

"Ready?" he presses a button on his treadmill several times. The speed picks up to where he starts to run. A light jog really with the length of his legs.

I take a deep breath, finding the same button. I press it until I have no excuse but to start a jog. The change in pace is jarring at first but my lungs and legs adjust quickly, easily keeping up with the faster speed. Before long, we reach the tenth minute. Surprise flushes through me as I start to feel sweat start to build up on my forehead. It feels like my body's natural reaction to this level of exertion of energy, but my lungs still keep an even pace like they've been doing this for years. I meet Arlo's eyes in the mirror, and he smiles proudly back at me. He presses the button again, the beeps increasing the speed to where he's in a full sprint. His cheeks are only slightly flushed but not a drop of sweat beads on his face. Never breaking eye contact, his treadmill beeps more, a challenge.

My hand finds the button again making it beep accordingly. As the speed heightens my legs start to ache at the pace. It's the familiar ache, one that I haven't felt in years. Looking down, I see the red numbers show that we're nearly at two miles.

How that happened so quickly, I'll never know.

My breaths start to come out in quick bursts as I look back at Arlo. He watches me intently as I keep sprinting along with him for several minutes. Before my lungs start the flame in my chest, my hand hovers over the down arrow. I give Arlo a look, asking for permission to slow the pace. He nods, at least I think he nods... its hard to tell with the bob of both of our heads.

I slow the treadmill anyways.

Through my panting breaths, I hear beeps coming from Arlo's treadmill. I slow to a light jog, finally able to fill my lungs fully again. Sweat drips down the side of my face as my jog turns into the same brisk walk we started at. Looking down, a giddy feeling rises at the numbers staring back at me. 15 minutes and nearly two and a half miles.

"See, instincts," Arlo says, now standing next to me on the floor. He reaches up, stopping the treadmill and it reverts back to sleep mode.

"Wow..." I pause, wiping the sweat from my forehead with my sleeve. "That was actually... easy? Felt good really. And I've never, EVER, said that before about a run."

"Good, now weights," he turns to head to the rack of weights.

My legs shake slightly once I step off, back onto solid ground. I may not be invincible after all. Watching Arlo walk away, there's still not a lick of sweat on him.

"That was nothing for you, wasn't it?"

His shoulders rise and fall in a shrug.

"Eh, I wanted to see how long you could go until you gave up. I usually have to tap out at around mile 20. The sweat starts then, and I can't stand that."

"Right..." I say. Still wiping my own sweat from my face, I roll my eyes at his back.

Once we get to the weights, Arlo talks me through several different moves. We go through several rounds, progressively increasing weight and reps until my limbs start to shake. We take a break at that point and I rush to chug some water. Arlo grabs water occasionally but mainly waits for me to be ready to go again. By the fourth round, my body nearly gives out. I sit on one of the benches, flexing my hands, open and closed, over and over, a motion Arlo told me would help bring some life back to them. Rolling my wrists, my wing stares back at me.

"I was wondering..." I start, breaking the long silence between us.

"Yeah?" he prompts casually.

I pause, nerves coming up and waking my tired arms.

"Well, I was wondering about... your story... why are you *here?*"

I hope he understands with my inflection that I don't just mean here in this gym but here as in, Earth. His eyes shift to someplace far away over my head. They glaze over slightly as he absentmindedly rubs at the wings on his wrist.

"I mean, yesterday was a lot and explained some but you know... why?" I awkwardly fill the silence between us with word vomit.

"Heaven isn't exactly all that it's cracked up to be... it's been corrupt there for a while now," he starts. "You would be surprised. Most angels and, well we can call them 'management,'" he throws his hands up in quotes in the air, "are only concerned with the count, soul count that is..."

"Soul count?" the words foreign on my tongue.

"Yeah," he nods his head slowly. "The number of souls that are in Heaven. Souls are very powerful resources," he pauses. "I wonder if you could feel it yesterday... Could you feel how powerful Howard's soul was?"

That must have been what the buzzing was. I knew it was more than just a sound, it felt too big to just be something simple. The way I felt drawn to it, like it was pulling me with it. I couldn't put it into words when I saw it but I spent all last night trying to find the right words.

I nod.

"I knew it... Anyways, most of the big guys in charge have never been here. Far too consumed and glutinous with the need to have more. They don't understand the beauty of Earth and its inhabitants. When they see humans, they just see another number instead of a person, a story... its tragic. Some of them have even gone so far as to reap souls before they're ready," he shivers, "which causes a ripple and a soul that needs to be contained in Heaven, instead of enjoying the paradise that it is. Or that it can be..."

"There are more angels than just the Protectors?" the question tumbles out of me without my own control.

"I'm not sure how much your mother has told you... Have you talked with her since your birthday?"

Guilt rises in my throat, making me choke on my words so I shake my head instead.

"Hmmm..." he says thoughtfully. "Well aside from the Lights, excuse me... the Nephilim and us Protectors—"

"That's you and my mother, right?"

"Right, but there are more of us too. There's another faction of angels, the Guides. Or the Overseers."

"You mentioned the Guides before... that night..." the word jogs the memory of the musty basement and the three rogue angels that kidnapped me.

"Yes, I did. They are our management—" more air quotes float in the air. "They're higher-ranking angels who communicate directly with the angels on Earth, us – the Protectors. They're the ones passing down the rules, where to go next to reap another soul, and pass along messages from our Mother."

"Mother?"

"I think you would call her 'God,'" he shrugs but the word is heavy with multiple meanings that I can't quite decipher.

"Wait, you're telling me the capital G, God, is actually a woman?" my mind is effectively malfunctioning. Everything I've ever learned anything that has ever been said about God made it seem like they were a man. But here I am with an angel in front of me telling me that that's complete bullshit.

Arlo smiles slightly, "do you need a moment?"

I nod as I take another sip of my water. In a way, it makes sense that God would be a woman but damn I wasn't expecting that.

"Okay, I'm good," I say to him.

"Anyways, the Guides being pencil pusher assholes, just stay in Heaven and bark orders at us. Which not surprisingly has caused a bit of division between us. Those Protectors who follow every rule out of the Guides' mouths down to the T – for example, the three who kidnapped you – will do anything for the will of Heaven, including reaping souls early, without a second thought. The rest of us, have taken a stand against those aggressive measures in favor of enjoying our thousand years here in harmony..."

"A thousand years?" I tilt my head with the world shifting in the same direction. The lights start buzzing loudly above us, but I try to drown them out by focusing on Arlo's words.

"Yeah. Before the Protectors were chosen to come to Earth, it was decided that they would only serve 1,000 years here. With the mission to protect and guide humans to the light instead of the darkness, intervening when needed from the demons here that are trying to corrupt as many souls into the darkness as possible, and only to reap souls when they are ready. But it seems like, over the years, a lot of them have forgotten the true mission... It's sad really... But once our term is over, we can return to Heaven to watch over the souls we brought into the light during our time here," he smiles fondly at the thought.

"That's what yesterday was..." the words fall at my feet.

"Yes, but we only take souls when they're ready."

I think his tone is supposed to be reassuring but it still sits strangely in my stomach. If he has reaped souls, then my mother more than likely has. She has taken people's essences from them. The one thing I'm still fighting to keep for myself, she has taken from someone else. My head spins with the idea, with the fact.

"Yesterday, you seemed surprised that I could see Howard's soul... why?"

"It's pretty rare for a Light to be able to see souls but it's not unheard of. I suppose there are some factors to consider as to why you are able to... maybe your bloodline lets you... maybe it's something else completely..." his voice trails off causing a shiver to run down my spine.

Seeing a soul reaped from a person, to see them die, wasn't a pleasant experience.

Understatement of the century Nola. My subconscious chastises me. Even though she is battle ready, sitting in a similar sweaty hunched position that I'm in, she grimaces at the thought. At the memory really.

"Does it hurt?" I ask the question that has been repeating in my head all night.

"It does when you reap too soon. Most of the time though, I don't think it actually hurts them. It's just like drifting off to sleep, at least that's what I'm told," his eyes lift up towards the ceiling as he considers it.

"But some angels are taking souls before their time? What happens to the person?"

"They die. We don't leave anyone soulless... not like the demons..." his face morphs with disgust.

"How? Why do they do that?"

"I guess it's some sort of game, or joke to them. Or maybe they just don't care. They don't care if the shell of a person walks around without their... substance... what makes them, them. It causes more chaos," he pauses, thinking about something far away. "If you look at some of the worst people walking around soulless: murderers, rapists, politicians," he winks, "you can see the damage they can cause. It only benefits them to leave them walking around. Because leaving them soulless invites more darkness spreads it like a disease..."

My thoughts drift as my stomach flips. Bile rises in my throat as I think of all the different kinds of people who are probably walking around soulless right now. How much darkness there is in the world. It makes me want to hurl the muffin I ate a while ago and also fight even more so for our side. The side that holds the light.

"How do you know if someone is a demon?"

It's a question that's been in the back of my mind for a while now. Ever since I found out what I was and about the creatures that lurk in the darkness. To be honest, the constant on edge feeling, looking over my shoulders at every turn is getting tiresome. I need to know more, and I need to know how to be prepared for when the time comes that I may have to face a demon.

"It really comes down to instincts again," Arlo gives me a non-answer. "If you feel in your gut that you should run, that's probably the best indicator. Oh, and you have this," Arlo reaches over to me, taking my left hand in his. Touching lightly on the inside of my wrist, my wing.

"This will guide you."

I don't understand what he means by that no matter how simple his words seem. How is my wing supposed to tell me who is a demon or not? Somewhere in the back of my mind, a connection is made. Several faces pop up. Jase and Azel flutter through my mind. But worst of all Blake's face flashes to the forefront. His burning blue eyes stare back at me. Memories of my wrist, my wing on fire when around him. There's no way... no fucking way....

My body moves, leaving my spinning mind and confused pounding heart on the bench. Arlo moves with me to grab the weights. He doesn't say anymore and I'm grateful for the silence as we continue with two more rounds of lifting.

Once we finish, Arlo breaks the silence again, "Up for a bit of a one-on-one?" his mood lifted from our prior conversation and sounds almost hopeful.

I bite back on the refusal that sits on my tongue. Maybe it'll help get some of these emotions out.

"Sure."

Arlo and I walk to the matted side of the gym. He helps me get some padded gloves on my hands before he does his own. Slowly, he shows me how to hit from several different angles on both my right hand and my left. I pick it up quickly despite the sore ache starting in my arms.

Nevertheless, Arlo knocks me on my ass during the first round. I get a few decent hits in on the second round and both of us are pleasantly surprised when I actually get him down to the floor. The third round doesn't go in my favor, my legs and arms finally giving way to the exhaustion and lack of stamina to keep up. They still held up longer than I thought I ever could, but this just means more training will be needed to build me up enough to keep on my feet.

"That's the only time you'll beat me," I promise as we step through the gym door back out into the alleyway.

The sun is now high in the sky. Cars pass by at a steady pace along with people on the sidewalks at the end of the alley. I check the time on my phone, nearly 11 in the morning.

"Yeah, sure," Arlo says with a smile on his face, rolling his eyes back at me.

"I never asked, how do you know about this place?"

"It's mine."

"You own a gym?!"

"Don't act so shocked darling," he throws an arm over my shoulder, the space in the alley becoming increasingly smaller. "Besides, it comes in handy from time to time."

"Right. Used only for training sessions with a helpless Nephilim?" I joke sarcastically.

Arlo laughs loudly as we turn the corner back onto the sidewalk, heading back to the café. Several heads turn and stare at his cackle.

"Exactly," he finally gets out.

The blocks back to the café seem shorter and yet my muscles scream at me with every step making even the smallest moves feel like they drag on for hours.

"What are your plans?" Arlo asks as we cross the last street.

"Huh?"

"For the rest of the day?"

"Oh, I guess... homework?" the word sounds ridiculous.

How normal and trivial. Yet I do have to keep up appearances and I have a photography assignment to finish by Monday so I should probably work on that.

'*Find color in a world of grey,*' Professor Bryan's words fill my head again.

"Borrrrinnnnggg..." Arlo drags out as we enter the café. I laugh at his dramatics. Several students turn their heads, most of them looking with eyes glazed over. Still working through hangovers from the night before or already working on projects. Is there really a difference?

Arlo smiles politely at the patrons and continues to walk to the counter. Pierre looks up from the drink he's making and smiles brightly at Arlo. Nothing but love reflects in his eyes. They embrace with a swift kiss and tight hug. The act makes my heart flutter. Maybe there are some moments of peace, moments of normal to be had still.

"How did everything go?" Pierre asks once he breaks free of Arlo.

"Great!" Arlo shouts before I can get anything out of my mouth. He starts walking toward the back of the café, through the door to the kitchen.

"That's great!" Pierre praises, pride shining through his smile at me.

"Yeah, I think I was more surprised my body didn't give out sooner," I shrug.

"Well, you guys have been gone for hours. I was starting to get worried, but it's good that you stuck it out for that long. Pretty good for a first session," Pierre goes to make another order.

"She was fantastic," Arlo reappears, now dressed in a button-down shirt and jeans. He throws a sandwich at me, and I catch it in the nick of time.

"Now go have fun doing your... homework," he feigns a shiver in fear.

A smile splits my face.

"Oh and Nola," Arlo says as he puts on the small brown apron on his waist. "Call your mother, okay?"

My smile fades. He's right. I should call her and talk through more of this. Hear her side but I'm still not sure if I'm ready for that...

I nod instead, not trusting my voice to fully promise that I will.

"Thank you for this morning, Arlo," I say to him. "For everything really," meaning more than I could put into words.

Arlo nods knowingly, waving goodbye.

I grip the sandwich close to my chest with one hand and wave with the other. My muscles protest against the push of the door of the café that is now significantly heavier than this morning.

Fuck, this is going to suck.

I form plans to soak in the tub to relax the muscles and stretch more as I pull out of the parking lot and head back to my apartment. Too bad I can't stretch to relax and quiet my brain from spiraling.

THIRTEEN

My study room breathes with peace around me. The music coming from my laptop next to me changes to a new song. In the silent moment that follows, soft footsteps echo outside the door followed by a light knock on the other side of the door. I'm used to this kind of disruption of the peace as it happens every so often when the library staff does their rounds, checking on the rooms and seeing if there are any books that are needing to be restocked on shelves.

"Come in!" I say just loud enough for the person on the other side to hear.

As the door creaks open, I look up expecting to see a flustered sophomore fumble through the door and apologize for interrupting but instead, I'm hit with the soft smell of sandalwood.

Blake stands in the doorway, dressed in his signature dark jeans and an open button down with a dark t-shirt underneath.

My heart jumps in my chest and I can feel the heat rise to my cheeks.

"Hello Nola," he says casually, a smile dancing on his lips.

"Umm... hello?" I say hesitantly, not sure why he's here.

His smile widens, touching his eyes, as he takes in my confusion and surprise. He steps through the door, letting it close behind him. He grips the chair on the opposite side of the table and looks up at me, asking permission if he can sit. I nod.

"Curious that even here you're studying," he shrugs as he puts his hands on the table in front of him.

"Why is that strange? It's the library..."

He laughs lightly like I just told a joke. Tilting my head at the sound, I wait for him to compose himself and explain.

"I suppose that physically this does resemble the library on campus," he looks around taking in the tiny room – my tiny room.

"But that isn't what I'm talking about," he starts to grab for my papers in front of me. "What are you studying anyway? Ahh. Abstract art over the years."

"So, we're just going to brush over what you just said? What do you mean?" I press, refusing to get distracted.

He sighs, frustrated that I'm not letting this go.

"I mean that it all looks and feels real, no? But at the same time, it feels off, right? Both tangible and intangible?" he gestures around the room as he speaks.

I look around trying to follow what he's saying. Rubbing the table in front of me, the texture changes beneath my fingers. One moment I can feel the scratches and marks from heavy writers, the next it's far too smooth, marks disappearing beneath my fingertips. I look up at the window and see the sun set behind the trees quicker than I've ever seen it or thought physically possible. The moon now competes with the overhead yellow fluorescents to fill the room with light. In what seems like three seconds, the music changes playlists four times before it settles on classic rock.

Looking back at Blake I notice he's intently watching me. Blue eyes boring into mine, watching every move. Aside from his intense gaze, he looks all but uninterested by our changing surroundings, focused solely on me.

"So, you study art?"

"Um, yes," I say, thrown off by his intensity. "My major is uh Art History and minoring... in Photography, hence all of this."

I look down at the papers and notice that they're all blank, all my scribblings and text gone.

"What's happening?"

"Just focus on me," Blake says softly.

"We don't have much time," he reaches over the table and grabs my hand. The burning electricity shoots through me, forcing me to meet his eyes. A part of me wants to pull my hand away but another part is grounded by the small touch.

"Why art and photography?" he asks curiously, head tilted slightly to the side.

"Well, I love it. It feels like some sort of timekeeper. A single painting, sculpture, or photo can hold so many words, a whole story really. All of them can take a while to make, all to just capture a single moment in time. A single moment that comes with a novel of a story," I smile down at our hands. "Each piece of art has its own story created out of conflict, hatred, moments of peace, or..." I hesitate, watching his thumb gently rub over my knuckles, each stroke sending a new wave of electricity. "Love..."

"That is very poetic."

As I look up I catch him smiling down at our hands as well. Does he feel the electricity too?

"I would also have to agree with you," he looks up, meeting my eyes. His eyes burn softly. "I've never put it into words as poetic as yours, but I feel like my drawings can speak more than I ever could."

"You draw?"

"Yeah. Maybe I could show you sometime? Outside of here of course," he gestures around.

I vaguely notice the sun is back in its place in the window. Hmmm... what is going on with the weather today?

Meeting his gaze again I see his eyes are lost looking at something over my head. He lets go of my hand and gets up to walk around the table. The heat rises in my face again as he brings his warmth to my side of the table. Stopping a few inches from me, he leans against the table. I follow his stare to the painting on the wall behind me. I stand beside him, moving the chair away a few inches to keep the same distance.

"What about this one?" he asks.

I've stared at this painting more times than I can count, having written a paper about it as well, but I still find new things every time I examine it. The painting captures a moment from the Battle of Edge. One of the many battles fought in this town, but this one was the bloodiest and the longest. It waged between the citizens of Edge, led by General Victor Edge, and the citizens of Cross, led by the esteemed and highly decorated General Nathaniel Cross.

While the reason for the battle's start is heavily debated, some historians claim it was taxes and land while others argue that it was a battle between the two families over love.

Very Romeo and Juliet.

It's said that the bloodshed ended when both generals died at each other hands, only then did the families strike a deal. The land was divided and cash was handed over, to allow the lovers to be together. If that side of history is true, it's almost impossible to imagine those lovers were able to live with themselves after nearly 17,000 citizens died for their love. How can a love be so great that you could allow that many people to die for it?

Looking at this painting always reminds me of that theory. In the foreground, a soldier is laying on his back on a cot, bandages around his head and torso. The red paint bleeds through the whites of the bandages and covers most of the cot and floor beneath him. Holding his hand is a nurse, dressed in a white gown that's dirty and stained with blood. Her head is down, resting it on their clasped hands, completely oblivious to the dark and bloody surroundings. Above them, casting the only light source in the painting is an angel. Its arm outstretched toward the soldier. What I never noticed before is the bright light that I thought was only being cast from the angel in the image is actually coming from another source. A bright orb right in the hand of the angel.

"I love this one," I sigh, examining the darker figures in the background. They're so dark that they almost blend into the background, becoming ghosts of the image as well.

"You do? It seems a bit dark and... pretentious."

"I guess it is in a way... I'm assuming you know about the Battle of Edge? The story of the lovers?" I pause and watch him nod, still examining the painting.

"I like to think the artist sides with the story about the lovers and this is their way of expressing it. Showing the two lovers in the light of the angel while the world of darkness, chaos, and blood wages around them. It's dark but also romantic and hopeful, no?"

I look over at Blake and notice him staring intently at me again. His blue eyes blaze causing my breath to catch in my throat. He closes the distance between us quickly, his face only centimeters away from mine.

"You know you light up when you talk about art," he smiles softly as his hand reaches up to caress my cheek.

All at once, the mixture of his scent and the burning becomes so overwhelming that I have to take a step back, trying to catch my breath. He steps with me until my back hits the wall behind me. His eyes search mine, again asking for permission. Before I nod, something else takes over. Call it curiosity and just plain want but I throw my arms around his neck, crushing his lips against mine. Surprised, it takes him a second to recover from my attack, but his lips move with mine, melting into mine with matching heat. The electricity crackles through me and above our heads. His hands move slowly but hungrily from the side of my face down my neck to the small of my back, pushing us together.

I let my hands explore him as well. Feeling the muscles of his arms and back contract under his shirt. I grab the button-down shirt at his side just as the burning in my left wrist, that was manageable before, becomes unbearable. I pull away from him, breaking away from his lips, and stare down at my wrist. My wing stares back at me with fire.

There's something I feel like I should remember about this? What was it about my wing... The words are right there, right on the tip of my tongue...

Darkness starts to circle around us. Blake grabs my hand

and I look up to see him also looking at my wrist, concern written all over his expression.

"Looks like we are out of time," Blake says, slightly breathless.

I look up at him, partially confused but mainly consumed by the fire raging in my wrist. If my breath hadn't been taken from the kiss, it would be gone now from the pain.

Softly, Blake grabs the sides of my face and stares deeply in my eyes, searching for something else. My vision starts to blur around the edges from the tears filling my eyes.

"Why...?" I start to say but he silences me with a gentle kiss. He breaks away too soon.

"I'll see you soon," he promises as his eyes blaze into mine as he winks playfully.

I smile as my vision goes dark.

I couldn't tell you the moment I fell asleep, but I wake in a cold sweat as the fire still rages in my wrist. I shoot up. My back aching from the position I had fallen asleep in, hunched over my desk with my laptop still playing music. My papers are splayed out around me, a few sticking to my face as I sit up.

I get up, painfully, from the burning and the stiffness in my joints. It was only this morning that Arlo and I trained so my muscles are completely stretched to their limit and falling asleep like that did them no favors. The burning intensifies as I head to the bathroom. Not bothering to shut the door, I turn the sink to the coldest setting. I put my wrist under the icy water and the burning calms almost instantly. Keeping my wrist under the water I stare up at my reflection.

"It was just a dream..." I say to her.

But it was all so real... Arlo's words repeat in my mind: this will guide you. Is this what he meant? My wing... the burning... is that it guiding me? But why would it do this in just a dream? Is Blake a demon? The questions pile up in my mind with no answers. The only one who would know... Blake.

FOURTEEN

I stare at the bubbles that rise from the heat in the pot. Some pop as they reach the top, releasing steam, in unison. Disrupting their dance, I swirl the boiling water around, to not let the noodles stick. They settle for only a moment but quickly grow agitated again.

It's a cycle really. The whole process of cooking, that is, much like everything in life. Now my life is a new cycle and I'm not sure where it ends or begins again...

"I think they're done, Nola," Ash's voice comes from the other side of the island. Ironic that her voice sounds so far away, islands away... lifetimes away.

Another noise reaches me in time with her voice. A soft beeping. It takes me a moment to realize that it's the timer on the stove.

"Shit!"

I open the oven door, half expecting the bread to be burnt but instead I'm hit with the buttery garlic scent. They're perfect, golden. The color nearly triggers the memory that I've been trying to keep buried for several days now. Buried beneath days of training as my muscles protest me bending down just to take the garlic bread out of the oven. Buried beneath schoolwork which doesn't seem to stop. Finals are coming up and there's really no other time for me to think about that soul... Howard's soul and where it supposedly is now.

And now is not the time to think about it.

Ash and I have been having these dinners for longer than I can remember. It's something we would do at least three times a week just to catch up and actually eat some good food. Tonight is my night to cook so it's been a welcomed distraction. A reminder of what's normal, or what used to be normal.

"Dinner's ready," I smile up at Ash, even though she already knows. Placing the garlic bread down on the counter, she sniffs the air.

"Why does it always smell so much better when someone else cooks it?"

As I turn to grab the noodles, I lift my shoulders, shrugging in response. I had placed the strainer in the sink a few minutes ago in preparation, so I strain the pasta slowly, squinting against the warm steam.

"Maybe because someone else's blood, sweat, and tears went into it?"

I hear the clicks as Ash turns off the burners that the pasta and sauce are sitting on, behind me. The cabinet opens and she takes out two bowls, placing them on the counter next to her.

"That's disgusting Nola. If I wasn't starving, I would boycott this meal and ban you from cooking for... forever."

"That's a lie. You love when I cook," I wink as I put the drained pasta back on the stove.

Ash scoffs as she fills her bowl with pasta and the warm vodka sauce. She expertly balances two pieces of the garlic toast on top.

"I just love that you don't make me clean up."

Ash HATES cleaning. That doesn't mean that she doesn't clean up after herself, though. If that was the case, we wouldn't be on year three of living together. But... she definitely hates it. I never figured out why but I do know that she tries to avoid it or get out of it every time if she can. I on the other hand, kinda like the simple task. Cleaning and organizing has always helped me relax and gives me something to focus on when everything else seems out of control. It's something I picked up in my childhood between the hospital visits, rehab family therapy sessions, screaming matches with Sean... all of it.

So, Ash and I decided long ago that I would be the one to clean most of the time. With a few breaks when Ash cooks for us instead.

By the time I serve myself and sit at our tiny kitchen table, Ash is already halfway finished.

"What? We're not saying grace?"

Ash looks me dead in the eyes as she purposefully takes another bite of her bread. She chews slowly, then pats at the corners of her mouth. I start to shake my head as the smile spreads on my own mouth.

Finally, she swallows the mouthful and says, "hell no."

Taking my own bite of the buttery bread, I laugh at her response. But the laughter feels different this time. It's not light as it has been before with the same joke.

It feels heavier and maybe that's because now I know, and

Ash doesn't. I know I don't know everything, but the truth is right in front of me when I'm with Arlo or my mother or the others. Hell, the truth is inside of me, a part of me. Religion has never really been a serious topic of conversation with Ash and I. I've never really brought it up in our friendship and we both tend to avoid the topic altogether if it comes up with our mutual friends.

I feel the brick wall of realization before it hits me. If Ash finds out the truth, I could not only lose her as a friend, but I could shatter her entire worldview.

I should've known that...

"Right..." I say with a sad smile, twirling the noodles around my fork.

"What's been up with you the past few days?"

I meet Ash's eyes across from me. She's no longer eating, instead just watching me.

Okay, so we are getting right to it.

Obviously, I wasn't as subtle as I thought I was.

"What do you mean?" I play dumb, wiping at my mouth with a napkin.

"I mean," her brown eyes are serious, and I can see her trying to pick the right words behind them. "You've been out of it... like distant... for a week or so now. What's going on?"

Most days I love Ash's brutal honesty and skepticism. But not today. Now that I'm on the other end of it, I feel like I'm under a microscope and she can see every atom within me, but some of these atoms I can't let her see.

"Oh..." I feel the panic rising. I can't keep looking at her, so I stare back at my dinner. "I've just been really busy with finals coming up and all the assignments..."

Suddenly this bowl of untouched food in front of me is the

most interesting thing in the entire world. I poke at the noodles, twirling and untwirling them. My stomach has flipped on a switch from hunger to queasiness under her stare. The silence stretches between us for several moments before I feel brave enough to look up.

I regret it almost immediately because Ash hasn't moved. Her stare hasn't faltered. In fact, it's gotten more intense, if that's even possible. I know she can see straight through the bullshit, probably because we have most of the same assignments at least in our major courses and those are almost done.

I swallow around the growing lump in my throat.

"And there's..." maybe she'll take a half truth, "family stuff that's going on. You know fall break was, a lot."

Her whole demeanor changes in an instant. She loosens as her face morphs into a look of pity. It's the same look she gave me when I first told her about my father. She was the first person I opened up to with the real reason that I chose Art History as my major. I told her all about how fantastical my dad made art. The twirl of his colors in the world opened up my own colorful inspiration in choosing Edge to go to school. Ash softened at my words then just as she does now. It's never easy to talk about my father and even Ash doesn't know how dark it really got, just that he's gone now.

"I'm so sorry Nola..." she picks up her fork again. "I just assumed it was something else... I mean we didn't really talk that much after fall break about that. I guess we've both been pretty busy."

"Don't worry, I haven't really been up to talking about it. I know it's been years since... but every time I go back there, it's like being transported to the past. Like it was all just yesterday, you know?"

Ash sighs and looks down at her dinner. Maybe her bowl is now the most interesting thing in the room to her.

"I'm not going to lie to you, I don't know what that's like," she twirls her fork and looks back up at me. Her brown eyes still brimming with pity, but her eyebrows are pinched with seriousness.

"But I am here if you ever need to talk about it. Or anything."

"I know."

And I do. I know that I could tell Ash anything. It nearly bursts through my chest in that moment, everything. My father and his addiction. Sean and our relationship. Me being a Nephilim who can see souls. My mother being an angel. Arlo being an angel. Demons lurking probably too close for comfort.

But each thought, each possible sentence, tightens the ball of fear in my stomach and sticks in my throat. Just like with Harley, there's still so much I don't know. Dots that still aren't connected and I honestly wouldn't know where to start...

"So, what have you been up to?" I ask her, turning the conversation away from me.

We both turn to our dinner again. Ash continues eating but I can't seem to stomach it now. I move the noodles around in my bowl.

"Pretty much the same," she answers with a mouthful of noodles again. Her eyes are still skeptical, watching my every move but I can even see that fading.

"Just studying and oh!"

I jump slightly in my chair, "what?!"

"Don't hate me..."

"Oh god," I roll my eyes at her and the irony of the words that just came out of my mouth.

"There's a party," she continues, ignoring me.

"No."

"And before you say no," she smiles brightly at me. "It'll be super lowkey. I heard about it from Karen and Mitchell. It's at Mitchell's frat house and Karen invited me and I said you had to come with, and she didn't care so you have to come now."

"Back up, who are these people?"

"Karen is in our class... Blonde hair, thick black glasses?"

I tilt my head at her.

"Sits like two rows over?" The image of the classroom pops in my head but no one comes to mind.

"Wow, you really need to pay more attention to your surroundings, Nola."

She shakes her head as she takes another bite of food.

"Anyways, her and Mitchell are together and he's in the Alpha frat and there's a party... tomorrow night."

"Tomorrow night?!"

"And I'm pretty sure Jase is gonna be there..."

The ringing in my ears intensifies as my fork clatters against my bowl. I clear my throat, trying to restart my heart. I don't like this at all. Jase being around Ash again is not something I want for her. Even though nothing has happened, Ash seems to be really taken by him.

I also can't shake the feeling that there's just something about him and his brother and... Blake. How they are all connected, I don't know. But I know if I don't go, Ash will go by herself, and I can't let that happen. She won't be safe.

"Alright, I'll go."

"Wait," Ash swallows around her food, her eyes filled with surprise. "You will?!"

"Yes," I nod to solidify the answer.

Ash squeals with excitement, but I can feel myself turning inward with a flinch. I try to mirror her mood with an encouraging smile. She can't see how frightened I am or how much anxiety the thought of going to this party is bringing up. Still, it fills my chest and pounds in time with my heart. A small part of me is hopeful that it will just be another normal night with nothing involving my new world.

You know that's dumb, my subconscious chastises me. She's dressed in a workout outfit from our last training session with Arlo. She's bouncing on her toes getting ready to fight.

How silly of me to think that with Jase there, it might be a normal night. Since the last time was my birthday and that was far from normal. Hell, it turned my whole life upside down. But maybe now that I know what I am, and with these training sessions, I can let my instincts take over should anything happen. And if anything does, I'll be by Ash's side to protect her.

FIFTEEN

I stifle a yawn as I absentmindedly surf the internet for some new winter clothes. It's a mundane task, one that I've definitely been putting off but the chill outside is getting harder to ignore.

However, my mind continues to drift to the night before. The plan still stands that tonight Ash and I are going to the party, but it didn't stop my subconscious from flooding my dreams. It was a sleepless night filled with fiery blue eyes, the haunting feeling of being watched, and the faint burning sensation that's still lingering around my left wrist. I woke up this morning with the burning becoming almost unbearable just like several nights ago. The only thing calming it down has been cold water running over it on full blast.

I stare down at my wrist and my wing stares back with secrets that I still don't understand.

"I hope you're getting ready in there...?" Ash's voice

reaches me through my closed bedroom door. I check the clock on my laptop.

"It's only six!" I shout back at her.

"Nola," her tone shifts to one of playful annoyance. "Don't make me come in there and make you. And you know I would love to get you all dolled up."

I scrunch my nose at the thought of Ash doing exactly that. It sounds like torture.

"No thanks!" I shake my head, getting up from the comfort of my bed. "I'm getting up now!"

I grab my phone from the dresser, surprisingly it hasn't buzzed for the last day. While that brings me an ounce of relief, it's also curious. Even my mother seems to have given up on trying to get me to talk. And I don't think I've gone more than a day without hearing from him... Has Sean finally given up? Almost sounds too good to be true.

"Good! You should wear those boots again, from your birthday!" Ash's voice starts to fade as I hear her footsteps walking away from the door. "Oh, and don't forget to bundle up!"

"Ha," I laugh to myself. I scroll through my last text messages and tap on Harley's name. The phone only rings twice.

"Nola Rae! How's it going?" Harley's voice immediately fills me with so many fond memories. It's an anchor to home and I can't help but smile.

"Hey, Harl! Oh, things are good!" I say like we didn't just talk the other night. "Ash is dragging me to some party tonight and you know me and parties go so well together..."

"I'm assuming you are calling because you either A. Need help getting out of it or B. Need your BEST friend there to get you drunk enough to enjoy it," I can hear the eagerness in their voice.

"I would like to take option 1 for $200, sir."

"Too bad, you're getting the opposite. Be there in an hour," they hang up before I can protest.

Fuck, they're good.

An hour later, I've got my version of a full face of makeup on, foundation, eye shadow, and mascara. I fought with Ash – who came back to my room to tear through my closet – for a full 10 minutes about the pointlessness of contour and blush before she finally gave up and let me do the majority of my own makeup. I did mix it up and use a newer pallet of eyeshadow that I had been saving for something other than just going to class. As I tap the finishing touches on my eye shadow, blending the glittering gold with a soft silver at the corners of my eyes, there's a knock at the door.

I smile as I head over to open it. The mixture of excitement of seeing Harley and taking the chance to not think about everything angel related nearly has me skipping down the short hallway to the door. I swing the door open so hard that it makes a loud bang as it bounces off the wall, nearly shutting again. I cringe as Harley catches the door with their foot.

"Damn Nola, you trying to wake the whole complex!?" they laugh and Harley's lip rings move with their mouth. They shut the door behind them, almost as loud as the bang from opening it.

"No, but apparently you are," I laugh with Harley and hug them briefly.

I notice they're dressed in their signature jeans and black tank top with a jacket draped over their arm. Their tattoos cover their arms and I notice a few new ones on their right shoulder. Harley loves showing off their artwork, hence the tank top even when it's so cold out.

Harley has always been one to not give an absolute shit about what people say about them. I have always admired that, ever since high school. Harley was the one that stood up and stood out from others, always pushing me into doing new things. They were actually the one who pushed me towards photography and gave me one of my first cameras. Which I still have, buried deep in my boxes of high school things, still filled with our shenanigans.

"Alright, what are we drinking?"

Harley is already at the fridge looking through it when Ash walks out of my room.

We all look fairly casual, not bothering to get too dressed up for this party. Ash, still wearing her leggings and graphic t-shirt from today, and I, in ripped jeans and a loose-fitting long sleeve top. Which I made sure I put on before Ash came in if only to cover my new black wing. I'm still not up for that conversation... The only difference being that Ash and I are wearing makeup while Harley, who has never been one for makeup, isn't.

"I was thinking tequila?"

Ash shimmies her way into the kitchen, reaching up to the top of the fridge where my bottle of tequila is at. She wiggles her eyebrows at me, asking for permission but knowing that I would never refuse. She claps her hands together excitedly.

"Ughhh..." Harley groans. "I was afraid you were going to say that. Good thing I brought my own."

They pull out a small bottle of vodka from their bag. I notice a few more mini bottles in it along with their overnight things.

"Oh, you really planning to get drunk huh?" I poke fun at them.

"Listen it's not often I'm able to escape the mundane existence that is Low College," Harley throws back the mini bottle.

"You can always come here. Just transfer," I shrug.

"Ehh. I'm already too far into my assignme... major. Wouldn't be fun to start over again."

"Yeah, I get that! I switched my major in my second semester freshman year and I thought I was going to die with the amount of catch-up I had to do," Ash says as she pours two shots, one for her and one for me. She then roots through our fridge to find a chaser.

"Damn, we don't have anything in here!"

"There's orange juice right there Ash," I point to the carton on the top shelf.

"Where's the move tonight anyways guys?" Harley asks, opening up another bottle and throwing their bag on the couch.

"Some frat house..." I shrug and shiver with disgust.

"Don't mind her," Ash says, pouring half a glass each of orange juice next to the shots on the counter.

She looks up at Harley, "Nola just doesn't know how to have fun."

"You got that right... I've been trying to make her have fun since we were little!"

"I'm right here guys," I roll my eyes at the two of them.

Harley holds up their second mini bottle with a smile

playing on their lips and says, "Cheers to a great night out with beautiful friends!"

I lift my shot glass up and wince at the clink of the glasses. The liquid burns ever so slightly going down. It calms my nerves some but the weariness of what the night might hold still weighs down my excitement. Ash and Harley begin to talk about getting a cab to the party, neither one wanting to drive. My mind lingers back to my restless nights, and I hopelessly wonder if he will be at the party. But that's not why I'm going. I'm going to keep Ash safe from whatever Jase might be. I shake off the thought as I tune back into the conversation. Ash and I down one more shot, this one giving me courage, and we're out the door and into the silver car waiting for us in no time.

We pull up to the house no more than 10 minutes later. The poor cab driver had to deal with us, another group of college kids as we laughed at some silly joke, alcohol making us comedians. As we got out of the car, I poke my head into the passenger seat window to apologize.

"Listen," I continue to giggle. "I'm so sorry for my friends. Obviously, we should be heading to a comedy show instead of here, right?"

I laugh and the cab driver just smiles and waves, completely over our bullshit.

Ash pulls me away, "Come on now, save some of the flirtatious advances for the party!"

Her and Harley laugh together as I scoff.

"You're the one that is going to be flirting with everyone in there!" I shove her away and laugh. Turning towards the house I finally see the beast we're about to enter.

The house sits on the same street as all the other fraternity and sorority houses. It's oversized neon green and yellow Greek letters scream out against the house's tan facade. I'm sure the darkness of the night is concealing the true condition of the house. Dirty siding, shingles falling off the roof, and broken boards on the porch. If it's not the darkness using its mystical powers to make this house even the smallest bit inviting to enter, then it's the people.

I see several classmates milling about on the front lawn of the house. Some smoking, some taking a break from the chaos inside, and some are already far too drunk for their own good. As we pass by, I wave, and they raise their cups or nod in acknowledgment.

"Damn Nola, how many people do you know?" Harley says in astonishment.

"Know them? Not at all. But I've seen them around..." I lift my shoulders nonchalantly as we make it to the door. I'm immediately hit with the stale scent of sweat, cigarettes, and mildew.

I guess the darkness can't hide that.

The music that was only a whisper when we got out of the car is now overwhelming. So much so, the haze inside from the smoke ripples with the bass.

I look back at the safety of the outside at the same time I feel a hand wrap around mine. Turning back to the house, I see that it's Harley's.

They're smiling, "let's go Nola."

Harley tugs my arm and I can't help but laugh. With one

more brief moment of hesitation, I let them drag me into the fog and heat of the inside.

Hand in hand, Harley leads me into the overcrowded living room behind Ash. Swept up by some friends from class, Ash quickly disappears into the crowd. The only lights in here glow from the corners of the room, changing colors every so often from red to blue to green to white and the pattern continues over and over. Music blasts from the speakers that are on a table pushed against the wall. Actually, most of the furniture is pushed against the walls if only to make more room for people to dance in the middle.

"I need more alcohol! You?!" Harley shouts in my ear over the music.

"Yes please!" I shout back, wrapping my arm through theirs as we shimmy through the drunk bodies to find the kitchen.

The crowd thins out a bit as we head down the hallway at the back of the house and into the kitchen. Avoiding the heated game of beer pong on the island in the middle of the room, Harley and I grab empty solo cups. They rifle through the fridge and pull out two cans of soda and swipes a bottle of vodka from the counter. With a heavy pour, Harley makes the two drinks.

"Woah now, if I didn't know any better, I would think you're trying to get me drunk?" I tease.

"You already know I am. I can see you trapped in your head. Enjoy the night!"

Harley hands me the drink and we cheers.

Harley's right.

Of course, they are.

And it's terrifying that they can see straight through me most of the time. Reading me like an open book that they've read for years and years. Pages crumpled with words they've memorized.

But I have been in my head. Ever since I found out what I am. It's eaten away at me. This secret that I have to hold so close to my chest. This new responsibility of this new world is another weight I'm not sure I can carry by myself. But how am I supposed to tell Harley, my best friend, all of this?

Not to mention, ever since I met Blake, I can't seem to shake him from my thoughts. Both when I'm awake and when I'm dreaming. He has consumed my mind and I only have more questions. Questions that may or may not get answers, if I even want that...

I take three hearty sips of my drink, nearly finishing it, coughing slightly as the vodka burns my throat and nose. Feeling confident as the alcohol finally kicks in, I head back to the center of the party in the living room.

I ignore all the people already dancing and drag Harley with me to the center of the room.

"There's my girl!" Harley shouts over the loud music.

The beat takes me away and we start dancing like two poorly trained toddlers in their first class. It's not pretty but it's fun.

"Where's Ash?! She needs to get in on this!" I wave my arms around, gesturing to our less than terrible dancing.

Harley laughs and shrugs, still dancing to the music. I look around, expecting to see Ash in the room but I don't see her in the immediate area. As I stretch up on my tiptoes just to get a bit taller to see over a few other heads, I scan around the room once more and finally see her.

Leaning against the front wall, Ash is chatting with someone. I watch as their conversation gets more and more flirtatious, she laughs at something the person said, then they laugh. She lightly touches their arm, and they wrap their arm around her shoulders. The lights change in the room briefly and I notice in the brighter light that the person is Jase.

A pit in my stomach forms as I remember the warmth of his hand, reminding me of a similar heat. Everything hits me again, all at once. I actually stopped thinking about Blake for a little while but now seeing Jase, it all comes flooding back. He whispers something in her ear, and she smiles, nodding. Jase walks away towards the kitchen; I can only assume to get them another couple of drinks.

I look back and notice that Harley has found some company to dance with. I point over to where I'm headed and they nod absently, too preoccupied with their admirer. I shake my head incredulously, of course, they would both find male specimens to enjoy this evening with.

Walking towards Ash, I stumble as the ground shifts ever so slightly. The responsible side of my brain takes note of how drunk I actually am and stores it next to the sign that says DO NOT DRINK MORE. Far more determined to get to Ash and see what that conversation was about, I keep pushing through the sweaty bodies.

"Hey!" I say as I finally reach her. She looks up from her phone.

"Oh my god! Nola! I was just about to text you and ask you where you were! One moment you guys were right behind me and the next, nothing," she slurs over the music.

I lean against the wall next to her if only to give me a bit more support from the tilting of the room. Never mind how much the bass of the music rattles not only the walls and floor but my vision, making everything more out of focus.

"Yeah! You got swept up in the crowd and Harley and I just went to go get more drinks."

I shift my focus back to the hallway just when Jase comes back into the room with a single drink in his hand. His eyes seem to scan the room quickly, landing on one of the guys in a small group, all laughing and wasted. The Greek letters on their shirts match the glowing ones on the outside of the house.

"So, what were you and Jase just chatting about?" I ask absently as I watch Jase approach the group of guys.

"Nola! He is just the best!" she gushes. "We are just talking about everything really. How I got into Art History. What he was studying. He wants to take me out!" she smacks my arm excitedly, causing me to jump, and break my gaze.

I rub my arm, "Ummm... ouch!" I fake hurt in my voice, but she's far too excited to care. "He wants to take you out already? This is your, what? Third conversation?" I ask, turning back to watching him.

Is he really good enough for her?

Through the bodies, I see Jase pull something out of his jacket pocket. The lights go dark for a split second so I can't see what it was. As the lights come back, it's brighter and I see what looks like white or maybe blue pills in a small baggy in the frat guy's hand. Now in Jase's hand, cash.

"Hey, when you know you know, amiright?" Ash nudges me lightly this time, but I barely notice. Did I just see what I thought I just saw?

"Besides, we decided on something casual for our first dinner so I'm not completely sure it will go anywhere. But there's something about him... I wonder where he is with our drinks..." Ash continues talking about their upcoming first date.

That's not going to happen if I have anything to do with it.

Jase quickly turns, heading to the side of the room with the speakers and other furniture lined against the wall. I push off the wall behind me, staggering slightly, and start pushing through the bodies once more.

"Hey! Where are you going now!?!" I hear Ash call after me. I down the rest of the drink in my hand as I barrel through the crowd.

Using all of my focus and might, I reach Jase just as he's handing the cash to a hooded guy on the couch. I yank his shoulder to turn him around to face me.

"Listen here, Jase!" Jase turns to look at me, shocked. "I don't care what you do in your free time. If that's dealing drugs or whatever. I don't care how nice you are! Stay away from Ash! She's too good for you and doesn't deserve to be put in the middle of whatever game you've got going on here!" I gesture around wildly.

Pointing aggressively at his chest, pushing him with every word, "Stay. Away. From..."

"Nola?"

Through the haze of red, I didn't notice when the hooded guy stood, but I would know that voice in my sleep.

"Oh shit."

SIXTEEN

"No, no, no..."

I look at Blake as he takes the hood off his head. His eyes glow even in the darkness of the room. It's hard not to notice that my heart skips a beat as I look at him. Shaking my head, I look down, away from his burning blue eyes. I land on the money, still in his hand.

"You're a part of this!? What are you some sort of drug dealer!?" my voice rises, anger and the pounding music making it higher, a few heads around us turn to look.

"Calm down Nola. You don't know what you're talking about," Blake says ever so coolly. His hand slips into his pocket as he glances over at Jase.

Before I can say anything more, Jase leaves and heads for the back of the house.

Good riddance, Ash deserves so much better than that. I think to myself.

"Don't tell me I don't know what I'm talking about! I just saw it all!"

Looking back at Blake, his face changes to look at me as if he's looking at an injured puppy.

Suddenly, the room shifts and starts to spin. I need to sit down before the world forces me to the ground itself. A burning hand grabs my arm to hold me steady. I try to yank away, but he grips tighter.

"Let me help you get outside at least," a forced smile playing on his lips.

The room continues to shift, and my feet struggle underneath me. Maybe some air will help. I nod slightly, tripping over my own feet. He shifts beside me trying to put one hand on my waist as he guides me out of the house. His warmth is almost as overwhelming as that first night with him this close. The feeling of his body around me makes me as dizzy as the alcohol. He pulls me in, holding tighter, as the crowd continuously bumps into us. His hand on my waist grips tighter and I feel an electric current shoot through my stomach, up my chest, and down to my wrist where his other hand is holding me.

The shock of the electricity is quickly replaced by the burning at my wing. There it is the same burning sensation every time I've been with him. The same burning that's happened in my dreams...

Finally, outside, I pull myself away. The feeling dissipates the farther away I am from him. The music fades but my ears still ring from the abuse. My head becomes clearer as I breathe in the cool air and glance down at my wing. Stumbling my way through the lawn, I start to rub my wrist, pushing away the last ache of the burning sensation.

"What are you trying to tell me?" I say to myself.

"What was that?"

Blake's voice causes me to jump, which comes from a lot closer than I expected him to be. Looking around, I see that the small front yard has only a few drunk students milling about. A couple smoking on the porch, a couple sitting beside the house, far too interested in each other to care what was around them.

"You'll think I'm crazy," I say, turning back to Blake.

His eyes lock in on my wrist, still being held by my other hand. Something shifts behind them, but his eyes are back on my face in an instant.

"What if I already do?" he smiles a crooked smile.

Don't look at his mouth. Don't do it...

I curse the rational side of my brain as the alcohol that made me so confident is also making me want to give in. From the slight stubble on his jawline to his cheekbones and the endless blue flames that dance in his eyes.

Whatever you do, don't think about his lips on yours...

"You wouldn't be the only one," I say sarcastically back at him.

"Well, I do think that a few people in there," he points back towards the house, "would think that you were with the way you were just shouting."

Like a switch being flicked, the protective anger returns.

"Ash shouldn't be getting involved with him. And you... you took that money? What are you? A dealer?"

"It's a bit more complicated than that," he runs his hands through his hair, watching my face carefully.

"What's more complicated? I saw Jase give those guys some pills and then he handed you the money and it's still in your pocket! Is this why you told me to stay away? To run? Because you're involved in this?"

Suddenly it all makes sense. I should stay away if this is what he's a part of. I've seen enough of the gritty, dangerous side of this world and what it can do to a person. What I haven't seen is a dealer with enough of a conscious to tell someone to stay away.

What is it about this guy?

Blake's lips part slightly as he takes a deep breath.

Stop thinking about his lips, Nola.

A battle seems to play in his eyes as he thinks of what to say next. His eyes become steely as he settles on some resolve.

"Yes," he starts to turn away.

"Wait," I call after him. "That's it? That's all you're going to say?"

I grab his arm to keep him facing me, the electricity and burning shoots through me again. I release his arm quickly, taken aback. He seems shocked as well but recovers quickly.

"What more do you want me to say? The less complicated version is that yes, I deal. And you should stay away. It's not safe."

"What do you mean the less complicated version? I know this life all too well and know that it's not safe and wrong, but I can see that you're not telling me everything. All these vague threats and warnings. You have to give me more than that, then I can decide for myself," I cross my arms over my chest.

He smirks again.

"Ever the stubborn and curious cat," he winks at me.

My heart skips in my chest again and a feeling of deja vu hits me.

"Wait... Didn't we already have this conversation? I could've sworn we have..."

Confused, I search his eyes for anything he will give away.

The alcohol not helping me read his face, as well as sober me, would. But he's cautious and amusement dances in his eyes.

"Possibly..." he shrugs. Amused as he watches the shock take over my face.

"That's not possible because it was a... a dream..."

"Nooollllaaaa!"

A voice rings out behind me causing my whole body to go rigid.

It can't be... He shouldn't be here.

A chill runs through me as I turn to see Sean crossing the street, stumbling slightly on the curb. His dirty blonde hair is longer, a bit shaggier than I remember. He's still reliving the glory days in his signature high school football hoodie and blue jeans. Once he gets close enough, I can see that his brown bloodshot eyes are still the bottomless pits they always were.

"Nola Rae. Babe. I've been looking for you all over! You're one tricky bitch to find," his words slur.

Of course, he's drunk. He only does this stupid shit when he's wasted.

I flinch as he reaches up to wrap his arm around me. I take a couple of steps back to get out of his reach and back into Blake, still standing where he was. His cautious warmth is far more welcoming than the wave of chilling fear coming from Sean's direction. Although it's been years since I've seen him, the old fear returns. Seeing him here and now, I'm immediately transported back to all of our time together. All the abuse, the hiding, the pretending, the covering up... It's far easier to ignore the pain when he's just words on the screen of my phone. But now... it's right here... he's right here in front of me, backing me in the cage that he kept me in for so long.

His hand drops to his side.

"Come on now Nola. Don't be like that."

The liquor wafts from his breath making the pit in my stomach turn over its own alcohol contents.

I take a deep breath to settle myself, but I find myself still uneasy.

"Sean..." I can taste the acid on my tongue. "You shouldn't be here. You need to leave."

Hopeful, I reach back and find Blake's hand. It feels reassuring, even with the burn, that he's there. Interesting, that I feel more comfortable with a complete stranger, who happens to be a drug dealer, than the man standing in front of me.

Sean's eyes shoot down to watch my hand in Blake's. He cocks his head to the side, the motion reminding me of a dog, trying to understand what he's looking at. His brow furrows as anger takes over his features. It's a look I've seen plenty of times, the switch from cordial Sean to irate Sean. It's a look I thought I had left in my past and yet here it is, standing right in front of me. I flinch back from it like so many times before. Disgust fills me with my own reaction.

Why does he still have this much power over me?

"What... the fuck... is this?"

His words are slow and deliberate as he looks behind me to size up Blake.

Blake takes a half step in front of me.

"Look, Sean, was it?" Blake says nonchalantly. "I think you should do what Nola says and leave," making no effort to hide the warning in his voice.

"Oh yeah? Why don't you make me?"

Sean takes a step forward as well, bringing them almost chest to chest.

I can see where this is going.

"Oh, I very well could make you leave but I would rather this be amiable since there's a lady present," Blake squeezes my hand.

"There's no lady here," Sean scoffs as he looks me up and down. "That fucking whore is always fucking around. Like she's fucking around with you!" Sean quickly lifts up his hands, shoving Blake.

Blake staggers a step back, taken off guard, and yanks me with him.

Shit.

Rage radiates off Blake as he releases my hand, closing the distance between him and Sean. He lands a punch on the left side of Sean's face with a crack.

"STOP!" I shout to no avail.

The fight breaks out before I can comprehend what's happening. Sean lands a few punches on Blake, but they don't seem to be having much of an effect.

"Guys stop it!"

I wedge myself between them, trying - and failing - to get them to stop. A small crowd has started to form around us, but no one steps in.

"Blake! Stop it!" I say as I try to pull him away.

It's no use. He's far stronger than I am, shrugging me off effortlessly as he hits Sean again. Suddenly, another pair of arms come in. I look up to see Jase trying to get a hold of Blake as well. With his help, we're finally able to separate the two.

Sean looks at me, with those bottomless pits wildly searching my face. Smiling sadistically with his busted lip splitting more, he grabs my shoulder hard enough that I know it will leave a bruise.

"Bitch," he says, spitting blood in my face.

He shoves me hard, and I fall on my back hard enough that it knocks the wind out of me.

I can't seem to catch my breath as Sean laughs, but it's quickly covered by a loud crunching noise and a thud as a body hits the ground.

Through the stars in my vision, I see Sean laying beside me. For a moment, he's so still I think the worst. My stomach nearly empties itself, but he faintly stirs.

Good, he will feel all of this tomorrow.

I look around as my vision returns and see the small crowd has already moved on, now that the excitement is over. Pushing up on my elbows, I wince at the pain in my shoulder. The ground shifts under me again from the sudden change and the alcohol sloshes in my stomach, making me feel sick.

"Let me go. I'm fine now. He'll be fine too. Dick. Could've gotten worse."

I look up to see Blake shaking out of Jase's grip. Also next to Jase is Azel. When did he get here?

Looking back at Blake, I feel like I'm looking at a completely different person. Maybe this is the person he's warning me about. The darker side. I've had enough darkness in my life. The darkest part is still coming too on the ground beside me. Blake's eyes meet mine and they shift from the burning blue rage from the fight to a melting concern.

I wince as I try to sit up. He closes the distance between us with two strides, leaning down so that he's on my level. The warm wave hits me again and makes me smile slightly. Maybe I'm being naïve but the feelings this guy gives me are terrifying, intriguing, and oddly comforting all at the same time.

"Are you alright?"

He reaches hesitantly towards me, but I flinch away. Still

unable to control my bodily reactions to having Sean so close to me. I look up to see his face scrunched up in concern.

"Yeah... I will be... I always am." I try to give him my most reassuring smile.

Still unsure, he slowly puts his hand out to help me to my feet. I take it without hesitation this time, ready to get off the ground and away from Sean who's now groaning in pain. The urge to help him flashes through me, as I've helped him so many times before. Blake slowly pulls me up and away from my groaning past and my old habits.

I stagger a bit, but Blake holds my hands steady.

"Maybe, I should take you home?"

"I think that would be best. Wait, no. I came with Harley and Ash. They would kill me if I left them!" I start to panic, looking around for them.

"I can take them home," Jase chimes in.

I shoot daggers at him, and he lifts his hands up defensively.

"Hey, scouts honor. No funny business. They'll get back to your place safe and sound," Jase gives me a boyish smile.

It softens me a bit but not enough to make me feel totally comfortable. The world shifts around me again and I'm reminded once more of the alcohol weighing heavy in my stomach. The only thing holding me together is Blake's hand in mine.

"Come on. Let's go," Blake says softly.

SEVENTEEN

The walk along the sidewalk is silent aside from the occasional passing car, dogs barking as we pass their houses, and our footsteps echoing on the concrete. The noise from the party is fading as we continue down the street, Blake leading me to wherever his car is parked. But even with the music gone, a slight ringing has taken its place.

The thought crosses my mind that I'm trusting a man who I barely know to lead me through the dark to his car. A man who's involved with who knows what with a world, a violent world, I thought I left behind.

Great, good going Nola... how are you going to get out of this one?

I look around to assess any escape routes. I could knock on one of the doors of the houses we've passed. I pull out my phone and check the time, two in the morning. Well, I'm sure that would go over well. A frantic girl knocking on strangers' doors this early. Logically, I could go back to the party, find

Harley and Ash, and just go home. But going back to the party would mean risking the chance of running into Sean again if he hasn't already cleared out.

Another thing pulls me forward: the possibility of answers.

A faint car horn followed by the clicking of car locks turns my attention back to Blake. He's holding the passenger door open, waiting. I hesitate, taking in the sleek black car. It looks similar to the one I saw him get into the other night we ran into each other. A chill runs through me and my hands start to shake slightly. Even as I grip my hands into fists, they tremble slightly.

Looking up, I catch Blake's eyes, slightly glowing in the streetlamp's light. He's watching me intently; I'm assuming waiting for me to collapse or scream or run in the other direction.

Granted, all those options have crossed my mind in the past few seconds.

I'm sure he can see my hesitation and gives me a slight crooked smile. He tilts his head to the side, welcoming me into the car. The gesture is sweet, reassuring, and it warms the chill still going through my body.

Here I go... trusting this guy.

Trusting the known and the unknown.

"Don't make me regret this, Blake," I say as I walk toward the open car door.

He chuckles slightly, "I wouldn't dream of it." He winks as I get into the car.

The door shuts before I can get another word in, silencing the outside world. I feel the cool of the seat through my jeans. It smells of new leather and sandalwood. I never made the connection until now but that's exactly what Blake smells like. I smile slightly as the driver's side door opens.

"What are you smiling about?"

"Nothing... well, it's just your car smells like you. I guess that's not out of the ordinary but still..." I let out a little laugh, blushing as I catch myself.

I can't look at him, *that was so stupid to say...*

"Maybe you are crazy..."

I hear a smile in his voice. Feeling braver, I look up at him.

"Yeah... and now I'm stuck in your car, at your invitation might I add."

He shakes his head incredulously, "Maybe I like them crazy."

My heart thumps in my chest. No way... no way he just said that to me. He can't like me; he doesn't know me. Doesn't know who, or what I really am. He must be joking, still poking fun at me. He smirks at my silence as I stare at him. I try to collect myself as he turns over the car engine. It purrs to life much steadier than my little car. Classic rock fills the car from the speakers at our feet, making the seat rumble with each guitar strum and drum hit. Blake turns it down slightly, then puts on the heat to warm up the inside. More of the sandal-wood scent blows in my face mixed with the heat and briefly, I wonder if this is what it would feel like for his hand to caress my face like the heat from his car. I blush and shake off the thought.

Focus Nola. Don't let this guy get under your skin. He's no good, violent. We don't need any more of that in our life. I nod at my subconscious, she's always making valid points.

We take off, a little faster than I'm used to and he barely rolls to a stop at the stop sign on the corner.

"So, you're a drug dealing vigilante who likes classic rock?" I accuse.

He flinches at my words, staring ahead at the road, "yes."

"But there is more..." I prompt.

There's silence for a moment as the song fades out and a new one begins. I recognize this song as one that my brother used to play when he was doing yard work at the house.

"Yes," he sighs.

Resolve fills his voice, but I can also tell that there's a guard up and something else... pain maybe...

"Are you going to tell me?" I frown at him.

"No," he says firmly, still looking out at the road.

I stare out at the window, watching the streetlamps pass in glowing blurs. The quick flashes of yellow light to pitch blackness makes me dizzy, and I'm reminded once again of the alcohol still sitting in my stomach.

"Why?" I question, pulling my attention away from the dizzying lights outside.

His chest rises with frustration.

"You're just not going to let this one go huh?" his voice rises with anger.

"Why can't you just leave well enough alone and know that whatever it is, it's better that you don't know or get involved?!"

I notice that he grips the steering wheel tighter making his knuckles that were red from the fight stark white now. I cringe away from the rising anger. Momentarily, I flashback to one of the many fights with Sean. Having him so close this evening has really opened some old wounds that are going to take a while to close again. From the corner of my eye, I see Blake look over at me. I flinch again, afraid to say anything more. I know

I'm stronger than this but I can't help but revert to the helpless feelings of the past.

I hear Blake take a deep breath.

"Look..." his voice has changed drastically, becoming more nurturing.

"Look at me please."

I hesitate for a moment as I feel the car come to a stop but the warmth in his voice convinces me.

"There you are," he smiles as his blue eyes stare longingly into mine. "So, I'm at a crossroads."

I tilt my head, confused.

"Part of me... well, really it's most of me, hates to see you cower away from me. Flinching and afraid that I would ever do anything to..." he hesitates and takes a deep steadying breath, "to hurt you when the only thing I want to do is protect you. But the other part of me, that wins out most of the time, wants and needs you to stay away. You've caused a real fucking battleground in my head," his expression is sincere, and I can see the torture behind the blue flames.

A car blares its horn behind us, startling me to break away from his stare. He takes off again as I try to process what he has just said. I hate to think of myself as someone who needs protecting because I feel like I manage pretty well on my own. Especially now that Arlo and I are training more. But I can't deny the blind spots, the weak points I have. Like tonight.

"Thank you," I say, staring out at the streets in front of us.

They're familiar now. We're getting closer to my apartment.

"I mean, thank you for tonight. Coming to my rescue and all but I am sorry you had to. I can't believe he showed up like that. It's not really surprising... he has a tendency to reappear just when things are alright," I sigh, leaning my head against the window. The bumps of the road rattle my memories, maybe this will help me forget them.

"I assume he's an ex?" he questions, a poisonous edge to his voice.

This time it's my turn to take a deep breath, "Yes."

"But there's more..." he throws my line back at me.

I look over at him, rolling my eyes.

"Yes."

Two can play this game. He smirks at me, and a dimple emerges on his cheek. He's amused by me playing along.

"Am I going to get more than that?" he turns serious again, curious.

Sean's someone I don't talk about. Harley might be the only one who knows most of what Sean has done to me. Mainly because they were there through it all. But even they don't know what happened behind closed doors. The damage goes beneath the surface, and I've only just started to come to terms with it. Would it be fair of me to tell this guy I barely know about one of the darkest parts of my life when I haven't even told my best friend the whole story? Granted they did just meet fist to fist so maybe a bit of honesty is warranted.

Maybe honesty is what we need in this car if I'm going to get some answers.

"You know those people that are in your life that you just wish would stay in the past, but somehow they worm their way back into your present, trying to force themselves into your future?" I pause and look over at him.

Blake scoffs, "Ha. More than you know." He says more to himself than to me.

"Well, that's Sean... wait. What do you mean?"

"Never mind..." he says, almost surprised that I heard him, "Continue."

"Always so evasive... You know that's not fair right?" I cross my arms over my chest, defiantly.

He looks over at me, assessing the situation. Blake must know by now that I'm not going to talk anymore until he gives something away. His eyes flick over my body, causing butterflies to flutter in my stomach and a shift in the warm air around us. His eyes land on mine.

"Fine, you continue telling me about that fucker Sean and I will answer one question," he promises.

Giddy with my small victory I almost forget that now I really have to open the wound that is Sean. The car comes to a stop and Blake puts it in park. I look around, surprised that we're already in the parking lot. A pit forms in my stomach from the thought of telling Blake about my past and the fact that we're going to part ways here shortly.

I feel his eyes on me as I clear my throat to make myself sound confident.

"Well, Sean and I were high school sweethearts. We grew up together. Going to the same elementary, middle, and high school. I knew he had a crush on me long before we actually got together. Always hanging around me and my friends and well, I had a crush on him too," it's like a river flows through my mouth as the memories flood back.

"I remember when one of our mutual friends brought up how much we liked each other during a Halloween party our freshman year of high school. She basically told us to get over it and kiss already. I was mortified and I give it to Sean for taking the reins, he just grabbed me and kissed me," I blush as I look up at Blake.

He watches me intently, his expression stone but I can see a flash of anger in his eyes. Sometimes he's so easy to read and other times, I'm just as confused as the day we met.

"Anyway, long story short, we became the 'it couple,'" I throw my hands up to put quotations in the air around the term, "he was the typical jock, and I was popular enough with the drama and art department. We spent nearly every day together from school to living streets away from each other. We were young and stupid. He was there for me with everything with my dad..."

I hesitate. I don't know if Blake notices but the rest of my words seem to stick in my throat as the grief constricts against my heart. My father isn't a story I'm ready to tell. Especially not with Blake. Not yet.

"Sean was a good guy, at least that's what everyone saw, and I can't help but feel guilty at feeding into that mirage. It was shortly after we got together that I started to see his possessive tendencies. But me being young and naïve, I wrote it off as nothing. It was all him showing me how much he cared right? It took me years to realize how manipulative he was, only wanting me to be around my friends when he was there, judging me if I went out in outfits he didn't like..."

The anxiety rises in my throat, choking me. I want to scream because even the memories of Sean can make me feel like I'm right back there with him. His words fill my mind and his hands on my skin that I may never be able to wash away from my body no matter how much I scrub. I feel the tears hot in my eyes. Embarrassed, I wipe at them before they can fall and take a few steadying breaths trying to ground myself. I tune back into the classic rock coming through the speakers to help ease my mind.

I hear Blake shift in his seat before feeling his warm hand grab mine. The electricity shoots through me once again and the burning on the inside of my wrist returns, more prominent than at the party. It's not the most comfortable feeling, but it's manageable. Bringing with it a comfort I wasn't expecting. I turn my hand over in his, looking curiously at my wrist, where I know hidden under my long sleeve, my wing is there.

Why does that keep happening when he touches me? What are you trying to tell me?

He squeezes my hand, encouraging me to go on.

"Ummm…" I continue, trying to find my train of thought again. "When it was all said and done, it wasn't a great relationship and it just continued to get worse…" I hear Blake take in a breath and his hand trembles. Heat radiates from him, making the hot car rise a few degrees with his anger.

My mind flashes back to a particularly nasty memory. The night of prom our junior year… It comes back in fragments: the party, the stench of alcohol and sweat, torn clothes, swollen eyes… bruises. I shudder at the memory.

This time I let the tears fall freely, letting the memory go with each drop.

"From then on, the mask was put up. Covering up the marks and pain. Playing happy but I knew I had to get away. So, I found solace and sanctuary when I chose to come to Edge for school. Away from Sean but still close enough to go home…"

I smile thinking about my mom, one of my safe havens, back in Cross. I should really call her soon…

Blake grabs my chin to urge me to look back up at him.

"You have a beautiful smile. Breathtaking really…"

He searches my face while wiping away the tears on my cheeks. I flush as his finger gently caresses my face and the electricity that was shooting through me, crackles in the air between us.

"I hate that you went through that. And it's taking everything in me not to go back and find that guy and do worse than knock him unconscious. But you should be proud of how strong you are for getting out of that... relationship," he swallows around the word. "You do have some whit's about you after all," he jokes lightly.

I smile, leaning into his hand, finding comfort in this small contact. His eyes shift down to my mouth and he runs his thumb along my lips, tracing them. They part involuntarily. The air shifts again, electricity palpable. He looks back up into my eyes searching for permission. His eyes are now a deeper blue. Indigo pools of water.

Somewhere in my mind, a sober version of myself is yelling at me for the thoughts crossing my mind. Screaming about how Blake is dangerous and involved in a world that I know nothing of and yet too much of. How I'm not in my right mind when Sean was just so close a few moments ago.

But she silences herself as I nod ever so slightly, wanting him closer to me.

He closes the distance between us quickly, stopping only a few inches away, eyes still watching my every move. I'm hit with a wave of heat and sandalwood. Desperate to have him closer, I reach up, pulling his face to mine. My hand rubs over the stubble on his jaw and he shudders. I feel his breath on my face as I close the distance and kiss him. The only sounds in the car are our unsteady breaths and the music.

I lose my breath as the electricity explodes around us. The burn in my wrist changes from a dull ache to a full-blown fire, but I try to ignore it. In an instant my phone vibrates loudly, he pulls away almost too fast, and a chill runs through me as all the heat moves with him to his side of the car.

Both of us still not able to catch our breath, I look at my phone screen to see Harley's name.

"Shit," I say under my breath.

"Yeah, you should probably go."

I look up, confused at how cold his voice is now. He's staring out through the windshield, looking anywhere but at me.

I'm a fucking idiot.

"Yeah," I say defeated as I reach for the door handle, rejection and shame washing over me.

I hop out of the car at the same time Blake shifts into drive.

"Wait, I never got to ask you my question."

"That's right..." He looks over, a gleam in his eye as it clicks.

"You never had any intention of answering my questions tonight, did you?" I say in shock.

"Not tonight, no. But maybe tomorrow?" his voice is hopeful.

Hope springs in my chest. He wants to see me again...

Don't do it, Nola... You know better.

"Tomorrow then," I agree, drowning out the sober me. She'll thank me eventually for getting answers with a clear head.

"Great, I'll pick you up at four. Be out here then," his voice has shifted to someone making a business deal.

"Oh and Nola?" I look at his burning blue eyes, glowing in the dark. "Sweet dreams."

A shiver runs down my spine as he takes off out of the parking space, the passenger door shutting with force.

The lock clicks at the same time the front door of my apartment flies open. My keys, still in the lock, are ripped from my hands. I look up and see Harley's panicked expression.

"What the hell Nola?! I was worried sick about you! I heard what happened at the party..." their hands fly up in the air around them.

"How could you get into a car with him!?"

I look back, dazed, not remembering how I crossed the parking lot or went up the stairs to the apartment. Hot tears start to force themselves out of my eyes. Harley's words sink in slowly as I remember everything that happened over the past two hours. Fear, longing, curiosity, and embarrassment weigh down my stomach. The tears flow freely over my red-hot cheeks, I finally meet Harley's eyes.

Their expression shifts from panicked anger to over-whelming concern. Before I can react, they pull me into the apartment, enveloping me within their arms. I know Harley isn't one for physical affection so in these rare moments when they show this side of them, I know that Harley understands when I need it more than their need to be distant.

"What happened?" Harley's voice is softer as they lead me to the couch.

Wiping at the tears, I take a deep breath to settle myself. Bringing my knees up to my chest, I hold them, trying to make myself as small as possible. Harley sits facing me on the cushion beside me. Their brown eyes hold nothing but concern and patience, waiting for me to begin.

"Where do I start?" I laugh under my breath.

Will they think I'm out of my mind? Crazy for liking yet

another guy who seems to be nothing but bad news. But he's also a guy that I still feel safe with, a guy who sends shivers down my spine but also fills my body with electricity. Not to mention the strange burning that has been happening lately when we touch. Absentmindedly, I touch the inside of my left wrist, tracing the edges of my wing on my cool skin. Harley doesn't respond, just waits.

"To start with, I think I had too much to drink." I smile as they roll their eyes. "I was talking with Ash, who was gushing over Jase... wait, is she here?" panic rises in my throat.

"Yeah, Jase dropped us off about 10 minutes ago... It was an awkward goodbye." Harley scrunches their nose in disgust. I've seen that face more times than I can count when we would pass couples out shopping or in school getting too close for comfort. It almost makes me laugh. "I thought you would've beat us here since you left before so when you weren't here, I freaked out."

"I'm sorry I had you worried," I mean every word. Faintly, I can hear Ash snoring from her room. Harley shrugs but doesn't say anything else.

"Anyway... I saw Jase at the party handing some pills to a few frat guys and I went to confront him. Probably a stupid decision but I had to, you know..." I think back to Harley comforting me after another one of the harder nights with my father. The Harley of now nods their head encouraging me to keep going.

"Well, Blake was there, Jase handed him the money and everything. Then he tried to calm me down by taking me outside, which helped a bit. Helped to clear my head only for it to get fuzzy again when he touched me..."

"Oh?" Harley raises their eyebrows, curious.

"Yeah... It's hard to put into words but I will try. Plain and simple, he scares me. But there is also something so mysterious. It's like I know who he is, and it's just out of reach, behind the walls he has up. Though now, I can't help but feel like it's all in my head." I look down at my hands, remembering the feel of his skin under mine.

"Why do you say that?" Harley says, startling me out of my daydream.

"He doesn't feel real. It's like he's a character out of a story instead of the guy I just made out with."

Harley's sharp intake of air nearly makes them choke as it suddenly fills their lungs.

"You did what now?!" Harley shouts breathless.

I smile at their absurdity. "Yeah... we made out a bit in the car just now but then he just acted really strange when we stopped. Like, he didn't want to be there anymore or like he had a better place to be. I'm probably reading too much into it at this point..." I feel the tears well up again in my tired eyes as my chest tightens and hands start to shake. "And then there was the fight..."

"Yeah, that's right. I heard about it... Do you have any idea why that ass-wipe would show up here?" Harley dances the fine line between concern and rage.

"I have no idea. I would probably go mad if I tried to figure out what went on in his mind. I just wish he would leave me alone..."

"Well, you know my thoughts on this situation," they're back to being serious.

Our many conversations about going to the police and filing a restraining order, moving to a different state or even country, flash through my mind. The "extreme measures" we called them. Sure, it would work but what would be the consequences? Him retaliating in life-threatening ways... Me being forced away from my family and friends over what? An egotistical, manipulative, abusive, psychotic boy? No, he held too much power over me for too long, I can't let him have any more.

"I do know where you stand and I'm pretty sure you know where I stand," I give Harley a knowing look and they nod in agreement. We had settled this argument long ago that in the end, it would be my choice.

"Yeah, yeah. Well, either way, I'm here to support you. If that involves holding your hand and wiping your tears, you got me. If it so happens to involve hiding a body," they shrug and give me a wicked look, "then so be it."

I can't help but laugh, Harley, joining in shortly after.

"You're definitely first on my 'hiding a body' call list. As well as my 'probably a serial killer' list." I nudge Harley in the shoulder as we continue laughing.

"Speaking of serial killers, want to watch one of the stupid romcoms that you love?" Harley's laugh bursts through as they take in my confused expression.

"I'm not sure how the two are related but yes! However, I need to shower first and get this day off me."

I unfold myself as I get up, noticing the tired ache in my joints. The extra stress of the day already showing its telltale signs.

"Alright! I'll get it all queued up!" Harley shouts after me, I smile even though they can't see.

The familiar creak under the floor is almost undetectable as I tiptoe down the hallway to my room. I grab my pajamas from the top drawer of the dresser, and the night repeats itself yet again behind my eyes.

I know that the electricity was there between Blake and me, that's hard for me to even fathom my mind making it up. It was there, almost tangible. The burning fire in the pit of my stomach and the burning ache on my wrist were also real. My head shakes incredulously as I put my clothes on the counter in my bathroom. Avoiding my reflection as I close the door, I head straight to the shower and turn on the water, knowing it'll take a minute to warm up.

Finally, I face the person in the mirror. My hair is slightly disheveled, sticking up in random places. Some is stuck to my forehead from the sweat and being tossed around at the party. My gaze falls down to my eyes. They're still bright green, some-times hazel, color though they feel brighter now, lined with red from crying. Unable to handle the stare, my bloodshot eyes shift to the makeup smudged under them. Robotically, I grab my barely used makeup remover, slowly and methodically I wipe away each dried-salt-stained smudge. The act is kind of thera-peutic, wiping away not only the makeup but each tear, each moment of pain, moment of anxiety, moment of fear, and moment of pleasure.

My muscles ache as I begin to shimmy out of my clothes. I wince at a new pain in my shoulder as I lift the shirt over my head. Looking in the mirror, now slightly foggy from the rising heat of the water, my bloodshot eyes land on my shoul-der. A dark red bruise is beginning to form in the shape of a thumb. I touch it slightly, cringing with the pain. Immedi-ately, anger rises, brimming over in my cried-out eyes. Anger for my own stupidity. It comes with all my insecurities and shame. This bruise is only one of many that Sean has left on me. A bruise that shouldn't be happening all these years later.

And yet the fucker can still get under my skin and leave his mark.

I stare down at the sink, watching the tears fall from my eyes onto the porcelain. Hating myself, my own decisions, and the situations I find myself in with every drop. A sob escapes before I can help it.

I jump slightly as a light knock on the door startles me.

"Hey, are you okay?" Harley says from the other side. Whether Harley knows it or not, they just pulled me out of yet another dark spiral caused by Sean.

I clear my throat, knowing that it'll be rough if I don't.

"Yeah. Sorry, I'll be out in a minute."

Looking up I wipe the tears off my cheeks, catching my wing in the reflection.

Shit... how am I going to cover this up so Harley doesn't see...

"Alright, well if you don't hurry, I'm going to start this movie without you. Or just go to sleep," I can hear Harley yawn dramatically through the door.

Rolling my eyes, I know they wouldn't start the movie, but they would fall asleep. If they did fall asleep, that would solve the panic rising about covering up my wing. I hop in the shower quickly, letting the scalding water work its magic. Releasing the tension in my muscles, washing away the day. If only it could wash away the memories and the marks on my body, but I will take what I can get.

Dressing quickly, I finish up my nightly routine and am out the door again shortly thereafter. I decide the best option is to drape my towel over my arm, covering my wing once getting out of the shower. I place it in my hamper in my closet and grab a clean hoodie to throw on. It covers the wing perfectly. I turn back to Harley, who has made themself comfortable in my bed, movie on pause on the tv.

"Are you ever going to explain the serial killer equals romcom comment you made earlier?" I ask, putting my phone on my charger and getting into bed.

"You cannot tell me that you don't see serial killer eyes in every one of the main characters. 'Specially the males. It's so obvious that if you put horror music as the soundtrack instead of frilly music, changed a few scenes, they would be murdering the girls left and right."

"You're saying to basically change the whole movie and then they would be murdering them instead of falling in love?"

"Not the whole movie! But, it's a fine line between murder and love, no? Or maybe it's death and love," Harley tilts their head in thought. "Both involve passion, all-encompassing passion for someone other than yourself. So much passion that it either consumes you or it consumes the other person..." they shrug a bit awkwardly, putting their hands behind their head.

"Which is which?" I ask, curious at their train of thought. "Is it murder that consumes you or the other person or is it love?"

"Exactly. The line between the two, so thin..."

I stay silent, letting their words sink in. We've had plenty of deep, existential conversations but this one is new and different. There's an underlying tone in Harley's voice, it's more grave than serious now. Sad almost. I can see a few thoughts go through their mind and worry on their face.

"Anyways, ready to start the horror movie?" Harley looks over at me, expression shifting to nonchalance. I nod, still not sure what to make of their comments and the changes in their mood.

Harley presses play on the remote in their hand and the movie starts. We both watch silently for a few moments as the female lead must move out of her big city apartment to the country, starting over in her own two-dimensional world. The moment that the male lead comes on screen, dressed in jeans and a slightly dirty plaid button down shirt, I can't help but laugh. He was just chopping wood out in the back of the barn where he works and threw down the axe.

"Murder weapon," Harley whispers casually.

I can't help but laugh more as they're not entirely wrong that he gives off some murderer vibes. We continue to watch, Harley commenting where he would be hiding the bodies, and how he is getting away with it all. I laugh along with them for as long as possible but eventually, the exhaustion takes over and I feel myself sink deeper into the bed, drifting away to fiery blue eyes.

EIGHTEEN

Before I know it, I'm standing outside of my apartment complex waiting for Blake. The day both seemed to drag on and yet take no time at all to get to four o'clock. Mostly, I wandered around the apartment doing mundane tasks. Cleaning, avoiding conversation with Harley... more cleaning. Before Harley left around noon, I caved, knowing I couldn't avoid them for long, I made us some tea. Lost in thought while stirring my tea, I jumped when Harley finally broke the silence that surrounded us.

"I was thinking about what we were talking about last night..." Harley said from their seat on my couch.

From Ash's room, there was some stirring, but she's never been known for getting up early on the weekends, so I wasn't expecting her out in the living room for another couple of hours.

"What?" I said, straightening up from the counter I was leaning over.

"I was thinking about what you said about... what was his name?" Harley looked over at me. "The guy that whooped Sean's ass?"

My heart skipped a beat in my chest. Bringing the cup of tea to my lips, I hoped that Harley wouldn't notice me stalling. The memory of the fight from the night before fills my mind. The fear never really went away, it was just simmering underneath the surface with the anger and disgust from seeing Sean. This morning, all those emotions were muddling together with Blake's name as well.

"Oh, and you made out with him..." Harley shook their head, as they took a sip of their tea.

"Ha. Ha. His name is Blake," I said, rolling my eyes.

"Right, Blake. Anyways, you mentioned last night about how you were feeling and what happened between the two of you and I just wanted to make sure you were alright? It all sounds very intense..."

I know that tone. Harley was concerned about me, and maybe they have a reason to be...

"It is very intense."

"And you're alright?"

A loaded question that I've been avoiding for too long with the people around me and myself if I'm completely honest. I'm not ready to answer it truthfully. There's still too much to process with the angel stuff, the human stuff, and sifting through all my emotions and thoughts when it comes to Blake. Honesty, in this case, doesn't seem like the best policy.

"Yeah," I lied. "I'm alright."

Now, the remaining rust brown leaves on the trees bordering the parking lot of my apartment complex rattle with the cool breeze. I shiver and wrap my arms around myself, pulling my hoodie tighter around my body. The shiver rattles through my very core and I feel the butterflies startle awake. I can't tell if they're excited because Blake should be here any minute or if they flutter with anxiety at whatever comes of our conversation. Either way, they're determined to make me throw up right here on this sidewalk.

His jet-black car pulls into the parking lot just as I feel like I'm going to double over. It stops right in front of me. Blake steps out in a simple black hoodie and dark jeans. The outfit is oddly similar to the one he was wearing at the party.

Did he not change from last night?

His burning blue eyes meet mine, the dark blue bags under his eyes answering my question. He must not have even slept. The thought bothers me a little more than it should. Why didn't he sleep? Did he go back out? Was he... with someone else?

A cruel monster raises its head deep in my belly.

"Hello Nola," Blake gives me a soft smile as he stands awkwardly beside the driver's side door.

"Hey," the word harshly cuts through the air between us.

Stop Nola. There's no reason for you to be jealous. Get out of your head.

Blake clears his throat, the only visible sign of his discomfort at my venom. He walks to the other side of the car, and I follow. Opening the passenger side door, he waits for me to step in.

"You ready?"

I can't help but notice the timid tone in his voice. He's scared... That realization smacks the jealous monster in its face and softens me. I nod as I get in the car, sitting in the now familiar seat.

Blake gets in the car, and we take off without another word. My hands shake uncontrollably, the only visual sign of my anxiety bubbling out of me. It feels like I'm on the precipice of my world shifting and changing around me. The only thing grounding me is the warm air flowing from the vents in front of me. They drown me in warmth and the soft sandalwood scent of Blake beside me. I'm grateful that Blake decided to drive in silence, the only sound now is the rhythmic pounding of the tires on the road and our small shallow breaths.

I can feel the tension rolling off Blake next to me. Chancing a glance towards him, he's staring out on the road ahead, his knuckles whitening around the steering wheel. His tension strikes a new spark of anxiety that's swirling in my belly.

Do I really know what I'm doing? What I'm walking into?

The questions continue to spin in my mind. Looking away, I start counting the streetlights as they pass, anything to keep my mind distracted. They're just starting to turn on as the sun sets along the horizon behind us.

We continue through downtown Edge in silence. Several times words try to escape from my chest, but I stifle them quickly. It seems silly to try for any small talk now, besides I'm so trapped inside of my own head thinking over everything. It was just supposed to be another normal night, a college party... totally normal. Did I go to keep an eye on Ash and Jase? Yes. But it was still supposed to be a fun night. But now Blake is some sort of drug dealer and Sean... I can still feel his hard grip on my shoulder even now. I shift in the seat pulling my arms back around myself. Blake shifts slightly and I feel his eyes on me. I'm brought back to the present as the road lifts, continuing in the air as we cross a bridge to the more residential part of the city.

Looking outside the car window I'm overwhelmed by the sea of black that meets me there.

When did it get so dark?

During the day, the bridge is beautiful, the channel of water flowing freely below it. Waving blues and greens at the cars above it. But now, just past sunset, in the dark nothingness, there's no telling where the coast meets the water. Where civilization meets the dark watery unknowns.

Before I can dwell on the dark shadows taunting me from under the bridge, we're on the other side, turning down more streets. These streets are newer and the road quiets more on the newly laid asphalt.

"Where are we going?" I ask, startled by my own voice.

"Oh umm..." he takes a deep breath. "I figured it would be easier to talk about, well everything," he shrugs. "At my place."

New nerves jump in my stomach.

"Oh..." is all that comes out.

We turn down a residential street, the houses getting progressively larger the further we go. The houses at the beginning of the street were similar to the ones downtown, more apartment/single family type homes. These are double in size and grandeur. Even in the darkening night, I can still see that they're all different colors and styles. Some are Spanish-style with stucco while others are more modern red brick. Fences and gates carton off where one massive house begins and the other ends. I notice some of the smaller grand homes have started decorating for fall/Thanksgiving while the truly massive mansions have opted to avoid such cheesiness.

Blake stops the car, throwing it in park in front of one of the last houses on the street.

"You live here?!"

I stare up at the house, well really, it's more of a mansion, out of my passenger side window. My face nearly presses against the glass as I try to get the full view of its three stories. It's dark, darker than the ones around it. The exterior nearly blends into the surrounding night. Lining the property is a large iron fence, it must be about eight feet tall with large spikes on the tops of each iron rod. Everything about this house screams "Do Not Enter." And yet, its tough exterior doesn't shake me off. I feel myself drawn to the inside wanting to know more about what the interior holds. Enticed by the warm yellow light pouring from each of the windows.

"Yeah, it's not much," Blake answers casually next to me.

"Not much!?" I gape at him. "How in the hell can you afford such a place?! Family money? Drugs? Prostitution?"

My questions make me giggle the more I list them off until I fall into hysterics. It all sounds ridiculous. Laughter that doesn't sound like mine fills the warm car.

Have I officially lost it?

I choke on the last laugh as I catch Blake's glare out of the corner of my eye, not amused by my silly questions.

Definitely lost it, you idiot. And now he knows. My subconscious chastises me.

"Ha," he offers as anger, shame, and hate flash behind his flaming blue eyes.

"I'm... I'm sorry. I don't know what is wrong with me..."

I stare down at my hands, the wing catching my attention. Sometimes I wish that with one wipe it would be gone, and my world would be right again. If only it was that simple.

The slam of his car door rattles through me. I look up, watching him walk around the front of the car to my side. He opens the door, letting the warmth of the car rush out, instantly being replaced by a cool salty, ocean breeze.

My senses awaken as Blake stands propped against the door, waiting for me to decide, but it all swirls around in my head. A part of me wants to go back to normalcy: college, degree, job, family, grow old... But in choosing normalcy, what would I lose? Then there's the other part of me, the angel, gaining a stronger pull with every breath that doesn't want to run. It doesn't want to hide away. It's hungry to know more, to embrace this new world and it terrifies me.

My legs swing out of the car, landing on solid ground. I grab Blake's hand, ignoring the burn that shoots through me, and give him a slight nod, letting him lead me to the front door. The iron gate squeaks open, and clangs shut definitively behind us as we walk through the small front yard up to the steps to the entrance. The dark wooden door is lit only by two flaming lanterns nestled on either side of the door. I can see from the orange light of the flames that the house is actually a deep royal blue color instead of the dark black that it seemed to be from the street. Blake uses his free hand to turn the doorknob, letting the front door swing open with ease. A wave of nervousness rolls over me, making me feel like I'm about to enter the belly of the beast. Blake looks back at me, his blue eyes dancing in the flames with anxious hesitation.

Swallowing the nerves, I take a deep breath, releasing his hand, and step through the threshold ahead of him. Determined to know more. To embrace whatever the light in the dark house is going to show me.

∽

Hushed voices drift from the back of the house along with the clatter of dishes.

Huh, must be the kitchen back there. I think, peering down the long entry hallway trying to spot the room where the voices are coming from, but I can't see that far.

Glancing to my right I take in a large room with décor that's surprisingly light. Two oversized cream-colored couches occupy the middle of the room, both facing a grand brick fireplace. Atop the fireplace is a painting of a sunlit field adorned with colorful flowers and trees. On either side of the fireplace are oak bookcases with books placed neatly on each shelf. Taking a half step into the room, I see on the back wall is a large window overlooking the darkened backyard. A small table with two chairs sits in front of the window. Unsure where to go next, I look back to find Blake still standing in the hallway. His gaze is intense as he watches me carefully. A warm blush creeps up my neck, embarrassed that I overstepped somehow.

"Sorry... I..." I start to say.

Staring down at my hands, I notice his movement through my eyelashes. Blake walks past me with a half-smile on his face. I follow him, continuing down the hall, closer to the voices. Before we get to them, he turns, heading up a set of stairs.

On the second floor, we emerge in another living room. This one is smaller than the one below, only one light brown couch occupies one wall and a TV is mounted above an entertainment center. More bookshelves, but these are a bit more cluttered, less organized than the other ones. Grabbing my hand, Blake leads me down another hallway. We pass by several closed doors, idly I wonder what's behind each one. They must be bedrooms or bathrooms but why are there so many? How does he live in a place like this?

Finally, he stops in front of a door at the end of the hallway. Turning to look at me, a wicked expression plays on his face, but I can see some hesitation behind his eyes. He turns the doorknob, opening the door. I peek around, expecting to see a room but instead, I see another set of stairs, half illuminated by the light from the hallway. I squint my eyes at the darkened stairs, trying to see the top but there's no hope, it's a stairwell to darkness. Blake steps aside and motions for me to go first. With a few breaths of hesitation, my subconscious shaking with her hand on a shield, I take a few steps up the stairs. My hand tracing the wall next to me for balance.

Suddenly, the light from the hallway below vanishes and I'm plunged into darkness. My breathing becomes ragged as I stand completely still, willing my eyes to adjust to the dark. Burning hot hands wrap around my waist, and I yelp at the burn flashing through me, flames licking at my wrist. Slowly, his warmth starts to envelop my back as he moves closer, placing his chin on my shoulder.

"Do you trust me?" his voice growls in the dark.

That is the question, the ultimate question. At the moment, my heart pounding in my chest, I feel like I'm being led to my death at the top of this pathway of darkness. But it's Blake. There's nothing to be scared of.... right?

Fearing my voice in the dark, I simply nod knowing that he will be able to feel my body shifting under his chin. With a slight push, he moves my body so that he can slide past. Releasing his grip on my waist, he's gone somewhere in the dark before me. I can faintly hear his footfalls on the steps ahead, but I don't follow, too afraid to move. His steps stop several feet away as I hear the click of a door opening. Light floods in and I'm blinded for a moment. Blinking a few times, I stare up at Blake's back, still silhouetted in the dark. As if he can feel my stare, he turns. I take a half step down as I take in his eyes. I've always been enamored by them but now, they're glowing like the blue flames they are in the dark. A sheepish smile spreads across his face and he blinks away, turning to walk through the door.

I'm up the last couple of steps quickly and bounce through the door. We're in yet another living room. Except this one is darker; a dark blue couch sits in the middle with a brown leather chair next to it. The walls are lined with shelves from corner to corner. Some books are lined precisely, and others are strewn about haphazardly. The room is less of living space and more of a personal library.

"Sorry, I probably should've cleaned up..." Blake says, heading towards the shelves.

"Oh, it's alright. It's actually quite impressive," I say, feeling drawn to the collections. Curious as to what stories fill his mind.

"Most of them are classics. Part of being an English major."

"You're studying English?" I ask incredulously.

I reach up to run my hand over the worn spines. Bronte, Shelley, Lee, Austen, Fitzgerald, Tolstoy, Dickens, Wilde, Stoker, Melville, Orwell... They're all here.

"Don't act so surprised," Blake laughs.

"No... it's just, not what I expected," I shrug. Continuing to browse the collection.

"Kafka?" I ask, pulling the worn book from the shelf.

The Metamorphosis.

I open it, flipping through the frayed pages, the binding barely holding itself together. I see some notes in the margins, questions about the plot and what it means, some comments about Gregor.

"Ah," he says, now in front of me. He reaches out and takes the book, smiling at it fondly. "My father actually gave this one to me."

His smile drops as his eyes become pensive. He recovers quickly and closes the book, placing it back on the shelf. I watch as he turns away, moving to go pick up more on the other side of the room. This is the first time I've heard of his family and it's obvious that it's a touchy subject. I turn back to the shelves trying to find something else to talk about.

On the shelf next to the one filled with the classics, I spot a shelf of smaller books, ranging in earthy tones with no titles or author names. I grab one off the shelf and notice a piece of paper sticking out of it. Pulling the paper out, I try to make sense of the drawing.

It's a rough sketch, trees lining the sides of the page, and in the middle is a girl with a camera held up to her face, taking a picture of the viewer of the sketch. Something familiar nags at me about the trees and clearing...

It can't be...

"What's this?" I say, hands shaking slightly.

Blake is back in front of me in an instant. He grabs the book and drawing out of my hands.

"Um... I can explain..."

"What are these?"

"These are my journals, some with writing, some with... drawings."

"And why... or how do you have a drawing of a dream I had?" I accuse.

He pauses, looking down at the sketch. I remember the

dream, he was in it, the dark figure lurking in the shadows of the trees as I took pictures of the changing leaves in the park area near my apartment. This sketch is from his perspective. That shouldn't be possible.

Blake takes a deep breath as he places the journal back on the shelf. He turns his back to me and crosses the few feet to the leather chair in the middle of the room. His burning blue eyes stare up at me expectantly. He glances between me and the couch next to him, telling me to sit in so many words. I walk to the couch and sit on the opposite end, keeping my distance.

Here we go...

"The simplest answer is that I can dream walk," Blake says matter of fact.

"Dream walk?"

"Yes, well it's closer to a manipulation of your subconscious."

"Wait, you can read my mind?!" I nearly shout, embarrassment flashing through my mind, flushing my cheeks.

Blake laughs in response, "No, I can't read your mind. But that isn't very hard to do either. You're not hard to read, you tend to wear a lot of your thoughts and emotions in your expressions."

"Oh," I recover, this is something I already knew. "Okay. So, dream walking? How does it work?"

How my voice sounds so even, I'll never know because I don't feel level headed. Far from it really.

"You have to be asleep for one," he smiles, and I relax some. "It took me a while to learn and master, but I have to go into a deep meditative state, somewhere in between consciousness and unconsciousness, extending my mind out. Reaching out to where and who I want to see. You were this... bright beacon of light. I couldn't resist."

"So, those dreams about you... The park? The library? Were actually..."

"Actually me? Yes. Unless you were having other dreams about me that I don't know of..." he smirks cheekily at me and the heat licks at my cheeks.

"You're a dream walking demon?" I ask bluntly, finally letting the word sit out in the open space between us.

It's just a hunch, something I've mulled over the past few days since Arlo told me to trust my wing, my instincts. The word played in my mind over and over again trying to attach itself to Blake, but I never wanted it to. I never let it.

I watch as his smirk falls and his cheek twitches in a flinch. There's my answer.

"More like a demon who can dream walk," his voice loses the lightness from before.

The truth rattles in my chest as all the air in my lungs leaves in a huff. Subconsciously, I wanted this... needed this confirmation but now that it's in front of me... I'm not sure how to feel.

"How long?" I ask hesitantly, uncertain where to start with my questioning.

My mind flashes to all the books I've read and movies I've watched about creatures of the night. All of them living longer than normal lives. But what about me? I'm something not completely human, what does that say about me? Panic rises in my chest. There's still so much I don't know... Another question to ask Arlo, or Lawson if he ever gets back to me.

"You're going to bolt if I say 100 years, right?" he asks, amusement making his tone light again.

I meet his eyes watching them gleam with his suppressed laughter as another smirk pulls at the corners of his mouth. I roll my eyes at his expression. Of course, he could see me spiraling.

"I became a demon when I sold my soul at 16," his voice returns to seriousness. "So, roughly 5 years."

"You... You sold your soul?"

"Yes," he looks down at his feet, his brow furrowing in concentration. I stay silent, hoping he'll continue.

"My mother was dying..." he hesitates, gathering strength with a deep breath. "Cancer. It was a very aggressive brain tumor. We did everything that science would allow. I remember my father and I would sit in the chapel at the hospital during her countless surgeries and treatments," he takes in a steadying breath. "I think we were on surgery number four when I couldn't stand it anymore. I was tired of praying to someone or something that wasn't listening. I left the hospital, leaving my father on his knees in the chapel."

"I ended up sitting on a bench outside, burying my head in my hands, listening to the ambulances come and go. I remember thinking about how many lives, how many souls were being carted in. Just a constant flow of souls coming and going," he hesitates, twisting his hands together over and over.

My own memories of sitting outside of the hospital so many times with my father fighting for his life inside, thinking almost the exact same thing fill my mind. Except this time, a younger Blake is sitting next to me crying some of the same tears I did.

"Anyways, I don't know how long I was out there but when I looked up there was a woman sitting on a bench across from me, just staring at me. She smiled at me, and it made me oddly feel comforted but also sad. There was something about her that reminded me of my mother. Maybe it was the kindness in her eyes, but she drew me in. She got up, walked toward me, and sat down. She asked for my name and wondered what I was doing out there by myself. She brushed the hair from my forehead, and I broke down, telling her everything."

"I guess she pitied me..." he continues. "Because she just sat and listened to my story and let me cry. After I was done, she lifted my head up and asked if I would do anything to have my mother back, healthy, and happy again. I remember nearly shouting at the top of my lungs that I would about a thousand times. She smiled and wiped away the tears on my face. It was so comforting, just that simple motion. I don't really know what happened after that because everything went black."

"Next thing I knew, I woke up on a couch in an overly decorated house. She was there and told me what happened, what I did, or more like, what I was, what I needed to do now... I couldn't believe it at first but then she took me to my parents," a sad smile breaks through the memory.

"My mother was healthy, laughing with my father. I watched as the doctor came into the room and told them it was a miracle. I remember the look on my father's blank face when he saw me standing in the doorway with no idea who I was and that was that."

I try to imagine the younger version of the man sitting across from me. Smaller than he is now, innocent but broken by everything around him. My heart aches for the boy with bright blue, tear-filled eyes. A wave of discomfort also hits me as I think about how the woman took advantage of him. A broken boy only wanting to save his mother and now, he's this, a demon. Forced into a life of whatever choices are already laid out for him. I wonder if she's still in his life. Maybe this is the house he was talking about... I wonder if she was one of the voices downstairs... A fierce protectiveness roars through me as I look back towards the door. Would he stop me from going to find out?

I turn back to Blake, preparing to ask about the woman who manipulated him, but his expression stops me. He's staring off, seeing something far away from the bookshelf his eyes have landed on. The heaviness of his words, his story, hangs thick in the air. The pain in his eyes is palpable. I slide to the other side of the couch, feeling a strong need to comfort him.

Settled on the other side, I reach across the small gap and grab his hand on the arm of the chair. The familiar burn flares but I push it to the back of my mind. His stare breaks as he turns to me. He pulls my hand towards him, forcing me out of my seat so that I'm standing in front of him. Yanking me down, I put one knee on one side of his legs and the other on the other side so that I'm straddling his lap. My heart leaps at being this close to him again.

Blake brings my hand up to his neck and I intertwine both my hands behind his head. He, in turn, wraps his arms around my waist. I place my forehead against his and close my eyes, reveling in the warm embrace.

We don't say anything but so much is said in the small gesture because, for whatever reason, we're drawn to each other. Drawn by the comfort of just being. It pushes every hesitation about who he is, what he does, out of my mind.

I open my eyes and pull my face away. Bringing my hands up to either side of his face, my mind flashes to the broken boy, the pain still in his eyes reflecting the past. I wish with all of my heart that I can take that pain away. I need to take it away. Bringing his face to mine, I lightly brush my lips against his.

Hesitating for only a moment, he crashes his lips against mine, kissing me deeply and passionately. Maybe he needs me as much as I need him.

A few moments pass, consumed by our proximity and how he holds me like I'm the last thing in the world holding him here. I can't help but reciprocate because, in all the craziness of the past few weeks, he has kept me centered, even while my world around me cracks and shatters.

Suddenly, his phone vibrates against my leg, bringing me back down to Earth.

I break away, breath ragged.

"Is that a phone in your pocket or are you just happy to see me?" I joke a bit breathlessly.

Blake smirks.

"Both."

He winks at me causing my heart to flutter again. He kisses me again, swiftly this time, and shifts my weight so that he can get the phone out.

Who could be calling him right now?

"Yes?" he answers, not bothering to look at who it was, never taking his eyes off of me.

The person on the other end says something. It's muffled so I can't make it out but everything about Blake shifts. He becomes rigid and serious. Jumping up suddenly, he nearly tosses me backward but catches me before I hit the ground. I stare at him, confusion stirring in the melting pot of my mind. He paces to the other side of the room.

"Yes, okay," he whispers to the person on the phone.

"Are you sure?" he asks, hands running through his hair. "No, no sir. I'm not questioning you."

He frantically glances every so often back to me, then back

to his feet as he continues pacing. His distress only heightening my anxiety.

"Yes, father," he says with finality, hanging up the phone.

"Father? I thought you just said that your father didn't remember you?" I ask confused.

He takes a deep breath.

"Yes, my father, my real father doesn't remember me anymore. That was, well that was my father now..."

"Your father now?" fear bubbles in my stomach, making me feel sick.

"Yes. I think you would call him the Devil," he says flatly. "Giving me more orders."

"What do you mean? What orders?" my voice comes out stronger than I feel because part of me is already halfway out of the house and down the road screaming for help.

"More souls to corrupt and collect for him," he shrugs, but he can't mask the disgust in his voice.

"Do I even want to know?" I ask out loud, more to myself than to him. I watch as he shakes his head in response and my stomach turns. Something clicks.

"The drugs..." I say, half a question but already knowing the answer.

He nods, "They help the process, sure."

"Oh my god. I think I'm going to be sick."

I start to pace to the other side of the room. Trying to create as much space between us as possible. I knew that Blake had these other sides of him, but am I ready to see that? The fear and disgust makes my stomach roll. Blake doesn't move from the other side of the room, making no effort to come and comfort me. I'm grateful he doesn't, I'm not sure I could control my body's reaction to him getting any closer.

"I think I should go," my pacing stalls at the door we came through, back down the stairwell of darkness.

"Nola, wait," Blake hesitates.

"Please Blake, I just want to go," I say sternly, trying to keep the spiraling in my head from coming out.

"Okay..." he takes a few steps towards me.

"At least let me drive you home?" he asks, concern laced in his voice.

I pause, weighing the options. I could call a cab but the cost might be ridiculous right now. Walking isn't an option.

"Fine." I agree, my hand already on the door pulling it open to reveal the darkness below.

NINETEEN

I jolt awake, feeling the car come to a stop. I must have dozed off on the way back. Which is not completely shocking with how this weekend has gone. Hell, how these past few weeks have gone since I turned 21... It all came with a lot more baggage than I was expecting.

I look over to Blake who hasn't spoken the whole car ride. He's tense like before, but this is different... His eyes are looking everywhere into the darkness that surrounds us.

"Um, thank you for taking me home," I say, my voice thick with sleep.

Blake simply nods in response. I guess that's that, I won't get any more out of him tonight.

"Well, goodnight," I say a bit aggressively, placing my hand on the door handle.

A burn suddenly radiates up my arm and my head flies to the source. Blake's hand on mine. He's staring down at our hands, examining my wing. His face, still pinched with tension, starts to break with a new somber mood as he frowns slightly.

"Goodnight Nola," the finality in his voice sends a cold dagger through me.

Looking up, he meets my eyes and something deeper than the pain from just a half hour ago when we were in his library is there. Despair. That's what's in those burning blue eyes now. Reaching up, he runs his thumb over my cheek, pulling my face to him. Dipping my head down, he kisses my forehead.

"What's wrong?" I say to his chest, worried by his sad demeanor.

"Nothing for you to worry about," he says flatly, voice catching at the end.

"You're not going to tell me."

"Not right now," he pulls away as I frown at him.

"I'll see you soon," he says as he taps the sides of my head and winks.

I roll my eyes. Of course, he would dream walk tonight. Maybe then I can get some more answers.

"Fine," I say in a huff.

Brushing my lips against his in a swift kiss, I turn, leaving him in the car.

Quickly, I'm up the stairs to my apartment, fumbling with my keys at the top. I hesitate at our door, hoping that Ash is back asleep or at least in her room. She had only emerged earlier today right after Harley had left. We had a quick conversation about the night before and what her plans were for the day, which mainly consisted of schoolwork. I made up some excuse to leave at four to run some errands. If she is back in her room, that's one conversation I can avoid. The only thing worse than the drowsiness that's weighing down my bones is the façade I keep in place now with Ash.

I turn the key and open the door slowly. Peering through the door I can see that the lights are off in the living room and kitchen. I tiptoe through, closing the door behind me. The lock clicks loudly despite my prayers for it to be silent.

"Do I need to put a tracking device on you, Nola?" Ash's voice comes from the darkened room, causing me to jump at the sound.

"Fuck! Ash, you scared the shit out of me!" I whisper shout at her, turning on the light of the lamp next to me.

"I could say the same. I was so worried about you! I was about 10 seconds away from calling the cops just now. You said you were just going on errands," her voice getting progressively louder with the anger rolling off her. "And then I went to take the trash out and saw your car still in the parking lot! What the fuck Nola? Where were you?!"

The air sticks in my lungs.

Shit. Fuck. Shit shit shit shit.

I should've taken my car or moved it or something. *Fuck.* The anxiety from earlier blinded me from this one very obvious flaw in my lie. I feel like a complete idiot for not seeing all the sides, covering all my tracks. How could I be so stupid?

I ball my hands into fists at my sides, feeling the slick sweat starting to form on my palms. My cheeks flush with my rising pulse. Panic ringing in my ears drowning out all noises making it hard to focus.

But you need to focus. How are we getting out of this? My subconscious paces the buzzing space in my brain.

She's right. How am I going to get out of this? Another lie on top of this one won't help. I know that. But I can't tell her the whole truth. That would mean revealing everything about me and I just can't...

"I'm so sorry Ash..." I start, swallowing around the knot forming in my throat. "I didn't mean to worry you—"

"Where. Were. You?" Ash cuts me off. Her voice is steady, almost calm with her anger. I've never seen this side of her, and it's frightening.

"I didn't go run errands..."

"Already gathered that," she crosses her arms across her chest.

"Blake picked me up and I went to his place," I try to make my voice sound strong but it's too soft when the last words leave my mouth.

Isn't the truth supposed to ease some of this panic in my chest? If so, why does it tighten more with every syllable?

"Blake?" Ash tilts her head. "The guy from the party who got into a fight with Sean?"

Flinching at the memory, I nod.

Her tone shifts to disappointment. "You can't be fucking serious! Why would you hang out with him?!"

"Ash... it's... complicated."

"It doesn't seem very complicated. In fact, it seems perfectly straightforward, this Blake seems dangerous and VIOLENT, and you just willingly went to his house and didn't tell me for what?" she gets up and starts pacing the living room. "You could've been hurt!"

"I was fine. Blake... he wouldn't hurt me," I say and I hope these words are true.

"Whatever Nola says goes huh?"

My defenses fly up as I say, "what's that supposed to mean?"

"Just that you're 'fine' hanging out with someone who's violent and yet you can threaten Jase to stop seeing me."

The defensive fists my subconscious was holding around her face drop on a dime as my stomach flips. Okay, so she knows about that...

"You don't understand..."

"Enlighten me then."

"Jase..." I search for words. What is Jase? I know now that my wing burning around Blake has to be something more than the burning in my stomach when I'm around him. Is that what it means when a demon is near? Is Jase a demon? If so, that means he's not good for Ash.

My head spins even more.

"Jase is dangerous," I say to her.

"Ha!" Ash throws her hands in the air and turns back to me. "Are you going to keep avoiding the real questions here?"

I open my mouth to defend myself once again, but she cuts me off.

"Actually, don't answer that because I already know. You're gonna keep being evasive like you've been these past few weeks. Honestly, I'm done with this conversation... It's exhausting trying to keep up with you Nola."

I feel hot tears start to fill my eyes and spill over before I can stop them. The ball in my throat that was panic is now a sob choking its way out.

"I'll be here when you're finally ready to talk honestly but why don't you let me make my own decisions about Jase just as you can with Blake," Ash's anger dissipates around her. Her brown eyes rim with wetness as she turns away from me, heading to her room.

"I am glad you're back in one piece though," she says over her shoulder, her door shutting with finality.

Her words ring in my ears as I stumble my way through the hallway to my room with blurry eyes. One piece. I don't feel like I'm in one piece. Maybe physically I'm fine but emotionally and mentally I'm shattering. Ash and I have never fought like that. She knows what I told Jase... He must have told her. Did he tell her everything? About the drugs? About him?

Somehow, I muddle my way through a shower. It replaces the salty tears on my cheeks with fresh water. I roughly towel dry my hair and brush out the tangles once I'm out. The task of getting ready for bed seems mundane but it ticks all the boxes of relaxing some of the stress away.

I hoped Ash didn't feel the same strain on our friendship that I was beginning to feel. Now the façade has cracked, and I don't know what to do about it. How can I tape and glue this back together to where we were before? Is it hopeless to think that we could go back to before now that I'm something new? I don't know how I'm going to do it, but I have to fix this. I can't lose our friendship when I need it the most.

Sleep eventually overtakes my senses but doesn't silence my worry.

I run my hands over the sand, watching the impression of my fingers create their own divots in the earth. Scooping up the sand, I let it flow between my fingers like a silk sheet back to the ground. The sun is setting on the horizon. I watch the colors, fiery yellow, and orange fizzling out to pink and purple, dancing in the sky reminding me of another sunset I've seen before. In another life.

Except this time, the colors don't look quite right. The purple is too bright and the pink too dark almost as if someone is shifting the color hues of a picture. Trying to get the right temperature of the image just right. The sun slips behind the horizon and dives deep into the ocean there. The embrace gives me that same bittersweet feeling again. The feeling of something coming to an end but also the thrilling feeling that the unknown of the night brings. I always loved how beautifully simple sunsets are. They're predictable and reliable at the end of a glorious day or a day that seems to have no end in sight. The close of a day, a year, a life in a single sunset. I close my eyes, breathing out the anxiety of the day and filling my lungs with the sweet salty air. It never gets old. This moment before the dark envelops me like a warm embrace.

The sand shifts beside me.

Hmm... that's new...

I open my eyes lazily, curious as to who's decided to join me. I know I shouldn't be as shocked as I am but there he is, as beautiful as ever. Blake. Wearing dark jeans, books, and a black t-shirt. His dark hair is tousled by the salty air but somehow, he still looks perfect. He wraps his arms around his knees casually and stares out at the water. I notice a tattoo peeking out his shirt sleeve as it shifts up with his movement. I don't remember ever seeing that before...

"Funny seeing you here," I smirk at him.

He cocks his head to the side, dimples on full display, eyes glowing against the darkening sky.

"You really do pick the most beautiful places to come to," his eyes shift from mine to the sand still in my hand. "The way your mind captures everything around you. It amazes me," he looks back out at the water.

The dark waves lap the shore, but they don't make a sound. *Odd...*

"Edge is a beautiful town if you know where to look," I shrug and turn to the water.

It really is beautiful. Sunrises and sunsets that could fill the pages of books. History that has done just that. Charming people, great schools, and places to live. If I didn't know any better, it would be a wonderful place to settle down and start a family. I smile to myself as my mind wanders to the thought of children, my children. How funny would it be to have my own little munchkins running around and playing like Max does? The chaos they would cause...

Shaking my head, I try to shake away that dream. So far out of reach, just as the sun is on the horizon. I frown at the sun for not only setting here and now but for setting on the fact that I'll never be normal again.

"Things are different..." I say to myself, digging my finger-nails into the sand in front of me.

I see Blake shift next to me from the corner of my eye. He reaches across, grabbing my sand covered hand. The heat shoots through the mark on my wrist.

"Things are about to get far more complicated," he says somberly.

"What do you mean?" I say, meeting his anxious gaze.

"Do you remember the phone call I had earlier tonight?"

Earlier tonight? My brain tries to process what he's saying. Suddenly, I can't remember how I got to the beach or how long I had been sitting here, or even what day it is. The familiar panic rises, rattling my hands.

"Nola. It's okay, you're dreaming," Blake says, grabbing my hands firmly to stop the shaking. The grainy sand no longer coats my fingers.

"It's the safest place we can talk right now. Inside your head," he offers a warm half smile.

"I'm dreaming..." I say, trying to convince myself.

"Yes, and so long as I'm here, no one else can get in. We are safe here. Which is so important for what I'm about to tell you," the urgency in his voice doesn't stifle the panic.

"The phone call?" I question, trying to pull my conscious mind into my subconscious. I remember the dark house, the bookcases, our kiss... Then everything changed with the ring. It all feels like a lifetime ago. Picking through the memories is like looking through a fogged window on a rainy day.

"The call where I got orders from my father. Come on Nola, you have to remember," his voice is desperate as he begs, then everything clicks.

"Yes, I remember," I nod, the window becomes clearer.

"Good. Well, the orders weren't the usual kind."

"Usual kind?"

"Mainly a party I have to go to and deal to kids," he shrugs but his jaw sets with disgust.

"Oh."

"Yeah..." he hesitates, looking around to the water, anywhere but me. "These orders were about you."

"Me?" shock pushes the word out of me in a gasp.

"Yes. It took me a moment to piece everything together, but he wants your... your soul."

His words fill my mind, and it takes a moment for me to process what he's saying. "My soul? The Devil wants MY soul... Why?"

"That's what took me a moment to figure out. I didn't understand why he was so urgent on the phone. Talking about some Nephilim. A strong one. One that hasn't been around for generations. One of a noble bloodline..." he hesitates and I can feel him watching me carefully.

I can hear some hopefulness in his voice. Maybe he hopes that what he's saying isn't true. I stay silent and watch the hope die in his eyes.

"So, why does he want my soul?"

"From the stories I heard over the years, he has been searching for this special Nephilim because he wants to open a portal between Hell and Earth. I've never seen it, but they say that Nephilim souls can be doorways between Heaven and Hell to Earth."

The cold salty air burns my lungs as they inflate quickly but the air isn't there for long as it vanishes quickly with a sharp exhale like I've been punched in the gut. The cycle repeats as I start to hyperventilate. I guess that explains why we're being picked off by both sides.

"Why me?" I ask firmly between panicked breaths.

"Well, if I'm right in my assumption. You're that special Nephilim..." the pain returns in his voice as his face crumples with it. "Your soul is rarer and far stronger, which means it... you... can withstand being held open for longer," his voice breaks at the end.

"Open for longer means that more... people? Or whatever else comes through, right?" I voice my fear out loud. Whatever is on the other side, can't be good. If what I can remember from the nights in church, what's in Hell is not particularly friendly.

"Yes, more darkness than you could even imagine would be let free on Earth," he confirms somberly.

"Why are you telling me this? Aren't you just supposed to follow orders? Why give me this warning?"

He sighs, shaking his head slightly.

"Do you really want me to say it?" he stares at me incredulously. Blue eyes burning intensely.

I nod silently.

"Because I can't let anything happen to you Nola," he says firmly, reaching up to brush my cheek. My heart skips a beat with his words.

"But believe me, I'm torn. Part of me, the demonically instinctual side, has no issue ripping your soul from your body. Fulfilling orders and moving on," he shivers slightly. "But my heart - if I still have such a thing - the part of me that still remembers love, is fighting hard against it."

It's funny how even in this sudo-reality of my dream, my world can still shift and tilt on its axis around me. Blake continues to shatter my world with not only his confession but with the earth-shattering news that my life, my soul, my essence of existence is in danger. But despite the part of him that wants to act on instinct, he's fighting. Fighting for me. Fighting for us. How can I resist and not fight alongside him? Not to mention that if the devil has it his way, who knows what kind of darkness will be unleashed on this world. A pit forms in my stomach as I think about my friends and family, they're all in danger if I don't fight.

I stare out at the pitch blackness on the horizon. There's no telling where the sky and ocean differ. They've been married together in the darkness. Is that what the world would look like? A shiver rattles up my spine as the resolution becomes rock solid in my mind.

"Then we figure out a way. We fight, together," I say, feeling stronger with every word.

"While I admire your spark, I'm not sure if that would be wise."

"Blake, I'm not going down without a fight," I say sternly, gripping his hands tightly, holding on to them for dear life. The conversation with my brother comes flooding back. I had to convince Lawson and now Blake.

"I don't see any other options. For you, my family, my friends, for me... I have to fight. I can't let my soul be the reason the world comes to an end."

I watch as he sighs, letting my words sink in. He stares down at our hands, turning mine over, he stares at my wing. Gently, he rubs his thumb over it and the fire blazes through my arm on a new level of intensity. I gasp as I see stars through the pain. He stops and drops my hand quickly.

"I'm sorry," his words are heavy with so many emotions.

"Don't be," the words come out as a breathless whisper. I reach for his hand, ignoring the dull ache.

"Are you with me?" I say, full of hope that this guy that I love will love me enough to fight alongside me instead of against me.

A half smile plays on his lips as he lets out an exasperated sigh.

"Of course," he meets my eyes and smiles lovingly. "But we do need a plan. We have to be smart about this..."

"Right. I think I have an idea about that. We're going to need help for sure. I don't think just the two of us can fight the Devil."

He laughs and I can't help but join in with the rare joyful sound. If anyone else was on the beach with us, I'm sure they would think we were two insane people laughing about the Devil. Good thing this is all in my head...

Not that that makes me feel any better.

"You're going to be the death of me," he says between the fits of laughter.

Blake squeezes my hands again, sending another burning wave through me. Suddenly, he vanishes before me, and I wake.

TWENTY

"Where's your head at Nola?"

Arlo stands on the opposite side of our makeshift ring., boxing gloves disposed of in a pile next to him. I lean on my weapon of choice, a long wooden staff, feeling the sweat trickle down my back. We're almost done with this training session, and every muscle in my body can feel it.

I tried to pour all my nerves and anxious thoughts into every move I made during this training session, I guess I succeeded. My fight with Ash is still hanging over me, unresolved. The thought of the fucking Devil coming after me drove the last several punches I threw to land harder than I expected on Arlo. Now, as I try to catch my breath in lungs that seem too small for the amount of air I need, Arlo wants to talk.

"That's a loaded question..." I say between pants.

"Wanna talk about it?" Arlo places his dull sword on the bench beside him as he sits.

I fill my lungs with as much air as I can as I sit across from

Arlo. Avoiding his gaze, I reach down and grab my water bottle, taking a long purposeful sip.

"Yes," I say, letting the cold chill fill my insides. "But I think someone else needs to be included in this conversation."

Reaching underneath my bench, I pull my bookbag out. It's doubled as my training bag for a while now. Fiddling with the zippers, I know exactly which one I need to pull. I need to talk with him, even if he isn't ready to talk to me. My phone springs awake as I tap on the screen. Maybe I'm dragging this out because I know the moment I tell him, he's going to tell our mother.

I tap on the tiny outline of a phone next to Lawson's name.

Here goes nothing...

The phone rings twice before my brother picks up.

"Nola? What's going on?" Lawson's voice is full of breathless worry.

"Hello to you too Law," I say back to him. I lock eyes with Arlo who pinches his eyebrows together in confusion.

"I'm so sorry Nola," Lawson becomes defensive. "I've been meaning to talk to you. It's just... there are things going on and..."

"Well, there are things going on here too," I cut him off. I don't want to hear his excuses right now.

Arlo tilts his head at me but says nothing, curiosity, and patience filling his eyes. I can't help but wonder if Lawson's brown eyes would have the same look.

"What?" Lawson's voice cracks on the other end of the line. "What's going on?"

Rip the Band-Aid off Nola.

"Long story short..." I look away from Arlo and down at my

feet. My heart beating loudly in my chest, it'd be surprising if Arlo can't hear it from where he's sitting.

"The Devil is coming for me. Well, my soul really."

If there was music playing, the record would've scratched.

The line goes unearthly quiet that for a moment I think Lawson hung up or the call dropped. Arlo, on the other hand, stands and begins pacing the small area. His face is unreadable, but I can feel the tension every time he passes.

"Nola, what are you talking about?" Lawson's voice is level on the other end, too calm.

"I mean exactly what I said... the actual Devil is coming for me."

"How do you know this?" Arlo asks, stopping in front of me.

He crosses his arms as he waits for me to answer. It's odd how calm he is. How calm Lawson is too. Like I didn't just drop this bomb on them. They're acting like...

"You already knew," I say to Arlo. "You both knew."

"No, we didn't know," Lawson says defensively.

"There were rumors though," Arlo finishes for him.

"Rumors?" I stand, holding my ground. "And you didn't think to let me know that, oh I don't know... the fucking Devil is trying to reap my soul to create some sort of doorway for darkness?!"

My voice rises, echoing to the ceiling. I'm grateful that Arlo's gym is private and secluded from the outside world. If we were at the café, I'm sure someone passing by would think I was insane. Hell, I feel insane and even now, after everything, they're all still keeping me in the dark.

"Nola..." Lawson's voice finds me in my rage.

"No, Law. Shut up," I grip my phone tighter to try to stop

my hands from shaking. "I thought we were past keeping secrets like this. You know, you both know, that I want to fight. Hell, that's why we've been training, right Arlo?" I pause but not long enough for him to answer. "And yet, here we are. You guys knew these 'rumors' and didn't tell me."

"It's a lot more complicated than that Nola," Arlo chastises. "We were trying to find out the validity to the rumors before we brought it to your attention because we didn't want you to worry."

"Well, news flash, I'm worried."

"Nola," Lawson starts. "How did you find out about this?"

The knot in my stomach tightens. I knew this conversation would take this turn, but I still hoped it didn't. I hoped I wouldn't have to tell them how I knew about this.

My brain stalls with the words that don't seem real.

Now I have to figure out how to tell them what happened in my dream with a demon.

"Umm," it's my turn to pace as I search for words in the space around me.

"Blake told me."

I stare at my reflection in the mirror on the other side of the gym. She looks as terrified as I feel. Green eyes wild with secrets. I barely recognize the person looking back at me. While she's scared, she's also strong. Strong enough to hold her ground during all these training sessions with Arlo, but I don't know if she's strong enough to go up against the Devil.

At least not without help.

"Blake?" Arlo and Lawson ask at the same time.

"Yeah," I swallow, turning away from the girl in my reflection. "Blake, he's... he's a demon."

"A demon?!" Lawson shouts through my phone. "How

could you get involved with a demon? Nola, you know the risks! Even after I told you to be careful!"

"Seems a bit hypocritical, Lawson, when you spent who knows how long in Europe with demons. You said so yourself," I counter. "Besides, he wants to help."

"Help? How's a demon," Arlo says, disgust on the tip of his tongue, "supposed to help in a situation like this?"

"We're still working on that, but that's why I wanted to tell you guys. I'm not going down without a fight and I know it's a lot to ask..." I look into Arlo's eyes, trying to gauge how he's processing. "But I think I need all the help I can get."

It's too much. Asking them to put their lives on the line, for me. To join me in this crazy mission. For a moment, I wonder if they won't help me. It'll just be me and Blake against the Devil. But our best chance is if I can convince the angels to help in some way.

"I'm in," Arlo says with conviction.

"Arlo! You can't be serious!" Lawson's panic bleeds into every word.

Arlo takes a few steps toward me, holding out his hand and I place my phone in it.

"Lawson," Arlo says to my brother, back to business. "You know our mission. We have to."

Those seven words shut Lawson up quickly. I can almost hear the thinking on the other end and see his nervous ticks as he more than likely is rubbing his hands together or pacing whichever room he's in now. At this time of night, it's probably his study filled with books he's collected over the years and some of our father's from all over the world. Maybe some of those books are the ones he's been meaning to give me.

"You're right," Lawson says sadly. "If this is true and we can trust this demon, we've got a lot of work to do."

Arlo nods to me, handing back my phone.

"Keep up the training with Arlo and I'll be in touch soon."

Lawson hangs up without another word. The panic that had lodged itself in my throat constricts then releases with some relief. So, they're going to help. And with that comes a new fear. Fear for all of our lives. Fear for all of our souls and those here on Earth. This isn't just a fight for my own soul but for everyone. I have to keep the darkness at bay.

"You ready for round three?" Arlo picks up his sword but instead of holding it like he was during our training session, he holds the handle out towards me.

His eyes are determined but I can see a sliver of fear in them.

"Let's do this."

I grab the sword, feeling more than its weight dragging my body down.

TWENTY-ONE

I cross my room, toothbrush still in my mouth, wincing slightly as I lean down and slide my finger across my phone, effectively turning the alarm off. It's been a long week. Long several weeks really.

These training sessions every morning and evening with Arlo have kicked my ass and last night was no exception. But after every session, Arlo seems pleased with my progress, and I would be lying to say I wasn't giddy every time I beat him in our sparring matches. I would also be lying to myself if I didn't enjoy the distraction that these sessions provide. I haven't heard from Blake since the other night and the anxiety won't leave me alone about that. Wondering if he's alright if we are.

So, it helps to get out, to work out the anxiety.

After another successful session last night, Arlo decided to give me a bit of a break from training in the gym with him on the grounds that I still did some sort of training. I opted for running. Something I used to dread, now feels so freeing. He also made me promise to focus more on my schoolwork, getting caught up, or even getting ahead if I can. I'm grateful because college never seems to let up.

With finals looming next month, it just seems like these professors enjoy throwing more assignments at us. I have to get through two classes today and then right to the library until I can't see straight. Grabbing my laptop from my desk, I shove it into my bookbag. My sore and stiff muscles haven't made it easy this morning to get everything done. It's no exception when I lift my heavy bookbag over my shoulders, wincing at the pain that radiates down my back.

Great.

I head to the kitchen as quietly as possible. Ash doesn't have class until later today so more than likely, she's still sleeping. I know that's another conversation I need to have but hopefully not this morning. I grab a protein bar and a water bottle from the cabinet, slowly easing it shut so it doesn't make a sound. Slipping the protein bar into my back pocket, I fill my water bottle.

My hand jumps at the sound of a knock on our door and my heart instantly starts to stutter.

"Fuck," I say to no one as the water drips from my hand onto the counter. "Who the fuck is knocking on our door right now?" I continue to the air.

Grabbing a dish towel, I head to the door. Anger and curiosity canceling out the anxiety of a possible stranger on the other side of the door. I open it just enough for half my face to show through the crack.

"Jesus," the relief floods out of me as I open the door fully.

"Not quite," my brother says smugly.

"Lawson, you scared the shit out of me. What the hell are you doing here?"

"Well, I was hoping you could skip out on class or whatever you have to do today..." he says as he steps through the threshold. He sits on the couch, making himself comfortable.

"On the one day, I have to just focus on school?"

He shrugs.

"I understand. I just thought you would want to come along. I think I have a lead on the Euch."

Curiosity bubbles up in my chest. The Euch is what Katherine and her company were after the night of my birthday. I hadn't heard that word since when my mother and I talked about it. I had no idea that's what my brother was doing...

"I'm assuming it's not with mom?"

"No, that was the first place I looked. Turns out she hasn't seen it for years. She thought it was lost until you brought it up to her," his voice trails off.

"So, is it here?"

"In Edge? No."

"Are you gonna tell me where?" I say crossing my arms over my chest. He smiles, enjoying dragging this out and testing my patience like he always does.

"It's in Cross. I believe. With a faction of Protectors. But I was hoping you would come. It may help to smooth things over..."

"How so?"

"Well, it could help with trying to encourage them to join us. If they have the Euch, who knows what other weapons they could have. It could help us to have more numbers and

weapons, if this is going to be the battle, I think it's going to be...
And since you're the chosen one—"

"No, I'm not," I cut him off. Cringing at the term.

"Okay, but you are. You're the one who can wield the Euch
and use it at full power. You can't deny that. This has been a
long war and maybe you can give these Protectors some hope
that the end is in sight," he shrugs but there's an edge in his
voice.

"Okay."

"Okay?" he tilts his head at me.

"Yeah, I'll go with you. Just give me like 5 minutes to get a
bag together."

I turn, curiosity driving my feet back to my room. I nearly
knock a bleary-eyed Ash off her feet in the hallway.

"What's all the shouting about?" she says, rubbing her eyes.
Her hair is a mess, and her sleep shirt is falling down her
shoulders.

"Oh shit, sorry Ash. Lawson is here. He, um, was in town
on a case and he is here to, um, take me to Cross," here I go
searching for the right words to feed to her. "We're surprising
my mom," I lie.

It hurts to lie to someone who has been there for me
through so many ups and downs, but I haven't figured out yet
how to tell her about this. This whole other world. This whole
life I now have. Sure, she's been suspicious about all my
training sessions but luckily, I've been able to divert her questions every time. Making up some stories about study sessions
or late nights at the photography studio. She gives me the same
look now as when I tell her those stories, her eyes squint a bit,
not quite believing me.

"Okay. You're skipping class?" she questions.

"Yeah, it'll be alright. I can afford it with all the studying," I offer with a half-hearted smile.

"I'll see you soon," I say as I squeeze past her on the way to my room. She nods and my heart breaks as I watch her accept my story.

I turn away, not able to keep up the façade any longer. Back in my room, I hesitate, debating on whether or not to take my schoolwork with me. Maybe I'll have some time to work on it... I shrug, deciding to leave it all in my bookbag instead. Grabbing another overnight bag from my closet I shove a few outfits in the bag and am back out my door in a matter of seconds, shoving my chargers into the bag on the way out.

"See you later," Ash calls from the counter in the kitchen.

She's putting her mug under our Keurig, and I notice a bite to her voice. Maybe I should figure out what I'm going to tell her by the time I get back. She looks up with a new intensity in her brown eyes.

Yep, definitely need to figure that out.

She's not going to accept these stories much longer.

"Bye Lawson. Always a pleasure. But maybe next time, not so early you dick," Ash directs her gaze to him now.

He just laughs. It always makes me smile at how casual their banter is. Ash and her family have spent several breaks and mini vacations with mine since we've been roommates. My family quickly welcomed her with open arms. It helps that Ash basically clicks with everyone she meets.

Lawson waves back at her, "See ya later Ash."

"Yeah, yeah. I'll see you at Thanksgiving," she gives him a half wave bringing the hot coffee to her lips.

Fuck, Thanksgiving is coming up... Will Ash even want to come to Thanksgiving once she knows? Hell, will we even be friends? I could lose my home... My heart beats against my ribs as I usher Lawson out the door, closing and locking it behind us. What if I never told her? Would I be able to keep up the lies? My mind spins with questions and before I realize it, I'm in the passenger seat of my brother's SUV.

"Let's do this," he says with a wide smile, but his eyes are watchful.

We drive in silence other than the quiet music from the radio filling the space. I can feel my brother mulling over something in the driver's seat. After about 45 minutes, I can't take the tension rolling off him.

"So, how are Flynn and Max?" I blurt, breaking the silence.

"Huh?" Lawson's response comes quickly, startled out of him and whatever deep thoughts were in his head dissipate before my eyes.

"How are your wife and kid?" I say sarcastically.

"Oh, they're good. Flynn has been busy with work. With the semester ending with her kids, she's deep in grading and planning for the next semester. And Max, well he's growing like a weed. Smarter and smarter every day," Lawson's face breaks into a loving smile. "You know the other day, he explained to me all the planets in our solar system. One by one, he went over each planet and a fun fact about each one. Blew my mind."

"Are you sure he's only four?"

"Yeah, more like 34 with a Ph.D. already."

We both laugh.

"That's one degree you or Flynn don't have. I'm sure you guys would be thrilled if he got one."

"Honestly," Lawson starts with fondness and contentment in his voice. "I would be proud of him if he chose to go to college or if he chooses another path outside of academics. Who knows, he may be better off in a trade school or just learning and training on the job," he shrugs, still smiling.

"That's very... progressive of you."

"Hey! I've always been progressive. Had to be with you for a sister," his eyes leave the road long enough to wink at me. I roll my eyes back at him.

The laughter escapes in short bursts as he sticks his tongue out at me. He's not wrong. I would always get into debates in school and when I would get into trouble, I would always come back home to rant about all the many wrong ideals that were spreading throughout our small town. I remember Lawson sitting there just shaking his head at my absurd outbursts but occasionally I would see him nod in agreement, mom would nod along as well. And dad... when he was still good, he would nod and smile along but then there were times where he would be so far gone that he wouldn't know what words were coming out of my mouth, he would just stare.

"Does... does Flynn know?" I ask, changing the subject and pulling the needle on our joyous record playing. "Like does she know about you? About us?"

"You honestly think I could keep something like that a secret for this long?" he asks doubtfully.

"I guess not..." I peel my eyes away from the road ahead and look down at my wrist, my wing. My mind wanders to the pressing concern of having to tell Ash. And then there's Harley... how am I going to tell them?

"When did you tell her? How did she react?" the questions are barely a whisper.

"Well, we met during what I like to call, my denial phase," his voice is even, comforting. "I spiraled about it all for a while and when I met Flynn, it was just easier to keep pretending because I wasn't even ready to accept it all for myself. But once I knew what we had was something more, something serious. I couldn't keep hiding. She was surprisingly accepting; I mean I think we all know she's always been that way," he smiles knowingly at me. "But it took a lot of deep conversations about my world, what it all meant. She wanted to understand, still does but I can see sometimes when she doesn't fully get it and she just worries. Worries about me, and Max."

"Worried that Max will become like us?"

"Partly. I think that's something that will be over our heads until he turns 21 for sure. But I don't think it'll happen to him. It's very rare anyways. He only has a fraction of my soul in him," his voice has turned more calculating, business-like.

"Ah," the sound breathes out of my lips in agreement.

I catch sight of a sign out of my window, only 30 more miles until we get to Cross. Another question scratches my mind.

"Did you tell mom?" the question weighs heavy in the air, and I hope that Lawson catches what I mean by it. If he asked mom about the Euch, she must know something. We only just talked yesterday about the Devil coming after me. Did Lawson keep that from her?

"No. Not explicitly," he confirms. "I think she knows something is up though. I figured you would want to tell her yourself. It's your idiotic plan anyways. Have you talked to her?"

"Not since my birthday..." guilt crashes down on my chest.

"You really should. I know how you found out sucks, trust me. But mom, she's always done what's best for us."

"I know," agreeing wholeheartedly. "I would also like to remind you that you're going along with my idiotic plan too."

"Yeah, I know, and I second guess it every second. Following my baby sister and some demon into battle against the Devil," he rolls his eyes at the road, voice laced with disgust.

"Blake," I correct. "His name is Blake."

"Right... Blake..." Lawson drags out his name. "What's going on with you two? Is it... something I should be concerned about? Is it serious?" his face scrunches up in discomfort.

I feel a hot blush creep up my neck, past my jawline, flushing my cheeks, and stopping right at my temples.

"We're..." I stall, waiting for the words to come. Are we serious? Are we in a relationship? The definitive answer is that there is nothing definitive about it. Somehow, it feels beyond labels, beyond any human word that I know. It feels eternal and something just beyond what we can grasp. It's a love that I've never felt before with someone I didn't even know existed two months ago.

"Yeah. It's serious," an oversimplification of the electricity that courses through Blake and me.

"That's it? That's all you're going to give me?" Lawson puts on a pout.

"Yes," I say definitively. Ignoring his persistence, I watch as the familiar exit signs start to appear over the interstate.

"Ugh!" he groans. "Fine. I just hope that he's better than Sean. How funny... hoping that an actual demon is better than that piece of garbage," Lawson scoffs watching the exits now too.

"Ha! I think the Devil himself is better than Sean," my

stomach twists at the thought of both Sean and the ominous 'father' of the man I love.

But the truth is there still that I would rather face a being hell bent on using my soul to open a portal to hell than another day in Sean's grasp. Maybe that's a bit extreme but with Sean, I was alone. I couldn't tell anyone what was going on. I didn't have anyone in my corner.

Now, with this new threat, I know I'm not alone.

"You might be right about that one," Lawson agrees as he turns off an exit. "Are you going to invite Blake to Thanksgiving?"

"Wait, what?"

"Yeah, I mean if it's serious...? Not that I approve at all. But I thought you would. I'd like to meet the kid," he shrugs but I recognize the familiar overprotective tone.

"I honestly haven't thought of it... Hold on, where are we going? Are we not going to your place? Or mom's?" I look at the exit number. We are still a few exits away from either one of their exits and I can't help the nervous knot.

"Nope. We're meeting up with the others first," he says simply.

"The others?"

TWENTY-TWO

Lawson parks in one of the empty spots in the small parking lot. Surprisingly, there aren't many empty spaces. The parking lot is already occupied by a couple large black SUVs, a small silver sedan, and a dark blue crossover that I recognize instantly.

Mom.

The building attached to the lot is small with weathered and worn bricks disintegrating on its exterior. As I get out of the car, I can see how warped the red wood front door and frame are. This building has seen many years and all that comes with them, people, storms, wars. Above the door is an off-white placard with bold black letters.

"OLD CROSS LIBRARY" I read the name out loud. "It certainly is old. Why did you take me here?"

"Aren't you always the one saying, don't judge a book by its cover?" Lawson teases closing his door a bit too aggressively.

"Come on. You know how I hate to leave people waiting."

Not bothering to lock his car doors, Lawson walks towards the front door. I follow his tense shoulders closely. With a hearty yank, the wood door shifts open with a loud creak. A small bell chimes overhead.

Seems a bit pointless, I think to myself, *a bit concerning if whoever is inside can't hear someone enter with the loud groan of the door.*

Stepping through the threshold, I'm smacked with the overbearing scent of worn leather and paper. The same smell that most libraries have, pages of books that have been touched by thousands of people. I expected a small room from the size of the exterior, but I'm pleasantly surprised to see that the room is actually larger, going back farther than I realized from the outside. There are two small aisles leading all the way to the back wall with shelves nearly touching the ceiling lining the isles. All four walls are just shelves stacked with books.

Lawson continues down the aisle on the right and I have to jog slightly to keep up. I glance down some of the stacks, catching the different genres as we pass.

Fiction

Non-Fiction

History of Cross

Authors of Cross

Religion

Demons

The name jumps out at me making my steps falter. There's a whole section dedicated to demons... that can't be right. I look down further and sure enough, **Angels**. My feet move down to that section even though my mind is still trying to yank me back to the demon section.

I head down one of the aisles and run my fingers on the

worn spines.

I stop at a red spine and tilt my head slightly to read the gold lettering, *The History of Angels in Cross*.

"You've got to be shitting me," the words tumble out of my mouth as I pull the book from the shelf. It hits me all over again that there's still so much that I don't know about my family and now the town I was raised in.

So much that I don't even know about myself.

"Nola?" Lawson's voice comes from the main aisle, startling me even in his hushed tone. He turns the corner and finds me. His eyes shift from my face to the book in my hands.

"Oh... yeah, I know," his voice becomes forlorn as his face drops to the ground. "Come on. You can take it with you, but they're waiting."

He turns quickly on his heels and a new determination drives my feet to follow him. I tuck the book under my arm, ignoring the nagging need to explore the rest of the stacks. At the back of the library, it opens up to a small seating area and a round counter. Behind which, a plump man with round glasses balancing precariously on the end of his nose leans over completely engrossed in the book in his hand. Lawson clears his throat, startling the man so bad that he gasps, nearly jumping a foot in the air. The glasses fly off his face, clattering onto the counter.

"Oh, Mr. Saint!" the man says with familiarity, slightly breathless.

"I'm sorry about that Jerry. Are you alright?"

My brother's tone is light, and I can hear the hint of amusement. The same tone he uses when playing a practical joke. He knew that would happen, *poor Jerry*.

"Yes, Mr. Saint," Jerry collects himself, straightening his

glasses back on his face. "The room is ready, and everyone's already here."

He nods his head and looks past us.

I follow his gaze to a dark door nearly camouflaged in the stacks of books.

"Thanks, Jerry. And again, sorry about startling you," Lawson puts on sincerity as he tilts his head down. Turning around, I can see the smile playing on his lips.

"Now that's just cruel," I say under my breath to him as we head to the door.

"He's an easy target," Lawson shrugs as he reaches for the door. "Ready for your first council meeting?"

"My what?" my voice rises with the sudden panic.

Lawson's smile turns devious as he turns the handle. Voices flood out in hushed tones, but quickly silence as the door opens. The first eyes that find mine are our mother's, her kindness crinkles at the edges and relief floods her features as she looks at me. She takes a hesitant step forward, around the large wooden table that occupies the majority of the small conference room.

"Hey baby," she says, closing the gap of space and wrapping her arms around me.

I can't help the sudden rush of comfort that comes. Her arms are the same as they've always been except maybe now, they feel a bit stronger, sturdier. Everything I felt growing up comes back tenfold.

Closing my eyes, I relish in the warm love.

"Hey mom," I say, wrapping my arms around her tightly. I didn't realize how much I needed this, needed her comfort.

"It's okay Nola. It's going to be okay," she whispers in my ear.

"Be careful Laine, she may hurt you," Arlo's voice comes from next to us. I open my eyes just long enough to roll them at him.

"It's okay if you're still butt-hurt at me winning our last few matches," I shoot back at him.

I feel my mother's shoulders shaking with laughter as I loosen my hold on her. She shifts to my brother, giving him a tight hug as well.

"Okay, okay, enough with the mushy stuff," a familiar voice comes from the other side of the room.

"Harley?"

My eyes dart in the direction of their voice and I find them leaning on the back of one of the chairs around the table. They're dressed in a simple black tank top and dark jeans. Their short hair framing their face perfectly. Harley's face is split into a wide grin.

"Didn't think you were the only special one, did you?"

They wink at me, holding up their left wrist, and they're surrounded by a pale halo is a single black wing.

"No fucking way!"

The words are out of my mouth before I can stop them, and I hear several intakes of air around the room. Blood pools in my cheeks from the embarrassment.

"Shit, my bad."

Harley slaps their hand around their mouth to stifle their laughter, while Arlo covers his with a cough. I shoot daggers at both of them causing them to laugh harder.

Harley catches my eyes, nodding slightly and I nod back.

We have so much to talk about.

Someone else starts to clear their throat and I finally let my eyes find the others in the room.

Aside from myself, my mother, Lawson, Arlo, and Harley; there are six other people in the room making it feel smaller. I eye the three figures standing close together in one of the far corners, immediately recognizing them.

"Nola, I'm sure you remember Sister Katherine, Sister Hannah, and Brother Abraham," Arlo starts.

Katherine and Hannah are standing so close they're almost holding hands, Katherine standing a half step in front of her. Protective. It's obvious who's making her so on edge as her eyes flick between me and the other three standing on the opposite side of the room.

"And this is Jeremiah," Arlo lays his hand out flatly towards the tall man on the other side of the room.

His face is sharp, too angular with high cheekbones. He's dressed in a simple white button down, black tie, and black dinner jacket. A white coat, the same length as a doctor's coat, is draped over his arms. He looks to be in his forties but the wrinkles around his eyes age him further. His dark eyes are deep set at the top of his cheeks, and I can feel their judgment as they rake over my face. I nod, keeping my head up.

"Zera," Arlo continues.

A young woman shifts at Jeremiah's side. She's much smaller than Hannah or my mother but the way her face is set gives me the feeling that she could murder us all without even blinking an eye or breaking a nail. She's dressed simply in dark blue scrubs. She wears her age in her eyes as well, even though her face would say early thirties or even late twenties, her pale blue eyes shoot their years at me. I try to swallow around the lump that has formed in my throat, still trying to find the strength and confidence to be in such a small room with all these angels.

"And Cael."

The man on the other side of Jeremiah steps forward. He's a few inches shorter than Jeremiah but of the same slim build. His features are softer, indicating his youth, with kind hazel eyes behind dark rimmed glasses that crinkle slightly with a small smile. His chestnut brown hair is tousled effortlessly, yet still looks like every hair is in its place. He can't be more than 25, wearing dress slacks and a striped button up. The sleeves of which are rolled up to his elbows, showing off toned muscles on his forearms. Cael lifts his hand in a wave. I anticipate seeing two dark black wings but instead, I stagger a bit when I only see one. My head tilts at his wave.

Another Nephilim. He smiles politely, lowering his hand.

"Hello Nola," my name sounds strange in his mouth, but it awakens something different inside of me. "It's nice to formally meet you. I know, if I may speak for Jeremiah, Zera, and I; we've waited a long time for you."

"You've not waited longer than the rest of us," Jeremiah's deep voice corrects Cael, confirming my suspicions. Cael breaks eye contact with me, dipping his head low as he takes a step back.

"What are we here for Brother Arlo?" Jeremiah turns to Arlo with disinterest. "We already knew about the Nephilim."

His eyes flick to mine, repulsion laced through his voice. My mother tenses beside me so I take a step back thinking maybe some more distance will stop the judgment, but the walls are closing in with it.

"Please, let's all take a seat," Arlo motions for the chairs around the table, now looking far too small as the tension in the air shifts.

For half a second, no one moves. I could swear that no one even breathes, but maybe that's just me.

Arlo scoffs loudly as he pulls out the chair closest to him. Sitting with a huff, he waits for everyone else to follow suit. My mother moves next and sits at Arlo's side. Lawson moves to place his hands on her chair. I follow his lead and stand behind Arlo. Harley passes behind the trio with Jeremiah, keeping their distance, and settles in next to me. Katherine moves, bringing Hannah with her and they sit as far away from us and Jeremiah's trio. Abraham only moves a few feet forward, still keeping his distance in the corner.

Jeremiah moves last, making a show of pulling out the chair, ignoring the squeak of the wheels. Once he sits, Zera and Cael flank him, both still standing. Cael's eyes find mine again with a sudden intensity. I shift slightly under his uncomfortable gaze. Jeremiah clasps his hands together on the table, the sleeves of his shirt rise a bit, revealing the tops of his wings.

"Alright, Arlo. What's going on? I don't have all day," Jeremiah tilts his head from side to side like he's stretching out a particularly annoying muscle in his neck.

"We have it on good authority that the Devil is working on making his move," Arlo cuts right to the point.

Abraham gasps loudly from his corner and Katherine shoots up at Arlo's statement. Harley stiffens next to me. The hairs on the back of my neck stand to attention. I knew in the pit of my stomach that this is why we were here, but the chill runs up my spine in anticipation anyway. The only person who doesn't look uncomfortable or shocked by the news is Jeremiah. Even Cael and Zera share a similar shock, with wide-eyed expressions.

"Whose authority?" Jeremiah asks calmly, eyes never leaving Arlo.

"Mine," the word escapes from around the lump in my throat.

Jeremiah's empty eyes find mine.

"And how do you know?"

"Becau..." I clear my throat, forcing strength. "Because he's after me."

"Hmm," the sound coming from Jeremiah. "So, he's planning on opening a portal."

He nods thoughtfully, but his tone remains disinterested like he's discussing the rise and fall of stocks and not my life or every other humans' life on Earth.

Anger bubbles up inside of me at this angel sitting in front of me.

"I'm not going to let that happen," I say, my hand grips the back of Arlo's chair and around the book still in my other hand.

"Oh yeah? You're nothing but a child," he spits back at me. "How are you going to defeat the greatest darkness? One that we've been after for a millennium."

"We're going to fight," Lawson speaks up, protectively taking a step closer to me.

Jeremiah's eyes shift to him. A cold, dead laugh erupts, filling the room and my head with the sound.

"But we can't fight without you all," Arlo raises his voice over Jeremiah's dying laughter. Jeremiah lifts his head up to Arlo.

"Imagine it, finally getting the chance to kill him... What we've been working for all this time," Arlo continues before he can get cut off. "You can't tell me you don't want that brother."

A new emotion flicks behind Jeremiah's cold eyes, hunger.

Hunger for victory. An eager smile spreads across his face, making his cheekbones rise higher, if that's even possible.

"And how do you suppose we do that? The weapon that we would need hasn't been seen for generations."

"Actually," my mother speaks up from her seat, her voice strong and steady. "I've found the Euch."

"Ah Sister Laine..." Jeremiah's eyes find my mother, his voice filled with fondness that flips my stomach. "You've been holding out on us."

"I thought you said you didn't know where it was," Lawson leans down towards her, talking low.

"I didn't," she turns her head to him, her eyes trusting. "But I remembered something that Michael told me once. And after you three," she turns her head pointedly at Katherine who retreats, tilting her head down to the table, "decided to kidnap my daughter. I knew I had to follow that hunch. Anyways, it doesn't matter how I got it. I have it now and we need you to stand beside us," she finishes matter of factly.

"Hmmm..." Jeremiah lets out the same thoughtless noise as before.

"How," he turns to me, "how do you know this? How do you know he's coming for you?"

He squints his eyes, judgment once again waving off him at me.

My brain scrambles. This doesn't seem like the best place to mention Blake, knowing what he is... It can't be safe to bring him into this even though he might be in the middle of this one day.

"There's a demon..."

Fuck.

The shaky words come from Abraham in his corner. "I saw him watching you that night. It was that demon wasn't it?"

One at a time, everyone's eyes turn to me. Everyone except Arlo and my mother, they stay still as statues in their seats. My stomach flips with the sudden attention and my hands are slick with sweat. I feel a brush of concern from Harley before they turn back towards Jeremiah. Just another thing we have to talk about.

I catch Cael's curious eyes watching me.

"We're trusting filthy demons now?" Jeremiah spits. The anxiety of the stares quickly forms into a white-hot ball of anger in my chest.

"As hard as it may be to understand," Lawson speaks slowly. "There are some who are on our side. Or at least want the same thing as us."

I can't believe he's defending Blake right now, especially with how he felt last night.

"That is very hard to understand. To believe," Cael speaks up in an even tone.

"I've seen it," Katherine's high voice pierces the air around us. "I've met a few over the years... maybe there are more. It wouldn't hurt to have some eyes and ears on the inside."

My jaw drops to the floor. Katherine, the one who orchestrated my kidnapping with Ash, is willing to be on our side and work with demons.

"Ugh!" Jeremiah slams his hands down on the table. I can feel the force in my feet as my ears ring with the sound.

"Not only do you expect us to trust these rats, but YOU also want us to fight alongside them in a battle led by... by a child!?"

Jeremiah's words bounce off the caverns in my mind and I

can't tell if the echo is coming from inside my head or the room. It's disorienting but the anger in my chest keeps me centered.

"I'm. Not. A. Child." I spit the words back at him.

Squaring my shoulders, I brace against Arlo's chair.

"You have two choices from where I'm standing. You can either join us, be a part of the winning team that just so happens to be comprised of angels, demons, and a Nephilim that's going to defeat the Devil. Get all the glory," I say pointedly at his ego. "Or you can be a coward and turn away just because of who you're fighting with."

Silence hangs with my words in the air. My eyes never leave Jeremiah as my words sink in. He leans back and crosses his arms over his chest, a devious smile playing on his lips.

"Hmmm," that fucking sound again. "You have some fight in you after all."

"Does that mean you'll help us?" I question.

"I'll have to run it up to the Overseers. Besides, it's going to take more than our factions. What's the plan? How much time do we have?" Jeremiah's tone is back to disinterest but there's a slight undertone of excitement.

Relief washes over me, *did I really just get this asshole to agree to fight with us?*

"Nola will be ready in a month's time," Arlo answers.

The worry knot tightens again.

A month... A month to get ready. To get everything in order, just in case.

Reality sinks in, this may be my last month alive.

"Then what?" Zera chimes in.

"He's after me," I answer far too quickly. It's something I've thought about but never voiced out loud. "I don't think it would be hard to lure him out. Somewhere away from Edge and

Cross. There are a few farmhouses about an hour away, middle of nowhere. If I can get him there, that's where we will fight."

Jeremiah nods in thoughtful agreement.

"I can get you a month. See to it that she's ready," Jeremiah says to Arlo. "Cael, stick around and keep an eye on things."

He stands and quickly, everyone else follows.

"I don't need a babysitter," I shoot over at him, now having to look up at him.

"Regardless," he says dismissively. "I like to have my own eyes and ears around."

Without another word, Jeremiah turns to Zera. They share a look, then head for the door, leaving Cael behind without another thought.

"I'll wait outside," Cael says shyly as he follows Jeremiah and Zera out the door. Katherine, Hannah, and Abraham follow quickly behind.

"I'm... I'm sorry for, well you know," Katherine forces as she stops next to us, Hannah and Abraham continuing without her. I nod my head, it's probably best to forgive someone who is choosing to walk up to death's door by my side.

"We'll be in touch Sister Katherine," my mother says, now beside me.

Katherine nods back and is out the door quickly. The room suddenly feels too big as all the tension leaves my body in a huff.

"Fuck Nola. What have you gotten us into?" Harley says. They let out an exasperated sigh and rub at their temples.

What have I done? I'm doing exactly what I don't want to do, putting those I love in harm's way. I know that I need them. But do I need them because I need help or because selfishly, I don't want to be alone in the end?

TWENTY-THREE

Outside of the library, the cool breeze chills the sweat that had started to drip down my back. With my hands on my hips, I take a deep breath, hoping to calm the nerves fluttering around in my stomach. I feel a hand on my back and turn quickly only to find my mother by my side, concern in her eyes.

"I'm fine," I assure her.

I have to be.

"Good," Cael's calm voice comes from behind us. He's leaning against the old brick building casually, arms folded over his chest.

"We have a lot of work to do," he continues, kicking himself off the wall.

"Look," I start, catching Harley, Arlo, and Lawson filing out of the door. "I appreciate it, but I don't need you. Wouldn't want you to waste your time."

"It's not a waste of time when it's orders," he chooses his words carefully.

"I'm getting really tired of being a part of people's orders."

"Luck of the draw," Harley says sarcastically, throwing their arm around my shoulders.

"Right," I roll my eyes at them but lean into their comfort.

"Nola, it may be beneficial to have Cael here helping out," Arlo says walking around to us. "I've read your combat reports, kid. Impressive. Cael can help out with training when Lawson or I aren't available. You, Harley, and Cael can all work together."

"Lovely," Harley chimes in beside me, their gaze fierce on Cael. "I'd love to see this skinny kid try and take me down."

Their voice is low so that only I can hear. Laughter bursts through me but it's short lived when I catch my mother's glare.

"Okay, what now?" I ask everyone.

"Sister Laine, you said you had the Euch? I think we should start training with it," Cael's voice and eyes are eager as he takes several steps toward us.

"If it's all the same to you, I would love to spend some time with my daughter. The training can start tomorrow," she puts on her motherly tone, daring anyone to argue.

There's a conversation that's waiting for us when I get home. There's no avoiding it now.

"I see," Cael, using the brains he seems to have, backs down.

"Come on Cael," Arlo walks toward him. "I would love to talk about strategy for tomorrow. I can take you wherever you need to go since it looks like your ride left you."

Hesitantly, Cael takes his eyes off me and follows Arlo to his car.

"See you tomorrow," Cael says, only to me.

My curiosity about the guy follows him. Why would he be

with a group of angels who so clearly hate Nephilim? And follow them so blindly? Maybe he is skilled in combat but there's something off about him. I box up my curiosity and place it in a new room in my mind. Something to figure out tomorrow.

"I have to head out or Flynn will kill me," Lawson breaks me from my thoughts. "Besides, I'm sure you three have a lot to talk about."

His eyes dance between Harley and me, then finally settle on our mother.

"I'll be around this evening though, mom," he reaches out, taking her in his arms in a tight hug.

"Love you, baby," I hear her say in his chest.

"Love you too," he kisses the top of her head. Lawson releases her and turns to me.

"I know I threw you into all of that... but you should be proud. I'm proud of you."

His eyes are earnest, assuming the role of both big brother and father. He wraps his arms around me, and I groan back at him.

"Please don't kill each other while I'm gone," he says in my ear.

"I'll try not to," I say back to him, squeezing his shoulders.

We release each other as he starts to turn away.

"See ya later Harls," he calls over his shoulder.

"Gee thanks, was starting to feel left out of the lovefest," they shout back to him.

"Ha!" Lawson laughs as he gets into his car, taking off a bit too quickly from the small lot.

"Shit. He has my bag in his car," I say, staring at his disappearing taillights.

"He'll be at the house later like he said, don't worry," Harley shrugs and heads towards my mother's car. I guess they came together.

"Hey, mom..." I say, catching her before she can walk away too. She turns back, green eyes sincere.

"I'm sorry... for being M.I.A. I just... I needed – "

"You needed time. Space to process," she offers, finishing my sentence perfectly. "I understand. I would never blame you. What's important is that you know that we're here. Always and especially now," she says sternly as she reaches up to wrap her arms around my shoulders.

I welcome her comfort like a much-needed blanket on a cold night. Like so many times before, she knows exactly what to say, how to calm a raging storm, especially the ones inside my own head. I wrap my arms tightly around her and squeeze my eyes shut just so the tears don't fall.

"Ouch Nola," she laughs a bit breathlessly. "You're getting stronger, so you have to watch yourself. Especially when you dig a book into my spine."

I drop my arms immediately. I had completely forgotten about the book that I was using as a lifeline.

"Damnit, I never checked it out..." I say looking back towards the door.

"It's alright. Jerry won't mind," she looks down at the book cover and nods. "I suspect there's a lot we have to talk about..."

The cover stares back at us... *The History of Angels in Cross*. The stories this book must hold. Stories I can't wait to devour no matter how much they terrify me.

"Yeah..." I rub my thumb over the beveled title.

"But I think you and Harley should catch up."

Right on cue, a loud horn honks in the small parking lot. I

turn towards the noise and see Harley leaning over the middle console of my mother's car, hand hovering over the wheel. They sit back, tap a vacant wrist, and then mime eating a large burger.

"Lunch first it is," my mother shakes her head incredulously as she starts towards the car.

I laugh at Harley feigning an absurdly dramatic famished state in the backseat but my stomach growls in agreement. A reminder that breakfast never happened since I was too nervous for whatever Lawson was dragging me into. Now, I could use all the sustenance for what's coming next.

"So, turns out I'm adopted," Harley starts, mid chew of a bite of their sandwich.

I nearly choke on mine. We had taken our respective sandwiches outside on the back porch of my mother's house to talk through everything. Now, coughing to clear my airway of bread, I almost drop the sandwich from my lap.

"I'm sorry what?" I say, eyes wide, trying to find some kind of joke in their eyes.

"Yeah... Well, I didn't know until I turned 21 and then this showed up."

Harley holds up their hand, revealing their wrist with the small black wing.

"I knew something was off before that, but I just wrote it off as bad days or whatever," they shrug. "Then it was my birthday, and something felt really wrong and the burning... it was all too much... I know I wasn't much fun that day."

I think back to the hot August day. It was right before we both went off to our junior years. One last hurrah. I remember Harley not wanting to have a big celebration, just wanting to go to our favorite restaurant and get a margarita. They typically served us without carding, but Harley made a big show of taking their ID out and placing it in the waiter's hand. I stuck with water.

I try to rack my brain to figure out what, if anything, was off about them. I guess the only thing that felt off was Harley not wanting to go out and celebrate. They had told me that they just wanted to feel more refined, and we laughed.

"I never thought anything of it..." I say, back to reality. I wipe my thumb at the corners of my mouth.

"I guess I hid it better than I realized..." Harley gives me a sad smile. "Anyways, Lawson came to me the next day and told me what it all meant. Explained that I was a Nephilim, left at a fire station as a baby. Talk about fucking world shattering. Finding out that not only am I not human, but my parents also aren't really my parents. Worst of all, I can't tell them. And I'm stuck on assignment at Low College."

My heart breaks with every word. Harley was alone... I never noticed any of this was going on with them. Maybe I should've paid closer attention. Should've asked more questions. I should've been there for them. My breathing starts to choke up in my throat like my sandwich was just trying to do. I want to apologize but something else catches in my mind and the only thing that comes out is a single word.

"Assignment?" I ask around the lump in my throat.

"Yeah, I'm keeping tabs on a small group of demons there. They seem harmless but it feels like something is stirring. I guess I have you to thank for that. You and your boyfriend," they smile deviously at me but there's a prickling edge in their brown eyes.

"Ah..." the sound hanging in the air around us. "I really am sorry. I don't – didn't think that this is what this would all turn into. Who would've thought this was the world that we were a part of?" I search for words as I try to absorb her truth.

None of it makes sense, hasn't made sense since my birthday, but I find some comfort in Harley being by my side. A pit of sadness opens at my core, Harley went through all of that alone and all the while my brother knew everything. I can't help the pang of jealousy but also relief that he was there for them, always the big brother to both of us.

"Why... why didn't you tell me?" I ask.

"For the same reason, you're probably struggling with telling Ash. Maybe even me before this morning," they say thoughtfully.

The different scenarios run through my head. Me telling Ash. Her conversation is more difficult. Probably world shattering. The possibility of having her walk out of my life knowing all the things that go bump in the night is high on my fears. Or worse, her sticking by my side and something terrible happening. The same scenarios played in my head before this morning with Harley as well. Ash has already experienced so much because of me. But my mind goes darker, both of them ending up cold... dead.

A shiver runs up my spine.

"Maybe it's better if she doesn't know. Safer so she isn't dragged into it all," Harley continues, seeming to have read my mind.

"Yeah, maybe..."

The somber reality seeps in. Maybe I can keep up the

façade, at least until the immediate danger is gone. But with Ash wanting to be with Jace... how much longer until the threat is right in front of her?

If we don't all die.

My subconscious, who has been suspiciously quiet, chimes in from her armored throne. I smack her back down.

"I'm sorry that you had to go through all of that by yourself though Harl. I wish I was there for you..."

"You were."

Harley reaches over, placing their hand over my shoulder, their eyes speaking volumes.

"Besides I had Lawson. He may be an asshole but he's a good man," they push my arm and we both laugh, relaxing into one another.

"Yeah, he is," I smile out to our childhood backyard.

Jealousy washes away, replaced by gratitude for my asshole brother.

Dinner passes in a blink. Lawson came by for a quick bite, to drop off my bag, and to make sure everything was alright. I hugged him a bit tighter as he was leaving.

"Thank you. For so much but for right now, everything you've done for Harl," I say quietly to him. He nods knowingly against my shoulder.

We break apart quickly.

"Have fun at training tomorrow!" he waves back to us, looking pointedly at Harley and I.

He had so slyly bowed out of training, opting to spend the Saturday with his family. The lucky duck. But I couldn't stop the darker thoughts that popped into my head. Maybe he's spending this time with them because he thinks he won't have much longer with them... I shake it off quickly.

"We will! Can't wait to beat that Cael guy's ass!" Harley says excitedly, nearly foaming at the mouth.

"Hey!"

My mother slaps their arm but doesn't hide the smile spreading across her face.

"Goodnight, guys," Lawson grabs the front door and is out the house in the same beat.

It feels like a piece of me leaves with him. My big brother, sticking by my side like he always has – when we weren't fighting against each other. I can't help but love the man that my brother has turned into. Even with his overprotectiveness, that's always been his heart. And he has a big heart, one as big as our father's. If things were different, I can't help but imagine if our father would be by our side just as willingly as Lawson and our mother has. Would my whole family stay by my side as we face possible death?

"So, what are we doing now ladies? Since the old boring married guy is gone. Shots?" Harley spins in the hallway around us.

My mother and I share a knowing look as we all giggle.

"I think I'll be heading to bed," my mother recovers from her fit of laughter. "As should you both. Rest is important for proper training," she puts on her mom voice that is never too far away, demanding yet kind.

"Ughhh!" Harley groans. "Okay *mom*," they roll their eyes but smile fondly at my mother, giving her the usual sass.

"You guys are so boring, but I love ya."

"We love you too Harley," my mother says before I can.

"You're all set up in the guest room. I'll see both of you off in the morning," she turns, heading up the stairs to her room.

"Okay now that she is gone..." Harley turns to me eagerly. "Shots?"

A short burst of laughter springs from my chest.

"I wish! But I think she's right. We should get some rest. I could use it," even now I can feel the familiar ache in my bones, but there's something else drawing me to my childhood room.

"Fine. Goodnight party pooper."

Harley shoves my shoulder as they pass heading towards the same stairs my mother went up, and I shove them right back.

"Geez, you are getting stronger. Maybe it's you who I need to worry about tomorrow," they rub at their arm dramatically.

"Yeah, yeah. Goodnight!"

I quickly do my rounds on the first floor, making sure doors and windows are locked, a habit I've become more anal about since the shadows started moving in my mind. Turning off the lights, I take the stairs two at a time. In the safety of my room, my eyes fly to the book sitting squarely on the nightstand.

The History of Angels in Cross

Picking up the book, I flop on my stomach and run my hands over the title. Odd, it's the only lettering on the cover and spine. Flipping it over, there's nothing on the back except a sticker with the barcode. There's not even a by line. Nothing but the title.

Taking a deep breath, I open the book. Just another simple title page followed by a couple of blank pages, then the Table of Contents. My eyes scan the list and automatically stop.

"No way..."

At this point, I feel like nothing should shock me, but I turn the pages ferociously only stopping once I find the page:

~

The Battle of Cross 1622-24 (Later known as The Battle of Edge)

Since the beginning of time, Cross has been holy ground protected and governed by Angels, under the jurisdiction of the Holy One's personal guard. Cross was a place where Angels lived in peace and harmony with each other.

That was until the Holy One introduced man...

Many in Cross were concerned that the lesser beings would only bring about destruction because they did not know or understand their ways. Many from the old guard rebelled and fled the Holy City.

One Angel, Lailah, her faction, and followers, stayed to protect Cross. For several generations, all was still peaceful. The few Angels left in Cross helped man advance and they were grateful.

But peace was short-lived when a radical group of men from a southern town called Edge ventured north into Cross in 1619. The men presented many goods for trading, goods that came from the water. It wasn't long before an argument broke out between the group of men and another trades group of Cross. Lailah came to intervene and the argument dissipated.

Shortly after, Lailah was scarcely seen around town and whispers started that she had run away with one of the men. When Lailah was seen again, she had a small child with her. A boy. Some kept their distance from the strange new boy but eventually, he was welcomed into the town.

Lailah confided in few that the child was hers. Little was known about a child of an Angel and man and soon everyone was talking about what the boy might be. It wasn't long before The Fallen arrived. Led by Eligor, they confronted Lailah about her child. She refused to give him up, instead choosing to fight those who were once her brothers and sisters.

And thus, the Battle of Cross began.

The Battle waged for two years. Prolonged by man's involvement from both Cross and Edge. Both towns had welcomed the child and so it was their fight to protect him against Eligor's faction. The Battle was bloody with many lives lost. The final count is unknown, but it is said that some 70,000 souls were lost. All men and only a handful of Angels were among the lost. In the end, all accounts state that there was a blinding white light, like an explosion, and then silence.

Those who could see through the light, tell of what happened: Eligor held the child with one large hand clasped around his neck, the other plunged deep into his chest. At the moment of impact, the explosion of light consumed them both. It is said that in the silence, one could still hear Lailah's wail for her lost child.

Her boy, the first Nephilim.

I read and reread the last paragraph until it feels like the words are no longer on the page but instead, branded into my mind. The images flash before my eyes, an angel falling in love with a human, a baby, the angels coming back refusing to accept the small child, a bloody battle... the same battle from the painting in my library room. I can see the angel reaching out to the man bloodied on the bed. Maybe the image is less spiritual and more literal... or both I guess.

Closing the book, I stare up at my ceiling, but the images are still there, even in the grooves of the textured ceiling. The darkness behind my eyelids isn't helping either. A nagging pull to keep reading nearly forces me to open the book again but the image of a small boy being ripped apart by angels refuses to leave my mind.

Is that going to be me? Will I be ripped apart with everyone I love dead around me?

I dig the heels of my hands into my eyes until I see stars. At least that's better than the boy. Better than my own self being ripped apart. Somehow, sleep comes. It's restless and panicked, but it's sleep. My own arms reaching out to the boy but never able to get to him. And then, my own arm plunged into the boy's chest, his pale unseeing eyes looking up at me as we're taken with the light.

TWENTY-FOUR

"Are you alright Nola?" Harley's voice reaches me from the other side of the kitchen table.

I force my tired eyes away from the half-eaten bagel in front of me.

"Yeah," I lie. "Yeah, I'm fine, just didn't sleep well," I add, so it's not a total lie.

"Right," Harley's skeptical eyes peer into mine, always watching. I know that they can read through me.

"Alright," my mother's voice comes from the bottom of the stairs. "It's time for you guys to get a move on. Nola, you can take my car. Harley knows where to go."

She rounds the corner, surprisingly cheery, even at this ungodly hour of the morning. I glance at the window behind her, yep, the sun is only just starting to rise. She's holding her arm behind her back, something she only does when she would give us presents when we were kids.

"Make sure she doesn't leave here without a snack,"

Harley's voice now coming from next to me. They shove their thumb toward me. "I don't want her to be cranky from lack of sleep or lack of food."

Harley leaves the room quickly but not before they grab a banana from the bunch on the counter. Distantly, I can hear them bounding up the stairs, they must be getting a bag or something before training.

"Here," my mother pulls the chair out next to me and sits.

From behind her back, she reveals what she's holding. A brown leather sheath with a golden handle sitting at the top of the opening. She holds the sword out to me.

"Is this what I think it is?" I ask timidly, but my hand reaches for the Euch without me telling it to do so.

She places it into my outstretched hands.

"Yes," she answers simply.

The leather is smooth like the other sheathes I've been working with. Feeling its full weight, I'm a bit surprised at how light it feels. Lighter than the others. I wrap my fingers around the golden handle and feel the familiar burn flash through my wing. But this burning isn't uncomfortable, it's not the warning that I've grown used to when around Blake. Instead, it relaxes the constant knot of emotions at my core. I can feel the strength of it coursing through me. Slowly, I pull the handle, revealing more of the silver blade. It looks sharp and deadly, but the fear of that thought doesn't come. At the base of the blade right under the handle, there are several lines inscribed on the blade.

"It means 'The Light,'" my mother's soft voice translates the scribbles.

"Wow..." I search for the right words. "I mean, I thought it would be different. Like, look different, grander maybe? But it feels..."

"Good? Like it was meant for you?" my mother finishes, every possibility correct.

"Yeah. Exactly," I push the sheath back up the blade, feeling a strong protective urge over it.

"I should get going. Shouldn't keep Harl waiting too long," I stand, gripping the Euch tightly.

There are so many things I want to say to her. I want to apologize for how I've acted over the past month. Apologize for being distant and not knowing the right words. Apologize for being angry at her for just keeping me safe. And the biggest apology, or maybe it's thanks, for her walking into this battle at my side. I wish more than anything she didn't have to, that none of them have to. But my gratefulness overshadows the underlying fears that threaten to overtake my body.

I can feel all of the words right at the tip of my tongue but all that comes out is, "Thank you, mom... for everything."

I throw my arms around her in a quick hug. Breathing in her comforting scent and feeling her warmth, it takes me a moment to let her go.

"You're going to crush me, honey," she says, patting my back in mercy.

"Oops. Sorry," I let her go, giving her a shy smile.

"Go on. Arlo will have my head if you're late," she places her hand at the small of my back, pushing me towards the door.

"Love you!" I call back to her as new excitement buzzes through me from the Euch.

Let's see what this baby can do.

The drive to the gym is short. We hit every green light on the way and with no traffic this morning, we fly through the streets. Harley yells directions over the pump-up music they've chosen, refusing to turn it down even one notch. I throw the car into park outside the gym and my ears are blessed with a moment of silence when I cut the engine. Harley nearly bounces out of the car before it's fully stopped. There's only one other car in the lot that I immediately recognize as Arlo's.

"Wonder if that Cael guy is here..." Harley balances on the curb with arms outstretched.

They look more like the kid that used to come over every Christmas to play with all the new toys we had than the 21-year-old badass Nephilim of recent.

I smile and shrug as I open the back door to get the Euch out.

"I really hope not. I can't stand the idea of having someone babysitting me. I already have enough of that with you all."

I roll my eyes as I pass them, grabbing the handle of the gym door.

"Yeah, and we don't even get paid for it!" Harley scoffs, skipping through the door.

Our laughter bubbles up and echoes in the high beamed ceiling.

"Oh, so good of you two to grace us with your presence!" Arlo's deep sarcasm reaches us from the other side of the gym.

The set-up is fairly similar to Arlo's gym down in Edge. The only difference being that this gym is larger and more open with windows lining the wall perpendicular to the mirrors. Instead of matted flooring occupying half of the gym, there is a boxing ring here. Next to the ring is a case and large tin drum filled with different weapons. The equipment is still the same, a row of treadmills, bikes, ellipticals... everything you would need for cardio. And mountains of weightlifting equipment.

"Apologies for the delay sir," I say just as sarcastically. "Had to get this bad boy," I hold up the Euch.

"You have it..." Cael's deep voice comes from next to me. I nearly jump out of my skin but some instinct in me pulls the sword closer to my chest.

"Fuck!" Harley shouts. "Where the hell did you come from?!"

"Sorry," he looks down, his cheeks flush a bit. "I was standing right there when you walked in."

He shifts his hand towards the weapons in the corner and I follow his exposed muscled arm towards the space.

"Is that actually the Euch?" he asks, turning back to me.

His emerald eyes explore mine. I notice that now without his glasses, there are flecks of orange and yellow in them.

"Um..." I peel my eyes away from his intensity. "Yes, it is."

"Good, then Sister Laine came through on her promise," Cael's voice hinting at a bit of surprise.

"What's with the doubt?" I squint my eyes at him.

He shrugs dismissively, turning towards Arlo, as my stomach twists with distaste.

"Are we ready to get started?" Arlo asks excitedly now standing in front of us.

Harley claps their hands together.

"Born ready," they answer, rubbing their hands together.

The session starts, as usual, cardio. And lots of it. Mileage and speed having increased over the last several sessions with Arlo, it takes a solid hour before I start to feel any sort of exhaustion slipping into my muscles. Once sprints are done, it's on to weights. Harley cracks jokes every once in a while, breaking focus just to have a laugh or make a snotty remark about Cael. I try my hardest to keep my eyes off of his muscles flexing under his shirt. But every once in a while, I catch his eyes in the mirrors. The intensity is similar to Blake's but totally different at the same time.

Blake... the dull ache of panic flares in my chest, I haven't heard from him and I've been so consumed with everything here. Guilt bubbles up as I stop mid rep, not caring what number I was on. I walk away from the weights and start pacing. The past couple of nights I went to sleep with a bit of hope that maybe I would see him. So that I could tell him everything that is going on here, tell him how I may have gotten some backup. But he never came to see me in my dreams. I lift my arms over my head to stretch my muscles or maybe to cover up my racing thoughts. The ache burns with longing to see him again or to even hear his voice, to feel his familiar burn.

"Earth to Nola!" Harley nearly shouts next to me. I look up to see them holding out a water bottle for me.

"Sorry," I say sheepishly, grabbing the offering.

"Wanna watch me kick Cael's ass?"

"Like you even have to ask," I smile at them then gulp down the cool water.

"Actually," Arlo starts walking up to us. "I hope it's not too big of a disappointment, but I thought we would spar together Harley. Mix up the playing field?" he shrugs nonchalantly.

Harley looks him up and down, making a show of it, then shrugs a bit deflated.

"I'll go easy on you," they tell him coolly, starting past him towards the weapons.

"Ha!" Arlo's laugh travels up to the high ceilings with ours.

"I'd like to see you try," he turns to follow Harley to the corner.

"Guess that leaves us," Cael says, walking towards me.

"Guess so," I don't bother paying attention to see if he follows me back to the bench where I left the Euch.

Arlo and Harley are already in the ring, Harley with a long wooden staff and Arlo with two small knives. Cael starts towards the weapons; I watch him carefully as he examines several before deciding on a sword. With a determined set to his shoulders, he walks back to me and holds out the sword to me.

"Oh no, I'm good," I say, my hand holding tightly around the handle of the Euch.

I let it fill me with the same energy as earlier, easing my muscles and my mind.

"Just hold it for me for a second."

"Okay..."

I grab the sword noticing the weighted difference. He leans around me and starts to push the benches around us away about five feet. Making our own makeshift ring. Out of the corner of my eye, I catch a couple walking along the windows with a small child.

"Isn't this a bit too open?" I say nodding towards the windows.

"Don't worry, they can't see in. There's a large mural of the town out there covering the windows."

Refocusing, I can see the small circles on the other side of the windows, the different shades creating a large picture.

"Oh."

"Ready?" he holds out his hand to me expectantly.

I nod, placing his sword back in his hand.

"Alright, go to your corner," he tilts his head to look behind me.

I move quickly, the adrenaline pumping in my ears. This part has quickly become my favorite part of training. Feeling all the strength in my muscles coil then explode with each blow. Learning each move before Arlo can land them, but this isn't Arlo, this is someone new. A Nephilim only here to watch me, test me, and figure out what I'm really worth to report back to Jeremiah.

I nod at him.

Cael nods back.

We start in a circle, each of us sizing up the other. My hands feel slick against the golden handle with sweat, but the energy continues to vibrate up my arms burning brightly at my wing.

I lunge forward, but Cael blocks me quickly with a loud clang of our swords together. He smiles brightly at me as he pushes me back. I falter only a step then lunge at him again, this time going lower for his legs. Again, he steps out of the way, easily blocking my move. I huff and quickly shift my weight to strike again once to his right, then again to his left. He blocks the blow to his right but is thrown off by the swift blow to his left arm. He advances then, sword high, I block him just before the sword can land above my head. While my arms are still in the air, he takes advantage of this by quickly shifting the point of his sword to find the middle of my chest. I feel the point, but he doesn't dig in, he knows he won the round.

"Again," I huff at him, anger building with the loss.

He nods, moving to his corner, a small smile playing on his lips.

I turn back to my own corner and nod at him once I'm

ready. The second round begins just as swiftly. Except for this time, I wait him out and he makes the first move, a swing to my left. I move quickly and doge out of the way having anticipated the move by his half step forward. He swings back quickly to my right, and I throw the Euch up. With the same loud clang as before, I know it was a good block. I push him back with my elbow. He only shifts slightly as my arm digs into his chest. With a grunt, I shove him with my shoulder, using my weight and the strength coursing through me with the Euch. He stumbles backward a few steps but before I can get my sword up to his center, his foot knocks my legs from under me. I land hard on my back, all the air leaving my lungs. The tip of his sword stops right above my heart, and he smiles down at me.

I'm getting really tired of seeing that stupid smile.

My subconscious finally agrees with me, her armor shifting as she stands. I stand with her knocking his sword away. The anger has fully shifted to rage, I know Cael is going to report back to Jeremiah and they're going to laugh as they leave us in the dust. Leave us to fight and possibly die alone.

I can't let that happen.

My mind shifts tactics. Obviously, Cael is a worthy opponent when it comes to combat but maybe a distraction could work to my advantage.

"So, what's Jeremiah's deal?" I start, focusing on each step Cael takes in our circle. I counter each step with my own.

"What do you mean?"

His question is casual, but his eyebrows pinch together. A tell for how thrown off he is by my conversation mid sparring match.

"I mean, why does he have a stick up his ass?" I tilt my head at him. Amusement dances briefly behind his eyes before he throws up his business-like persona again.

"He's not so bad."

"Oh yeah?" I counter. "He's not all candy and rainbows from what I can gather and you're stuck keeping tabs on me."

"I needed the workout," he shrugs. "And there are worse things I could be doing."

He lunges quickly. The move catches me off guard and I'm almost a second too late at the block. Maybe this conversation thing wasn't the best move.

"Besides, I owe him."

I shove back at him.

"Yeah? And you're what? Paying your dues by being here?"

"Kinda," he resets his shoulders as he lifts his head up. "He got me out of a really tricky situation when I didn't have a home to turn to, took me under his wing. He's been the only parental figure I've known."

Again, he shrugs like he didn't just tell me he was an orphan.

"Oh..."

He lunges again but this time I expect it, blocking and responding with my own quick move to his right, he ducks just in time.

"And when he tells me to keep tabs on a Nephilim," he says the word like he isn't one, with the similar distaste that Jeremiah said it.

"No matter how beautiful..." he pauses, letting panic flash across his face. I feel my heart stutter in my chest. No way he just said that... He recovers quickly and starts circling around our ring again.

"Err, or a Nephilim who has gone and put a target on her

back with the Devil by getting involved with a filthy demon," he spits the word at me as his face turns up in a snarl.

Suddenly, all I see is red. The world tilts as a white-hot rage flames through me. I swing the Euch with every ounce of strength in me. I swear I can feel every cell in my body exploding with it as I swing and lunge blow after blow. Cael blocks some but most catch him off guard. I try to find anything in me to care if I actually hurt the guy, but nothing comes. This guy not only thinks less of me because of who I am but because of who I love. My rage knocks Cael to the ground and I kneel on his chest, the Euch at his neck. My lungs quickly fill and deflate with exertion, but I don't care. I stare at the blade digging further into his neck. He grunts back and I falter.

I'm no killer.

At least not now. Not ever... if I can help it.

Definitely not Cael.

No matter how annoying and infuriating he is. He's like me no matter how much he hates it and there are only so few of us left. Suddenly, the dreams from last night flood back into my mind. My hands through the small Nephilim's chest.

No.

I pull back, lessening the pressure of the blade on his throat. He brings his free hand up and rubs at the red line there. Slowly, he smiles up at me.

"Good."

He approves of my rage, the thought twists my stomach in knots. I get up quickly, adding just a bit more pressure to his chest as I do so, and head back to my corner. Ready to go again.

~

"That Cael, while an absolute dick, isn't bad to look at," Harley says casually, staring out their window on our drive back to the house.

Harley and I had been driving in silence for a few minutes before her comment. The rage from earlier still simmers under the surface but it dims with every passing second, every new mile that distances us from the gym. Mixed with the simmering rage, something else starts to bloom, intrigue maybe...

"Yeah... maybe..." I answer Harley, trying to shove all those thoughts about Cael in a steel box and chain it up in the corner of my mind.

To be forgotten.

Just then my phone vibrates in my jacket pocket. I glance at it quickly, trying to keep my eyes on the road. It's a number I don't recognize and my thumb hovers over the decline button. But something in me stops myself from pressing it.

"I mean if you're into the nerdy jock type..." Harley continues, and I can hear the smile on her face.

My phone vibrates one more time in my hand before I hit the answer button.

"Hello?" I say to whoever is on the other end. I feel Harley shift to look over at me.

"Hey Nola," Cael's voice comes from the other end. "I'm sorry to call like this but Arlo gave me your number."

Damnit, Arlo.

"I wanted to compliment you on today's training session, I was... impressed," he says smugly.

"Thank you?"

Harley waves their hand over at me. They mouth, 'who is it?' with their hand up to their ear like they're on the phone. I roll my eyes back at them as I mouth, 'Cael.' Harley wiggles their eyebrows at me. I stop a little short just to get them to stop.

"You're welcome," Cael says. "Anyways, I wanted to ask if you were available tonight?"

"Um..." I try to ignore the extra thump in my heart and focus on the confusion that fills my brain. "Possibly, why?"

"Well, I have a mission that I could use some help with, and since you did so well today..."

Relief flashes through me. Of course, he wouldn't ask me on a date. But he's asking me to go with him to help with whatever this mission is... I wonder if it's going to be like the hospital, reaping a soul. Nerves rattle in my stomach. I've never actually reaped a soul. Is that what I'm supposed to do during this mission?

It's a test, this is all a test.

Cael has probably already reported back to Jeremiah about our session and now this... whatever it is. They're still testing me, making sure I'm worthy enough to fight with. I know it.

I can't give them any doubts.

"Okay," I say, turning into my neighborhood. "I'm in."

TWENTY-FIVE

I stare at the address for a few seconds before looking up from Cael's text to the house in front of me, the ball of nerves tightens in my chest.

Definitely the right address... but where's Cael?

It's a part of Cross I've only ever driven through. The houses were too nice to actually stop at or know anyone when we were growing up to be invited to places like this. This is the side of town with debutante balls, country clubs, and private parties. I knew a few people from here in school, but we were never on a first name basis. They passed by in the hallways dressed in name brand flowy blouses, skirts, clean pressed button ups, and slacks. Heels clicking on the dirty tile floor without bothering to glance in my direction.

Several people walk by dressed like those kids from school except there's no restrictive dress code here. Well, maybe there is because no one is dressed like me. I feel completely out of place as I pull down the waist of my hoodie nervously.

I would've found something from my mom's closet back home if I had known, but that would've delayed me further. And I already tried to delay as much as I could by begging Harley to come with me to this place if only for some kind of support, but the conversation was short with Harley insisting that they needed to get back to school.

"You'll be alright," Harley had said with conviction filling their brown eyes. "Sure, you'll have to deal with that stupidly attractive asshole, but you'll be fine."

I don't know how they were so convinced I would be fine because I don't feel fine. I feel unwelcome by some of the small glances from the people walking by.

Where is he?

"You look like a lost puppy."

Looking over, I see Arlo stepping up onto the sidewalk from crossing the street.

Okay, so I caved.

When Harley couldn't come, I thought I would be fine alone, but on the way here, the racing thoughts got the best of me, so I called Arlo.

Seeing him now, a warmth floods through me and loosens the tight ball of nerves. Even with the smug look on his face right now, I know I made the right decision.

"Thank you for coming," I ignore his comment, smiling at him.

"Of course," he smiles back at me and buttons his suit coat.

"Oh, so you got the memo apparently," I pinch my shoulders together. Something as comforting as my hoodie now feels so profoundly uncomfortable.

"Pshhh... this old thing?" He asks as he runs his hands over the front of his coat like he's brushing off dust but ironically, it's perfectly clean.

"Had it for years. Just happened to pack it for this trip," Arlo shrugs.

"Right... So, you had no idea about this? And I'm not talking about when I just called you to come with me."

Arlo sighs deeply, a smile still playing on his lips as he straightens his shoulders.

"I knew there was a possibility of them testing you. But I didn't know it would be this," he looks up towards the large, overpriced house that several people dressed in chic outfits are going into.

"And what is this?" I ask Arlo, but my eyes stay on the house consuming the designer people.

Just then Cael comes out of it dressed in a fitted black suit with a white shirt and matching tie. The steel box that houses the way Cael's muscles flexed during training this morning rattles in its padlocked corner of my brain. His hazel eyes lock onto mine from behind his glasses as he takes the few steps down from the front door.

My heart flutters.

Fuck, stop that, Nola.

"You could've put more effort into your outfit Nola," Cael says in a loud fake whisper.

My heart instantly freezes over. Guilt, shame, and hatred for this guy flashes across my face. Blake was a bit rude at the beginning, but he had a reason. Even if I didn't know it at the time, he was trying to keep his distance because, well because he's a demon, and he... But he was never this big of a dick.

"It doesn't matter," Cael continues, his judgment shifting to Arlo beside me. "I wasn't expecting you here."

"Nola asked me to join—"

"It doesn't matter," Cael repeats, cutting Arlo off. "I could use both of you in there. We will have to make do with whatever you're wearing."

The hostility rolling off of him in waves meshes with his business attitude. I've never seen someone switch personalities so quickly before. The softer, more reserved, Cael from the council meeting is nowhere to be found in these harsh eyes looking me up and down.

"This event is being hosted by Mayor Madeline," Cael turns, facing the house with us.

Of course, I noticed its size being comparably larger than the others in this ritzy neighborhood, but I didn't think it was the Mayor of Cross's house.

"They're raising funds for the new children's hospital. At least that's the cover."

"The cover?" I look over at Cael, his gaze still on the house. Watchful of everyone going in and out of it.

"Well, our lovely Mayor has been soulless for several years now."

I feel Arlo tense up next to me. The air shifts causing a chill to run up my spine. The Mayor of my hometown is soulless... I mean, I guess that's why I never really aligned with her stances and policies she's been trying to put in place. My heart skips in my chest with fear. How am I supposed to walk into someone's house who's soulless? I always expected the worst case possible when Lawson mentioned soulless people. I never would've thought that someone of power, someone this close to my home, would be one

"And while they might be raising some funds from some of

the people here," Cael continues matter of factly. "Much darker things are going on inside."

"Wait, can we take a few steps back?"

Cael audibly groans but I take that as my opportunity to keep talking out all the swirling thoughts trying to escape my mouth in a rush.

"The Mayor has been soulless for a while now, right? Why haven't you guys done anything? Like why is she still, I don't know the Mayor of Cross?"

"You're not asking the right questions, Nola," Cael shakes his head, then finds my eyes. "And we can't interfere like that. Getting involved in cleaning up every mess the demons make, especially in politics, can get complicated."

"We have to pick and choose our battles, Nola," Arlo chimes in with agreement.

I nod. It makes sense but it still doesn't sit well with me.

"Right, and we're here to stop the darker things going on?"

"You're going to need this," Cael holds his hand out in front of me.

Ignoring the brush of his fingertips on my palm, he places a small knife in my hand. Its energy pulses through me. It's not as strong as the Euch felt earlier today, nowhere near as strong, but its warm energy gives me enough strength that I feel like I could walk through these large white doors ahead of me and fight. Nerves pushed aside; I feel ready.

I slip the knife into my hoodie pocket.

"Alright, so what's the plan?"

I catch Cael's smile out of the corner of my eye.

"There are a couple of demons working this party," he answers, all traces of the smile now gone. "They work closely with the Mayor and are here to sell and solicit to the patrons.

We're here to stop them but not make a scene. Do you understand?"

A couple walks by hand in hand. They look about mid-forties and are dressed exquisitely. The man dressed in a black tux and holding his partner's sparkly clutch in his free hand. She has a floor length evening dress on with lace accents complimenting the blush of her dress and her skin. They're beautiful. Smiling at one another, they walk the short steps up into the Mayor's house. They have no idea what they've just walked into a party with darkness lurking inside.

I nod, looking back at Cael and Arlo.

"Yeah, I understand."

"Let's head in then," Cael says, already taking a step forward.

Arlo locks eyes with me as he follows.

"You're alright?" he whispers only to me.

"Yeah," I reach into my pocket and grip the handle of the knife there, letting it give me strength. "Yeah, I'm good."

It almost doesn't feel like a lie.

My feet push me forward as I follow them up the front steps. The warmth within the house coming from the open door invites us in. We walk through without any trouble, and I let out a breath. It's odd there doesn't seem to be any security here. But I guess with demons walking around, the Mayor might not want anyone intervening with any of the chaos she's agreed to have tonight.

The house opens up into a giant foyer with grand staircases on either side leading up to a second floor. I look up and am almost blinded by the massive crystal chandelier that's casting bright beams of light all over the room. The beams dance around the room, reflecting off all of the shiny dresses and crystal glasses. Illuminating the subtly textured wallpaper, ornate portraits, and landscape paintings that cover the walls. I recognize some of the portraits from past Mayors to the founding family of Cross. Even the landscape paintings, ranging from the war to the city skyline at sunset are all familiar to me. I've seen all of them either in history books in school or in the art books my father used to show me when I begged him.

I feel the dig into my shoulder, bringing me back to reality. A woman in a dress sparkling almost as much as the chandelier barely spares me a glance of apathy as if she didn't just bump into me. Anger bubbles up in my chest at the annoyance. I hope she can feel my eyes burning in the back of her perfectly combed hair. She walks briskly, arm and arm, with a tall hand-some man. I watch as they reach the bottom of the stairs on the right side of the room, but I don't follow as they ascend because my eyes have already drifted to another part of the room.

Beneath the stairs something dark moves. My heart stops as a chill freezes my core. I have to blink a few times to adjust to the only dark spot in the room. Two figures emerge. They're young, early twenties maybe. The guy is dressed in an untucked white button down with a loose blue tie, the girl in a simple black minidress. They blend, almost too well, but the chill in my stomach thaws with the phantom burning on my wrists.

"There they are," Cael's voice is a hypnotic whisper right in my ear.

I didn't realize he was right there but ignoring the unease at his proximity, I tighten my grip on the knife in my pocket, letting its power drive my feet forward. Right towards these two demons.

Don't make a scene... Get them alone, outside of the party...

My head buzzes with the plan and the rest of the party falls away. My subconscious is in warrior mode, with armor, and the Euch in her hand. Her eagerness is heightened by the knife in my pocket and it's intoxicating.

Somewhere in the distance glass shatters.

It takes a moment for my feet to stop moving forward. It takes even longer to register that the high-pitched noise that followed the glass shatter is a scream.

I peel my eyes away from the couple of demons and turn around to the sound. I half expected the whole party to stop but some people seem to have not noticed the scream, too enthralled with their conversations or the sparkly drinks in their hands. But several people have turned like me towards the noise.

A small crowd moves in the direction, out of the large foyer into a room on the right. I follow closely behind, hand still on my hidden knife. It seems to be some sort of living room, but all the furniture is gone. The only decorations are a massive brick fireplace and more paintings.

Another scream pierces through me.

I wince against the sound to find its source. Shoving past a few people, I see her.

Her midnight blue dress wrinkles around her waist and pools on the floor around her. Her once perfect makeup flows like a muddied river down her cheeks with each sob. Tearstained eyes seeing nothing but the boy's face in her hands.

He can't be more than 18.

I watch as his body twitches on the ground, releasing the knife in my pocket as my body locks in place. Bile rises in my throat, and I want more than anything to be able to look away, but I can't. My body won't let me.

So, I stay, staring into the boy's pale brown eyes.

"Help me!" the woman pleads through sobs, holding onto the boy. "Someone please help me!"

I know what's happening. I've seen it more times than I can count.

The scene before me shifts. Instead of this unknown boy's brown eyes, it's my father's eyes no longer seeing me or the world around him. I came to show him a beautiful painting in my art book. He always loves them and tells me stories about the painting or another painting he's seen a million times, the colors dancing on the page with every word. But this time, he didn't move, didn't even blink. Even at 10, I knew something was wrong. The memory of my scream for help scratches at my throat. I can still feel my mom's strong, sure hands on my shoulders. I didn't know at the time that this wasn't the first time she'd brought my dad back from the brink.

"Get out of the way Nola," Cael's voice comes out in a whispered growl behind me.

He shoves past, snapping me back to reality. Or some version of reality. The boy is still overdosing on the floor in front of all of us. He's still staring at the ceiling, becoming paler by the second and the woman is still holding on crying for help. I feel just as helpless as I did when it was my dad in the place of the boy on the floor. Except now I don't have the comfort of my mother.

Instead, Cael reaches the boy and leans down. He offers some words of comfort to the woman that I can't hear as he places his hand on her shoulder. His other hand moves to the boy's neck. Feeling for a pulse.

My breath stills in my chest and clinches my throat.

I have to do something. Why won't my body move!?

All the fight has drained out of me, replaced by ice cold fear. Cael reaches into his suit coat and pulls out a small square package. Flipping it open quickly, he pulls out something small that looks like a vial. Tears fill my eyes as I watch Cael move the boy so that he's laying flat on the floor. If I blinked I would've missed how Cael administered the medicine into the boy's nose. The exact same way my mother did all those years ago.

"Someone should call 9-1-1," a man's voice says behind me.

"Already on it," comes a response.

I have no idea where the person is on the phone, my eyes staying locked on Cael's hand rubbing against the boy's chest. After a moment, a groan escapes the boy's blue lips. It should give me some sort of relief to hear some life coming from him but my heart stops as I finally peel my eyes away from the boy.

Something moves in the shadows of Cael's arms. It's a spiny dark mist and for a moment I thought it was just his shadow. But it moves on its own, stretching out towards the boy. I want to scream as I watch it wrap itself around the boy's torso but no sound comes out, still trapped within my throat. The boy twitches on the ground again as the mist disappears into his chest.

This can't be what I think it is...

I don't think everyone else saw what I just saw, well maybe Cael, but everyone goes silent as the boy stills. It feels like an eternity before the boy slowly blinks, finally coming to. A few audible gasps and sighs come from the small crowd around. Even I feel a gasp escape my throat as my lungs fill quickly with new air.

But looking into the boy's eyes now, something's off. They aren't unseeing like they were just moments ago, now they are colorless... lifeless. Everything about this boy has lost its vibrancy and that can only mean one thing.

His soul is gone...

The realization hits me at the same time laughter from the other side of the room finds my ears.

My head snaps over towards the shrill sound, nearly giving me whiplash. I find them quickly, leaning up against the wall on the far side of the room. The woman locks eyes with me and I feel my fire start to blaze within. Instinctually, I reach for my knife again but this time I pull it out of my pocket, holding it at my side. They did this... These demons gave this boy whatever it was, then took his soul. Red spots begin to cloud my vision.

The woman's dark eyes travel down to the knife and I swear she looks surprised. Her eyes move back to mine. She tilts her head with curiosity, a wide grin spreads across her face. I brush off the tense ache in my muscles as I take a step toward her. This time I don't need the power of the knife to drive my feet forward.

I don't get more than a step forward before a warm hand wraps around my wrist, pulling me back.

"What the fuck?" my voice is rough in my throat. I look back to see the source of the hand is Cael. He pulls harder but I pull back.

"They did this," I try to keep my voice even through the anger.

"Stop," he pulls again and tilts his head towards the entryway of the room.

Some of the crowd has moved on to other parts of the house, enjoying more of the party. Others have stayed to comfort the woman and to keep the boy, who is sitting up now, comfortable while they wait for paramedics. Near the door I see Arlo.

His watchful gaze is filled with concern that unsettles my stomach.

"Let's go," Cael says. This time when he pulls, I let him lead me away from the room.

"We're not going to do anything about them?"

There's a moment's pause as we reach Arlo.

"No," Cael answers, looking between Arlo and I. "We've been made. The mission is compromised, no thanks to you."

His eyes move to the knife still in my hand. He takes it quickly and skillfully puts it back in his jacket pocket.

"There's nothing we can do without a fight. Which I'll have to deal with later I'm sure."

The disappointment comes off him in waves. With every crash, I feel the pull of the weight of the evening. I knew coming into this that it was a test. A test to see if I could actually be the Nephilim that's going to destroy the devil, but now Cael is going to report back what a complete and utter failure this was. The failure that I was. There's no way the angels will back someone who freezes the way that I did. I can almost see Jeremiah's face, smug with contentment that he was right all along.

I feel the prickly fear creep up my neck. I'm going to be alone with Blake in this fight and we're definitely going to die if that's the case.

"She'll be ready next time," Arlo says with confidence, seeming to have read every thought and emotion that's rambling through my head.

"Oh she better be ready for the fight ahead," Cael nods in

agreement and turns to me. "We will be seeing more of each other very soon."

Something flickers in his eyes. Maybe he isn't going to tell Jeremiah what happened tonight, but then again, maybe that's just hopeful thinking.

"I need to get back in there and clean up more of this mess," Cael turns stiffly back towards the room. "You both should get out of here before you cause any more of a scene."

Without another glance, Cael disappears back into the room with the boy. Arlo wraps his hand around my upper arm, leading me back into the foyer and out the front of the Mayor's house.

"You did really well, given the circumstances," Arlo says once we are back out on the sidewalk.

Given the circumstances... everything in me starts to shut down. I just watched a boy overdose and lose his soul. And I couldn't do a damn thing about it. I don't feel like I did well at all. Instead, I feel the terrible weight of guilt and responsibility for what happened tonight. It's something I haven't felt in a long time and I don't think I can handle feeling it right now. I wipe away the tears that refused to flow in the house that has now freely decided to fall.

Maybe there is some hope that the angels will still back me. That's the hope that I have to hold onto if I'm going to be anywhere near ready to fight the biggest darkness that's out there waiting for me.

TWENTY-SIX

The blink of the camera shutter closes, capturing a perfectly wilting yellow dandelion growing from the cracks of the concrete sidewalk. Color in a world of gray. That's my final assignment for my photography class.

I snap a few more pictures of an overflowing window planter. The small purple, orange, and yellow flowers reach up as much as they can, trying to find the sun amid the concrete jungle. It's no surprise that these flowers are still holding on, still alive despite it being the middle of November. In Edge, the biting winter doesn't blow through until January. So, these small batches of life still glow their colors of summer.

I look up toward the sky, closing my eyes against the sun's warm embrace. If I try really hard, the sun can somehow wash away the past weekend's events. Or maybe if I throw myself into schoolwork, it'll all somehow disappear. Every anxiety, fear, and trauma of the weekend can live somewhere else outside of my mind. At least that's what I told myself when I finished all my homework earlier today. Now all that's left is finishing up this assignment I forced myself out into the city to do.

Just a couple more snaps of the flowers before I head to the photography studio on campus to start editing.

It doesn't take me very long to get back and I quickly offload the images from my camera onto my hard drive for the class. My hand clicks the mouse on the computer, making the image bigger. Clearer to work on the finer details of color and image corrections. It's not even one of the pictures I just took, it's from a few weeks ago. Lost in a moment on the beach. The large trunk of driftwood on the sand occupies the majority of the image. Its partial mossy green underbelly counterbalanced with its exposed bleached white top facing the sky. The light was coming in from the west, just before sunset, the burnt oranges and pinks weren't there yet. The sky here is still a deep bright blue. I drag the intensity up, the blue quickly changing, morphing into something otherworldly and yet so familiar.

"That's beautiful Nola," Blake's voice comes from behind me. "Though I think your obsession with me is showing."

I turn, having forgotten that I'm in the photography studio that just about anyone can walk into. Even annoyingly handsome demons. Meeting those burning blue eyes, the connection clicks with the enhanced blue of the image on the screen.

Oh, this is gonna be a problem.

I get up and roll my eyes.

"Hey," I smile brightly at him.

I can't help my body moving closer. Reaching up, I wrap my arms around his neck. At this moment, it's easy to forget everything else around us. Everything that we are. He closes the distance, wrapping his arms around my waist. His lips find mine and the burning electricity crackles around us, centering itself at my core. I ignore the familiar burn of my wrist, pulling him as close as humanly possible.

He breaks away with a soft kiss.

"I missed you."

His words are just a soft whisper, yet I can feel the relief rushing off of him. My heart swells with the same relief.

"I hope it was worth it," I kiss him once again and feel a smile turning up the sides of his mouth.

He pulls away, taking his warmth with him.

"We'll see about that... It was productive. But you first."

He grabs my hand as he pulls the chair out next to where I was just working at the computer. The screen has since gone dark and silently I pray that the last changes saved. If only to remember that shade of blue forever.

"What were you up to?" Blake asks, bringing me back to him. He sits, pulling my hand down with him. I sit back in my chair.

My mind quickly brushes over everything over the past couple of days. How long has it been since I saw him last? Since he told me the Devil was coming after me?

"A lot," comes from my mouth in a whisper.

I think back to my first training session with the Euch, with Cael. I now have to see Cael just about every day as he has so graciously come back to Edge with me to be my main sparring partner. The Mayor's party, which I've tried to keep locked away in my mind, jumps to the forefront. I can still see the boy on the ground lost in the void and brought back but with his very being taken from him. The faces of the demons there have haunted my dreams, dreams that Blake has been vacant from.

The ball of anxiety that had started to unwind clenches

tightly again with all the memories. Whether I like to admit it or not, Blake is a demon. Plain and simple. Another thought that I've kept buried is the fact that Blake could be just like the demons at that party. Reaping souls. Innocent lives shattered because of him...

"I've been training... and it's been intense..." I hesitate, staring at the door of the room. We're the only ones here, but I can't help the paranoia of being overheard. Or maybe I'm just stalling.

I push my back against the back of my chair, creating a chasm of distance between us.

"Yeah?"

"Yeah," the words left unsaid stay locked in my throat.

He reaches his hand across the distance between us, laying it on my knee. I flinch at his touch. He hesitates a little, then removes it.

"What's wrong?" he asks with an edge to his voice.

"No, it's... it's nothing."

Blake folds his arms across his chest revealing the tip of the tattoo from my dream. He leans back against his chair, that way he can fully face me.

"Tell me," his voice is stern.

The words beg to come out, but I don't know how he will take it. Will this push him away? I swallow around the lump in my throat, I need to talk about this.

"I've had a lot of eye-opening experiences lately... involving souls. Reaping souls in particular," I blurt out.

"Oh," he pauses, his face contorts in disgust.

"Yeah."

"And..." Blake prompts, feeling the pause in the air.

"And..." I repeat. "And I wondered, are those your orders?

Reaping souls before their time? Is that what you were doing at the party a few weeks ago?" my voice becomes stronger in his silence.

"Is that what the 'dealing'" - my hands shoot up in air quotes - "cover is for? Have you – have you taken someone's soul?"

Something deep inside me knows the answers to my questions already. But that doesn't stop my hands from shaking with a perfect melting pot of nerves as I watch his every move. After what feels like hours, his burning blue eyes find mine again. Resolution as thick as his lashes oozes from his eyes.

"Yes."

With that single word, something inside me shatters. The perfect mirage of what this is clatters to the ground.

"I have a feeling you already knew that answer though," he continues, his voice softer. "I have done some unspeakably horrible things but it's not like I had a choice... It could've been much worse," he trails off, coming from somewhere far away.

The sound of his voice, bitterly nonchalant rings in my ears – bouncing off the shattered glass still fracturing on the floor of my brain. Maybe he really didn't have a choice. Maybe he never had a choice from the moment he sold his soul to save his mother. Did he even have a choice in that decision? But the thought still creeps in that he has more than likely caused some irreversible damage. What that damage is... I don't know if I could stomach that.

The room starts to spin with the glittering spiral of panic. Suddenly, Blake is too close and yet much too far. My hands start to drip with sweat. How can this be my life now?

"Hey, Nola," Blake's voice breaks through, reaching out to

stop the spiral. He doesn't move a muscle, but I can feel it in his tone.

"You have to believe that what I've done, what I had to do, I didn't have a choice," he says firmly but still gently. "But you – you've helped me look past that. Helped me see a speck of light in the darkness that I've caused, the darkness that I've called home for so long."

Blake's mouth turns down to the ground at the corners as his eyes rake over my face. My heart flutters at his sincerity.

"I just – I..." words becoming increasingly difficult to find.

"I know..." his head tilts down sadly for a second before it snaps back up. Hopefulness flashes through his eyes.

"Let me take you out."

Shock slaps me across the face.

"Wh-what?" I stutter. "What do you mean?"

"Let's go to dinner. Right now."

My stomach grumbles against the sides of my torso at the thought. Dinner. With Blake. It sounds nice and human.

"I don't know. Don't you think it's kinda... normal?"

"That's the whole point. One meal isn't going to change the world. Maybe a couple of hours away from this is what we need," he shrugs as he stands to his feet.

Still processing the confirmation that I was right about my assumptions about Blake and his demon dealings, I can't help but adore the man in front of me. A man shrouded in darkness but still grasping for the light, for me. My stomach wins out.

"Fine, but I'm driving."

He nods and smiles back at me as I break away from his gaze and turn around. My hand shakes slightly as I shimmy the mouse, waking up the computer. I triple save the image on my hard drive for my own selfish reasons. Still wanting to make sure my schoolwork is done if it even matters anymore.

My subconscious carefully places the picture of Blake on the table next to her, one more caress of his face and she turns away. Back to her armor to get ready.

Gathering my things quickly, I stand and head for the door, not bothering to check if he's following.

TWENTY-SEVEN

We decide on a small restaurant near the water but still within the city. It's casual and low-key. Most of the restaurant is open air with half of its seating outside so there's a view of the water. I'm sure that during the summer, the place is busy with tourists, but since it's the end of fall, there's hardly anyone here. There are still some tourists, who I'm sure are trying to escape the bitter cold winter already beginning up north, occupying a few of the tables inside. Heaters stand tall in front of the massive ceiling fans outside, working hard to fight off the chill of the ocean.

Blake and I sit opposite each other at a table farthest from the groups of people but still inside the open building. It doesn't stop the shiver that goes through me when a gust cuts around the corner.

"Drinks?" Blake asks, with a smile on his lips. Those beautifully distracting lips.

"Um, yes please," I pause, and he looks at me expectantly. "A margarita, please."

"You got it."

Blake stands to head toward the small bar when it smacks me upside the face. We are on a date. An actual date. I haven't been on a date since, well, there have been guys here and there throughout my years here but nothing that ever felt like this. The butterflies beat themselves against the walls of my stomach making me queasy. I try to distract myself by looking through the limited menu in front of me, but it slips through my sweaty palms back to the table.

Normal, this is normal.

"You alright? You look like you're either going to be sick or run out the door?"

Blake returns, placing a small glass in front of me.

I take it and take two steadying gulps. My nerves subside as I place the glass back down, half of the drink now gone.

"Better?" he asks, a taunting smile splits across his face.

I nod my head. "Yes. I'm sorry, I don't know why I'm so nervous..."

"It's because I'm gorgeous."

His eyes glint as he winks at me. My heart flutters.

"Well, obviously," I roll my eyes. "We're doing this whole normal thing and I guess it just hit me how long it's been since I was asked out or even went on a date."

"I find that hard to believe," his brow furrows with skepticism.

"Well believe it," I shrug.

Just then a 30-something waitress comes up to our table.

"How are we doing here? I'm Claire and I'll be taking care

of you guys tonight. I see we already have drinks, anything else I can get for you?"

Her brown eyes flash politely between the two of us.

Shit. I scramble to look through the menu quickly.

"I think we can start with the nachos. Nola?" Blake looks over at me. My saving grace.

"Yeah, that sounds good," I fumble out, placing the menu back down.

"Sounds good. I'll be right back with that," she turns quickly on her heel.

"So, tell me about you," Blake starts, clasping his hands together around the glass of brown liquid he got for himself.

"About me?"

He nods, seriousness making the humor that was written all over his face earlier fade to the background.

"Umm... I'm an Art History major and Photography minor..." I twirl the tiny black straw in my drink.

"I already know that," he says, interrupting me.

"You already know?" my head tilts with the question.

He simply taps the side of his head.

"Oh right... the dream..." The dream of us in the library comes flooding back. The painting. The kiss. Heat rises from my stomach and it's not the alcohol.

"Ehmm..." I clear my throat, trying to clear the feeling of his lips on mine from my mind. "Well, what do you want to know then?"

"What do you want to do with your degree?"

"Oh..."

The question pulls me in another direction, away from the table, back to my 'normal' side. The human side of me stretches. I've been asked this question all throughout high school, more so once I declared my major. I always knew what I wanted to do, and what my plan was for a career. Of course, that was all before. Before I found out who I am, what I am. Before my life was being threatened by the Devil himself. Now I'm in the after, and I don't know what comes next.

If there even is a next.

"I always wanted to be a teacher. A photography or art teacher. Maybe a professor if I got my Ph.D.... if I had the time..."

My voice trails off and I start to swirl the ice in my glass. I take a small sip, letting the cool liquid flow through me. Doing nothing to help the chill at my core. Will I have more time?

"I can see it."

Blake's comfort finds its way to me in the deep recesses of my mind. I look up and his eyes burn into mine with fierce reassurance. He gives me a small hopeful smile. If there are any cracks of doubt, I can't see them.

Claire returns with a spectacular overflowing platter of chips drowning in queso, shredded cheese, tomatoes, guacamole, salsa, sour cream, and chicken. As she places it down, some lone chips fall to the table and my stomach growls uncontrollably. Protesting against filling it only with tequila.

"Here we are. Would you like another drink?"

She looks down, concerned at our nearly empty glasses, and back up at us. Blake tilts his head, no need to ask.

"One more wouldn't hurt," I say shyly and he nods back encouragingly.

"Great. I'll be right back with those!" Claire leaves us yet again.

"Have at it," Blake motions his hand towards the magnificent pile between us. Greedily, I grab a chip heavy with all the toppings.

"Are you – can you eat?" I ask, realizing I've never actually seen him eat.

Is it a demon thing?

To answer my unasked question, Blake picks up a larger chip, filled even higher than mine with toppings, and throws the whole thing in his mouth. He grins and his cheeks protrude like a chipmunk.

"Noted," I say and quickly do the same with my chip.

His childish smile as he stuffs his face more nearly makes me choke with laughter.

"Here you guys go," Claire's back and places the new drinks down. "Anything else I can get for you?"

She smiles at both of us.

I shake my head, trying to quickly swallow the remaining food in my mouth.

"No. Thank you so much!" I say politely.

"Not a problem. Just wave if you need anything," she nods and disappears again.

"What about you? What's your major? You're going to classes at EU right?" I put another chip in my mouth as I stare at Blake expectantly.

"Yeah, I am," he nods. "Double major in English and Illustration/Graphic Design."

"Explains all the books and drawings then," I say mostly to myself, remembering the bookshelves in his room littered with books and journals.

"And your plan for that?" I press. If we are being hopeful for the future, he must have some plan for himself.

"I guess an Illustrator for a big corporation like the one with the overzealous mouse or something," he shrugs.

"I didn't know demons would work at a place like that..."

I think back to all the children's cartoons I would watch growing up and the amusement parks with roller coasters and castles.

"Oh, you'd be surprised," he counters, a flash of something wicked passes over his expression.

"Do I want to know?"

"Probably not..." he answers quickly, picking up another chip. "What about your family?"

He switches subjects as he devours more of the platter.

"My – my mom is a paramedic," I hesitate but still smile with pride. "Always overworking. But I guess that makes more sense now with what she has to do... Or what I've learned over the past few weeks what she does..."

Reap souls, the connection hits me like a ton of bricks and now since I've chosen to be on their side, it's something I'm going to have to learn to do. The memories of the golden soul swirl with the muddied blackness from the boy. It's two sides of my life that I'm not sure if I'm ready for.

But whether you're ready or not, it's coming. My subconscious reminds me as she hangs up her armor with care.

"Um, my brother is a lawyer," I continue, ignoring her. "Super protective and an asshole at times. He's married and they have Max," I smile as the little blonde headed boy runs through my mind.

"And your father?"

"He... uh... he..." I wipe at the drops of condensation on my drink. Suddenly, I'm no longer hungry.

When he first passed, I could never bring myself to talk

about it, with anyone really. I would just shut down. The words stayed trapped in my chest while the tears flowed freely. I know I probably worried a lot of people... my mom, Lawson, and even Harley. Maybe even Sean if he wasn't too busy being another pillar of torment in my life at that time. 18 was only a few years ago but in some ways, it feels like a different life. A lifetime has passed and yet the words are still trapped in my chest. The tears threaten to flow every time I think about my father. How his world of color seemed to die with him.

Blake's hand wraps around mine, trapping me between fire and ice.

"I'm so sorry."

The same pain of when he was talking about his family laces in his words. He can understand the loss, maybe not entirely but he lost both his parents with his soul.

"Thank you."

"Of course."

He smiles, rubbing his thumb over my knuckles. The simple movement is so comforting it nearly blocks out the sadness. Instead replacing it with a pulsing burning to my wrist and a hot electric static in my belly. The flush creeps up the back of my neck as I move our hands to lock my fingers with his.

"I'm finished if you are," he says suddenly.

I look up confused, breaking away from the pull happening at my core. He tilts his eyes down to the plate in front of us and I follow. I hadn't realized he hadn't only eaten all of his side but had started making his way to mine. I had made a decent dent in the nachos but there was still enough left over to feed another two people. I grab my drink with my free hand and quickly down it, ignoring the fuzzy feeling of the alcohol. To counter it, I eat several more chips, never letting go of his hand.

He watches me intensely with a smile. I wipe a napkin to my lips and smile back at him.

"Finished."

"Great."

He throws his free hand up in the air, never breaking eye contact or letting go. A new kind of hunger blossoms in my stomach.

Thankfully, Claire arrives in seconds.

"Can we get the check please?" he asks.

"Of course. Here you go."

She places the billfold on the table then starts grabbing the plate and glasses. Quickly and effortlessly, Blake pulls out his wallet placing a card inside. Not even bothering to look at the amount.

"Thank you. I'll be right back," Claire leaves, balancing the platter with glasses and check in her other hand.

Blake continues to stare directly at me, his eyes full of lust, burning a darker blue. Or maybe it's just the dim lights. He runs his thumb over the palm of my hand, the waves of electricity crashes against me in time with the waves on the beach in the distance. Too quickly, and yet not quickly enough, Claire returns with the check, receipt paper sticking out the top of the black billfold. Blake shifts his eyes down to write and I'm suddenly stripped of the warmth of his stare. He hands it back to her.

"Thank you. You guys have a good night!" she cheerily adds and scurries away again.

"Shall we?" Blake asks, the wickedly lustful smile plays on those beautiful lips.

I nod, not trusting my voice or mouth from saying something stupid.

"You're good to drive right?"

He hesitates as we both stand, hands still locked together. I quickly access, making sure.

"Yeah, I'm good," I say confidently.

It's too quiet in my small car. The only sounds coming from the short directions Blake gives to his house. Both of us are aware that the night is coming to an end. Do I want it to end? The warm electricity crackles around us and it's so very hard to ignore. His quick glances at me that I catch in the corner of my eye, full of something darker.

Tempting, my subconscious licks her lips.

After 20 minutes of silent tension, I throw my car in park on the street outside. The house has its usual ominous glow against the dark sky but still has every light on inside, inviting me in.

"Thank you for tonight," I shift to face him. "For our 'normal' date," my hands go up in air quotes, fingers slicing through the electricity in the air.

"You're welcome."

Blake turns his too big body, looking far more out of place in my car than I do. His teeth glow against the darkness around us and his eyes flick dark blue.

"I should-" my throat goes dry with need. "I should get back..." voice coming out hoarse.

"Or..." he says, moving his hand slowly, he finds my thigh.

The heat of his hand radiates through my jeans and up into the deepest parts of my belly.

A part of me wants to flinch away. Smack his hand and fight this demon sitting next to me. I know this side of me well, she's the logical one. My gut that tells me when and how fast to run. I've relied on her quite a bit over the years and for good reason.

But unfortunately for her, the tension has muddled the logic like a murky blue lake.

"You could come in," his voice comes out deep, deeper than I've ever heard it before. It rattles within me.

"I could..."

The words come out of my mouth before I can stop them. My mind has already made itself up as my hand switches the engine off.

Blake's heat is all-consuming and welcoming as we sit together on the couch. Even though we're sitting close enough that our thighs touch, it isn't enough.

At the same time as I lean down to place my nearly empty bottle of beer on the floor, the front door of the house opens up. Several voices drift into the living room Blake and I are occupying. It takes me a moment to realize that one of the voices is Ash.

"I had so much fun tonight," her singsong voice floats through the doorway.

I shift, moving further away from Blake. His heat vanishes with the distance, but I can still feel the electricity simmering between us.

"Ash?" I call out.

We haven't seen each other since I got back from Cross. Granted, it's only been a day and maybe I've been avoiding her. Or avoiding our inevitable conversation. I know she must want to talk to me with how she looked at me before I left this past weekend.

"Nola?"

I can hear the confusion in her voice as she steps through the doorway, trailing closely behind her is Jase.

Everything in me tenses as the hair on the back of my neck stands on end.

Blake, and everything that was crackling between us, is left abandoned on the couch as I stand. My hands clench into fists at my sides, it grounds me as the room tilts slightly, alcohol rushing to my feet.

"What're you guys doing here?"

I surprise myself with how harsh the question comes out, bubbling with the fierceness that's in my chest.

"Woah," Ash releases Jase's hand and lifts her hands in defense. "Nice to see you too..."

"Shit, I'm sorry Ash," I say, sheepishly meeting Ash's eyes.

"It's alright, but you do know that Jase lives here too, right?"

Jase leans against the door frame, not bothering to come into the living room. Well, his living room. His and Blake's... Azel must be here too. It all clicks. The weight of fear with all these demons being here crashes down on me. And Ash is here, right in front of me.

"I didn't... but I guess it makes sense—"

"Nola," Blake's voice cuts me off. His warmth right behind me stops all thoughts.

"It's alright Blake," Jase says softly from where he stands. "She knows."

I feel my eyes start to bug out of my head. Jase... told Ash what he is? How could he? How could he put her into this world?!

Anger clouds my vision, but I hold steady, watching Ash's face.

"You know?" I ask, only to her.

She looks back at me, confused, and says "that Blake and Jase are cousins?" her eyes leave mine and look between the two boys. "Yeah... you didn't?"

Something within me loosens with relief. So, he didn't tell her everything... told her a lie instead. A lie I can follow. It makes me like Jase a little more, but the protective anger still simmers under the surface.

"Oh right..." I recover, looking fully at Jase, "yeah, I knew that."

"Ash, honey," Jase peels his eyes away from mine and takes a step towards Ash, "why don't you go get us some water and I'll be right behind you?"

Ash seems to be completely unfazed as a loving smile spreads across her face. She turns on her heels, looking back to Jase.

"Sure," she turns back to Blake and me, "can I get you guys anything?"

Always polite, even in awkward situations like this one. Suddenly, the room spins, a reminder of the alcohol still flowing in my bloodstream, and I stagger back into Blake. His hands on my hips hold me steady. Water sounds perfect, cool, and sobering.

"Yes please," I give her a reassuring smile.

"Be right back."

Ash quickly grabs Jase's hand and squeezes it. She's out the door in the next beat.

Jase is left behind, his hand still outstretched. Painfully slow, he turns back to us. His eyes filled with worry as he meets mine. Faintly, I can hear Ash in the kitchen at the end of the hall.

"Cousins? Really?" I question the whole room.

Almost automatically, Jase lifts his hands up in defense.

"Would you rather I told her the truth?"

The weight of the truth beats with the rising panic. Blake is a demon. Jase living here, I can assume that he's a demon as well. He and his brother Azel, are both demons. Who knows how many demons are in this house... Fuck Ash is in the kitchen by herself... I take a step forward, out of Blake's steady grip. I ignore the tilt of the world around me, focusing all my might on the noises coming from the kitchen.

"No," I spit at Jase, anger driving everything, "no, you can't tell her."

"Nola..." Blake's voice is calm, too calm.

"Don't you think she has a right to know?" Jase questions right back to me.

His words hang heavy in my head. He stays silent for a minute, letting me decide on an answer.

"I know she can handle a lot. Hell, she can handle a lot of my shit, but she shouldn't be involved in this," my hands move in the air around us, "this world."

"Look, Nola," Jase sounds like he's talking to a child. "What you and Blake have, it's special. Do you think you'd still be here if he kept what he was a secret? If you weren't what you were..." his voice trails off. "Ash and I... well, I think I'm starting to fall for her. I can't keep her in the dark," his eyes glaze over with loving adoration.

Ash who was just here with the same look in her eyes. I can't deny the connection between the two of them but I had no idea that it was love... Is that what's between Blake and I? I turn around and meet his blue flames, letting their burning heat flow through me. Would I still be here if I was only human? It's hard to say. The situation would be completely different, I'm sure of it, if I was only human and he was still a demon.

Would he fight as hard as he is now to protect my soul? Would I?

I shiver at the thought.

Ash is just a human, one of my best friends, I can't let anything happen to her.

"Damnit Jase!" the words pour out of me. "You're not making this easy. Everything in me wants to tell you to fuck off and leave Ash out of everything..." I run my hands over my face, trying to clear away the jumbled thoughts and find something coherent.

"But it's not fair of me... I know that..." even as the words come out of my mouth, they fall defeated on the ground. I know there's nothing I can say to change Jase's mind from telling Ash what he is. That just means I have to fight even harder to protect her and hope that he will be there to protect her too.

"Thank you," Jase says with relief.

"Don't thank me just yet," I look up not realizing he had moved farther into the room, his hands on the back of the couch Blake and I were just sitting on. "Because if you hurt her, *in any way*, I will personally rip you apart limb by limb and burn you alive," I say matter-of-factly.

"Descriptive..." he says with a mock shiver.

I roll my eyes back at him.

"What the fuck Nola?"

I didn't hear Ash come back into the room and by the look

on her face, she just witnessed me threaten the boy she really likes life like it was nothing.

"Shit, Ash... that was – it was just a joke," I scramble.

"Didn't sound like a joke Nola," she says, and I can see the anger building in her eyes, her walls going up. "It sounded pretty fucking serious."

It was, my subconscious chimes in just when I don't need her. Jase knows it was serious. Hell, even Blake probably knows I'm not joking. But Ash... since she doesn't know the full truth yet, she can't know just how serious I was.

"It was a terrible joke," I try to diffuse, "come on, you've said stuff like that about Sean... if not worse."

I know almost immediately that that was not the right thing to say. Ash starts to shake from where she stands in the doorway.

"You can't be fucking serious... I've – you're really about to compare Jase and Sean?"

"What? No!"

"Babe," Jase's voice gets lost in the anger radiating from Ash.

"That's really fucking rich coming from you. You're gonna threaten Jase's life who's been nothing but nice to you and yet you stay with him," Ash's eyes flick to Blake beside me, "who beat the shit out of Sean not a couple of weeks ago?"

I flinch. It's a memory that I tried to keep buried away. The fury that rolled off Blake, I never want to see that again.

"Ash, you don't understand..."

"I obviously don't," she says with finality. "I don't under-stand *you* anymore."

Hot tears fill my eyes, blurring my vision, with the truth of her words.

"Ash, I'm sorry. Please let me..."

"Stop Nola," she lifts her hand, "just stop."

Ash clinches her jaw, her eyes finding Jase. She places one of the glasses of water down on the small table just on the outside of the door.

"Jase, can you take me home?"

Jase starts to walk over to her. I feel his eyes on me for a moment, but I don't look away from Ash. This can't be happening right now. All the truths sit on my tongue, everything about Jase and Blake, everything about me... This whole conversation would be different if she knew...

But nothing comes out except, "Ash..." as I hold back a sob.

I feel Blake's warm hand wrap around my wrist. Holding me back as I watch them walk through the door without another look back. It feels final, like a piece of me is walking away. All I want to do is run after her, tell her everything... I can't keep the tears in anymore.

Blake's warmth wraps around me, leading me to the couch again. Being the one solid piece when a shattered piece just broke away and walked out.

"I can't believe..." I stare down at my hands in my lap through my cloudy vision. That fight was by far the worst fight Ash and I have had and I feel helpless.

"Shhh..." Blake's comfort comes through the ravine of hurt I've nestled in. "She'll come around Nola."

"You don't know that," I counter. "There's so much... too much that she doesn't know about... about all of this!"

My chest rises and falls with quick sobs. Instead of feeling choked, I feel lightheaded with the quick bursts of oxygen filling me.

"And if she finds out..."

"She has to find out, Nola. She's making her choice; Jase is making his choice... just like we made our choice."

"It's different... this is different," I wave my hands in the air between us.

"Maybe..." Blake reaches across the electrified distance, lifting my face to his. He wipes his thumbs across my salty wet cheeks and the motion buzzes through me.

"But as much as you may want to, you can't control them," he gives me a small smile.

His statement hits me like a punch to the face. The blow softened only by that damn smile of his. *Fuck.* He knows what he's doing. As much as the truth hurts, it's also sobering. If Jase talks with Ash tonight or not, I can't stop him. I can't stop whatever comes next in more ways than one. I know I won't be able to stop the inevitable conversation with Ash now.

"So much for our 'normal night,'" apologies lace my voice, becoming clear of the sobs from earlier.

Blake leans back on the couch, hand back around his beer. His smile widens but the joke doesn't quite reach his eyes. He's still watching me with concern.

"Ahh, what's a date night without a threat of someone's life and a little bit of a fight?"

"Maybe..." I say, smiling at his nonchalant shrug.

"There she is," he smiles back at me as he takes a sip of his beer. "Do you want me to take you home?"

Home. The thought of going back to my apartment right now, opens a fresh wound in my heart. Home is the last place I want to be.

"No," I say, reaching down to grab my own beer still on the floor next to the couch.

I take a sip and we lock eyes. Suddenly, the air around us

shifts. The charged feeling comes back from before, stronger than ever. Maybe it's the energy that's still lingering in the room from the fight, or maybe it's just because we're alone again. Regardless, it's a welcome distraction.

A needed distraction.

"I guess I won't be going home any time soon..." I sit up straight and look over at Blake. His lips glisten slightly from the beer.

In one swift move, he reaches across me, his chest nearly laying on my lap as he reaches down to place his empty bottle where mine was. I stop breathing and suddenly feel very sober. Slowly, he sits up, his face only a few inches from mine. His burning blue flames flick over my face, alternating glances between my eyes and lips. Pure hunger, but still asking his silent permission. To answer, I reach up and lock my hands behind his neck, pulling his face to mine. Ravenously, I let my mouth crush against his. He takes a half second to respond but kisses me back just as deeply. Our mouths open together, granting each other more access, letting our tongues explore one another. He tastes like a combination of beer with a hint of mint.

My hands find his shoulders and I push him back against the couch. Moving to where my knees are on either side of his hips, I lower myself down to straddle him and he responds with a satisfied groan in his chest. He wraps his arms around me, holding me close.

"God-" his voice is hushed but deep with lust. "I. Want. You. So. Bad." Each word punctuated with a soft kiss.

My heart flutters and a deep need pulls at my core.

"Me too," the words startle me, and it takes me a moment to realize the thick voice is my own.

In another quick move, his hands cradle under my ass as he lifts me with ease. I want to protest against the move but there's no time before we're out in the hallway.

A giggle escapes my mouth, still pressed against his when I realize where he's taking me.

"You are NOT carrying me up two floors," I pull away, giving him a wink.

"I most certainly could," he smirks at me.

"I'm sure, but I'm good with walking."

"Have it your way," he says as he slowly places me back on my feet. His hands never leaving my body.

My cheeks blush with the waves of heat flowing through me. I grab his hand, needing to stay connected even in a small way. All the butterflies from earlier flutter at the thought of what's about to happen. I push away everything else, everything that I am, what Blake is. This moment, this night, is meant to be just how it is. And boy is it perfect.

We don't make it up the last set of stairs before our bodies are connected again. Lost in hands and lips. At some point, he picks me up again, carrying me up the last few steps and through his small living area. My back hits the door as our kisses deepen. Holding me up with one hand he opens the door behind me quickly. Once inside, he slowly places me back on my feet, our mouths never breaking apart for long.

Slowly – deliberately – clothes are removed layer by layer, finding a new home on his bedroom floor. I step back, lungs heaving to take in the most air between us. Which is difficult when my eyes rake over the specimen in front of me. He really is beautiful. Now I can fully see his tattoo that I've only gotten a glimpse of before. It covers most of his left shoulder and half of his upper arm. It's a rope draped and twisted around his arm.

Knotted together at the top of his shoulder with a metal bracket, locking it in place. I run my fingers along the rope, making my way up to his shoulders and across his chest. Meeting his eyes, they burn with undeniable passion. He too had been steadying his breath but with my touch, he's stopped breathing altogether.

Suddenly, his mouth is back on mine, hands raking and devouring my entire body. The backs of my knees hit the hard surface of the edge of his bed and he pushes me down at my waist. His body, burning hot, presses down on top of me. Our breaths uneven. Our bodies, hands, and mouths not able to get enough of one another. He pulls away slightly and presses his forehead against mine. His panting breaths fan over my face as he looks deep into my eyes.

"Are – are you sure?" he asks between breaths. This man – this demon – is asking me for consent. A smile spreads across my face at the joke that this is. I grab the back of his neck and pull his lips back to mine. Not able to take the small distance between.

"Yes," I say, strong and steady between kisses.

It's undeniably hot. Every second of it. He pushes and I pull. The electric pulses increase, becoming blinding stars around us. Together we climb higher and higher until we can't take it anymore. Reaching the summit all at once and together. The feeling is overwhelming and all consuming. I know I'll never be able to get enough. I'll never be able to get enough of him. I'll never be able to get enough of us.

We collapse together in euphoric bliss. His arms wrap tightly around my naked torso, and I feel as his breathing steadies against my back. His lips press against the back of my head in a soft kiss.

"That was... amazing," Blake says into my hair. His voice still thick and deep.

"Understatement," I respond. He snorts with laughter and I can't help but join in. Letting the high from one another fill me with joy.

How we got here, I'll never understand. If anyone saw us together in public, they wouldn't bat an eye. Hell, the waitress from tonight probably thought we were a normal couple. But they'll never understand or know that Blake is a demon, a creature of the darkness. And that I'm a half angel. Still learning how to be the light that is inside of me. But maybe we can be the normal couple that everyone else sees because right here and now, is one of those perfect human moments. The ones I've been jealous of when I steal a glance at couples around me or when they are captured in pictures and paintings and books. I smile at the darkness and press my back closer to Blake and he sighs with pleasure. That sound and tonight are things that I'll hold onto forever.

My own version of normal.

I focus on Blake's even breathing as my eyes close. Slowly slipping into one of the most peaceful sleep I've gotten in weeks.

TWENTY-NINE

My fingertips gently caress each spine of the books on the shelf. The texture changes from smooth, to rough... to hot and cold. I didn't know books could feel like that. My hands linger on *Metamorphosis*, running along the lettering. The color of the spine changes from black to a smoldering orange like molten lava. The book stays where it's at, on the shelf but with the heat radiating off of it, you would think that it would combust or melt right there.

"I'm humbled that you chose to come here," Blake's voice comes from behind me. I turn, startled out of my exploration of his books. He's sitting on the couch of his living area.

"Or I should say, you chose to stay here," a slick smile plays on his lips. "Though, I'm a bit disappointed that we're clothed again," his eyes rake over my body hungrily.

My eyes in turn glance over to his, he's back in his black t-shirt and dark jeans. He's still stunning but the undressed version of Blake is heart-stopping.

"I would have to agree with you there," I lick my lips as I cross the small distance, choosing instead to sit on top of him again. My legs straddling his. The fire in my wrist bursts into flames but I try to ignore it.

"I'm assuming I'm dreaming?" I ask, brushing my thumb over the stubble on his cheek. He closes his eyes and leans into my touch.

"Yes," he breathes out. "And I hate to ruin the mood, but we need to talk about the plan," he smiles apologetically, tone turning more serious.

My hand freezes on his cheek, heart thumping up to my throat.

"Wha-what do we have to talk about?"

I guess our "normal" night is over. I knew it couldn't last forever but I hoped it would. Hoped we could live in this bubble of date nights and be wrapped in each other's arms forever.

"If you're serious about fighting my father, I think I have a way. Jase, Azel, and I were talking through it..."

Our bubble of happiness continues to crack at the edges. I stay silent, letting his words sink in, breaking through the weak points. We're talking about the Devil now, his father. The father of all demons, one of which is sitting beneath me.

I slide off his lap and find a cool spot on the other side of the couch.

"From what I've gathered," he continues, adjusting the way he's sitting so now he's facing me. It's too professional, too guarded. "We're going to need some kind of sword..."

"The Euch..." I wrap my arms around my knees.

"You know it?" a weird combination of fear and hope flashes through his eyes.

Know it? Even now I can feel its pull. Arlo had suggested that he keep it at the gym when we got back to Edge, but I wanted to keep it close. The fact that it's not right by my side right now, makes my palms itch. I clench my hands together around my shins.

"Very well."

His head moves up and back down in a tight nod, "Right..."

"Yeah, I have it-"

"Don't," Blake says, cutting me off. "Don't tell me anything else."

"Why?" I tilt my head at him in confusion.

"Well, the Euch is deadly to all of us," our bubble completely shatters, "but would only wound my father if wielded by just anyone. In your hands," he reaches across, taking my hands in his, they feel rough against mine, "a Nephilim as strong as you are, pure of heart and soul... You would be unstoppable," the fear now marries with pride as he looks down at our hands.

"I guess it's a good thing I've been training with it," sarcasm oozes into the half joke.

He coughs a laugh at me.

"It is because this isn't going to be easy. We have to be careful, very careful especially when we talk about all of this. Here," he gestures around the room, "in your dreams, it's probably the safest place we can talk."

"What do you mean?"

"Because out there, we have to be careful who we talk to. My father's body is still in Hell, but that doesn't mean he isn't still around."

"What... what do you mean?" seems to be the only logical

question that keeps repeating out of my mouth. A shiver runs up my back as it goes rigid with fear.

"I mean that while he's not at full power, he can still possess his children... us..." he swallows, leaving the word unsaid. "And even in his limited power, he can dream walk but not to the extent as when he's at full power. When he's at his strongest, he can manipulate what you see and cause harm, if not death, to your waking body. Trapping your mind in a perpetual nightmare..." the edge in his voice tapers off into something else. Fear maybe.

"How do you know that he's not, you know, here?"

"Because he can't be here while I'm here," his fear filled voice sounds almost nonchalant.

"And how do I know that you're... you? I mean you can't just tell me that you could be possessed and then honestly expect me to trust you..." I move my shaking hands out of his grasp, wrapping them back around myself. The absence of his warmth is like sticking my hands in an ice bucket.

"That's a bit complicated but for now, you have to trust me," he moves his hands back to his lap, letting me have the distance. "When we wake, I can show you. But two words, holy oil."

"Holy oil?"

My brain pictures the three wise men from the bible story.

"Yes, shit burns like hell. I would know. But demons who aren't possessed by our father, we can touch it, some even wear it..." he reaches up and touches the collar of his shirt. I never noticed the small black string leading below his shirt. "And it stings but it's tolerable. But when possessed, the body of the demon can burn up. Specifically..." he takes a deep breath, swallowing hard, "the body part that touches it, blisters and catches fire. Obviously, it does little to my father in that form but it's not pretty."

My stomach lurches with bile. Trying to imagine someone burning up makes my head spin. Our surroundings actually physically shift. After all, this whole thing is in my head. I watch Blake glance around and then turn back to me.

"Nola. Focus on me."

He breathes steadily and, involuntarily, my breathing follows along with him.

"Good," he gives me a smile. "Now, do you remember what you mentioned the last time about needing people to help?"

I nod, focusing on not letting the room tilt, just my head.

"Yeah, I... I have some people."

"Me too," he gives me an encouraging smile.

"You do?"

"I went on a trip recently to get some help. I knew I needed to talk with others I can trust... people I met long ago..."

More words, stories, left hanging in the silence between us. I want to ask. I want to know everything, but I hold my tongue. We can talk about it later... if we have a later.

"And?" I ask through a new panic rising in my throat. Whoever these people are... they have to be like him, like Jase and Azel. Demons...

He reaches back across and this time wraps his arms around me so that my head is cradled against his chest. I know he's supposed to feel warmer, but the feeling is muted, like trying to feel him through layers of fabric. I close my eyes, thinking that maybe if I focus, I can feel him better.

"And they agreed to meet up," he rubs my arm, the motion feeling strange, "this weekend and I want you to come along."

My cheek moves against his chest in a nod.

"Wait," the room around us starts to disappear around us. "You want me to come with you? To meet other..."

"Yes," the word is almost a comforting shush as he kisses the top of my head. "You're gonna be okay..."

His voice rings deep in my ear. Faintly another sound starts to creep in. The sound is high, repetitive, and vaguely familiar.

My eyes fly open and for a moment, the room is foreign. It takes a couple of breaths for me to come back to reality. Actual reality.

And I'm burning up.

Blake's heat comes over me all at once and his arm feels like a lead weight over my stomach. I try to wiggle out from under him, but he groans as he hooks his hand around me, pulling me closer.

I can't help but smile.

"If you want me to turn the alarm off, you're going to have to let me go."

The only response I get is another groan deep in his chest. Reluctantly, he releases his hold and rolls onto his back. I quickly get up, throwing on his black t-shirt that's still on the floor. I glance back at him on the bed, his eyes still closed. His chest and stomach are exposed and the sheet is bunched at his waist. From here, he looks – for lack of a better word – like a god. From his messy dark hair down to his stubble dotting his jawline and his full lips, I really don't understand how he could exist.

How either one of us could.

"Are you just gonna keep staring or are you gonna turn off that stupid pinging noise?" his lips turn up in a smile.

Leaning down I plant a kiss on those lips. The kiss is quick but still shoots through me like an electric current.

"Sorry, can't help it," I smile as he opens one of his eyes to meet mine.

I lift back up before he can grab me again and head out the bedroom door. The alarm is coming from my phone which I find after a brief search on the floor in his tiny living room. How my pants ended up all the way out here... I don't know.

Checking the messages quickly, I pad back to the bedroom. A couple are from Jess asking me about my trip and where I am. *Oops.* I never let her know when I got back... Nothing from Ash. A small flicker of hope dies with that. One from Harley asking me to save them from the boredom of their school and asking me how I'm doing. I smile at the message. Arlo and Lawson even started a group chat with me, messages waiting about more training sessions. Even Cael has checked in about training.

Damn, I go off the grid for one day and come back to this... The whiplash of coming back to reality threatens to burst the bubble of everything from the night before. I thought I would have longer to revel in it all but now I have to figure out what comes next... preparing to meet with more demons. And I have to figure out how to get the angels on board.

Funnily enough, neither of those things scare me. My thumb hovers over Ash's name on my phone. Whatever happened last night, we have to talk through it. I just hope that conversation doesn't pour salt onto the wound.

"What's wrong? You've got that adorable little crease between your eyes," Blake asks from the bed, his arms now behind his head propping him up slightly.

"Huh?" I blink back up at him. "Oh, I guess, we have work to do," I give him a heavy sigh and quickly text back Arlo and

Lawson, confirming the training schedule for the week. "Are you going to tell me more about this weekend?"

Blake shifts, sitting up more on his bed. I ignore huge pull of my eyes to the slipping sheet at his waist. He rubs his hands through his hair. Sighing, he touches the edge of the silver necklace resting on his collarbones.

"I can't," his voice oddly sad. "Not right now at least, but I'll pick you up at eight on Friday."

"Right..." my eyes linger on the necklace. Holy oil... "Well, as much as I would love to stay here with you for, well for forever..." I smile at him, legs pulling me back to the bed. "I need to get going if I'm going to make it to classes in a couple of hours."

He frowns adorably at me.

"I hate that you're right."

"And don't you forget it," I wink at him as I lean back over the bed. We're eye to eye, blue flames staring into a jade green. Colors that beg to melt together.

His frown quickly turns into a large, beautiful grin.

It's been days. Two days to be exact. Two days of silence and tiptoeing around the apartment. When I got home from Blake's I thought for sure there would be an angry Ash waiting for me. Instead, the apartment was completely silent other than the faint sound of her tv playing in her room. I probably stood outside of her room, hand raised to knock, for about 20 minutes. But I chickened out that time and every other time since.

Turns out living with someone you've been keeping secrets from and trying to figure out where you stand after a huge fight, is difficult. Ash hasn't been making it easy either. Going out of her way to avoid any interaction with me before classes, leaving early and choosing to get rides with Jase or other classmates. She's been holed up in her room every night too. I only hear her come out occasionally to get sustenance.

I'm sure at this point the silence and avoidance may kill me.

"Focus Nola," Arlo's voice comes with a blow to my side.

Doubling over, I grip my ribs. The only thing staring back at me is the blue mat beneath my feet.

"I'm..." grunting against the pain, I straighten up to face him, "trying."

"You need to try harder."

His tough love is starting to get really annoying. Training this week has been increasing in difficulty. I've mainly been working with Cael, hand to hand with a multitude of weapons. I've beaten him several times, getting several approving nods from both him and Arlo each time. I can feel myself getting stronger, better. I hope that Cael is reporting only the good parts back to Jeremiah and the others. Not every time I fumble, which is still a fair amount.

"Especially if you're going to be meeting with several demons tomorrow night," Arlo holds onto his staff at his side.

That was a harder conversation to have. One I was only able to have with Arlo just a few minutes ago.

"I know you think it's stupid."

"It's not one of your smartest ideas," Arlo says.

"Yeah, but it's not a *bad* idea," I counter, leaning against the sword I've been using. It's not the Euch but it's about the same weight.

Arlo groans, turning to pace his side of the makeshift ring in his gym.

"No, it's not a bad idea," he finally says, back to me. "But I wish you would let me tag along."

"I'm sure if I bring an angel to a meeting with demons, that will go over well."

"But you're a Nephilim..." he turns to face me, panic brimming in his eyes. "To top it all, you're a wanted Nephilim."

Taking a deep breath, I ignore the pain still lingering in my side. Though the physical pain is more welcome than the brick of panic starting to sit on my lungs.

"I know..." boy do I know. "It's a stupid, risky plan. But with your training, I'll be fine. And I'll have... Blake."

"Ahh, the demon."

"Hey..." I squint at Arlo's disapproving tone. He awkwardly throws his hands up in response, one hand still holding onto his weapon.

"You can't honestly think I approve of the pairing right?" he pauses only for a moment. "I mean I'm all for love in all different forms but a demon...."

My body rattles with the red hot heat of anger. The power behind it makes me grip the sword even tighter. How dare he... He knows nothing about Blake, about our.. relationship. And frankly, it's not for him to judge.

"I'm not asking for your approval," comes through gritted teeth.

Arlo takes a step back, creating more than enough space between us. His knees hit the bench behind him. I watch as his eyes flicker through shock, sadness, and settle on guarded contentment.

"You're right," his voice calm as he stands a little straighter. "I still wish you'd let me come."

I take a deep steadying breath, letting the anger simmer out of my fingertips.

"It'll be alright. You know where I'll be so if anything should happen, you know where to find me."

He nods.

"And if it goes right, we could get some help on the inside."

"Which would be helpful," he nods again, "I'm still worried about how we can convince the others."

"I don't think there's much of a choice... this could give us a fighting chance, that's what you're going to have to lead with."

"Me?!" Arlo feigns shock. "You think I'm telling the others about your stupid plan?"

I sigh, ignoring his dramatics.

"I know you will. Probably right after I leave here."

Shrugging, I place the sword on the bench behind me and sit on the floor to start my cool down stretches.

"Is this what's got you so distracted?"

"What?" I look up at him, confused.

"Everything going on tomorrow night... you and Blake? Is that what's been distracting you during tonight's training session and the past couple of days?"

"Partly... yeah," I answer honestly.

"What else?"

His concern washes over me. It irks me some but not as much as his judgment from before. I feel the weight of it all...

"Ash and I got into a fight a few days ago..." maybe Arlo can help.

"Oh?" I barely catch the tilt of his head out of the corner of my eye. "What happened?"

"I'm not really sure..." the night replays in my head. "I said something really stupid and it all kinda blew up in my face. And I just don't know what to say from here."

"Well," his voice nonchalant, "did you apologize?"

"Several times that night. But it didn't seem to help..."

"Hmmmm..." he hums thoughtfully.

We sit in silence for a moment. I'm not sure what to say. If I should fill him in more on the specifics or just leave it at that. Ash just might be a puzzle I have to work out on my own...

"How, um..." I hesitate, switching topics... kinda, "how did you tell Pierre?"

"Ahhh..." he finally sits on the bench behind him. "So that's what this is about..."

My head nods of its own accord. I don't correct him or it because they aren't totally wrong. I have to tell Ash. If she already knows about the demons... what Jase is, then it's only a matter of time before what I am comes up.

"It was a heavy – and long – conversation," Arlo starts. "As you could probably expect, he was in shock for a little while. Didn't talk much and was just avoiding me for a while..." he looks down at his hands but I can tell he's somewhere else.

"It was by far the hardest part of our relationship. Which is funny because, at the time, two men getting married was so taboo that you would think that that was the hardest part."

"Wait," I cut him off, "you waited until you guys were engaged?!"

He smiles at the thought, or maybe at me, I can't tell which.

"Yeah, probably wasn't my best idea to hold off on having the 'I'm an angel,' conversation until then but something just stopped me every time. Maybe I just wanted to make sure... make sure that he loved me," his smile turns sad. "I wish now that I had told him sooner... it might have been easier in the beginning."

I nod, trying to absorb his words. I can almost picture the two of them having the conversation.

Almost.

Ash keeps sneaking in there, her back turned on me. The silence ripping a hole so wide in our friendship that it's irreparable.

"Eventually, he had a lot of questions," his eyes crinkle with joy at whatever memories are playing in his mind. "Some of them started some really interesting conversations. Some were just ridiculous."

My own stupid questions pop into my mind and I can't help but smile along.

"All in all, it could've been worse but it wasn't. You and Ash have such a deep bond, it may hurt at the beginning but I don't think that will last," he gives me a look of encouragement. "But the longer you keep this inside, it's only going to get worse."

It already feels pretty bad but maybe it can only go up from here?

She's still going to freak, my subconscious chimes in. I ignore her, deciding that if Ash does, I'll handle it.

"I know..." I say with resolve to Arlo and the annoying version of myself in my head. "I know."

THIRTY

Horizon is fairly empty. Well, empty being a relative term. There's still a crowd on the dance floor but instead of a DJ, like the night of my birthday, there's a band on stage. I can't help but correlate this with the fact that its main clientele is probably busy tonight with finals preparation. The open space by the bar eases some of the anxiety fluttering around in my stomach. A squeeze of my hand reminds me of my biggest lifeline tonight, Blake.

"Come on," his voice comes loud enough over the music. "Let's get a drink."

I smile, nodding my head at him, grateful.

His hand leaves mine as he heads towards the bar and like so many times before, he takes his warmth and flames with him. Turning to the band, the music is a bit more on the indie rock side and it's so good! The lead guitarist's voice is gravely as he sings about a couple falling in and out of love. I find myself swaying along to the words with the crowd in front of me.

A warm hand wraps around my waist, swaying with me.

"They're quite good," Blake's voice is hot in my ear.

His other hand appears in front of me holding two plastic cups one filled with orange liquid and the other a dark brown.

"Your favorite."

I can hear the smile in his voice as I take the drink, nearly inhaling it with a hardy sip. We stay like this, one of his arms wrapped around me and my back pressed up against him. Swaying together for another song and for a moment, it's easy to forget what we're here for.

That is until my wrist flares.

It's different from the burn I've grown used to with Blake. It's not electric. This burn is white hot like someone is holding a hot iron from the flames against my skin. It snaps me out of the trance of the music. I look around to see Jase and Azel walking through the door. Two more dark figures walk in after them.

I half expect to see Ash next to Jase, attached to his hand.

No, if she was, I may have to fulfill that promise after all.

She can't be here. Not now.

"You ready?" Blake says calmly in my ear.

I look up and follow his eyes to the two people on Jase and Azel's heels. They keep walking to the back of Horizon, leaving through the back door. Out of the corner of my eye, I catch Blake nod. I don't know who he's nodding to but it forces my attention back to him. His eyes are crinkled with worry but meeting mine, he gives me a small reassuring smile. I feel the others' eyes on me, but I focus only on Blake.

"As I'll ever be," I finally answer.

I take his free hand in mine, trying to act as casual as possible. We need to seem normal to not attract any attention. His grip is tight as he leads me through the dance floor we danced on not that long ago.

As we step outside, the cold fights its way against my jacket. Our group is the only one out here, there isn't even a bartender. I guess the crowd inside is preferring the band over the biting November chill. Glancing at the few round tables I notice quickly that this area is meant for smokers. The number of ashtrays littering the tables and bar is astounding.

As if on cue, one of the new demons with us lights a cigarette, taking a long drag. She lets out the dense white smoke slowly, her piercing brown eyes lazily meet mine and wander down to my feet then back up.

"So, this is the one who is supposed to save us all?"

Her voice is a bit gruff, probably from the cigarettes, and comes off with indifference even though it feels like the question is supposed to be a jab.

Blake's warmth envelops me as he moves closer to my side. His arm reflexively drapes over my shoulders, and I lean into his fire.

"This is Nola," he says to the two of them, ignoring the girl's remark.

"Nola, this is Fore Griffith."

The girl with the cigarette nods slightly. She seems young, maybe a few years older than us, but her tired features age her. I can tell that maybe her cheeks used to be fuller when she was younger but have since hollowed out.

"And this is Shaw Wilder."

The red headed boy nods timidly. He looks a couple of years younger than us, I'm surprised the bouncer even let him in. He stands a half step behind Fore. Her stance, while casual, does border on protective.

"Hello," I say, clearing my throat around the dryness.

"Thank you guys for coming and meeting with – "

"Yeah yeah," Fore cuts me off. "Well, we're sick of all the shit with father," she waves her hand dismissively, but her words are venom.

She takes another long drag of her cigarette. I try to find the right words to say... I wasn't anticipating just jumping right into it.

"So, what's the plan?" Fore asks, white smoke still pooling out of her mouth.

I watch as her hand shakes slightly as she brings it back to her mouth. The only tell in the cool mask she's wearing of how she must really be feeling. The urgency in her words continues to tighten the ball of anxiety at my core.

I look around at our group and realize that everyone's eyes are on me. Azel's filled with disgust. Jase's eyes are expectant with a hopeful edge to them, he gives me an encouraging smile. Shaw looks uneasy, while Fore simply looks bored. I square my shoulders, trying to feel confident facing these demons.

"It's me that he wants. The plan is to lead him to me."

I feel Blake stiffen next to me. A part of me feels guilty that I never disclosed this part of the plan to him. It's a part of the plan that I've thought about over and over since I found out. I knew then just as I know now, we have to have the element of surprise on our side.

"And what about us? What are we here for if you're just going to do it all yourself?" Shaw speaks up, his voice is shrill. He doesn't hide his panic as well as Fore.

"I hope you'll be by our side. I'm sure you know that we might have a fight on our hands," I pause, letting my words hang in the air.

"At least I... I won't go down without a fight," my voice is strong despite my hesitation. "So, I think our best chance is in numbers. Numbers he doesn't know about... But I know this isn't an easy decision to make, you have to know that..."

"We're signing death sentences?" Fore finishes my words with another drag of her cigarette.

I nod my head. She's not wrong, we all are signing on the dotted line.

"Well, we did that a long time ago."

Blake flinches next to me.

"Right..." I start, trying to process. That was too... easy... "I'll have to figure out how to meet him by myself first and then you all will be there and so will..."

"The angels," Fore once again finishes my sentence. It's off putting how nonchalant she seems to be about all of this like she truly doesn't care that we all might die.

I hear a couple of gasps of air coming from our group.

"Possibly... yes," I hold onto my strength, looking at Fore fully. "Like I said, numbers he doesn't know about."

"I'm so glad you have everything worked out, Nola," Blake's harsh words startle me.

With one look, I know that the rising heat coming from him is not from his proximity but from anger.

"But I'm not letting you go anywhere near him by yourself."

Fuck, okay... so we're doing this now.

"Blake, this plan will work. I can't let you get yourself killed for me. I'm actually trying to prevent any of you guys from getting killed because of me..."

Blake closes his burning blue eyes and takes a steadying breath. When he opens them again, his eyes are softer.

"Okay, but how's it believable if you're just out in the open by yourself?" he takes a step away, anxiously running his hands through his hair.

It's the first time I've heard him stumble over his words, "He would know that you know about him and his plans if you do what you're suggesting. He would already be suspicious seeing you alone. We have to convince him he has won... his prize."

A prize... I'm just the Devil's prize? My stomach flips as bile rises in my throat.

"How... how are we supposed to do that?"

The lump in my throat has grown three sizes. Blake tears his eyes away from me nervously. I'm cold, too cold, with him so far away.

"Tell her Blake," Jase says.

I keep my eyes on Blake, willing myself to be stronger than my shaking knees.

He raises his hands, pulling at his jacket. His calm demeanor all but washed away. I wait, heart racing as his hands are still at the back of his neck. His eyes meet mine.

"I bring you to him," the words are rushed, coming out all at once. "He's already anticipating that actually, he insisted that I bring you to him."

He takes a deep breath and drops his hands to his sides.

"In two weeks..."

"TWO WEEKS?" I nearly choke on the words.

I thought I had so much more time. Hell, I know Jeremiah hasn't given me much time to get ready for them to assess if they would be willing to join us. Who's to know what Cael is telling him about my performance...

"I... I was... Two weeks just... it's not enough time..." my thoughts come tumbling out of my mouth between rushed breaths.

"I know... I've been trying to give us more time but—"

"Wait, you've been trying? How long have you known this – this timeline?" my head tilts to the side.

"Oh honey, he's known since that first night you came to our house," Azel's words cut through me.

The memory of the phone call with his father flashes through my mind. The panic in his eyes, it's the same now. A flash of betrayal shoots through me. He knew there was an expiration date on my head. He fucking knew... My feet take a step back without permission.

"You, you knew..."

"Last call everyone!" a high voice comes through the door leading inside. Along with the voice, the last notes of a song float through, pulling me away from Blake.

"That's our cue," Fore says casually. Leaning down, she puts out her cigarette stub in the nearest ashtray. She links arms with Shaw.

"We'll see you in two weeks," she nods as she passes, sarcasm laced in her words.

Silence falls over our group again as the door closes behind them. The only noises are coming from inside Horizon. People chatting loudly, oblivious to what's just happened out here.

"Fuck Blake... This is... fucked," my voice shakes.

"Yeah. I know," he sounds sorry but there's no use denying the truth.

"I, I need to go home," I turn away from Blake, searching for another option for a ride. "Jase?"

"Nola, please," Blake begs behind me.

Ignoring the pang of hurt that comes with his voice, I hope

that Jase can see my desperation to get out of here, away from Blake. My hope dies as his eyes move to Azel.

"I'm sorry Nola... Azel and I came together. We could take you back to my car but that would be... kinda counterproductive being that..."

"The person you're trying to avoid lives there too," Azel waltzes by throwing his hood over his head.

"Nola, please... let me take you home."

Blake's hand hovers over my shoulder, filling the air between us with heat. Flinching, I turn back to him.

"Fine."

Turning around again, away from him, I walk back to the door leading inside. I don't bother looking back, but I can feel the burn following.

The tension bubbles in the small space of the car between Blake and me. He didn't even turn on the radio when we got in, both of us letting the silence hang in the air. I count the turns, only four more until I'm back home.

"Nola, I'm so sorry," Blake starts, sincerity breaking through. "I, I'm so sorry that I didn't tell you, but I was just trying to get us more time and get the right people on our side which you've so brilliantly done. You were great tonight, aside from the stupid plan of you being solo when meeting with my father."

I huff back at him. Why does everyone think my plans are stupid? Especially when their counterplans are even worse.

"Regardless, you did win over Fore and Shaw."

"It didn't seem like it took much... Like they were already

on board before I even got there... I mean I just told them what my plan is."

"Yeah well, they've been eager for a while," his hands tighten around the steering wheel. Staring straight out the windshield, the orange glow of the streetlights casts moving shadows across his face.

"What do you mean?"

"They've grown fond of humanity. They still remember it and have fallen back in love with it. They've grown tired of the oppressive orders of our father..." he ticks off like these are obvious reasons.

I stare out my window, two more turns. There's still so much I don't know about Blake. What orders he's done. And yet, he holds a piece of my heart already.

"Sounds like you know..." my heart swells more for him.

He takes a deep breath, hands letting the tension go around the wheel. His eyes never shift away from the road.

"Yeah, I do," the words sound like a confession coming from his lips. "But I guess they needed to see you, make sure you were real."

"Right because I'm the 'chosen one,'" I throw air quotes in the air.

"You are, love," he glances over at me, meeting my eyes.

"Sure. I'm just trying to make sure we all survive somehow..."

"We will. If you agree with what I said. It's our best chance," his eyes search mine as he makes the last turn into the parking lot of my apartment.

Betrayal aside, I can't help but see that he's right. It would be strange if I was there alone when his father shows up. We can't risk tipping him off to anything.

"Alright," I agree as he puts his car in park. I reach for the handle.

"Hey."

I feel Blake take my hand. My body doesn't recoil from the touch, instead, I relish in the electric burn.

"We're alright, aren't we?" Blake asks, his voice taking on a softer tone, apologetic. His eyes are on my wing for a second before they lift up to mine.

My heart swells despite everything.

"Ugh," I groan. "Yes. But you know two weeks isn't a long time... there's so much I have to do..." everything flashes before my eyes involving my two worlds.

Blake lifts my hand up to his face pressing my knuckles to his lips.

"You're cute when you panic."

I roll my eyes at him. The stupid and gorgeous demon who sends butterflies through my stomach laughs at me.

"We'll be alright," he reassures, pulling me towards him.

"Maybe..." my face now inches away from him as a mischievous thought crosses my mind. "But we have to survive Thanksgiving first."

He pauses, smile faltering as panic flashes through his eyes. "You mean..."

"Yep, you're coming home with me for Thanksgiving."

I shrug, thoroughly enjoying his expression. No longer is he the menacing dark shadowy figure from a month ago, he's now just a man who is panicking about meeting my family that just so happens to be a demon.

Oh, and I love him.

"Don't worry. We'll be alright," I deepen my voice, doing my best impression of him.

This time, he rolls his eyes at me. Laughter bubbles up in my throat.

He reaches up and takes my face in his hands. His thumb runs over my bottom lip, his eyes completely entranced. The mood shifts in the car. I take his thumb between my teeth and look up at him. I hear him take in a sharp breath, nothing is forgotten from before, but maybe this could be a fun distraction...

"Fine. I'll come with you," his voice deeper, laced with desire.

I release his thumb.

"Great! I'll pick you up next Wednesday," I smile with all of my teeth, pulling away, out of his grasp.

His face falls with the distance, hands balling into fists where my face was. I lean back in, giving him a quick kiss.

"You'll be alright," I say to him. "We'll be alright."

I pray with everything I am that I'm right. That we all will be alright.

We have to be.

I need to be ready, in whatever time I have left.

THIRTY-ONE

"You're going to be fine," I say to Blake, who's nervously sitting on the passenger side of my too small car.

His knee bobs up and down anxiously, the car shaking in his wake.

"You don't know that," his voice shakes slightly with his body.

I've never seen him this nervous. It's different than the other night.

This... this is adorable.

"It will be fine," I put as much reassurance as I can into every word

"You don't know that," he repeats, sounding more and more like a child not able to get his way. "I've never met anyone's family... not officially. Not as like a boyfriend."

The word hangs in the air between us. I smile at it, looking over at Blake, whose eyes are nearly bulging out of his head. My laugh almost steers us off the road.

"I didn't know we had defined this," I say between laughs.

He looks over, concern written all over his face.

"Well... I guess... I mean..."

I laugh harder at his fluster. A rare side of him that I haven't had the pleasure of meeting yet.

"Yeah, I get that" I take a breath. "Seems a bit silly to put a label on this..."

He smiles slightly, relief flashing behind his eyes.

"I guess it does..."

His hand moves to my jean covered thigh causing a wave of burning electricity to shoot up through me and center itself at my wrist.

"Sounds so... human."

He's right. Something in me sinks yet floats at the same time. How can something as little as a title of a relationship even apply to us? Two beings, who frankly I didn't think existed several months ago, do we get the same labels? Does any of it really matter? On the other hand, my humanity is giddy. Overjoyed at being able to call Blake mine.

For however long we have.

"Right, and we have something very human to do now."

I put my car in park in the driveway, lowering my voice as I turn to him.

"Meet the family..." I claw my fingers in the air towards him, feigning like I'm some wicked witch bringing him to his doom.

"You joke but this is terrifying," he stares out through the windshield at my childhood home.

"You really haven't met anyone's family before?" I drop my hands.

"No. I mean I didn't really have anyone like this... before.

And since, it's not something I entertained seriously..." his voice trails off. "On top of that, your family probably isn't going to like me being what I am ..."

His honesty cuts me to the core.

"Right..."

I look out at the front porch. It's not like my track record with bringing guys home has been so swell. My mind wanders back to Sean and his first meeting with my parents. It was messy, to say the least. My dad didn't seem to care that there was another person in the room while my mom played hostess. Lawson, on the other hand, grilled into him. Which later caused one of our bigger fights... This has to be better than the disaster that was.

"It's going to be fine," I repeat more to myself than Blake. Reaching over I grab his hand.

I give it a small squeeze and smile. His fearful blue eyes meet mine as he takes a deep breath. We both lean in at the same time for a quick kiss.

"Okay," the word comes out as a sigh.

Blake turns and opens his door, I follow shortly after. As we walk hand-in-hand up to the house, I give his hand one more encouraging squeeze before opening the door.

Immediately, we're assaulted by the millions of spices baking. I smile at the memories of my mom in an old apron preparing a five-course meal every holiday. Lawson and I would always try to help but then immediately get kicked out when we inevitably got in the way of the madness. Instead, we would gladly run outside and play with all the other kids, working up an appetite that only half of an overflowing plate would fill up.

In the present, my mother walks around the corner from

the kitchen and it's no surprise that the same old apron is around her neck. I swear it used to be white but now has a faint yellow hue and kaleidoscope of stains from the years of use. Right at the center of the apron is a small chef holding an over-sized bottle with a label donning 'XXX' on it. Around the chef are the words, "Comments to the cook can be hazardous to your health." I remember my mom telling me the story that my father gave her this apron as a joke anniversary gift, but she loved it and never wore any other apron during the holidays.

"My little light," my mother's warm smile shines at me from down the hall.

"Mom..." I feel the heat rising up to my cheeks at the name.

"Oops, sorry."

Her smile only wavers slightly as she reaches us. She throws her arms up around my neck and squeezes tightly. I release Blake's hand to return the hug.

"Umm. Mom," I pull away from her. "This is Blake Corbyn. My boyfriend."

The words come out awkward, but they feel right somehow.

"Ahh yes!" her voice doesn't waver in joy though, I feel a bit of apprehension.

"It's nice to officially meet you, Blake," she smiles, sticking her hand out.

Blake stares down at her outstretched hand, hesitating a bit. He recovers quickly with his cool mask neatly in place.

"Nice to meet you too, Mrs. Saint," he shakes her hand.

"Please call me Laine."

The exchange is awkward, to say the least. Both of them eye one another. Anyone from the outside would think that it's just a pleasant exchange but the slight tension in the air says otherwise.

"I should thank you, Blake," my mother says, breaking the awkwardness and turning away from us. "For keeping my Nola safe. A few times I hear."

Her words are methodical but still sincere. It shouldn't surprise me that she knows as much as she does given that I now have Cael as a babysitter. Granted, there were people watching me long before that.

I roll my eyes at the back of her head as we follow her down the short hallway. The deeper in the house we get, the stronger the scent of all the baked goods is. I can see the island in the kitchen is already overflowing with different ingredients and cooling cookies. The warm orange glow of the oven lets me know that there are several more batches and from the looks of it, a pie still baking away.

"Of course. Though I don't think she needs much of my help now."

Blake looks over at me from the doorway leading to the living room. He leans against the side, winking at me. His shoulders seem to have relaxed a bit making the tight ball of nerves in me loosen.

My mother hums in agreement, now busy with whatever's next on her list.

"Mom, you don't have to cook for a whole army you know?" I joke.

"With all of you in my house, I never know," she smiles up at me.

"Speaking of, when are Lawson, Flynn, and Max getting here?"

"They should be here any minute. I asked them to pick up a few more things and the pizza."

"I'm sorry..." Blake chimes in with his head tilted. "But why pizza when all of this looks amazing?"

"Thank you," my mother answers politely. "At least someone here is appreciating all the hard work I've done."

Her eyes shift from Blake to me giving her 'mom look.' I throw my hands up in defense, "Hey, I appreciate you!"

"Sureee," she drags out looking back at Blake. "It's kind of our tradition. I'm usually too busy with all of this," she waves her hand at the array of desserts for Thanksgiving, "to cook an actual meal before Thanksgiving so we do pizza."

"Ah."

Blake awkwardly shifts on his feet which I take as my cue to change the topic.

"I'm sure you don't want our help with anything..." I back away from my mother, hands now full of flour.

"No no. You guys go hang out!"

She lifts her head and smiles at the both of us. I think I'm the only one who notices when her smile falls slightly as she looks at Blake but it's still polite. Grabbing Blake's hand, I give my mother a warning look as we turn and head into the living room.

That sure was awkward but didn't go terrible. I had anticipated the meeting with my mother and Blake to go like this but I didn't expect the tangible tension. Maybe it's the whole angel/demon thing but it was something I've never experienced, especially with my own mother.

Blake stops at the mantel over the fireplace in the living room. His eyes looking over the family photos. A couple from Christmases long ago. Me and Lawson as children. Individual baby photos. My parents' wedding photo. Lawson and Flynn's wedding. Baby Max. A newer family photo with Lawson, Flynn, Max only a year younger than he is now, my mother, and I. The only person missing, my father.

"I'm assuming this is everyone that I'll be meeting tonight?" Blake asks his attention on the last family photo.

"Yeah, that's the gang."

"And this is your dad?"

My eyes wander back to my parents' wedding photo. My mother and father look so young and beautiful, both of them. They're holding each other tightly, all smiles at the camera as my mother's dress flows out behind her, mid dance. I can't help but smile with them.

"Yeah... umm yeah that's him," I swallow around the grief in my throat.

"You look like him," I can hear the smile in his voice. "I'm so sorry... about..."

Blake's fumbling for words only makes me smile. A new layer has been peeled away from the mysterious man all those months ago.

"It's alright. It was a while ago."

"I understand. I'm still sorry... Do you mind if I ask, how? You don't have to answer..."

Blake reaches over and lays his arm around my shoulders. The comfort shoots through me as quickly as the electric burn.

"Yes and no," I answer honestly. "It was an overdose. And I guess in a way, we could all see it coming but no matter how often the worst flashes through your mind, you're never prepared for when it actually happens."

For a moment, the sounds of the sirens and their flashing

lights resurface in my mind from the deep recesses I threw them in.

"I'm so sorry Nola... I—"

"HAPPY TANKSGIVING NO-NO!"

Blake is effectively cut off by Max running through the living room. I feel his tiny arms wrap around my knees and squeeze tightly. My legs buckle slightly with the pressure of his grip, but I don't care. I lean down and scoop him into my arms giving him a kiss on the cheek. He's getting bigger and heavier but with all the training it's easier to pick him up than before. Max wraps his legs around me so I'm enveloped in his warmth.

"No-No..." Max whispers nervously in my ear. "Who tat?"

I smile as I move Max to my hip. I see that the nervousness has returned to Blake's eyes as he takes in the wild Max.

"Max," I say, in the same whisper. "This is Blake."

Blake gives him a small smile but doesn't move another muscle.

"Hmm."

I feel Max's weight shift as he looks down at Blake's feet and then back up to his face.

"He you boyfriend No-No?" Max's tone loses some of his childish joy, replaced by childish judgment.

"Yes Max," I giggle. When did this 4-year-old get so bossy?

"But you'll always be my number one," I whisper to him, my eyes still on Blake who seems to have shaken off the nervousness, now feigning hurt.

"I guess I have some competition. Nice to meet you, Max," Blake nods at him.

"Hmm."

It's the only response Max gives him. He kicks at my hip

but never takes his eyes off Blake as I place him back on the ground.

"Max!" Flynn's voice finds us as she rounds the corner, arms full of grocery bags.

"Oh, I'm sorry. I hope he wasn't bothering you guys. Sometimes he just runs off like he runs the world. I mean he runs my world, but you know…"

Flynn throws down the bags and crosses the room to us. She reaches out, giving me a tight hug.

"He's cute," she whispers only to me.

I fight the urge to slap her arm for her comment when we break free.

"Flynn. Blake," I motion my hand between the two of them ignoring the flames of embarrassment on my cheeks.

They quickly exchange a handshake, hellos, and polite smiles. The interaction is the most civil with no underlying tension. But that's Flynn, she gets along with everyone.

"Lawson should be in shortly with the rest of the things from the store and the pizzas."

"PITZA!" Max shouts as he runs out of the room.

"Max, go get cleaned up and say hello to grandma," Flynn calls after him.

She turns back to us and gives an apologetic smile. My stomach growls as she leaves the room. With the nerves of the day finally giving way to hunger, my mouth starts to water with the anticipation of our traditional pizza night.

I turn to Blake, his eyes already on me.

"I'm sorry for all the craziness. Max is… well you've seen."

"He's great," Blake smiles fondly.

"Yeah, he is. Who would've thought he would be the one you have to win over tonight, huh?"

"I do have my work cut out for me on that one."

Blake reaches up and runs his hands through his hair. He shakes his head as he starts to laugh. I laugh with him, trying to imagine what kind of conversation would unfold between a demon and a 4-year-old.

Just then, Lawson comes through the front door.

He breezes through so quickly that I can only tell that it's him by his blond hair and trailing bags of groceries. I hear several cans hitting the tile floor as he enters the kitchen.

"Lawson?" Blake questions only to me.

I nod and head back to the kitchen. I hope that Blake catches the hint to follow me. My palms start getting sweaty again, not knowing how this one will go.

"Mom, where do you want me to put all of this?"

I hear him say as Blake and I round the corner. Lawson's back is to us, and I can see the edges of the pizza boxes still in his hands, the two grocery bags at his feet.

"Put the pizza on the table and we can put away the rest later," our mother answers with flour now up to her elbows.

It's really hard to not picture her as this, a normal mother, when in reality, she's an angel who seems to never take any shit from anyone and who I'm sure has had her fair share of badass moments.

"Pitza, pitza, pitza..." Max comes running through, chanting.

He nearly takes out his father's legs but Lawson steps sideways as he turns to avoid the 'pitza' monster.

Lawson looks up once Max safely passes. His eyes, our father's eyes, meet mine.

"Hey Nola," he smiles at me. "Would hug you but..."

He lifts his shoulders up, motioning to the boxes in his hands.

"It's fine. Lawson, this is—" I reach back for Blake's hand, but I don't feel his warmth.

"Blake," Lawson cuts me off.

His face is no longer filled with the same lighthearted kindness. I've only seen my brother with this hardened expression a few times in my lifetime. Once when a little kid knocked me down off the swings, that kid walked away with a bloody nose. The other time was when I came home from that awful prom night with Sean, and he could tell I had been crying. It took everything for me to convince him to stay and not go out and murder Sean. This face has been hidden for a while now that I didn't realize that Lawson still had it in him.

But here it is and now Blake has to face it.

My heart skips in a panic. I try to talk it off the ledge and chock up Lawson's expression to some macho overprotective brother thing.

Blake is nothing like Sean.

"Hello, Lawson. It's nice to meet you."

I turn and see Blake is nearly a foot away from me. He's eyeing Lawson, but his expression is nothing but friendly. Either missing the daggers being thrown at him or ignoring them altogether.

Lawson huffs at him. An audible noise of disgust comes out. I take a step back, not used to this kind of response from him.

"Lawson..." our mother gives a warning from the kitchen.

He rolls his eyes. It's so odd to see my brother act like this.

"It's nice to meet you as well," Lawson's voice like venom through gritted teeth.

Hatred. That's what this is.

I move closer to Blake when Lawson takes a step toward us. I'm not sure if it's a protective move or it's just so he can pass us. But Lawson doesn't give us another look as he places the boxes on the table.

"Pizzas' not going to eat itself," Lawson says, pulling out one of the chairs.

I catch Blake's eye and mouth 'sorry' to him, he gives me a half-hearted smile in response. Keeping his mask in place.

Dinner goes by awkwardly with the silence broken only by the occasional small talk. Not even Max's 'pitza' outbursts and imagination can cut the tension in the room. I would give anything to feel as carefree as Max does instead of the prickling stress tightening my back in knots.

"So, Blake, tell us about yourself. Any family around? Parents?"

This is my mother's fifth time trying to break the tension, having already breezed through weather, school, and a long conversation with Max about if he is excited to start school. Everything but the elephant in the room, my boyfriend.

"Umm. No, no parents," Blake's answer is honest and somber, cutting through my heart.

"Oh, I'm so sorry."

"It's alright," Blake gives my mother a small smile, his features softening.

"This is a lovely home, Laine. Thank you for having me," Blake says, changing the subject away from him. He looks around the room and lands back on the mantle of pictures.

"Nola was just telling me about your husband's passing, I'm so sorry for your loss," his eyes are so sincere it hurts.

"Yeah. Well, you should be."

Lawson's voice cuts through like a hot iron. My head spins to him just in time to see him throw the remaining crust he was chewing at on the plate in front of him.

"Lawson," the same warning as before hovers in my mother's voice.

"No, this is bullshit!"

My eyes shoot between the two of them.

"Oooooo, daddy said a bad word," Max chimes in.

"Flynn," Lawson looks at his wife.

I can see that he's trying to even out his breathing. They share some sort of silent conversation.

"Right. Max, honey, I think grandma may have gotten you an early Christmas present."

"Realllllyyy?!" Max's excitement bounces him right out of his chair.

My mother looks at him and smiles broadly but it doesn't reach her eyes like it normally would at his joy. She tilts her head mischievously towards the garage.

Flynn nearly has to sprint after him to keep up.

"How dare you come here and act like that!" Lawson's voice raises just as the door behind Flynn shuts.

I spin back, Lawson's face is fully flushed with his anger. Eyes never leaving Blake across from him.

"What the fuck Law!?" I feel my eyes bulging from my head at least that's what it feels like.

"Nola, I'm sorry but I can't keep up whatever charade mom is such an expert at with this fucker here."

"Lawson, what the hell are you talking about!?"

"Exactly Nola!" he throws his hands up. "That's what you've brought into this house. Our home... Hell. At least a scummy piece of it. A piece that has the fucking balls to sit there and apologize for OUR loss when he was the one who-"

"Lawson!"

Our mother's shout cuts him off. Her knuckles are almost as white as the napkin clenched in her fist. I feel the air slowly slipping from the room.

"Lawson don't."

"No, I'm not going to sit here pretending like the reason my father's dead isn't sitting right here."

Suddenly, I'm crushed under the weight of his words. Everything goes cold as the air is knocked from me. My world tilts and I do everything I can to hold on.

"What... what are you talking about?" the words come out as breathless as I feel.

I find my brother's eyes, searching for some kind of lie but all I see is rage and hurt. I switch to my mother; it has to be a lie. There's no way... She takes a moment to collect herself before meeting my eyes. Her eyes tell me everything that I need to know.

"No... what... what's he talking about?" I turn to Blake.

He doesn't look at me for a moment. Eyes still on Lawson. Slowly, for what feels like an eternity, he looks down and takes a breath.

"Nola, please..." Blake starts.

"Oh, here we go," Lawson lets out an exasperated sigh.

I ignore him. I need to know.

"What is he talking about Blake?"

"Nola, I was so young-"

"Bullshit."

Blake winces.

"I was so new... New to it all, to what I had to do."

"What did you do?" I can't look at him anymore. His close-ness, his warmth now feels suffocating.

"I, I was selling. And that night, she wanted me to take a soul... Your father, he was there, and I just didn't care. I think it was his first time buying anything and it was... it was easy."

The images flash through my mind. Blake is younger than he is now with my... father. Memories of the blackness from the Mayor's party... Was that how it was for my father? It was just the blackness, nothing like the golden soul from the hospital...

"You... you reaped my father's soul..."

I feel the pizza trying to make another appearance in my throat.

"Yes... but Nola. I'm so sorry... There are so many things from that... that time that I wish I could take back."

"Things?!" my eyes flash up to him, I feel the hot rage flush my cheeks. "My father was a person! A whole person, if flawed before you... you ripped him apart!"

"I know. I'm so sorry, you don't have any idea how-"

Blake reaches for me, and I nearly fall out of my chair as I stand to get away from him.

"I didn't make the connection until after we met... and then everything moved so fast. And then I saw him there..." his head tilts towards the mantle. "Nola, I wish I could take it all back."

"You knew?! You knew all this time!"

The crushing world around me now cracks at the edges. This is different from when I found out about who I am... this time, my heart shatters with it. The hot tears flow freely now, blurring everything in the room, every face.

I try to brush them away but it's no use. My hands rake themselves through my hair and I fight the urge to pull, to feel something other than the breaking of my heart. The betrayal and deceit unravel every moment. It all feels like a lie. How can the man that I love be the reason my father died? Be the reason that the spiral dug so deep so quickly.

Because he's a demon you idiot, my subconscious decides now is a great time to chime in. *He was doing what he's always done, what you even saw him do that night of the party.*

I shake my head involuntarily. She's right but I can't handle that right now.

All the warnings my mother and Lawson gave me about Blake. I always thought it was because he was a demon, but it was something more. It was this...

"You all knew..."

My eyes find my mother's blurry face.

"How, how could you not tell me?"

"Nola, honey, I wanted to-"

"Oh, that's right, you've always preferred to keep me in the dark," I spit back at her.

"That's not fair Nola," Lawson's voice is calmer, his attention fully on me.

"So, you're the only one who can have outbursts!?"

I throw my hands in the air, trying to find some room to breathe.

"Nola..." my mother speaks to me like I'm some wounded animal.

Maybe I am.

"Stop! You've constantly kept things from me, and this," I point around the room at no one, "this is huge! How could you not tell me?! The reason the worst thing that's happened to our family? Fuck all the little side comments, the warnings..." I pause, trying to catch my breath between the sobs. "And then tonight, what the fuck was all of that earlier Blake?"

I find him no longer in his seat but standing on the other side of the room. My heart rips further apart as I meet his burning blue eyes filled with regret.

"Nola, I'm s-"

"If you fucking apologize one more time..."

I cut myself off before I can regret anything. My voice breaks with another sob, the tears not wanting to stop. I wrap my arms around my chest. Maybe somehow that will stop the cavern from opening up where my heart used to be.

"I think," I take a deep unsteady breath, hoping that some strength comes with it. "I think you need to leave Blake."

Blake opens his mouth to say something but then closes again. A part of me hopes that he does stay, figures out some way to get past this. That part is shattered when his face changes. I watch as the hurt and regret slip back behind his mask. With one more look, he nods and then turns on his heels.

I wince with the loud shut of the front door. And then everything shatters.

"Nola?" my mother's voice is closer to me, reaching me from inside the cavern.

"Mom, please. I need some space."

I turn, forcing one foot in front of the other. Somehow, I find myself at my bedroom door.

Safely inside, the flood bursts through.

Sometime later... I think. It could've only been minutes, hours... days. The only way I know some time has passed is by the dried salt staining my cheeks, hair, and pillow under my head. I don't know when I got on the bed or how my light got turned on next to me. I don't know how my eyes haven't swollen shut with the puffiness or how I'm still breathing with an obvious hole in my chest.

A light knock comes from my door.

"Come in," my voice is no longer my own. It's someone else, hoarse and broken. I sit up, tightly wrapping my arms around my knees.

My mother's head pokes through. Her eyes are slightly red, but the green shines through. The only indication that she too was crying.

"My little light..." her voice breaks as she steps through the door, closing it behind her. She sits at the edge of my bed.

I don't say anything. I can't, not with the missing part of my chest.

"I'm so sorry Nola. I warned Lawson not to bring anything up, especially tonight. But we know how he can get sometimes."

She looks around, uncomfortable. I just stare at her, watching as she sifts through whatever thoughts are going through her head.

"I'm sorry that we kept this from you."

Her words fill some of the void and I feel new tears coming. I didn't think I had any more left in me.

"I had to come to terms with all of it so long ago. I tried. Nola, with everything that I had, I tried to help your father. To bring him back from the dark ledge I saw him slipping over. The lengths that I went to..." memories flashing behind her eyes that I don't even know. "Being what I am, I couldn't give up. But once he was gone... really gone... there was nothing I could do. And I... I lost him."

Her tears flow freely with mine. I had no idea. It never even crossed my mind what she must have gone through, how hopeless she felt. When she was supposed to be bringing goodness, someone she loved slipped away into the darkness.

"Mom, I'm so sorry," somehow, I find my real voice through fresh tears. "For tonight. For what I said. I didn't... know that you went through that and here I was just blaming you for keeping it from me."

"You were right to be angry honey. I wanted to tell you before but there was never a right time and there was so much already. Too much. And then I saw the way Blake was looking at you today. The way you looked at him. I couldn't get between you guys, between what was there... what is there."

She wipes at her tears and then reaches over to run her thumb on my cheeks.

"I don't know about that mom. I don't think I can see him again, let alone forgive him."

"Maybe... but I think he's holding more pain, hatred, and guilt about it... about everything he's done. I mean look at what he's planning on doing."

My mind flashes to our plan. The trap. How all of that is supposed to work in a week's time if all of this is shattered is beyond me.

"It's hard not to see how much he loves you."

Something flickers in the cavern. A small light of hope but I don't know if it's enough to fill what's been torn apart.

"Take some time..."

"Not that I have lots of that," I say, scoffing to myself.

My mother reaches up and places her hands around my face, guiding my face up to her so that we are looking eye-to-eye. The furrow of her brow telling me how serious she is.

"Then get some rest."

"Yes ma'am," I say, half as a joke, half terrified that she might smack me for that.

Instead, she smiles softly brushing her thumbs once more over the wetness still on my cheeks.

"Nola, my little light..." her voice turns more serious. "I'm really sorry. So sorry that you're feeling this much pain right now. And I'm sorry that I probably haven't helped in stopping that pain. I don't know if I can forgive myself for that..."

"Mom..."

"Let me finish. I've always just wanted what's best for you and maybe you can't understand that now, but I love you so much. Unconditionally and always. I hope you can see that, my little light."

She gets up and places a kiss on the top of my head. Something that she hasn't done for years. I'm not really sure how I can process everything. All of what she just said feels like something I've been waiting on for such a long time. I didn't even know I was waiting for it. And now that it's here, it's been said, it clicks. From deep in the cavern, it's still painful but maybe it's all been necessary. It'll take some time but maybe I will be able to forgive her for everything... and then maybe Blake...

But not yet...

"I love you, mom."

The emptiness closes in around me once more when she leaves the room. I hold onto the little faint flickering light in the void and pray that it'll turn into a raging fire. One that will bring me some of the warmth now missing without Blake.

Eventually, I curl up on my side, letting the darkness of the void swallow me whole. Somehow drifting into a restless sleep.

THIRTY-TWO

The darkness feels too dark if that's possible, but it also feels familiar. Like a room where the lights were just shut off and my eyes still haven't adjusted. Somehow it feels empty, yet full at the same time.

I stick my arms out, trying to feel for something, anything, but I flinch as a shadow moves near me. Or maybe it doesn't. Trying to get some orientation, I squat down and feel gravel and wood?

Suddenly, an overhead light flicks on and I blink against its orange glow. The halo of light surrounds me, illuminating only a few feet in each direction but it's enough. I recognize my surroundings almost immediately. It's an old, abandoned barn that I explored with Harley here in Cross between our freshman and sophomore years of college. I was on a kick of photographing abandoned buildings, the creepier the better, and the more beautiful the pictures came out. Playing with the light that would come through the cracks and the juxtaposition of the vines and overgrowing weeds against the faded brittle wood. Life trying to take over the dead.

But it's different now.

Outside of the safety of my light, the shadows breathe and move. A cold sweat chills my spine, locking me in place. My heart pumps with adrenaline at the same time my wing flares with burning fire. I squint at the darkness. The shadows can't really be moving...

"Nola?"

The voice is familiar, and my heart nearly stops with relief.

"Jase?"

I squint harder in the direction of his voice. He steps from the shadows that have stopped moving and into the soft orange glow. The moment of relief dissipates as I take him in, his eyes are wide with panic and fear.

"What's going on?"

"I'm sorry Nola. I... I promised Blake I would never do this. But I... I...." he starts hyperventilating. I'm nearly choked with the panic building in my chest.

"Jase... take a breath," I take a step towards him, ignoring the burn. "What happened?"

There is a moment's pause as he does what I say.

"We were on our way to come get Blake, Ash, and I. He sounded so broken up and drunk and Ash was with me... We were nearly there when we were ran off the road and they..." his breathing becomes erratic again. Tears fill his eyes.

"They took her Nola..."

My worst fear comes crashing down on me. It nearly crumples me to the floor.

"Who's they?" I spit the words out. Whoever has Ash, they are going to pay.

"Some rogue demons. I assume working with our father... I tried Blake, but I can't get a hold of him. And I figured I could reach you here..." he waves his arms around. The building starts to move like a mirage.

A dream. I'm dreaming.

The walls bend further with the realization. Maybe the shadows were moving after all.

"I promised Blake I would never come to you like this but... I need your help," Jase continues babbling but my mind is already made up.

"Jase, are you here? In Cross now?"

He nods. I look around, we're running out of time here.

"Where?"

"I... I don't know this building but it's off the highway..." he runs his hands through his hair and tugs in panic. "I wish I knew where we were, but everything happened so fast, and I... I couldn't save her..."

"Stop Jase."

I can't think the worst right now, not about Ash.

"I know where you are. I'll be there in 10."

I think he nods or mumbles something else, but everything goes black again.

I wake disoriented. It takes a few moments to remember that I'm in my childhood bedroom. The light beside me is still on and some other part of me catches the time as I grab my phone.

Three in the morning.

My feet bound down the stairs. The pounding in my chest matches in time with the sound of my loud footfalls. I can't bring myself to care about the amount of noise I'm causing because the only thing running through my mind is 'get to Ash'.

I hesitate only for a second at the front door, questioning whether or not to leave a note behind for my mother. But the adrenaline, fury, and panic guide my legs out of the house and into my car.

Typically, I would be against speeding, but my body has other plans. It takes me no time to turn down all the right streets of my deserted hometown. Before I know it, I'm throwing my car in park outside of the barn, only six minutes after I woke.

Despite the adrenaline, my breathing is even and focused as I sprint into the building. It's dark but not the same darkness from my dream. Several streetlamps outside illuminate the inside with their glow. The rest of the light comes from the moon shining brightly through the collapsed ceiling.

"Jase?!"

I shout, startling whatever wildlife that was calling this place home.

For a second, I hear nothing, and panic tips the scales in its direction. Maybe this isn't the place from my dream, where he said he was....

Suddenly, I hear the crunch of gravel behind me. I spin on my heels.

"I will say, Nola. That was far too easy."

Jase stands in front of me, but something is off. I expected him to be as panicked as he was in my dream, running with me to the car to go get whoever took Ash.

This Jase is calm. His voice is level, a smile playing on his lips.

"I'm a bit disappointed."

He shrugs, meeting my eyes.

The air suddenly gets knocked out of me as a raging fire

blazes up my arm. It's nothing I've felt before. Like sticking my arm in the middle of a volcano. I look down expecting it to be fully on fire, but it looks no different from my other arm. I clutch at my wrist, trying to stop the burning but no relief comes.

"Ouch. Looks painful. Sorry about that," his voice is still Jase, nonchalant.

"But it's so nice to meet you. Face-to-face."

I look up at his smile, it's wide causing a pit to open in my stomach. His eyes are no longer Jase.

These eyes, burn red.

"No..."

THIRTY-THREE

"How?" my voice shakes with terror.

From deep within Jase's chest, the Devil laughs. The sound slices through me, filling the abandoned building.

"It was quite easy actually. Just sorta slipped right in. Poor little Jase was none the wiser."

He smiles, clasping his hands together in front of him like he's giving a dissertation. Unbothered as he explains how he just possessed someone.

"I've just been here..." he brings one of Jase's hands up and taps his temple. "Watching... waiting... listening."

"So, you've known the whole time?"

"Oh no, my dear. Just the past few weeks. But I think that's been enough. You all were getting too eager, collecting those who were always loyal to me. I couldn't let that keep happening."

He waves his hand dismissively. The pit that opened up is

now a deep cavern in my stomach. If he's really saying what I think he's saying...

"You didn't..."

"Oh yes, I had to Nola," the smile never leaves his face... Jase's face. "I had to kill all those rogue demons that were plotting against me. One after one, they promised that they would be loyal soldiers once again, but I couldn't trust that. Poor Azel screamed for his brother to stop..."

The Devil shrugs in Jase's body, letting out a deep chuckle.

I want to scream or maybe cry... my bones ache to collapse within themselves.

"Azel is gone?" the words come out barely a whisper.

I feel hot tears spring to my eyes for the demon who was nothing but an asshole.

For all of them.

"You know, I think Jase secretly liked it. He begged to stop it all too from in here," again, tapping his temple, "but I could see that there was some joy in it."

I search his face for any sign of Jase.

"Jase is still...?"

"Still in here?" he meets my eyes, burning red into green, and shrugs again. "For now. It's actually quite annoying. Like a voice, I can't get rid of. Would be easier with my body here but you know, that's what you're here for."

The corners of his mouth turn up in a wide smile. It's a smile I've only seen in movies, the villain's smile... too large for his face. He takes a step toward me. Automatically, I stumble backward in a panic. My mind scrambles with fear and adrenaline, both fighting for the reins of how to handle the situation I've run into.

"Blake... did you kill..." my voice trails off. I can't think about it but maybe keeping him talking is the best way.

He groans with disgust but stops his advance. My heart swells with some hope.

"No. When Jase got his call, I thought that would be my opportunity to end that little pain in my ass. But then the human girl just got in the way."

"Ash!" my voice rises, gaining strength. I hope that if she's nearby, she can hear me. "Where's Ash?"

"Oh, the human is fine. For now. Depends on you."

He takes another step forward, predator stalking prey.

"How do I know you're not lying?"

"Hmmm," he tilts his head slightly.

I flinch as he sticks his hand out quickly. Two loud snaps ring through the air, then I hear a muffled scream and shuffling feet from one of the dark corners behind him. Ash is shoved into the light by two dark figures. Demons. My wrist flares with new flames.

Ash lands on her knees hard causing a grunt to come from her chest. Her arms are bound together behind her back and a large white piece of cloth is wrapped around her mouth. The top of the cloth is stained with blood. Her blood. I notice her left eye is swollen shut with a deep cut at the top of her cheek.

I take a step toward her.

"Ah ah," the Devil sidesteps to block me. "Now, now. You see that she's fine."

"Fine?! She's bleeding!"

He shrugs, "Like I said, she got in the way."

I shift to see her again and her one good eye meets mine. Her muffled sobs make their way through the gag as fearful tears flow freely down her cheeks.

"If you want her to stay alive, you can come without a fight. No need for this to get messy."

I peel my eyes away from Ash, the pit hardening with resolve. That's an easy choice to make.

"Okay."

"Okay? Really?" his eyes dance with excitement, a laugh bursting out of his chest. Loud and menacing.

"I wish your demon was here to see this..." he says. "See you give up so easily. See you at the end."

His wicked smile meets his eyes again.

I smile right back at him. I'm glad that Blake isn't here, he would only get in the way. Get hurt or worse... At least now, I know he's safe, wherever he is. Right now, I only have to worry about Ash.

My legs explode from beneath me in a sprint. I can see the confusion flash across the Devil's face in a moment, but I don't give it much thought as a sprint past him. Right to the two demons behind Ash. My fist flies out, connecting right in the middle of the tallest one's chest. I hit him with all of my strength and then some, using the momentum of my run. He falls almost immediately.

I turn away from him, lying motionless on the ground, towards the shorter demon. From behind his back, he pulls out a knife, twisting it in his hand, the gleam matching his smile. I panic for a moment, feeling very much unarmed, but that thought quickly passes as he lunges. His move is sloppy, all brute strength, and nothing calculated about it so I dodge it easily. My mind switches to all the training sessions. Keeping my hands up, I watch every move this demon makes. He favors his right side, leaving his left vulnerable.

He lunges again to his right, I shift to my right, out of his way, and hit him square in his jaw. I ignore the pain that shoots up my arm. He stumbles slightly, rubbing at his chin. Using the back of his hand, he wipes the blood spilling from the corner of his mouth. I don't give him much more time to recover before I advance, kicking my leg up, hitting him too in his chest. He falls backward with a thud. His grip loosens on the knife, and it falls about a foot away from him. I lunge over him, hand outstretched towards the knife.

Just as I'm wrapping my fingers around the handle, I feel a hot hand wrap around my ankle, pulling me back. The shorter demon now on his knees flips me over quickly and his fist connects with my right cheek in an explosion. I feel a crack and the warmth of blood starts down towards my ear. Blinking through the stars now clouding my vision, I kick my legs, fighting for some way to get his weight off of me. My knee finds the intended target and he gasps loudly. His weight shifts slightly, just enough to get my arm and the knife free. I shove upwards as hard as I can and feel the blade plunge deep into the demon's chest.

Through the stars, I meet his brown eyes filled with pain. He falls with a hollow thud, knife still in his chest.

"Valiant effort but such a waste."

The Devil is now standing behind Ash. With Jase's arm wrapped around her neck, he places his hand on the side of her face. Pushing slightly against her open wound, her neck straining. Her eye shoots between me and the knife still in the demon's chest. The tall one is still motionless. I can see as the fear twists her face, her eye wide.

"Wait!"

I hear my own voice meeting my ears through the echo.

"Please just let her go..."

"Why would I do that? You seem to have a hard time listening to me and you just killed two of my children. Seems only fair if I just..."

He pushes harder, twisting her neck further. My cheek pounds in time with my heart.

"No, please!! Jase please stop!!!"

For just a second, the red eyes flicker back to brown. My heart stops... Jase. He releases his hold on Ash and she collapses to the ground. Quickly, I reach for her, undoing her gag. She gasps, her head turning from me to Jase. He takes a few steps back.

"I'm so sorry... I'm so... sorry..." he repeats over and over, creating as much distance between him and the two of us.

"Ash," I grab her face, careful not to touch her wound. Her one eye meets mine; she opens her mouth to say something, but I cut her off.

"I'm so sorry for all of this..." I can only hope she can feel how sorry I really am... "For everything... but you have to get out of here."

My heart pounds in my chest as I look back at Jase. He's doubled over, grunting, fighting against the Devil, his father, all inside his own head. Pure adrenaline pushes my hands to act. We don't have enough time. I turn back to the demon with the knife. I swallow against the bile that fights its way up my chest as I yank the knife free. I bring it back to Ash and cut the cable ties around her wrists.

"Don't look back," I shove my keys at her, wrapping her hand around them.

"Go! Now!"

She hesitates for a second, unsteady on her feet. I help her as much as I can to stand.

"Go... please..." I whisper.

I can see she wants to say something, but we don't have time. She doesn't have the time. With one more look between the two of us, she stands fully and runs towards the door I came in from.

"ENOUGH!" Jase shouts, his voice is back to the deeper, menacing one.

I meet those fiery red eyes at the same time what feels like white hot iron plunges deep into my chest. All the air leaves my body as I look down and see Jase's arm through my chest. I struggle to breathe, but it feels like an eternity as the fire burns through me. I think I scream. At least I feel my mouth open, but nothing comes out. No sound. There's no air. I think I blackout. Or maybe I just hope that I will. I still see. See that smile that is no longer Jase.

Then, something explodes.

It's deafening and bright.

It feels like every fiber of my being is being ripped apart, one piece at a time. The smile is gone, everything is white. But also, not white. Like staring at the sun but seeing every color so brightly. Too brightly and it's everywhere. It takes me a moment to register that the light is coming from me. It's me. I'm the one exploding. Or maybe imploding.

This must be what death is like.

Through the explosion, relief, a calm I've never felt before washes over me. At least Ash isn't here. She's safe. Blake's not here to see this. To see my end. Harley, Lawson, mom... they aren't here and that's good. Good that they don't have to see me like this. They don't need that kind of pain after... dad.

Dad... my voice sounds strange in the blinding light. Unearthly.

Dad... Are you there? I pause, not really sure if I'll get any response but I continue into the light anyways. *I'm so – so sorry for everything... I wish I could've stopped everything that happened. Helped you more somehow... I was there but not really and I'm so sorry for that. But I also understand. I understand how you wanted to be there too and couldn't. I understand and it's okay. I'm okay... I miss you, dad,* warm tears fill my eyes. *I love you so much. I love you and mom forever... Mom... she did everything for us. She did everything... never faltering in her love... I know that now. I know mom...*

My back slams against something hard. I can tell it bends with the impact. The light vanishes as I feel air returning to my lungs. I look down, expecting there to be a massive hole. My arms feel heavy as I reach up to my chest. It's all in one piece. Whole.

Maybe I am dead...

"That's not possible," a breathless voice reaches my ears from the other side of the building.

I look up and see Jase again, leaning against the wall across from me. More light is flooding in and part of the crumbling ceiling is gone. I squint up, noticing the boards and beams are singed.

"You shouldn't... that should've worked."

I meet the red eyes.

Right, not Jase.

And not dead.

Slowly, I move my legs under me and push up. I can feel every muscle working together as I stand fully. It's painful like my muscles have been stretched too far.

"That's alright..." I groan the words out. It sounds like my voice. "Everyone has performance issues sometimes."

I smile as I shake my arms out, ignoring the lingering burn.

From across the room, a guttural growl, low and animalistic, comes from the Devil's chest.

"Pathetic child. You have no idea what you're up against."

He spreads his arms wide. I hear several feet shuffle through the gravel around us. Maybe around 20 dark figures step into the barn. From the burn, all demons.

It's not shocking… not really. I should've known that the two still laying on the ground weren't the only backup he brought. But the fear rises anyways. I'm completely alone.

Somehow, it doesn't stop me from doing what I do next. I square my shoulders and plant my feet, lifting my fists in the air in front of my face.

"Ha! You really think you can fight this?"

"I'll die trying," the words ring true through my chest.

"That you will."

He takes a half step forward, in time with his demons.

Suddenly, a rumble crackles through the sky.

I look up to see several figures coming through the hole in the ceiling. They land gracefully on the ground. I stumble several steps backward as I take in two large wings on each of their backs. They give off a shimmery bright light, illuminating the darkened building.

One by one, the lights vanish as the wings disappear into each of their backs. Replacing the glow is the sun fighting to rise through the cracks in the wood. My eyes are drawn to the back of one of the new figures. There strapped around their back, the Euch. I feel my body start to tingle with its proximity. The figure turns his head slightly, revealing just enough of his face.

Arlo.

He meets my eyes briefly. The corner of his mouth that I can see hikes up into a smile and he winks. I fight the urge to roll my eyes at his casual demeanor, literally in the face of danger.

With a few more steps, he's by my side along with a few other figures. Looking at their faces I see my mother, Jeremiah, Zera, and several others I don't recognize.

"So, you can fly?" I whisper to Arlo, just loud enough that he and my mother can hear.

"You thought these were just decorative?" he holds his wrist up, and the two black wings flash white.

"I just thought they were symbolic..."

"I believe this is yours," Arlo reaches behind him and removes the Euch from his back. I lean down as he puts it over my head. Its strength continues to buzz through me, filling me with its warm power.

I hear several feet rushing behind us. As if on instinct, I unsheathe the sword on my back. Power rushes through me tenfold. My muscles tighten with it, ready to explode. No one else on my side moves, their focus on the ones in front of us.

Why aren't they turning?!

My confusion dissipates as relief fills my heart when I see the new faces. Through the door, Lawson, Blake, Cael, and Harley run in. Each of them holding different weapons. Cael with his spear, Lawson with two long knives, Blake with a similar knife as the one the other demon had, and Harley has something with spikes. It's then that I notice the array of weapons on the backs and hips of the angels around me. None of which are in their hands.

Cael stops next to Jeremiah and gives me a short nod. My brother flanks on the other side of our mother eyes forward.

Blake fills the space between Arlo and me with his warmth.

His blue eyes scan over me. I see the flash of anger as he takes in the side of my face, now caked with dried blood. His eyes find mine. Everything, every word left unspoken between us almost floods out. Every 'I'm sorry.' Every 'I forgive you.' Every 'I love you,' sits right at the tip of my tongue. I would say anything just to reassure him that I'm fine, especially now that he's here. Now that they all are.

"My foolish son," the dark voice rings out.

Blake tenses as he turns away from me and towards the Devil.

"Hello father," Blake's voice is clear, full of venom.

"Now, there's no need to be hostile. Just hand over the Nephilim," his red eyes flick to mine.

"You know that's not going to happen," Jeremiah's dull voice comes from our side.

Red eyes shift from mine down the line to him. The wicked smile, showing all of Jase's teeth, changing every part of his face, is there again.

"Then I'll take it for myself," he spits back.

With a tilt of his head, the demons move.

In the blink of an eye, several of them are right on us. I hear weapons, knives and swords, clashing as the metal-on-metal rings out. The fighting is loud on our side, but I hear other commotion still coming from the other side. I quickly assess that everyone is alright around me. Peering around, I notice that some of the demons have turned on one another.

Hidden amongst his children, those still on our side.

A crack of pain spreads across my temple. Bringing me to my knees, my vision darkens as a ringing reverberates through my head. Another blow lands on my side, taking my air with it. I feel the snap that time more than I hear it. I try to take a breath and the sharp pain intensifies.

I blink through the darkness, trying to find my assailant. My hand finds the Euch in the dirt next to me. Its power masks the pain as I blindly swing up. Feeling the blade sink into flesh. My vision returns as the heat hits my face.

I hold onto the handle as I take in the stranger's face. Her face is twisted in pain, eyes no longer seeing. The blade is still in her side but from her wound, flames spread instead of blood. Consuming her as I pull the Euch out.

There's no time to process when I catch movement from the corner of my eye. I block a sword before it comes down on my head. The force rings out, rattling down my spine. I meet the demon's face. His eyes are wild, bloodthirsty and a growl escapes his crooked mouth. He's quick, shifting his weight to his right, he swings. I block the attack just in time. Twisting the blades around each other, I am able to throw him off balance. The demon trips on his own feet. I use his faltering steps to my advantage, driving the Euch into his back. Once again, the wound blisters with flames.

The pain in my side tingles as I try to catch my breath. My senses are quickly assaulted by the smell of copper, wood, and flesh. Several flashes of light draw my attention up, only to meet red eyes locked in on me.

Only a few feet away, I watch as he leans down, never taking those eyes off of me. His hands are clasped around a discarded spear and he twists it around in his hand expertly. Grasping it with both hands he points it at me. I stand tall, gripping the Euch tightly, letting every ounce of strength pour into me.

He takes a step to his left. I mimic the move to my right. We start in a tight circle, my eyes staying on the spear.

"I didn't think the Devil needed to hide behind a weapon," my voice is light but menacing. Someone else taking control.

He answers with a lunge, the spear slicing through the air making contact with my thigh. Hot blood drips and coats my pant leg.

I meet his eyes again; they dance with excitement and greed. This time it's my turn to lunge forward with power laced adrenaline and I swing the Euch, aiming for his side. He blocks my advance with ease and I feel his full strength as he shoves me backward. I trip, landing on my back. He's over me in the same motion, the spear coming down right over my chest. I feel all of its force drive through my right shoulder. The Euch falls from my hand and with it, the power vanishes, leaving nothing but blinding pain in its wake.

I fight back the urge to blackout. The blade of the spear holds me in place on the ground. I feel the blood leaving my body. The pain in my side comes back tenfold as he leans down, right on the cracked rib. I try to scream but I don't think anything comes out, muted by the pain.

"Poor little Nephilim. You really thought you had a chance," the Devil's red eyes are inches from mine.

I try to move, in hopes to get his weight off of me but the pain only intensifies, threatening to consume me altogether. He presses his hand against my chest again. My heart beats against the burn that comes with the touch. He lifts his hand back up and curls Jase's fingers into a fist.

This is it.

Death is only a breath away. For me and for everyone I've ever cared about. All here in this abandoned barn in the middle of nowhere. Somewhere far away, I know Max is still sleeping. The sweet boy who deserves to have a life well past these short four years. This fight, my last fight, was for him and I failed. Failed them all.

I fight against the urge to close my eyes, welcoming the darkness or whatever comes next.

Suddenly, something silver flies through the air between us. Landing right into Jase's arm. His weight shifts with the force of the hit, just enough that I can move as he lands next to me. Blake is over me now. I meet his blue eyes, his face covered in blood. I can't tell if it's his own or not, but that doesn't stop the concerned panic that fills my broken chest. He looks down at me, placing his hands over the handle of the spear still lodged into my shoulder.

"I'm so sorry love," his voice is everything I need. Strength, comfort, peace, *home.*

In one swift motion, Blake pulls the spear from my shoulder. My body reacts all on its own. Sitting up, my hand flies to the open wound. I look down at my hand, slick with my own blood. If I had anything in my stomach, it would be on the ground now. Fighting back the stars dancing slowly into my vision, I grab the Euch with my blood-soaked hand. Using it as a crutch, I stand, feeling the blood flow freely down my arm.

None of it bothers me as I turn to the Devil, laying on the ground.

The knife is still in his arm, he goes to move his other hand towards the handle and in a quick move, Blake slams the spear down. It lands into Jase's shoulder, stopping him from pulling out the knife.

I stand over him now, both hands wrapped around the handle of the Euch.

"Go."

I lift the Euch up, meeting the Devil's eyes.

"To."

The Euch now high above my head.

"Hell."

With all the power exploding from me, I slam the blade through his chest. I feel it shatter with the force as Jase's body bursts into flames. Limb by limb, the fire engulfs every inch. The last to burn, those red eyes.

I stare down in disbelief. I'm met with nothing but the quickly dying flames and glowing embers of where Jase's body —the Devil and the Euch was.

The adrenaline slowly flows out of me as I watch the last of the embers turn to ash. It only takes a few seconds but feels like a lifetime as the sounds around me die out. I don't bother looking up as I hear several feet scattering out of the barn. Just as the burn of the embers fade, so does the fire in my wrist. However many of the demons that were left, are now scattered into the woods.

We did it...

Warm fingers wrap around my good arm. I know who they belong to, but I can't pull my eyes away from the pile of ash in front of me.

"Come on love," his voice is low in my ear. "You did it."

The only thing grounding me, his voice. Blake's hand on my arm. I feel the last quiver of adrenaline leaving my fingertips and with it, all of the pain returns.

My knees buckle under the weight. Blake doesn't have time to catch me. I let out a gust of air as I hit the ground. The ash flies up in front of me. I choke on it as I try to take in a small breath through the pain. It settles around me and my heart stops.

No, no, no. That can't be real. He's dead, gone... I can't actually be seeing...

Within the pile of ash, a hand shifts. Covered in ash, it grabs at the air. My wide eyes break away and find Blake kneeling next to me staring at the unknown hand. Fear rises with the blinding pain. Neither of us move. Or even dare to breathe.

More ash shifts, revealing one arm, and then another. Ash covered blonde hair. Then a familiar face. The same face that just went up in flames. Jase's face. I watch as he blinks against the ash, pulling the rest of his body out. Slowly, he looks up at us. His eyes are back to his own, a kind brown.

I see Blake's hand move in a flash. Clear liquid flies through the air at Jase. It soaks his face, clearing away some of the gray ash. He wipes at it, smearing the ash, and looks down at his hand.

"It... it doesn't burn..." Jase's voice is gravely but it's his.

That wasn't water Blake threw at him, it was holy oil. The test. If it doesn't burn... that means...

"You're human..." I stare at Jase in disbelief.

It doesn't seem real, and yet, here Jase is. Sitting in front of me, covered in ash and completely human... My side flares with pain with every breath. I try to wrap my good arm around my chest, but it doesn't help.

"Nola..."

My brother's voice comes from a few feet to my right. I meet his eyes, my father's eyes. They're filled with fearful tears. Next, to him, my mother sits, her hands are soaked with blood,

Lawson's blood, still fresh as she presses down on his leg. Trying to stop the bleeding.

My eyes shift to the figure lying next to them. Singed wings cover his body. I only see a part of his face and that's enough. My body painfully shakes with the sobs fighting their way out of my mouth all at once.

But no tears come as I stare at Arlo's pale face.

THIRTY-FOUR

My hand cramps around the handles of two mugs. Carefully, I push open the office door with my good shoulder, the other useless in a sling. The hot liquid almost spills as the door gets caught on something.

"Hey!" Lawson's voice comes from the other side. Lower from his usual spot of standing at six feet tall.

For now, he's confined to a wheelchair. His right leg sticking out in a full cast. Just this morning he was released from the hospital. Under the care of Jeremiah, he should make a full recovery. Everyone came out of the battle two weeks ago a little worse for wear. Turns out my rib wasn't fully broken but it was cracked. The clean cut of the blade through my shoulder only required minor repairs, a simple non-invasive surgery, and once cleared to be out of the sling, plenty of PT with Zera and Cael.

But none of the positivity and talk of recovery helps my guilt.

It's just as crushing as the pain itself.

Every injury, however minor, is my fault. Every death is my fault. Arlo's death... my fault.

"Sorry about that Law," I sidestep his protruding leg and enter the tiny office at the back of the café.

I place one of the steaming mugs on the desk in front of Pierre, now sitting in the chair Arlo had sat in before. I grab the other scalding mug fully in my good hand. Maybe the minor burn will drown out the heaviness in my chest.

Pierre reaches for the mug. His eyes are still bloodshot, the tears are never far away. He gives me a small grateful smile and I feel the guilt sink like a rock in my chest. He puts his lips on the mug and looks back at my mother sitting across from him.

"Pierre, we're here for you however you need us. If you need help with... arrangements... the café, anything..." my mother's soothing voice fills the room with nothing but love, yet, every word breaks my heart more.

"I'm happy to help out with the café if you need it," the words tumble out of my mouth. "Opening and closing, anything for however long you need me to... I'm just... I'm so sorr-"

Pierre lifts his hand in the air. His wedding ring catching in the light.

"Nola, if you don't shut up..."

Silence falls over the room.

"Apologies," Pierre looks up at me. "Nola, you've said sorry so many times. I'm not exactly sure why you keep doing so... But you're holding onto too much. You have to let it go," his eyes bore into mine.

"Don't let it crush you."

I blink back the hot tears. It's not fair how easy everyone else seems to be able to read me.

"As for... arrangements... my, my Arlo had everything planned already. There's nothing else for us to do. Except for our parts," Pierre's voice becomes more formal. "I assume that he spoke to you, Laine?"

My mother's head tilts up and down in a tight nod.

"He'll come home... I'll bring him home."

Home? The word fills my head with confusion. It takes me a moment to connect that she doesn't mean home here... on Earth. She means Heaven.

Some of the guilt lifts. Maybe I'll see him again. At least that's what everyone says about Heaven. A place to see your loved ones again. Maybe Arlo's there.

"Right. Now to figure out what to do with everything," Pierre takes a thoughtful sip of the tea.

"Anything you need," I say to him.

"Actually Nola, I noticed the other day there was a box under the counter out front. It has your name on it, and I... well I didn't want to open it."

"Oh?"

"Please, take it. I suspect Arlo wanted you to have it."

His eyes shift to the door behind me as he gives me an encouraging nod. Curiosity, like the sneaky cat it is, leads me toward it.

"Of course, I'll get it packed up," I smile half-heartedly at him as he takes another sip.

I'm more careful this time, avoiding Lawson's leg and chair as I open the door next to him. If this is the small way I can help Pierre, then it's a done deal. Even if it doesn't stop the splintering of my heart at the thought that Arlo had already planned that this might happen to him. That he wouldn't make it out alive. He knew that was a possibility.

They all did.

I know that Pierre said not to let the guilt crush me, but it feels like the only thing I can hold onto. Just the painfully constant reminder that I'm still here and he's not.

I reach the counter and place my mug of untouched tea on it at the same time the front door chimes open.

"I'm sorry, the café is closed," I look up, meeting my favorite ocean eyes.

"I know. I wanted to check on you," Blake gives me his signature smirk.

There's still so much to work through with us. Forgiveness sits right there, between us but I still can't grasp it. Maybe that part of me is just being buried beneath the grief. But one thing is for certain, we can work through it together.

"I'm... well, I'm broken. Physically," I motion with my good hand to my bad arm, pulling at my sore side. "And emotionally."

Blake nods, his face turning down in a frown as he walks around the counter, but stops a foot away. He has kept a respectful distance away, trying not to break the damaged goods any more than I already am. It doesn't mean he hasn't been by my side nearly the whole two weeks. The smell of sandalwood and his warmth, never too far away.

I smile now as both hit me at the same time.

"Anyways, Pierre said Arlo might've left me something..."

I look down below the counter. There are several boxes, some filled with coffee cups and paper bags for food. I move some of those out of the way, only wincing slightly at the pull on my side.

Behind one of the boxes filled with lids, is a decent sized box with my name on it. Too big to pick up with one hand.

"Could you grab this for me please?" I point to the box and look up at Blake.

Aside from the several cuts and bruises on his face and his torso, he came out of the battle fairly unscathed. Each mark on him, each one marking a new notch of guilt.

He places the box on the counter with a small thud. Taking a deep breath, at least as best as I can, I pull the flaps of the box open.

Inside, my fingers dance lightly along the neat covers of several worn books. Every title jumping out at me. I remember several of them from the bookstore back in Cross. One of the books simply titled, *Archangels*, is riddled with multicolored tabs.

"He left you a library."

I hear the smile in Blake's voice. I can't help but smile along with him. Of course, Arlo did. He left me all the knowledge he never got to tell me. Hot tears fill my eyes and I feel my throat fighting to close with a sob.

"What's this?"

Blake reaches his hand inside the box and pulls out a white envelope. On the front in simple handwriting:

Don't let all the work go to waste.

I grab the envelope and open it, a bit clumsily with one hand. I tip the envelope over and a single bronze key falls out. Attached to the keyring is a strip of paper with an address and four-digit code on it.

I recognize it immediately.

The gym. Arlo's gym.

He left me his gym.

All of our training sessions break free from the back of my mind. It's like he's still here. Every mile ran side by side. Him pushing me to my limit over and over again only to find out that my limit was farther than before each time. Gripping the key tightly in my fist, I don't bother holding back the tears now.

"Nola?"

I feel Blake's warm hand on the small of my back. It's the first time in a long time that I feel his electric burn shooting through me, but it doesn't stop the grief from splitting open my chest.

"I—I need some air," I choke the words out through the lump in my throat.

Holding myself together as much as possible, I turn away from Blake. Leaving his warmth and nearly sprinting through the door.

Immediately, I'm hit with the biting December cold that Edge promises every year. I can't tell if my body shakes with that cold or the sobs that roll through my chest freely. I feel my chest heave with each breath or half breath between the sobs. My whole body feels like it's rattling, on the verge of breaking, but that's how I've felt for a while now. Like I'm always seconds away from crumbling with my world around me.

I look up and stare at the clouds, mindless and carefree, floating through the blue sky. I've never been jealous of atmospheric elements before, but I feel it now. I close my eyes, foolishly hoping that that will stop the tears from falling. It's no use.

"I'm so sorry Arlo," I say to the sky.

Slowly, my breathing starts to even out. But my body still

shakes with the cold. Even the warmth from the sun can't seem to breakthrough.

"Nola?" Blake's voice comes from the door behind me.

I turn to him and start to wipe away the tears, still falling. Will they ever stop?

"I'm sorry, I'm such a—"

All of the air leaves my body in an instant as something tears through my chest. I look down at a hand that's not my own protruding through me. The world around me stops as I watch the light, my light, start to leak from me.

"NOLA!"

Blake's shout rings in my head. I look up and meet his frightened blue flames.

His face is the last thing I see before everything explodes into a white light.

My world is consumed by it.

And then everything goes dark.

But I don't feel alone here. Through the darkness, I hear shuffling and a new voice.

"Hello, Nola."

ACKNOWLEDGMENTS

I want to start by thanking the people closest to me who suffered my chaotic tendencies while I wrote this book. My family. Thank you for sticking by me, raising me, and loving me anyway.

To my found family, my friends, thank you for slapping me down a few pegs to help me focus, which is a difficult task and I thank you a million times over.

To Kennedy, I truly wouldn't be here without you. Your push at every time I wanted to quit and encouraging words with every edit is the main reason this book is finished. Thank you for sacrificing your time and sanity dealing with me. (:

To Rachel, editor and book coach extraordinaire, thank you for helping me see Nola's story with new eyes and giving me the tools I needed to bring her life to the page.

To Toni. Thank you for being my first reader way back when this story was just ramblings on wattpad. You were the encouragement I needed then and I hope more than anything that this version made you proud.

Lastly, thank **YOU**. Yes, you, who made it this far. Thank you for spending time with Nola, Blake, Harley, Ash, and all the other voices in my head. Thank you for letting me live my dream.

ABOUT THE AUTHOR

S. Caro is an emerging author of YA/NA fantasy novels. This is her debut book, the first in a trilogy. Caro has a Bachelor of Arts in Communication from the College of Charleston where she blossomed into her love for writing. If she there's not a book/pen/paper/iPad/laptop in her hands, you'll more than likely find her hiding behind the camera.

instagram.com/scaro_writez